the EMERALD LILY

VAMPIRE BLOOD SERIES

the EMERALD LILY

VAMPIRE BLOOD SERIES

JULIETTE CROSS

This book is a work of fiction. Names, characters, places, and incidents are the product of the author's imagination or are used fictitiously. Any resemblance to actual events, locales, or persons, living or dead, is coincidental.

Copyright © 2018 by Juliette Cross. All rights reserved, including the right to reproduce, distribute, or transmit in any form or by any means. For information regarding subsidiary rights, please contact the Publisher.

Entangled Publishing, LLC
10940 S Parker Rd
Suite 327
Parker, CO 80134
rights@entangledpublishing.com

Amara is an imprint of Entangled Publishing, LLC.

Edited by Tera Cuskaden
Cover design by LJ Anderson/Mayhem Cover Creations
Cover photography by nadezhda F/Shutterstock
sibrikov/Deposit Photos

Manufactured in the United States of America

First Edition January 2018

For Kevin—
my own prince charming and happily-ever-after

Prologue

Long, long ago, there lived a king and queen who were deeply in love. Out of their infinite joy, they bore a daughter—lovely and fair. Unfortunately, the birth was too much for the queen's frail body, and she died. Though in mourning, the sad king still invited royalty and gentry from all over the empire to his palace, Briar Rose, to celebrate the birth of his beautiful child. For that was the dying wish of his beloved.

When the dark queen of Varis arrived in the great hall and peered into the bassinet with malevolent intent, she proclaimed that the infant must be betrothed to her youngest son. The king stood from his throne and declared that it would never be so. The king sensed the evil emanating from the empress and feared for the safety and well-being of his precious girl.

The empress stormed from the great hall, but not before she turned at the threshold and warned, "Mark me well. You will regret this injury you have done me."

The king said nothing, knowing the dark queen was capable of crooked, evil deeds to get what she wanted. The throne room fell into a hush as all present bowed their heads in sorrow.

Then...from among the crowd stepped an old woman—her hair, face, cowl, and cloak all a snowy white. And though she was old, her eyes glittered like emerald stones, and her smile was kind. "There, there, my king. Do not be afraid."

"How can I not be afraid?" he asked. "My darling child is in danger. The empress will stop at nothing."

"Fear will not save her, my king. But I can. I come bearing a gift that will do more than protect her. It will save the whole world."

"Who are you?" he asked.

She smiled. "All you need know is that I am a friend. Will you allow me to bestow my gift?"

An aura of peace hung about the woman, compelling the king to nod his approval. The woman bowed, then approached the cradle and gazed down at the beautiful babe.

She pulled from within her cloak a radiant stone, translucent and shimmering with myriad colors that glittered up to the vaulted ceiling. The crowd murmured in wonder.

"What is that?" asked the king.

"It is a fragment of the Stone of Making."

He gasped and whispered, "The hartstone."

The white woman did not answer, having eyes only for the infant girl, who peered up at her from wide, crystal-blue eyes. She held the stone above the baby and began to speak, her voice vibrating with power. With enchantment.

"You will grow even more beautiful and fair, yet you will walk in a waking slumber. When you are a woman, the dark queen will curse you with a living death."

"No!" he cried, stepping forward. "Please help her."

The white woman tapped the magic stone three times. Shimmering dust floated down in a magical whirl upon the babe's cheeks, eyes, mouth, and gurgling tongue. A mystical wind blew through the castle, rustling the skirts of the women who gasped in awe, and billowing the banner above the king's head which bore his sigil, the white dragon.

"But one day, darling girl, a prince will awaken your heart with a blood kiss. Not long after, you will drink fire into your soul and awaken the beast of vengeance and righteousness. And courage and hope." The baby cooed as if she understood the old woman's cryptic words, still resonating with magic and portent. The white woman pressed her thumb to the stone and then smudged the shimmery dust across the infant's tiny forehead. "And you, blessed child," she whispered, "you will awaken the white queen with emerald eyes and smite the evil one with one bite. You will be the savior of them all."

Then she vanished into a swirling plume of smoke, leaving them in heavy silence with only the soft cooing of the babe echoing in the hall.

One year later, on the road home from a long journey, the king and his men were killed by brigands. The baby princess, now motherless and fatherless, and her kingdom were put into the care of a steward.

Time went on. The king and queen were forgotten. So was the white woman. But it mattered not at all...for the hartstone never forgets.

Chapter One

Briar Rose cut an eerie silhouette in the moonlit night. Sharp turrets and massive battlements would be formidable to scale and climb for most men. And vampires. But not for Mikhail and his four brethren in the Bloodguard. They'd watched from the woodlands since sunset. Watched and waited.

Mikhail flicked a hand, signaling his men. As one, the hooded vampires melded with the shadows and flashed to the eastern gate. Gregoravich cracked the neck of the first Legionnaire guard, then severed his head with a clean, deep slice. Dmitri, the second. They dropped the bodies along the inner wall.

There were two ways into the well-guarded eastern tower, which most assuredly held Princess Vilhelmina. Either through the palace itself and likely two dozen guards, or through the tower window. They'd opted for the path of least resistance.

The heavy concentration of Legionnaires clad in red-and-black dress—denoting King Dominik's men guarded her rather than her own—was like a beacon shining a spotlight on her location within the castle.

Dmitri had asked Mikhail at sunset, "Incapacitate or kill?"

There was only one answer Mikhail could give with icy conviction. "Kill."

They would show no mercy to these brutal bastards who'd imprisoned the princess. Especially since they were under orders of the nefarious butcher king himself. The evil Queen Morgrid's announcement that her eldest son would take the captive Princess Vilhelmina as his bride set the members of the Black Lily into action. Friedrich, the Duke of Winter Hill, had told Mikhail why it was imperative that he save her at all costs. "The fate of us all depends upon the success of your mission. She cannot come into the hands of King Dominik or Queen Morgrid."

And so here they were, embarking on said mission. Beyond Friedrich's warnings, Mikhail had another reason for saving the Princess of Arkadia. One that bore so deep his blood hummed with the possibility that she could be the key to avenge the wrong done to him and his family. A wrong that still pricked with sharp teeth upon that tender organ beneath his ribs.

Slipping through the shadows to the wall beneath the eastern parapet, Mikhail gave a swift nod. Together, they climbed, finding the notches and grooves of brick to hoist themselves up in swift silence. With claws extended, for they'd all summoned their inner beasts to the surface, they made quick work of the wall. Upon their leap over the top ledge, they fell upon the unsuspecting guards with deadly swiftness.

Mikhail unsheathed his serrated dagger as a Legionnaire attacked. With little effort, he gutted the vampire and opened his throat before he'd even drawn his longsword. By the time Mikhail turned to his men, there was a pile of seven eviscerated Legionnaires. His men faced opposite directions to await more who would come when they smelled the blood. The only sound was the whipping of the Arkadian flag atop the corner battlement—the white dragon sigil roaring upon the forest-green backdrop.

Without delay, he slipped a sleek black rope from within his coat and looped it around a jutting square along the parapet wall. He'd estimated this post would serve well for his purposes hours earlier when they'd watched from the woodlands. He'd been right. Looping the other end of the rope around his waist and tying it with a slipknot, he stood backward on the edge of the parapet and leaped over the edge into the night.

His feet made contact with the wall, then he repelled with ease down the tower to the window. Peering through the mottled pane, he noted there were no guards within the chamber. With both feet on the ledge, one hand holding the rope, he pulled his razor pick from the leather strap across his chest, securing his tools of the assassination trade. Scoring one square pane along the frame, he then slid the pick back where it belonged. With one, two, three taps of his finger, the pane cracked then fell free, shattering a second later on the stone floor. After sliding his hand through the opening and popping the lock free, the casement doors swung open.

Once inside, he untied the rope from around his waist and looped it over the window latch to keep it from slipping away. No candles burned in the room. No fire, either, leaving the chamber in a wintry chill. Heartless bastards.

The circular room bore few furnishings. A table with a bowl and ewer along the wall, a chair, and a bed.

He approached the bed, where gossamer curtains framed the woman within. His heartbeat reverberated in his ears, a quickening drum as he beheld the princess entombed in her bloodless sleep. The Princess of Arkadia was known for her grace and beauty. Still, his breath caught in his throat when he pushed aside the bed sheer.

Resting upon her back with her arms draped across her abdomen—an unnatural position for one in sleep—she still appeared at peace. Dressed in a white nightgown and a green velvet robe that was fastened with a row of black buttons down the bodice, her lithe body appeared too thin. As any vampire would be, having been starved with only one drop of blood per week to keep her in this torturous state.

And yet, her face.

Mikhail inched closer. The darkness could hide nothing from his vampire senses. Waves of the palest yellow hair, like sun-bleached wheat when it's tall and ripe, draped down to her waist. High cheekbones, delicate nose, full lips. Overly full. He dragged his gaze upward to her lashes, black against her pale complexion. What shade of blue would her eyes be? All born vampires had blue eyes. Royal born, the bluest of all. A marked trait.

Her chest rose and fell steadily, even after being in this cursed slumber for months. He'd heard of powerful warriors being induced into the bloodless sleep who died within a fortnight. Wandering the darkness of their minds, confronting and reliving the nightmares that await there, had been enough to stop the heart of bigger, stronger men. Yet, here lay this pale beauty, soft and serene as if in a natural sleep. He hoped she survived the transition to reality. He'd heard of those awakening with their minds unhinged, never regaining full control of their sanity.

He and his brethren had discussed when to awaken her, but Mikhail had rejected all votes that they should wait until they'd carried her to safety. Mikhail had heard tales from survivors of the bloodless sleep. The dark agony of sensing everything going on around oneself but never being able to speak or open one's eyes or make any move at all. And all the while, an aching pain stabbed the sleeper's gut, ricocheted out, and rattled bones.

Sitting on the edge of the bed, he lifted a lock of her silken hair, sliding his fingers till it fell away. The sensual caress striking a vulnerable cord in his chest. He clutched his fist together. Her beauty made him breathless. The fact that she lay imprisoned in her own body cut through the tough veneer of the captain to the man beneath. No way in hell would he leave her in such a state of agony a second longer.

Awakening a victim from a bloodless sleep was a precarious job. He must be gentle, careful not to overpower her system and jolt her body to full wakefulness. She could go into shock. Friedrich had suggested the best-known method—the blood kiss.

Leaning close to her ear, he whispered, "Princess. If you can hear me, listen well. I must awaken you from this deep slumber. Pardon the intimacy and have no fear. I mean you no harm."

His canines fully extended, he bit into the fleshy part of his palm and smeared his lips with his own blood. Wrapping his other hand behind her slender nape, he leaned close, inhaling the fragrant scent of white jasmine and sunshine. He paused, faltering at the sweetness of her, an unexpected punch to his senses.

With tight control, he swept his lips over hers, wetting them with his blood and coaxing them apart. The slightest relaxing of her mouth gave him entry. Raising his palm, he licked a swath of his own blood across his tongue then angled his mouth over hers with firm possession, delving in to awaken her starving body. Sliding his tongue over and against hers, he slicked her thoroughly.

His pulse pounded an erratic beat. He heard hers quicken in timing with his own. Her senses stirred.

Unexpected arousal crashed through him, hardening every inch of his body. His fangs extended to their most painful length, demanding succor.

Bloody hell!

He'd come to offer his own lifeblood, not take what little she had. And yet his body trembled with bone-shaking hunger.

Stifling his rebellious body's needs, he sucked a few drops of blood from his palm wound and pressed his mouth to hers once more, letting the blood seep inside and down her throat. He couldn't help delving back in, licking the delicious taste of her onto his tongue.

A low moan emanated from her throat. He jerked away, remembering himself. By God, his thoughts spiraled down a dark, wayward path when his mouth was on hers. Panting, he leaned farther away, giving himself some distance.

She lifted a slender hand, her brow furrowing as she moaned a second time, rousing from her deep, paralyzing sleep. Her eyes shot open, and she sucked in a deep lungful of air. Her wide-eyed gaze landed directly on his. Mikhail was sure he'd slipped and fallen off a cliff, flailing helplessly.

Fathomless pools of blue, burning brightly. His father used to take him to the ocean shore during the summers as a boy. They'd walk along the sandy beach collecting shells. Once, he'd found the most beautiful clear gem washed upon the sand. *Sea glass*, his father had told him. A broken piece of bottle or jar that the ocean had tumbled and smoothed into the clearest, purest blue he had ever seen. That was what he thought of when he looked into the eyes of this princess who smelled like sunshine and tasted like heaven.

"Welcome back, Princess Vilhelmina." Steel clashed against steel on the battlement above. Footsteps pounded on the staircase leading to the tower. "Time to go."

Chapter Two

Mina's pulse thundered in her ears, as she stared up at the most stunning vampire she'd ever seen. Midnight-black hair. One blue, one green eye flaring bright in the shadowy room. His face cut too sharply to mark him as beautiful. Mesmerizing, more like. A memory flitted over her mind, a repetitive dream from her deep slumber. One where a dark prince would one day save her.

But this was no dream. Her skin burned, her muscles ached, her heart raced with his blood coursing through her body. She slid her tongue over her bottom lip, tasting the sweet tang of a drop left behind. His otherworldly eyes followed the movement, sparking with new fire.

"Who are you?" she demanded, voice cracking.

"No time, Your Highness." He leaned close, and before she knew what he was doing, he lifted her against his broad chest and carried her to the open window. He set her on her feet. "You'll have to forgive me, but we have approximately twenty seconds."

"For what?" she asked, her legs trembling as he steadied

her with a hand at her waist.

He lifted the end of a rope looped onto her window latch, tied it around her waist, and tightened it into a complex knot with deft fingers. He wrapped his hands around her waist, nearly spanning it completely. She hitched in a breath as he leveled his gaze on hers, lifted her, and slipped her out the open window. She should've been afraid, but some new powerful force inside her pushed all her fears away. Had it been him? This dark savior's blood kiss?

"Hold onto the window ledge for a brief second."

She gripped the ledge, knowing full well she couldn't hold her own weight. No matter. As soon as he let her go, he grabbed the rope with a tight grip. "I won't let you fall. Someone is at the bottom to carry you to safety."

She felt no dread even as she dangled from the tower while the sound of combat filled the night air. She gave a confident nod. Then she was gliding fast down the side of the outer brick wall. The chilly wind lifted her hair and billowed her skirts around her bare ankles. When she expected to hit the ground with a thud, her descent stopped just short of her feet hitting the ground. A vampire lifted her, a burly beast of a man, while another unfastened the rope around her waist. Then she was passed from the arms of the mountainous one to the other, who smiled at her. Something about the shape of his eyes was familiar. He looked like the one who'd just dropped her out the window.

"Pardon me, Your Highness." He tucked her tight against his chest. "I am Dmitri. You may want to close your eyes. My speed can be a shock to the system."

"I am an Arkadian princess." She heard the words come out husky but with confidence. "I can handle the speed of any vampire."

His mouth tilted into an infectious grin. "Let's get you the hell out of here then."

Three Legionnaires stormed from an archway and rounded toward them. The big vampire engaged all three at once with moves too graceful for a man his size. Mina had one second to recognize the Legionnaires wore the livery of King Dominik of Izeling, not her own colors or the queen's. Then Dmitri flashed into motion, moving in a head-spinning blur away from Briar Rose. Away from her home. And her prison.

Dmitri was right to warn her. Though all vampires had the ability of supernatural speed, even though she was too weak to do so on her own at the moment, he moved remarkably fast. She gripped around his neck and let her head fall to his shoulder rather than resist the force of the wind, too weak to do anything but allow herself to be taken away. While her body was weak, a vibrant pulse thrummed in her veins, shocking her senses with a potency she'd never felt in all her life.

She hoped these men weren't brigands, and that she hadn't exchanged one imprisonment for another. No. She reached out with her other sense, her vampire gift. The man who held her in his arms had no nefarious emotions swarming about him. Though the one who'd awakened her certainly kept company with darkness, he didn't resonate with ill-intent, either. Not for her, anyway. Of that, she was sure.

She held on tight as he flashed them deeper into the wooded Novak Mountains. The mountains kept some of their foliage, even steeped in winter. For now, the snow only reached the tip-top of the range that swept in a horseshoe around the seat of the Arkadian kingdom, Briar Rose.

The air was crisp, nipping at her ears and nose. When the queen had exacted her punishment, the trees of the Novak region had just begun to turn red and gold. How long had she been under? It seemed like an eternity.

Within an hour, she heard other vampires running

parallel to them, but Dmitri didn't seem alarmed. It must be his brethren. She couldn't help but wonder who'd hired them. Her first order of business was to discover who'd sent them for her.

After a chilling trip higher into the foothills of the Novaks, Dmitri slowed to a human pace. Barely winded, he walked toward a mound of heavy brush then casually stepped behind it, where the entrance to a cave was hidden.

"Stop." Mina gripped the rough leather of his coat at the shoulder.

Dmitri stopped suddenly. "What is it, Your Highness?"

"I smell bear."

"Oh, that." He continued on, ducking his head at the entrance. The interior was much more spacious than it appeared. "Don't worry about him." He set her gently on her feet. "We moved the bear last night."

"You moved...the bear."

Two more vampires entered. The hulking one who'd fought the Legionnaires so she and Dmitri could make a quick escape. And another she hadn't seen yet. Quiet with sharp, watchful eyes.

"Sure," added Dmitri. "Not much of a chore for us." He winked. "Eh, Gregoravich?"

"Just a wee cub," replied the big one, Gregoravich.

"That wee cub nearly snapped off your tree trunk of an arm," said a fourth vampire who entered the cave. His blond hair gleamed by the moonlight slipping in. He gave her a formal bow with a tilted smile that had most certainly charmed many a lady. "I am Aleksei, Your Highness. At your service."

"Bah." Gregoravich waved a beefy hand. "One punch to the jaw and he was out like a baby."

A fifth vampire moved into the cave on silent feet. The black-haired one who'd awoken her. Even while in the bloodless sleep, she'd heard his velvet voice whisper in her ear. She'd felt his fervent kiss. Her fingers went to her lips, then her legs wobbled. He was at her side, steadying her with a hand wrapped at her elbow.

"Enough," he ordered over his shoulder. "We'll rest for three hours. Gavril, you have first watch."

The quiet one nodded and fled the chamber in a blur. The others moved a little farther into the cave, sitting in the shadows and propping themselves back against the wall before closing their eyes. She couldn't imagine anyone comfortably sleeping in that position, but she'd never encountered men like these.

She swiveled back to the leader. His full attention rested intently on her face, accelerating her heart rate.

"Who are you?"

"Come," he commanded gently. "Sit down."

She didn't argue. She could barely stand. Even so, she protested. "I don't need rest."

"I know what you need, Princess." The rumble of his melodious voice sparked a warmth in her chest. "Please sit," he urged more gently, guiding her to a spot near the cavern wall where a circle of kindling was stacked neatly into a tent shape. Larger stones framed it in.

She sat and pulled her knees up, wrapping her arms around herself as the cold settled in. Vampires could easily regulate their body temperature, but only when well-fed. The vicious churning in her gut reminded her she needed blood. Soon.

"What's your name?" she asked softly, her voice still rough from lack of use.

He knelt and picked up two flint stones, cracking them together three times before a spark popped off onto the kindling. Leaning in, he blew the spark to life. A flame licked up quickly onto the dry tinder. He leaned to his right and lifted a log from a stack. They'd prepared this place for precisely this moment. A stop off in their escape.

He rocked back, crouching on one knee. "My name is Mikhail Romanov. I am Captain of the Bloodguard. We come by request of the Black Lily."

She sat straighter, still hugging her knees to her chest, quivering. She'd heard rumors of the Bloodguard. A covert and deadly band of mercenaries who didn't work for the crown or any single aristocrat, but only for men they chose—human and vampire alike. They swore allegiance to themselves alone and no one else. Some nobility snubbed their existence, saying they thought themselves too arrogant to devote their gifts to the kings of the land. Others called them heroic for taking the part of unfortunate humans who could not help themselves.

She wanted to know more about this captain, but her immediate interest was in whom they served now.

"Arabelle and Marius sent you?"

He nodded.

She smiled and exhaled with relief. A sudden wave of tender emotion swept over her, all of what she'd endured bubbling to the surface. In a single act of defiance, she'd broken her engagement to Prince Marius and encouraged him to go after the one he loved and the one who loved him. She'd not known the depths of the queen's evil. When the queen had discovered the truth, Mina's fate was sealed. The crown's Legionnaires had promptly escorted her back to Briar Rose, where she thought she would be on house arrest. She was terribly wrong.

As they'd crossed the threshold into Mina's own palace, Queen Morgrid's Legionnaires had slashed open her lady-in-waiting, Kathleen's, throat. Mina watched her one lifelong friend die before her eyes while she screamed in protest, in agony and heartbreak. To no avail. The officers promptly dragged Mina to the eastern tower and locked her inside. Not a soul returned until after she slipped into a coma from starvation three weeks later. The bloodless sleep.

She shivered. Mikhail stood and moved behind her, wedging himself in a sitting position between her and the cavern wall.

"What are you doing?" She'd never had a man so intimately close.

He stretched out his legs, bracketing her body. "Straighten your legs."

Though this man was a stranger, she found herself oddly compelled to obey him.

"Now lean back."

"What?"

He didn't wait for her to comply. Gripping her upper arms with firm hands, he pulled her back against his chest and wrapped his arms around her, pressing his legs closer to hers. Instantly, she was enveloped in steamy heat. His temperature was up from the exercise of combat. She closed her eyes, unable to withhold the slight sound of pleasure at the tactile heat of his body.

"Better?" His husky whisper was at her ear.

She stiffened. He gave her a light squeeze, one arm banding her waist, the other across her chest, where his hand gripped her opposite shoulder.

"Relax. Do not fear me. I'm only trying to get you warm."

"I don't fear you," she snapped, though the tenor of her voice sounded high and strained.

He chuckled, his broad chest rumbling against her back. "Defiant, aren't you?"

She didn't answer. "Why are we stopping so soon? So close to Briar Rose?"

"They'll be floundering for hours, trying to reorganize. We killed all of the officers in command. That's the downside to Legionnaires. They're a well-disciplined machine, which means the soldiers are completely lost without someone giving them orders."

He was right. "How do you know you killed all the officers?"

"They wear their pretty little bars on their lapels."

"Yes, but how do you know you got them *all*?" Her chin stopped quivering, but her body continued to shake.

"Standard Legionnaire operations. When a threat presents itself, the commanding officers meet the threat first, assess, and determine the best strategy to extinguish said threat. After Dmitri spirited you away, we waited to be sure we'd taken care of the officers so there would be no one left in command. For Legionnaires, it's much like cutting the head off the snake. The body will writhe uselessly, trying to find a direction to no avail."

"I see," she said, teeth chattering.

"You need to feed and rest before we move on. My blood will be enough to regulate your body temperature and give you strength till our next stop, where we'll get you a human bleeder for real sustenance."

His reminder drew awareness to her parched throat and the agonizing churn in her belly. Loosening his hold, he uncuffed one of his sleeves and rolled it up past his forearm. When she realized he planned to feed her directly from his arm, her pulse lurched into a gallop.

"I—I can't feed that way."

"What do you mean?" He finished rolling up his sleeve, baring a well-muscled forearm, a thick vein prominent. Her mouth watered.

"I don't feed from the flesh." She squeezed her eyes shut, his heat and heady scent pulling her canines from their rest, thickening her mouth.

"What other way is there?"

"I usually—that is, I mean, I've always had my host fill a cup for me."

Silence. Stillness.

"I've never…actually fed directly from a host."

Statue still for a moment more, he finally shifted behind her. He tilted her chin to face him as he leaned to one side. "I am not going to fill a cup for you, Princess. If you want to live, you'll drink from me. A natural practice for all vampires. No matter how low or high born the bloodline."

A challenge.

His unearthly eyes bore into her own, the firelight dancing on his sharp features, making him even more severe. He waited patiently. Unmoving. A steadfast wall of male vampire awaiting her decision. She became peculiarly aware that he was a man accustomed to giving commands and having them obeyed. But that wasn't what made her want to sink her fangs into his masculine arm. It was some primal need that sparked to life the second she awoke with the taste of his blood in her mouth. She wanted to taste more of him.

She perused his features again, noting his own fangs were long and sharp beyond his parted lips. Her gaze slid back to those piercing eyes, seeing the same emotion of desire shining back at her.

"Yes," she whispered. Not because she was unsure, but because there was an intimacy formed between them when he awoke her with his blood kiss. She whispered like a lover would to her paramour. "I will drink from you."

Pausing for only a second longer, he maneuvered back into position. With gentle fingers, she wrapped them around his arm and brought the fleshy part of his forearm to her lips. A gurgling rumbled in her belly as her vampire senses heightened, the scent of warm, sweet blood filling her nostrils. How could she explain to him that the idea of feeding directly from the flesh had once repulsed her?

Her wet nurse had said she'd never fed properly from her. When the nurse would offer her arm or neck, she would turn her face away, refusing to puncture with her infant fangs. It was her nurse who first drained her own blood into a cup so that the toddler princess could get the nutrition she needed. Ever since then, she'd fed the same way.

She'd never allowed her animal nature to come too close to the surface. But now, her primal urges took hold without her consent. The sensation new and wonderful and profoundly right.

Brushing her nose along his warm skin, she inhaled deep. The earthy scent of mulled spice and wood smoke and leather filled her nostrils. She had to open her mouth to keep her fangs from embedding into her own tongue. A slight sound of pleasure escaped as she latched her lips against his skin and slid her sharp canines into his skin, the sensation foreign but dizzyingly euphoric. His warm lifeblood spilled into her mouth, wetting her tongue and dry throat, sliding to all the parts of her that thirsted, that yearned, that longed for succor. Pleasure, pure and strong, shot through her body.

His muscles bunched beneath her suctioning mouth. She clenched her nails to keep him still, a predatory sense spiking in her body, urging her to keep hold of her prey. It frightened her—and aroused her. His arm that was looped around her waist tightened as he dropped his forehead to her shoulder, cursing with sudden sharpness. His masculine groan urged her on. She moaned, sucking him deep.

He murmured so low she might not have heard, "Fuck, that feels like heaven."

His blood replenished her body lightning fast, amplifying her senses to brilliant vibrancy. The potency she experienced when her eyes shot awake was nothing like this. His blood was like a honey of the gods, sweeping her into a place of ecstasy. The heat of him—body and blood—wrapped her in a sensual embrace, making her want even more. The sudden thought of what he'd feel like on top of her, inside her, snapped her back to the here and now.

She broke her bite, crimson blood trailing down his forearm, a few drops falling into her lap. She quickly licked his wound; the healing component in her saliva would seal it.

He wrenched his arm away with a firm tug. She let go. He lurched to his feet, facing away from her while swiftly rolling down his sleeve and buttoning the cuff.

"I'm sorry," she whispered. "Did I take too much? Did I hurt you?"

He scoffed, still facing away. "No, Princess. You didn't hurt me." With a fierce glance over his shoulder, his gaze roved her face, her throat, and fixed on her mouth. "Get some rest. We leave soon enough."

He left, heading into the night. She stared, wondering if he sensed her heightened desire during the act of drinking from him. Once more, she thought this sudden change in her should provoke some sense of unease or fear. It didn't. Rather, a swelling of confidence poured through her being. A sense of rightness she couldn't explain, even to herself.

Soon, the hypnotic pull of satiation and the heat of the fire on her skin made her drowsy. She tried to fight it, staring into the crackling flames, but eventually lay on her side, pillowing her hands beneath her cheek.

So that was what it was like. Now she knew, understood on a primitive level why so many vampires lost their humanity and gave into the beast to bleed a host dry. Not that she believed she could ever do such a thing, but someone without conscience and with less willpower might easily be lured to commit such a crime. To experience such pleasure.

She touched her fingertips to her lips, relishing the strength of her body from his virile blood. What a wonder. Was it the fact she extracted the blood directly from the source? Or was it him? The answer swirled and mixed with the heady concoction pouring power into every artery of her body. Her empathic sense felt the trembling residue of desire flowing in the blood that was in his veins moments before. She wasn't sure where this path would lead, taking her back to the Black Lily. But she knew for certain her fate was now inextricably bound to the vampire named Mikhail.

Chapter Three

It had been over two hours since the princess had bitten him and drank his blood. He'd relieved Gavril and taken watch, needing the chill night air to cool him off. It had done nothing to extinguish the fever she'd ignited when her elixir poured into his veins. A punch of erotic adrenaline took the breath right out of him then shot straight to his cock. It had taken every ounce of willpower to hold still and not ravage her on the cold cave floor.

He had his answer about her surviving the sleep with her mind intact. Not a touch or sign of insanity. Quite the opposite. She appeared as lucid as if she'd been napping for an afternoon. Amazing that such a woman should endure a deep, dark sleep, and to awaken with a vibrant spark of fire in her eyes. This was not the norm for those so cursed. Of course, she was a royal. A sinfully sensual royal princess.

Dangerous. This was dangerous. He needed to protect her if he was to avenge his family for what the evil queen had unleashed. But now, he wasn't sure he could stand to be in her presence without the need to feel her pretty fangs in his flesh, without wanting to put his own in hers. Without putting himself inside her.

"Stop," he snapped, turning on his heel back to the cave.

Unaccustomed to feeling out of control, he needed action to dislodge this edge of uneasiness. They'd rested long enough. Time to move on to the next stopping point, where they could all feed and rest up for the last stretch of the journey to Silvane Forest.

He stepped through the cave, his gut clenching at the sweet silhouette of the princess lying on her side, the orange embers glowing on her flawless skin. Tearing his gaze away, he sought his men. Finding Dmitri first, sleeping in a sitting position, something they'd done time and time again, he shook his shoulder.

"Brother, it's time to go."

Dmitri's eyes snapped open, alert as ever. His brother's vampire senses were remarkably acute. The others stirred at the sound of movement. He returned to Vilhelmina, still sleeping, a golden-haired beauty, an innocent temptation he needed to keep at a distance. And yet, here he was, lifting her in his arms to carry her to the next stop.

"You got her, Captain?" asked Gregoravich, the physically strongest of the five of them.

Tamping down the desire to growl his response, he cleared his throat and replied softly. "Yes. Let's move."

She stirred in his arms as they exited the entrance. "What…?"

A pall of gray light rose in the east. The smell of a storm pressing down from above.

"We'd best move quickly," said Aleksei, nose to the wind.

"Agreed. Lead on, Aleksei." Mikhail finally met the gaze of the wide-eyed princess. "I know you have some strength back, but it's best if I carry you to be sure. Plus, you don't know the way."

When he thought she would protest, she didn't. Rather, she linked her arms around his neck and tucked her head in the crook of his shoulder. He knew it was for practical reasons, to hold on and to keep from injuring her neck against the force of the wind, yet a raw emotion swelled in his chest, an unfamiliar, indefinable emotion that gripped him hard. He might have called it possessiveness, but that would be foolish.

He took off after the others, moving through the gray haze, letting his instincts guide his swift feet, and chastising himself for wanting something, someone, he couldn't have.

Foolish, indeed. The blood oath he'd made as Captain of the Bloodguard doused his desires with icy finality. He recited the words in his head to stave off the lure of the woman he held in his arms. The promise to sacrifice marriage and family for the sake of the Guard and his brothers at arms.

He would not, could not allow himself to form an attachment beyond duty and service.

And yet, the blood kiss still haunted him, his lips against hers, his tongue stroking inside. Even worse, the feeding. *Fucking hell.* When she sank her slender fangs into his flesh, he'd nearly lost his mind with the primal need to take her. This fair-skinned, golden-haired beauty who appeared to be molded and created and divined by the stars for him.

He sped faster, willing his inane thoughts away and focusing on the task at hand. To get the princess to the safety of the Silvane Forest and the Black Lily.

They descended out of the Novak Mountains and crossed the vast plains to the northeast, skirting around villages. After a few hours, they slowed and dipped into an open valley with wide fields and sparse woodlands. The trees were naked now in the dead of winter. The heavy clouds pressing down promised sleet or snow sometime today. Having moved out of the deep south, the temperatures had dropped markedly.

Aleksei led them to a paved road lined with tall oaks,

their thick branches stretching out like arms welcoming him home. None of them had been home since before Mikhail had sought out their role as guardian to Friedrich Volya, the Duke of Winter Hill. That plan had worked out just as Mikhail had hoped, forming an alliance with the one royal, other than Prince Marius, who was covertly working with the Black Lily against Queen Morgrid and her son King Dominik.

They slowed to a walk as the paved road widened at a tall wrought-iron gate.

"You may put me down now," said the princess, jarring Mikhail from his thoughts.

He'd forgotten he was holding her.

"Of course."

He set her on her slippered feet. He'd have to find her warmer attire before they ventured to the Silvane Forest. The winter had curled a colder hand around Varis than usual, as if the queen herself controlled the weather with her wicked intentions and black magic. The heavy snows made it more difficult to assemble their armies and train. Deep cold made no difference to healthy vampires. But for humans, which the vast majority of their army was made up of, it did.

"This is your home, Aleksei?"

They walked closer to the three-story manor house.

"Yes, Your Highness. Welcome to Wentworth Hall."

The gargantuan door flew open. A lovely fair-haired lady, a vampire with Aleksei's distinct features, launched down the portico steps and into his arms. Aleksei laughed boisterously and spun her around, her skirts fanning wide. Mikhail couldn't help but smile.

"Easy, Irena." He set her on her feet. "You'll strangle me."

"Damn you, Alek." She punched his shoulder with the heel of her hand playfully. "Six months? That's entirely too long."

"What? Mother isn't good enough company?"

"Mother is lovely. But you know she has no sense of humor. And the winter has kept everyone away from visiting. I'm bored senseless."

He chuckled again. "Come then. Meet my friends."

"Friends?" She arched a brow. "You mean your fellow assassins, don't you?"

He grinned affectionately down at her but didn't answer. Apparently, Aleksei's sister knew more about the Bloodguard than most.

She tucked her arm in the crook of his when he offered it, then he led her to where the rest of the party stood off to the side.

"May I present my sister, Lady Irena Lukov."

His sister curtsied in greeting.

"Irena, this is Gregoravich, Dmitri, Gavril, and my captain, Mikhail."

Her eyes widened when they landed on him, a common reaction from women he newly met. He was aware that his unusually sharp features and his peculiar-colored eyes drew attention.

"And this is Her Highness, Vilhelmina Dragomir, Princess of Arkadia."

Irena's cool eyes widened even further. She dropped to a deep curtsy, almost to the ground. "Forgive me, Your Highness. I didn't know—I wouldn't have behaved in such a—" She shot a scathing look up at Aleksei, who merely grinned.

Vilhelmina stepped forward and took her hands. "Please stand. There's no need to worry yourself. I imagine you didn't have warning we were coming."

"No, Your Highness." She stood, shooting another death glare at her brother. "We had no warning at all."

"Then I beg your forgiveness."

Aleksei interrupted. "Irena, perhaps we can get the princess inside. She's been through an ordeal."

Irena finally took in Mina's nightgown and velvet robe. "Yes. Please come inside. Mother will be anxious to meet you all."

Aleksei led the way, passing through the door, where a butler stood, stiff and unaffected by the surprise visitors.

"Hello, Marshall."

"Lord Lukov. It is a pleasure to see you again." Though the butler's stern features didn't show pleasure of any kind.

"And you."

"Mother will be in her drawing room," said Irena, hurrying ahead with long, swift strides.

"A bit spirited, your sister," said Dmitri.

Aleksei glanced over, his smile fading at once. "Dmitri, stop looking at my sister that way."

"Or what?" he asked, still watching Irena farther ahead.

"Or I'll punch your teeth in."

"She's a lovely girl."

"Yes," snapped Aleksei. "Girl, not a woman."

"Hmph." Gregoravich scratched his grizzled beard. "She must be twenty at least."

Aleksei's fury turned to their hulking comrade. "*Twenty-one*. And that's hardly more than a girl in vampire years."

Vilhelmina dipped her head low, hiding her smile.

Aleksei grumbled as they entered a bright, high-ceilinged parlor draped in pastels of blue, white, and gray. Irena had already summoned her mother to her feet. She was a mature vampire, perhaps three hundred years old, her features denoting a lovely woman who was wise in years by the set of her all-knowing eyes—crystal blue—the same that Aleksei and Irena bore, which settled on her son first.

She opened her arms. "My son."

He embraced her warmly. "Mother."

"I've missed you so." She pulled back to gaze at his face, a look of love and adoration shining bright. She cupped his cheek as she might have done when he was a boy. Aleksei didn't shy away but let her gaze her fill. "Now." She turned toward the rest. "Who have you brought with you?"

"This is my mother, Lady Galena Lukov."

She swept her gaze across them then gasped when she landed on Vilhelmina. "Oh, dear child." Stepping forward, she curtsied deep before the princess. "I had word that you were—" She stopped the rest of her sentence and glanced back at her son. "Did you all take her from Briar Rose?"

"It's best you know as little as possible, Mother. If I could've kept you from meeting her at all, I would have. But we had to stop here to rest and to feed before we move on."

She stared at the princess with a nostalgic smile. Then it hit him. A flash of memory that was not his own, but the woman's before him. *She stood in a grand hall filled with royals and nobles around the throne of a king Mikhail didn't recognize. A baby in a bassinet—sweet and lovely. The black-robed Queen Morgrid storming from the hall, people parting for her as if from a plague. A woman draped in white leaned over the bassinet, cooing kind words to the infant. Fathomless deep blue eyes stared up from the round, innocent babe. The princess.*

Mikhail inhaled deeply, snapping back to the present. His vampire gift—a heightened intuition about other people, often accompanied by flashes of their memories—seemed to always jar him for a moment. Dmitri frowned at him, recognizing when he had a vision. The flashbacks occurred sporadically and only when someone exerted powerful emotion.

"Son, you will invoke the wrath of Queen Morgrid," pleaded Lady Galena.

"Yes." Aleksei squeezed her hands. "We know," he

replied with confidence.

"Why?" Her voice cracked with despair. "You do this for your father? He is dead, Aleksei. Nothing will bring him back."

She might as well have been speaking to Mikhail himself. All of the Bloodguard had a vendetta to set right. Blood for blood. Death for death. And a few Legionnaire guards at Briar Rose wouldn't fulfill the debt owed.

Mikhail's mission would right all wrongs and do away with the queen—the heart of evil across the land—for all time. He'd not put her into a bloodless sleep. Not her. That would be too kind. His gaze slid to the princess, standing quiet and demure and perfectly poised. Her calm eased the anger riding him at the thought of the queen.

Aleksei embraced his mother as she began to weep. Irena quickly stepped toward the princess.

"Come, Your Highness. I'll find a place for you to rest. Gentlemen, if you'll come with me as well."

They quickly filed after her, eager to give Aleksei some time alone with his mother. Mikhail shadowed the princess, needing her proximity to keep him grounded. He frowned at the sensation.

"Your Highness, I believe we are close to the same size. If you wouldn't mind wearing one of my dresses, though I doubt they're as beautiful as yours, I'd be happy to lend you one."

"That would be lovely." Vilhelmina smiled at Irena, her genuine appreciation shining in her honest face. "You are too kind."

That's what it was. Every move she made. Every word she said. It was honest to the bone. Beyond her beauty, her pure candor drew him ever more.

"And might we trouble you to find a few bleeders for us?" asked Dmitri. "We'll pay handsomely. We need to replenish our strength."

Irena glanced at Mikhail's brother, shyer than she was before when she first met him. Dmitri wasn't the charmer Aleksei was, but his confident air was no doubt attractive to the ladies.

"Yes." She cleared her throat, batting her eyes more than necessary. "We have several servants who I'm sure would be happy to oblige. If you'll wait in my brother's study through that door, I'll send Marshall in a few moments to find hosts for each of you."

Irena started up the stairs. Mina behind her.

Before Mikhail followed the others through the study door, he caught the princess glancing over her shoulder at him, a pinch between her brow.

"Princess, I'll bring a cup up to you." He couldn't help but let a smile slip. "If that is what you would like."

She paused, her delicate hand on the stair railing. "That would be lovely." She smiled, arching her brow. "Though I did actually prefer my last feeding."

Her gaze trailed down to his lips to his throat then to the arm she'd fed from. Her raw desire channeled straight to his cock, hardening it to stone. Sea-blue eyes flared bright, and her secret smile seemed to say she knew exactly what she'd done to him as she sashayed up the staircase.

She had no idea.

He was a man of control and power and strength of will. A steely focus guided his every move, allowing him to lead the Bloodguard to become the most feared and revered mercenaries across the entire land of Varis. The sole reason he'd kept such control over the growing guard had been his resolve to uphold the blood oath that set them apart. Of course, a guardsman could fuck as many blood whores as he liked. But attachment was against their laws, an essential rule that kept men from splitting their allegiance between family and the Guard. Not that he'd set his sights on marrying a princess. She'd likely have dozens of suitors once she finally takes her rightful place in Arkadia. And he wouldn't be one of them. Even so, he watched the tantalizing sway of her hips as she reached the top of the staircase and disappeared out of sight. Then he went in search of a couple bleeders.

Chapter Four

Mina watched the steam rise from her arms, draped along the tub's rim. A hot bath never felt so glorious, the jasmine petals and lemon-scented soap filling her chamber with fragrant warmth. The fire crackled, lulling her into contentment. Though still weak, she'd never felt so good. So alive.

From the second she snapped open her eyes in the tower, a sense of urgency, of need had washed through her body, through her mind. Even her heart. The captain's kiss, his blood, seared through her veins, jolting her primal urges to the forefront. It was as if the captain's essence had changed her. No, not changed. Awakened. Now her eyes were wide open, and she longed to let loose the vampire she'd kept restrained all her life behind a mask of nobility and proper etiquette.

For Kathleen's death and for her own wrongful imprisonment, she longed for revenge against Queen Morgrid. Apparently, the queen's son King Dominik had joined her ranks, for it was his men guarding her at Briar Rose while she lay helplessly in a bloodless sleep.

"Damn them all." She surged to her feet, the water sluicing down her breasts, torso, and legs.

A knock at the door. Mina froze, inhaling the tantalizing scent of leather and mulled spice. A responsive shiver thrilled through her frame. Stepping from the tub, she dabbed quickly with a bit of toweling and hurried into the thin, gauzy wrapper Irena had left for her. Knowing full well the fabric molded to her damp form, revealing more than it concealed, she walked to the door and opened it.

Mikhail lifted his bent head and froze, the goblet of blood in his hand nearly tipping over.

Mina pretended not to see his reaction, opening wide the door. "Come in, Captain."

He remained in place, his scowl deepening as he seemed to consider whether it was safe to enter her lair. She smiled innocently and waited. Finally, he took heavy steps into the chamber, his gaze falling to the tub, jasmine petals still floating on the water's surface.

"I brought you some sustenance." His voice was rough and slow, like the words were stuck in his throat.

"Thank you. You can set it over there." She waved to the sideboard as she walked to the vanity.

"You need to drink, Your Highness."

"Of course. In just a moment."

She busied herself uncoiling her braid and damp hair. As she brushed through the dampness in long waves, she watched him in the mirror where he stood with crossed arms, facing the window as the sun slipped away.

"Why were King Dominik's Legionnaires guarding me?"

His gaze flicked to hers in the reflection. Clearing his throat, he finally answered. "King Dominik has a vested interest in keeping you a prisoner."

Setting the brush down, she stood and faced him. "Which is?"

His stormy countenance darkened further. "It was announced not even a fortnight ago at his ball in Izeling that you will be his bride."

Mina flinched, the horror of such a thing catapulting her heartbeat into a gallop.

"I would never agree to a match with him." She shook her head, her unbound hair sliding over her shoulder and breasts. "How could he make such an announcement without my consent?"

He lifted the goblet and walked toward her. "He does not care if you give your consent." His low rumble was a rough caress against her skin. "He would take you by force and then take the armies of Arkadia for his own." His jaw clenched so tight she heard a pop. "Do not be afraid. It will never happen. I will not allow it. I will protect you with my life." He handed over the goblet.

She took it and stared down at the lukewarm blood, her stomach twisting with nausea. She laughed.

"What is it?"

"I've always taken my feedings this way. In a cup. Secondhand. But now—"

"But now?" He hadn't moved, yet his voice sounded closer, more intimate.

She looked up at him. "But now, I want to drink from you."

He froze, full mouth firming into a grim line. "You need human sustenance. To regain your strength."

"But that's not what I want." And she'd been setting her own desires aside all her life, hiding from her true nature for far too long. She set the goblet back on the sideboard and stepped closer to him. "I want to feed from you."

"That's not a good idea."

"Why not? You thought it was a good idea in the cave."

"That's because there was no alternative."

She stepped closer. His shoulders and chest stiffened. "I'll make you a bargain."

Amusement softened the lines around his mouth. "A bargain?"

"I'll drink the human blood. But only after you let me feed from you first."

The hot and heady scent of him stirred her desire to a fever pitch. Her chest rose and fell at a quickening pace, her fangs lengthening at the thought of sinking them into his flesh. Like a caged animal, he looked as if he might rush from the room.

Placing a hand on his biceps, she implored, "Please, Captain. I *need* it."

She spoke the truth. The fervent need was crippling her with hunger. Not for a cup of secondhand blood but for the pulsing hot fluid straight from this vessel of masculine power. She wanted it. She wanted him. She'd been a complacent *good little princess* all her life. Now, she wanted what she wanted. And she wasn't afraid to say so.

"Captain?"

"Lay on the bed." His command was terse and dominant.

Mina choked on a grateful sob. If she wasn't so consumed by her painful longing, she might have been embarrassed. All she could feel was relief that he'd give her what she wanted. Crawling onto the bed, she lay on her back, her robe falling open to reveal a bare thigh. She flicked the sheer fabric closed, but it did little to hide the curves beneath. The captain caught the flash of her bare skin, his gaze roving her body in a heated caress.

Unstrapping the harness of daggers across his chest, he let it fall to the floor with a clunk. Then he unbuttoned the top of his shirt and climbed onto the bed beside her. The sight of his bare throat sparked a tingling, pebbling her skin and raising her nipples. She squirmed, rasping them against the silky fabric.

Straddling her hips on his knees, his gaze flicked to her breasts and still she didn't care how inappropriate this was for a woman of her breeding. She only felt want, need…heavy, flaming desire. The proof pooled between her legs.

His nostrils flared. "I'm going to need you to promise me something if we do this."

"Anything."

"Don't touch me."

A shocking request. She frowned. "Why not?"

He laughed, but it sounded more like a man in pain. Gently, he gripped her wrists, his rough calloused hands dragging hers to the wooden slats cut into the ornate headboard.

"Hold on."

She did as he commanded and gripped two slender slats, his words launching her hunger a notch higher. Then he braced his hands on either side of her head and lowered his body, caging her in a wall of deliciously hard vampire. Pleasure spiked along her spine. She was sure she couldn't feel any sensation better than this.

But she was so wrong.

· · ·

Bloody, fucking hell. What was he thinking?

Her thrumming heartbeat and obvious arousal at the thought of feeding was the reaction of a newly made vampire, not a vampire born. Her sea-fire eyes blazed, dilating with desire. The sight of her was an aphrodisiac that threatened to strangle him with overwhelming lust.

"Mina, listen to me."

She licked her lips, her gaze focused on his throat.

"Look at me."

She did.

"I'm going to let you drink from my throat. You'll get more blood than from the thinner veins in my arm." And the ball-tightening torture of having her fangs in his flesh would end sooner.

She nodded. "Yes."

If she licked her pink tongue over her lips one more time, he was going to come in his trousers.

"It's natural to feel a certain amount of pleasure during feeding. Just go easy. Slow. Do you understand?"

"Yes."

He eased his weight on top of her, cupping the back of her head and lifting her to his arched neck. She licked his pulse. He hissed a breath between his teeth, his own fangs sharp and aching.

"Bite, Mina." His gravelly command did the trick.

With a sweet moan, she sank her canines into his throat. And his world came apart.

Molten, liquid heat flowed into his veins, her elixir racing straight to his cock. She sucked hard, the piercing pain rolling over into ecstasy. Her knuckles turned white where she gripped the headboard slats, but keeping her hands off him did little good. She arched her spine, pressing the supple mounds of her breasts against his chest.

Then she opened her legs, cradling his cock between them, the thin fabric doing nothing to hide the scorching heat of her body. The scent of her arousal filled his lungs.

She moaned, still sucking hard, and rocked her pelvis up, rubbing her sweet cunny along his rigid length.

"Mina," he warned. "Easy."

His warning seemed to have the opposite effect, for she whimpered and rode his cock harder. The wall he'd erected—his code of morals—was being bashed apart by the most sweetly sensual creature he'd ever known.

She broke free from his throat, pressing her head back into the pillow. The action thrust up her breasts and arched her neck, presenting him with the most vulnerable part of her. An act of submission. A temptation that commanded his sudden attention, calling to the predator inside him who wanted to pounce, to take. He imagined burying his fangs into her slender throat and his cock inside her, marking her for his own.

"For fuck's sake."

He pressed both hands into the mattress, leveraging to launch himself off her.

"No!" She let loose the headboard and gripped him at the shoulders, her nails sinking into his shirt. "Please," she whispered, tears pooling in her eyes. "I ache…please."

The despair in her eyes ripped his heart right out of his chest. He couldn't fuck her. She was a virgin, meant for her husband. Which would never be him. But he could ease the pain. Something told him she'd never done this for herself. To herself.

"Please," she begged again, closing her eyes as her body quivered with longing. He could smell it, taste it on his tongue. A tear slipped into her hair.

"Shhh. It's all right. I'll take care of you." He pried one of her hands loose from his shoulder, shifting his weight to her side. "I'll show you," he crooned.

Her panting breaths increased as he untied her robe and opened it at the hips. Taking her hand, he lifted it to her mouth.

"Open."

She parted her lips, her canines still sharp, her mouth reddened from his blood. A possessive thought flickered through his overheated brain. He pressed two fingers inside along her tongue. Cupping her hand with his, his index and middle finger along the back of hers, he slid her fingers down her body into her slick cleft.

She gasped, her mouth opening wider, her eyes tightly closed.

"That's it." He guided her own fingers around the swollen nub, sliding farther down to her entrance, then back up. "Just like that."

She rocked up to meet the downward trail of her fingers, her undulating hips dislodging the top of her robe. The flap over her breast nearest him slipped free. Her perfect, rosy-pink nipple jutted up as she rolled her body to the rhythm he'd set. Losing focus, his fingers slipped from atop hers, gliding into her drenched folds. Like silken heaven.

She moaned and thrust her hips up harder. He couldn't take his eyes off her writhing body—her thatch of dark-blond hair, pert breast, pale throat, and mouth open in ecstasy. A temptation no man could endure.

His fingers took control, gliding into her soaked folds, pressing against her engorged nubbin. Hot desire spiked his heart rate like a rocket, stealing his breath.

"*Yes.*" She clenched her fingers around his wrist, urging him on. "Please...more."

"Just a little taste," he murmured on a rumbling growl.

He lowered his mouth over her taut nipple, rolled his tongue in a circle, then sucked hard, grazing with teeth.

"*Mikhail.*" She cried out and thrust her hand into his hair, pressing him closer.

Sliding two fingers into her tight heat, he circled her clit with his thumb and flicked her nipple with his tongue, knowing for certain he'd lost his fucking mind.

Her panting cries filled the room, growing quicker, louder, as she plummeted toward her orgasm. Her nails dug into his scalp. He thrust his fingers faster, deeper as she pumped her pretty hips up to meet him. Pressing his cock into her hip to ease his own ache, he groaned at the pink flush heating her body. Then her fist tightened in his hair.

"Mikhail." A long moan let loose from her throat. Her sex squeezed and pulsed with her climax. He continued to brush his lips gently over her kiss-swollen nipple, easing her down as the ripples of her orgasm slowed.

When her breathing had evened, he removed his fingers gently and closed her robe. Her expression showed only a woman well-satisfied. No regret. He was glad of that. Though he wished he could say the same for himself. He crossed a line he should not have, and the torture of knowing her so intimately would only kill him slowly.

Easing off the bed, he picked up his harness and strode for the door.

"Captain."

He paused, the door ajar.

Her whisper was feather-soft. "Thank you."

He nodded without turning and left, knowing for certain he had wandered off the path he'd set for himself. For the first time ever, he felt lost.

Chapter Five

"Your Highness, you look so beautiful." Irena sighed. "I must've looked like a haggard witch in that dress compared to you."

Mina laughed and spun around, shaking her head. "Highly doubtful. You are quite lovely, Irena. May I ask a favor of you?"

"Anything." Irena beamed, standing in a gown of coral silk, the square neck accented with delicate lace. She truly was a beautiful young woman.

"Will you please call me Mina? I'd rather forgo all the formalities. It's been so long…"

Her thoughts wandered yet again to Kathleen, her lady-in-waiting. She swiveled back to the mirror, blinking away the tears that caught her off guard. Her dearest friend in all the world had been murdered right before her eyes by order of the queen. That bastard, her closest bodyguard Radomir, had gripped Kathleen under the chin, then slit her throat before she even knew she was in danger. When Mina had fallen to the ground, wailing in despair, he'd flicked his hands, and two of the queen's Legionnaires dragged her away. The last thing she saw was him grinning as they carried her off.

"Yes, Your High—I mean, Mina. I'd be honored to use your first name. I'd be honored to call you a friend. Though, if I know my brother, you won't be staying long."

"I doubt we will. But you may still count me as a friend." She admired the champagne-ivory gown with a heart-shaped neckline. She appreciated the clean chemise and undergarments even more. Mina had rested all afternoon after her encounter with the captain, until Irena's lady's maid, Therese, had come to assist her in dressing for dinner. Truth be told, Mina did little resting at all. She lay in bed, reliving the most glorious experience of her life. While Therese coiled her hair into intricate braids atop her head, drawing attention to her slender throat and delicate shoulders, Mina had tried not to laugh at her own lack of worldliness. The captain probably thought her pathetic for losing self-control so easily. And yet, she wanted to do it again with him. She wanted more, actually. A strange sensation for someone who'd kept herself locked so long within a shell of self-restraint.

She turned from the mirror and held out a hand to Irena. "I can't thank you enough. For making me feel so welcome. For everything."

"But, Your—" she stopped and bit her lip—"Mina, you are the Princess of Arkadia. The one we wish would rule the south. Not that damnable Steward Thorwald. I would do anything you asked."

Mina opened her mouth to reply, but then the door opened, and Therese stepped in. "Pardon, my ladies. But the guests have gathered in the dining hall and are awaiting you."

"Shall we?" asked Irena, leading the way.

"Absolutely." Therese closed the door behind them when they stepped into the hall. "I find it fascinating and wonderful that your mother keeps the proper routine of human dining.

Not many vampires do."

"Oh, yes. Mother loves food. Especially dessert. Sometimes, I have to remind her if she hasn't fed from her host in a week. Honestly, I think she forgets she's a vampire at times."

Mina laughed at that, admiring Lady Galena a great deal already.

They strode down the grand staircase together. Irena regaled her of what it was like having a brother who encouraged her to do all sorts of naughty things, like coerce her into sliding down the winding marble banister when she was little.

"And when my nurse caught me, she whipped me with a switch till I was black and blue."

Mina was laughing loudly as they strolled into the dining hall. All five men stood at once. But Mina's gaze landed squarely on one in particular. Mikhail. Her heart stuttered at the sight of him. His cheeks were ruddy from feeding, his sable hair glistening by the candlelight, his otherworldly gaze fixed intently on her. Like the other gentlemen, he wore fine formal wear. His black-on-black suit fit to perfection.

"Come, Your Highness," said Aleksei, seated at the head of the table as the master of the house. "Please take a seat."

"You all look so—"

"Yes, don't we mercenaries in the Bloodguard clean up well?" He winked.

Dmitri smiled and pulled out a chair at his side. "Please have a seat, Lady Irena." Gavril was on her other side. Aleksei shot Dmitri a dirty look, but the man just smiled amiably.

Mina broke her stupor and made her way to Aleksei's side to the empty chair across from Mikhail.

She examined these five men of the Bloodguard. She'd witnessed firsthand their use of deadly force. She couldn't deny that they were efficient killers, but underneath there was a resonating thread of nobility tying them together. For the first time, Mina looked at her saviors with new eyes. They belonged in this gallant finery, yet they chose a brotherhood of blood instead. She yearned to know why.

Lady Galena sat to Mina's right when she took her place. "You know, my dear, it was a shock when my only son confessed he'd joined the Bloodguard. Forgive me, is it all right if I address you without the title?"

"Please." Mina unfolded her napkin in her lap. "I would prefer that." She kept her gaze on Lady Galena and not on the man across from her whose intense stare heated her cheeks.

The footmen carried in platters and set down a bowl of rich beef broth before each of them.

Aleksei smiled seductively like the rogue Mina was sure he was. "You look well-rested, Your Highness. You have the prettiest rosy blush to your cheeks."

"Thank you, my lord. I believe it was the blood the captain gave me."

Captain Mikhail coughed, having just swallowed a spoonful of broth.

Mina froze with her spoon halfway to her mouth. "Are you all right, Captain?" she asked innocently.

He lifted a glass of wine and knocked back a big swallow. "Fine," he answered gruffly, eyes averted.

"Glad to hear Fanny's blood was to your liking." Aleksei swirled his glass of claret. "We need our princess on the mend."

"Truth be told—" Mina dabbed her napkin to her lips— "I feel absolutely divine. I've never felt better in all my life."

Mikhail sat back in his chair, glowering at her as if she'd said something monstrous. Rather than acknowledge his obvious distaste for the present thread of conversation, she lifted her wineglass and smiled at him over the rim.

"That's wonderful to hear, my dear." Aleksei's mother

had obviously recovered from her emotional episode earlier that day as her happy gaze alighted on her handsome son.

"I am delighted to know my son and the Bloodguard came to your aid. Aleksei never was an obedient child. A loyal son, to be sure, but never good. A scoundrel, more like. I'm happy to hear his escapades could be of service to the Princess of Arkadia."

"Oh, Mother. Don't go extolling all my virtues. Princess Mina will think you're matchmaking."

Mina smiled at his teasing smirk. They fell into silence, eating the soup quietly. But Mina was distracted. She stared at her broth, stirring it absently.

"What is it?" asked Mikhail, drawing her gaze across the table. "You have a question on your mind, Your Highness."

The footmen removed the bowls of soup and set down the next course, sliced roast pork and herbed potatoes.

"Yes, Captain." She took her fork and knife in hand, focusing on her plate. "Forgive me, but my reports of the Bloodguard have extolled your men as nothing more than mercenaries. That is obviously not so. You've saved me from the hands of the queen and King Dominik for the Black Lily. But, the Black Lily is the human resistance against the crown. I don't understand why you would involve yourself in such a venture."

"The resistance is not composed of only humans anymore." He held her gaze, hands in his lap. "Since you've been…asleep, others have joined their cause. The Duke of Winter Hill for one."

"And us," chimed in Dmitri.

Mikhail gave a nod of assent, a knowing glance passing between the brothers that made Mina think there was more they weren't saying.

"I understand you men wanting to help the prince and the duke," chimed in Lady Galena, her brow pinching together.

"But why would you risk your lives for a human revolution?"

Aleksei tensed. But Mikhail seemed calm as ever. Rather than address Lady Galena, he kept his focus on Mina—dark and serious focus.

"We saved you, Your Highness, because it was the right thing to do." His steady voice, rife with power and command, riveted her to his every word. "Because injustice, wielded by the hand of the monarch who proclaims to be protector of her people, is not only a crime, it is a sin. Because tyranny over a weaker people is the worst kind of corruption. Because murder inflicted upon innocents when the ruler of the land maliciously and intentionally spread the foul disease sanguine furorem for her own pleasure—" he paused, his voice vibrating with such fury it zinged along Mina's skin "—is the greatest depravity of all." He inhaled deeply and slowly exhaled, steadying the tenor of his voice. "And because we, the Bloodguard, though deadly mercenaries, fight for something greater than money or spoils of war."

Silence permeated the room. Mina sensed emotions beyond rage from the other men at the table—admiration and high esteem for the man fuming across from her. For their captain. She couldn't blame them. She yearned to know more of his strength and power, to feel it in his hands on her body. "Brother, you have a gift for spoiling the mood of a party faster than anyone I know." Dmitri raised a hand to the footman behind him. "More wine, please. I'm afraid I'll need it."

Gregoravich bellowed out a throaty laugh. Mikhail broke his fixed stare from her, arching a brow at Dmitri before returning to his plate without comment.

His warrior's hands, rough and lined with masculine veins, were now the center of her attention as he cut into his meat. When he brought a bite to his lips, he froze at the sight of her intent gaze, before bringing the fork to his mouth, a fresh scowl marring his brow.

"That's our fearless leader," said Aleksei. "Ever thinking of the cause."

"Hear, hear," said Gavril, the first words Mina had heard him speak at all. He raised his glass in salute, "Captain." Then he knocked back the remainder of his wine.

Mikhail gave him an approving nod.

"More for Gavril," ordered Dmitri. "I say we deserve a celebration. Irena, do you dance?"

"Of course, I dance. What kind of lady do you think I am?"

"Marvelous. It's been too long since I've had the pleasure of a dance partner as lovely as you."

"Dmitri," growled Aleksei, "are you flirting with my sister?"

"Of course, I am."

"Then stop. Immediately."

Dmitri whispered something low to Irena, which made her giggle. Before Aleksei launched his knife through the air down the table, Mina said, "I do have another question."

"Oh, no," said Aleksei. "Your Highness, please tell me this one is harmless."

"It is," she assured him. "How on Earth do you all have perfectly tailored suits at the ready here at Wentworth? I am sure I saw none of you carrying packs that would fit formal evening attire."

"Good planning," answered Aleksei, flashing his charming smile. "My tailor in nearby Crowley is the finest in the southern provinces. When I knew we'd be resting our midway point here, I sent ahead to have suits waiting for us upon our stop from Briar Rose." He forked his last piece of roast pork and leaned back in his chair.

Mina shook her head. "You were so sure you'd make it away from Briar Rose...unscathed?" She was careful not to use graphic language that might upset Lady Galena, but the mistress of the house was preoccupied, prattling on to Gregoravich about the fineries of fermenting southern wine.

Aleksei didn't answer. Mikhail did. "There was no doubt."

Mina found her gaze locked to his once more. The footmen entered with trays of lemon tarts, and the captain finally let her go. After dessert, they retired to the parlor for an after-dinner glass of blood.

Aleksei offered her his arm, and she gladly rose to take it, enjoying the view of Captain Mikhail strolling ahead of them. Entranced by the broad set of his shoulders, his shining black hair under the candlelight, the graceful way he moved like a patient predator who knew he'd catch his prey eventually, Mina exhaled a heavy breath.

"Are you all right, Your Highness?" Aleksei whispered down to her.

"Never better."

A lie. She'd tasted the virile man stalking ahead of them and heading straight for the liquor decanter, but it wasn't nearly enough. This afternoon, one taste of his sensuality sparked a flickering flame into a burning inferno. She wanted more than his blood. She wanted the captain as a lover. Her first lover. She'd never even entertained the idea of a lover outside marriage before he awoke her from the long dark. As if it was designed in the stars that he should be the man to awaken her, that he should ignite her primal urges, calling her vampire to the forefront to meet his as an equal.

The captain knocked back a tumbler of amber liquor. Mina smiled, for she sensed his internal struggle after their earlier encounter. A man of duty and honor simply didn't topple his moral code to seduce royal virgins. It seemed she had her work cut out for her. Time to put the sweet princess to sleep for good and let the passionate woman take the lead.

· · ·

While the others gathered around the piano—Aleksei charming them with his deep baritone voice, singing a lullaby about home and hearth—Mikhail filled his glass and took it out to the balcony. His blood was up after dinner.

Who was he fooling? His blood had been up since this afternoon, when he'd allowed the princess to sink her fangs into his throat and drive him to the brink of madness with lust. Staring up at the near-full moon, he tossed back a large swallow, thankful for the liquid burn and numbing effect of good strong whisky and the biting winter air.

"Do you mind a little company?"

Her dulcet voice stiffened every part of him. How a creature so soft could make him hard as adamant, he had no idea.

"Of course not," he answered, though he was well-aware his tone said otherwise.

She sidled closer but not too close, setting her gloved hands on the stone banister. "I wanted to speak to you about this afternoon." She dropped her chin, staring at the snow-dusted garden, the stone path silvery white under the moonlight.

Mikhail cleared his throat. "Yes. I wanted to apologize for my behavior."

"Apologize?" She looked up, her fairy-like visage luminous. "Please don't."

Stunned for a moment, he tore his gaze away and stared at the humped moon hanging between two peaks of the Novak Mountains in the far distance. The tension between them would only tighten if he didn't explain himself, and why there could be no repeat of what had happened that afternoon.

He blew out a heavy breath, the frosty air curling upward. "Fine. I won't apologize. I am pleased to have been of service to you."

She angled her body toward him as he kept his grip on the bannister. "I was pleased as well." Her tone held a teasing lilt.

Hardening his expression, he faced her finally. Her smile faded at once.

"It can never happen again."

Her lashes dropped. She swallowed hard before lifting her chin, a defiant glint in her eyes. "Was I so distasteful to you?"

He almost choked on air as he inhaled deeply with one hard shake of his head. "No, Your Highness. That isn't it."

"Then why must it never happen again?"

Shock didn't cover his reaction to this innocent beauty asking why they couldn't explore each other's bodies. Her primal nature had truly taken hold, her vampire playing the predator behind glass-blue eyes. Hell and damnation, if he didn't long to break every code to show her other pleasures. Deeper, darker, carnal pleasures. But his men depended on him.

"You are Vilhelmina Dragomir, heir to the throne of Arkadia. You are destined to lead the southern kingdom. And I am the Captain of the Bloodguard, who has sworn an oath, promised with blood, to lead my men toward victory."

"I see. Even so, you are a vampire...with needs. Are you not?"

Her pulse quickened as she waited patiently for an answer. He refrained from leaning closer to stroke his thumb along porcelain skin.

"Yes. I have needs. Ones that are fed quickly and without complication in a blood brothel."

She flinched. He hated himself for speaking the truth so harshly, but there it was. She must understand. Acid churning in his gut, he went on.

"Every member of the Bloodguard has taken a sacred vow of fealty to the Guard itself. Forsaking marriage or family or any kind of relationship with a lover. His loyalty, his focus must not be divided."

As she snapped her gaze away from him, he felt it like the cold slap of northern wind. "I see," she whispered. "You spoke of victory. What does victory look like for you?"

The need for revenge for his father, for his ancestors, for his men's families, burned hot in his chest, especially now that it was in his reach.

"It means the defeat of Queen Morgrid and King Dominik's army. It means the overthrowing of her reign altogether, preferably with her death and that of her brutal son. It means starting over for the land of Varis with just and benevolent rulers in place."

"And when you've achieved this victory? What then? The Bloodguard will continue on being mercenaries for hire?" She bit her bottom lip as if she regretted saying the last, but he knew he'd sparked her anger.

"The Bloodguard will always be needed, Your Highness," he said gently. "To maintain order for the new realm. To help those rulers who come into power to enforce a new way of life for the people." He softened his tone. "I have a duty."

"I understand." She faced him again, straightening her shoulders, gaze direct, mouth tilted in almost a smile. "Once upon a time, I would've swallowed my own desires and wishes, bowed gratefully, and taken my leave to do *my* duty as the obedient princess." She waved a flippant hand in the air as if shooing away a vision of her past. "But I am not that girl anymore."

She eased so close, her bodice brushed his waistcoat and his heart seized.

"Something happened when you awoke me in that tower. I can feel it as easily as I can feel your breath on my cheek or the winter chill at my back. It's real. It feels wrong to turn away."

She placed a gloved hand upon his chest, her feathery touch summoning his desire as if she cast a spell upon him, able to control his every thought. As if that wasn't enough, she slid her hand up his chest to cup his nape while he remained a block of marble. Her fingers brushed the short hairs, the sensation sending blood rushing to his cock.

"I know you feel it, too."

She smiled wider, kicking his heartbeat into a thunderous roar. Sweat beaded along his brow, but he said not a word. He couldn't, wouldn't confirm that she was right. He was the goddamn Captain of the Bloodguard. He had more control than that.

"Did you know I'm an empath, Captain?"

Closer still. Her perfect pink lips so near, all he'd have to do was dip his head a few inches and he could kiss her, drink from that sweet mouth. Slip his tongue inside and taste heaven. Or was it hell? He wasn't sure.

"My whole life, I've remained quiet in my little cage that Steward Thorwald kept me in at Briar Rose. I was forced into an agonizing bloodless sleep by that witch, Queen Morgrid. And apparently, I've been sold into marriage without my consent." Anger rode her words. "But *you* woke me up. In so many ways." She sucked in a shivering breath. "I know you want me," she whispered, her gaze roaming down to his mouth. "Like I want you. There's more here between us. And I won't ignore it."

Then she left him on the balcony. And heaven help him, as he watched her walk away, he knew he was doomed.

Chapter Six

"Thank you for your kindness and generosity, Lady Galena." Mina clasped hands with her.

"You honor us, Your Highness." Lady Galena stepped back.

Mina then embraced Irena warmly. "Thank you for everything. I hope we'll meet again."

"Oh, I hope so, too." She leaned in and whispered, "Perhaps a royal ball where my brother isn't invited."

Mina laughed. "He only wants to protect you."

"Smother me, you mean."

A sad pang swept over Mina. Other than her friend Kathleen, she'd never had anyone to love as Irena did. She held her at arm's length, clasping both her hands. "Count yourself lucky." Then she winked, "But I'll definitely invite you to the first royal ball I host."

"What's that?" asked Aleksei, stepping up behind them.

"Nothing," they said in unison, then laughed.

"We'd best move on," urged Mikhail.

Mina pressed her cheek to Irena's one more time. "We

shall see each other again soon. I am sure of it."

When Mina stepped aside, Dmitri took her place and swept a kiss over Irena's hand. "Until we meet again, my lady."

Irena flushed.

"Not if I can help it," grumbled Aleksei, shoving Dmitri onward. "Let's go, lover boy."

Gregoravich and Gavril were already halfway down the paved road to the gate.

"Snows will be here soon, Mother," Aleksei called. "Take care with the cold coming." He blew her a kiss.

"You take care of yourself," she shouted back.

Mikhail walked silently beside Mina, as alert and professional as ever. As if the intimate conversation and encounter they shared yesterday hadn't occurred. As if the heated tension wasn't strung taut like a bowstring between them.

"You look well enough to run and keep up," said Mikhail, observing her with a side glance. "Are you?"

"Yes. I am feeling quite strong now. Thanks to the refreshment you gave me in my bedchamber."

He winced. Mina smiled. She'd never been aggressive by nature, but something about this man made her beast want to come out to play. She wanted to bait him. To see what he would do. Hoping he would play with her right back.

"I am glad to hear it." His voice remained tight and controlled.

"And I see that you and your men have fed well. There's a ruddy flush to your cheeks, Captain."

He narrowed his gaze but kept his aim forward as they marched on down the tree-lined road. Mina was constantly aware of this new primal need swirling inside her bosom, a desire that seemed solely focused on the captain. However, beyond that, she longed to know more of the man himself.

Power emanated from his tall, broad figure as he moved with agile grace. Every step, every glance of his wary gaze appeared purposeful, deliberate. A misstep was not in this man's nature. And yet, she knew she'd made him misstep. Hence, the grave lines drawing his face tight.

"Tell me, when you feed, is it a manner of replenishing your body, or do you gain pleasure from the experience?"

His brow pinched together. "Why do you ask?"

"I'm curious. You seem a man of, how shall I put it, efficiency."

"That I am."

"Then you do not experience that extraordinary sensation of pleasure when you feed?"

He pulled her to a stop with a firm but gentle grip. "What exactly are you getting on about?"

"Well, seeing as my experience with you in the cave and yesterday afternoon were my first times feeding in the traditional or, um, *natural* way a vampire feeds, I was wondering if you felt that with other women. When you feed."

Envy twisted in her gut at the thought of his mouth on another woman, and yet she couldn't help but follow this line of questioning to see what he would say. And after the way he leaned imperceptibly closer, his vibrating intensity bristling along her skin, she was glad she'd followed her instincts.

"And what exactly did you feel when you fed from me?"

She adored the way his melodious voice dropped to a rough timbre, like shallow waters scraping the river rocks across a sandy bed.

"I felt a euphoric sense of belonging in that moment," she answered honestly and stepped closer, tipping her head back. "As if my whole life catapulted me to that sliver of time when my lips touched your skin, when my fangs sank into your flesh, when your blood rushed fast and hot into my body. It was ecstasy."

His eyes had dilated, covering his multihued irises mostly black. His nostrils flared, but he didn't move. Not a splinter-thin fraction.

"It's time to run, Your Highness."

"I think you're running already, Captain."

He narrowed his gaze, ignoring her gibe. She was certain he wasn't the sort of man who retreated. Ever. And yet he seemed eager to get away from this conversation. Away from her. The pulsating ripple of desire waving against her empathic senses told her she was right in this pursuit. Whether he knew it or not. The knowledge gave her comfort, even as he bristled at her nearness.

Most her life, she'd felt out of step with the world, with other people. Sure, she could sense their emotions and therefore knew how to react toward them, how to offer them sage advice, as she once did to Prince Marius, knowing he was in love with the peasant revolutionary, Arabelle. But knowing people's emotions and connecting to people were two entirely different things. She'd often felt isolated, because her steward kept her safe from too many visitors and because her empathic senses could be overwhelming and often made her long for solitude. But the bond between her and Captain Mikhail was as tangible as a silken thread wound about her body and encircling his, squeezing tighter every moment they were together.

It was like the cosmos had divined her to be a lone planet among fields of stars, until a dark moon finally found her, where he was meant to circle without end.

With a tilt of his square chin, he said, "Best keep up."

"Oh, I'll keep up." She smiled. "Lead on."

He flashed away, swirling the wind around her with the scent of mulled spice and wood smoke. That scent would be easy for her to follow. She ran in vampire speed, blurring past Dmitri and Aleksei, who were still bickering about Irena.

Then they were all flying together, following Mikhail. Mina laughed at the rush of moving with such strength, such speed, such power. She'd never had occasion to run as the dainty princess. Not like this.

The dormant beast in her body, in her blood, yawned and stretched, sniffing the air as if for the first time. And on the wind was the scent of her prey, calling her to follow faster, to catch him if she could.

Her heartbeat throbbing in her ears, she didn't simply follow the pack but chased the leader. The one whose beast called to her own, demanding that she take note, and that she finally awaken from her long slumber to take what was meant to be hers.

She was so focused on Mikhail, she didn't notice the danger flanking her on her left till it was too late.

...

Mikhail smelled them the split second before they attacked. He dropped back and launched himself into the vampire flying toward Mina. Gripping him around the waist, Mikhail and the attacker went tumbling into her, knocking her to the ground. She screamed. Mikhail's claws ripped through the attacker's skin, his fangs long and sharp when he sprang for the hissing vampire.

Pinning him on his back, Mikhail gripped his throat for control. The creature's eyes were full black with the blood madness. He bucked and clawed, slashing through Mikhail's shirt and gouging his chest. Crimson sprayed the air. Mikhail felt nothing, his sole intent on watching the man die. With a swift move, he gripped both sides of his head and snapped his neck. Unsheathing the serrated, twelve-inch blade he kept at his hip, he severed the man's head with three hacks. Vampires could self-heal from broken necks but not from decapitation.

A shriek pierced the woodlands behind him. He shot to his feet right as Gavril slashed another vampire's carotid artery. A third lay beheaded between Dmitri and Aleksei. Gregoravich kept a defensive stance in front of Mina. Within a second, Mikhail was behind Gregory and held Mina by the shoulders, scanning her for injuries.

"Are you all right?" He needed to touch her, to see that she was unharmed. He examined her face, her throat, opened her cloak to find nothing but a torn sleeve on her arm.

"I'm fine. It's nothing," she protested when he lifted the arm to observe if she'd been injured. "I'm fine. Truly. Not even a scratch."

Satisfied the beast hadn't marred her skin, he turned to his men grouped around the one at Aleksei's feet.

"Same dress as the huntsmen up north," said Gregoravich, his barrel-deep voice rumbling low, his beast primed and ready for more violence.

Their eyes flared bright ice blue with their vampire senses at the forefront.

"And in a pack of three," noted Aleksei, "like the ones who took Helena."

"Who's Helena?" asked Mina.

Mikhail cracked his neck, exhaling deeply and calming his monster still yearning for blood, itching to kill and maim anyone daring to touch her. He retracted his claws before facing her.

"Helena is the daughter of the Duke of Winter Hill's wife."

"His daughter now, as well," added Gavril.

"They took her?" Mina's face paled, her eyes wide.

Mikhail's heart clenched at her concern. "She's all right. We saved her."

"*Bloody hell.*"

Mikhail spun at the sound of his brother in pain. "What

is it, Dmitri?"

He gripped his left shoulder, trying to roll it back, bearing his canine teeth like a feral wolf. "My fucking shoulder."

"You popped it out of socket again."

"*I* popped it out of socket. How is this my fault?"

"You move too fast, Brother. On your knees." Mikhail maneuvered to stand behind him and gripped Dmitri's shoulder with his right arm and his biceps with his left. "I've told you before to control your speed in combat."

"Yes, that's easy for you to say. My speed amplifies when my blood is up, so don't lecture me—"

Crunch.

"Fucking hell!"

Gregory chuckled.

"There's a lady present," Aleksei warned with a smirk, wiping the blood from the flat of his blade on his trousers.

"Don't mind me," said Mina, smiling, though her brow was still pinched with concern. "Are you all right, Dmitri?"

"Yes, Your Highness." He rotated his arm and scowled at Mikhail, who lifted him to his feet.

She caught his gaze and offered him a tender smile, one of admiration that made his chest swell. He shouldn't be admiring or wanting her smiles. He shouldn't be wanting any of her. And yet, his body disagreed with his brain.

"Do you think these men were sent after us specifically?" asked Gavril, crouching down and inspecting one of the bodies.

"No. These have gone rogue. The blood madness will do that," replied Mikhail, glancing back at the one he'd killed, fangs still bared even in death. "That one was trying to kill the princess. The queen will want her alive and healthy."

"How do you know that?" she asked.

The men looked to Mikhail, who had no intention of elaborating on how he knew this to be true.

"Oh," she said quietly. "King Dominik."

There was more to tell her about Queen Morgrid's plans for her marriage to her son. Thinking about it poured ice into his veins. That was a detail he'd tell her in private.

"We need to clear out of here quickly. The smell of blood will draw predators. Including any other rogues in the vicinity."

Mina glanced warily behind her, so Mikhail edged closer. "Are you good to travel on foot from here, or do you need my help?"

He thought she'd simply shout defiance like many women would, but she took a moment to self-examine before drawing in a deep breath.

"I believe I'm fine. If I begin to weaken, I'll let you know."

"Promise?" he asked gently, retying the lacing of her cloak at the throat.

"Yes. I promise."

"Give me your hand."

Her brow pinched together like it did when she was puzzling something out, yet she offered her hand anyway. So trusting. He held it between both of his and closed his eyes, reaching out with his senses.

"Heartbeat is steady. No shakes. No tremors."

Opening his eyes, he stared into the infinite blue, feeling something slip inside, like he was losing himself, piece by piece.

"Steady under attack, Your Highness? I'll bet you'd make a wonderful warrior queen."

"Are you teasing me, Captain?" She arched a delicate brow.

"Not at all. I mean it sincerely." He sobered. "Deeply."

Their gazes lingered, deepened, causing his heart to kick up a notch. With a squeeze of her hand, he ushered her between the other men with a hand at the small of her back. "Dmitri, you're point. Gavril and I will take her right. Gregory and Aleksei, her left."

She moved within the circle of Bloodguard assassins, shielded on all sides. As one, they flashed into vampire speed, moving ever closer to Silvane Forest. Soon, she'd be within the safety of the Black Lily. Perhaps then, the temptation to drag her off behind a tree and devour every last inch of her would finally subside.

Perhaps not.

Chapter Seven

Mina warmed her hands at the fire Gavril had built. He placed another small log on the flames, nodded to her, then found a tree to lean against. That one was the most elusive of them all. He was polite but withdrawn. Mina wondered what tragedies these men had endured. One thing she knew for certain, it was their shared hardship that united them as one in the Bloodguard. She sensed the familial brotherhood binding them each to one another. She envied them.

Aleksei and Dmitri dozed, backs against tree trunks and arms crossed. If they fell under attack again, she knew they'd be on their feet in a split second. Gavril stared into the flames. Gregoravich was on guard down the small incline, facing the southwest in case King Dominik's Legionnaires should finally catch up to them, though none of them feared that they would. And Mikhail had gone to the nearby brook to wash his wounds from the attack. The others had done so already. Mikhail had kept guard, falling into silence—avoiding her gaze—while Gavril had tended the fire.

Mina glanced in the direction of the brook that trickled

softly nearby. She couldn't see him. Shifting in her cozy spot, she considered finding her way down to that stream where he was.

"Don't be anxious, Your Highness," said Dmitri, his eyes still closed. "We're safe for now."

"Oh, I'm not anxious."

His eyes slid open. "No?" A lopsided grin creased his masculine face. "You sure seem it. That heartbeat of yours is pumping hard."

Taken aback, she fiddled with her sleeve. "Though I've endured quite a bit, it's not often I'm attacked by rabid vampires."

He chuckled. "Guess not. Happens to us all the time." He winked. Glancing down to where her fingers pulled at the cuff of her emerald nightgown, he jerked his chin. "What is it with you royals and dragons?"

She stared down at the wide cuff where the white dragon sigil with emerald gems for eyes winked up at her. She'd embroidered this one herself.

She smiled, remembering something. "You know, there's actually a story behind the dragon sigils of the north and south?"

"Is there?"

"My nurse used to tell me the old tale when I was a little girl."

"Well, I'm no little girl, but I like a good story." Crossing his arms, he settled lower on the tree trunk.

"Very well." Mina cleared her throat. "Once, a long, long time ago, there lived a great silver dragon full of fire and magic. He lived in a kingdom in the clouds far from humans or vampirekind. There were no other dragons left in the world. Only him. And he was lonely. He yearned for companionship.

"So he decided to fly down from his pillowed lair in the

sky down to Earth. He searched and searched though he knew not for what. Until one day, he heard the most beautiful voice, a maiden's sweet melody, calling to his beastly heart.

"He followed the voice until he found the fair maid perched at the window of a single ivory tower with no doors anywhere, only one window. She wasn't afraid when she saw the great beast land upon the ground with a shudder.

"'You sing like an angel,' said the dragon.

"'Thank you,' she replied. 'You have beautiful wings.'

"'Come fly with me,' he pleaded. 'I will show you the beauty beyond the clouds.'

"She sighed sadly. 'I cannot. I have been cursed to stay in this tower until the prince of this land fetches me for my wedding day. If I should leave, great peril would come to me.'

"The dragon snorted with fury, black smoke puffing from his nostrils. 'But aren't you lonely in this tower?'

"'Indeed, I am. Perhaps you can visit me, dragon, and keep me company.'

"'I will come every day,' promised the dragon.

"And so he did. Every day for a full year, through winter, spring, summer, and when the leaves began to change in fall, he flew down from the heavens to visit his maiden. She sang for him. And he told her stories of old. She had captured his heart. And he hers. She was the only reason he rose each morning, eager for a new day.

"Until the one day when he landed outside her tower and didn't find her perched in her window, waiting for him. Rather, he heard her crying within. He peered inside and asked her why she cried, for the sound tore him in two.

"'I am to be wed to the prince tomorrow,' she whispered, 'but I love another.'

"The dragon's blood raced like wildfire through his veins. 'Who do you love, dear maiden?'

"She stepped into the morning light of the window. 'I

love the one who is devoted to me. I love you, dear dragon.'

"The dragon couldn't believe such joy existed in all the world. So he tried to give her the same joy. 'I love you as well, sweet maiden. Please come with me to my kingdom in the clouds, then you never need marry this prince you do not love.'

"The maiden stared up into the heavens, a sad but sweet smile spreading across her angelic face then she answered, 'Yes. I will.'

"The dragon was so full of happiness, he crouched down by her tower window and told her to climb onto his back. Gingerly, she stepped onto his back and held onto his mane. Then the dragon, full of joy and love, lifted off into the sky.

"But the maiden didn't tell him what would happen should she defy the curse. The consequence of leaving her tower before she was wed to the prince was death. But since her heart belonged to the silver dragon, she preferred to die with him in the sky than to live without him upon Earth. And so she did. As they drifted through the beautiful heavens, she cradled herself close to her dragon and whispered her love before she took her last breath."

Mina paused, always feeling somber at this point in the story.

"That's it?" asked Dmitri. "That's how the story ends?"

"Not quite." Mina smiled. "The silver dragon cried out with fury and sadness and plummeted back down to the world, landing in a dark forest. He lay his maiden love upon the ground and dug her grave deep with his mighty claws. When he lay her in the earth, he said, 'Without her, there is no use for this anymore.' He slashed his claws across his chest and opened up his flesh and ribs, taking out his still-beating heart and placed it in the earth, burying it with his love. Upon his last sweep of soil upon the grave, the heartless beast roared into the sky, screaming his rage and pain and loss to the heavens. Without his heart, he could not live, but he was still full of fire and magic. As he rocketed toward the stars, he suddenly split in two. The silver dragon became a black dragon of fire and a white dragon of magic. The black dragon, a beast of fury and hatred, soared to the north, trying to cool his burning blood. He landed in the northern mountains and stormed the peaks till he melted into them, becoming one with the rock and stone.

"The white dragon sought warmth and peace in the south. She finally came upon a fragrant, green place full of roses and life. There, she lay down and became one with the earth and let her magic flourish upon the land and its people."

The fire popped as the story ended. Dmitri stared at her, but his mind seemed to drift as he thought of the silver dragon and her maiden.

"The hartstone." He finally broke the silence. "The dragon's heart became the hartstone."

"Yes. That's how the story goes anyway." Mina shrugged. "My nurse used to say that the first king of Briar Rose lay with his bride upon the meadows there and conceived their first child upon where the white dragon reposed. That is why the white dragon's magic lives on in our blood." She laughed. "I always thought it a silly tale, but somehow true. Is that strange?"

Dmitri snorted. "I've seen much stranger things in my time." He tossed another log onto the fire. "Thanks for the story, Your Highness."

"You're welcome." Mina stood, catching sight of the dark red splotches upon her wrist. "I need to wash."

"Mikhail is down by the stream. He'll keep you safe." Dmitri leaned his head back, closing his eyes with a smile. "Trust me."

She moved off, mumbling, "I don't doubt it."

How could she after that display of expedient

extermination of the savage rogues that had attacked them. These five men of the Bloodguard had dispatched them as if they'd been sparring in a yard exercise. And from what Dmitri had mentioned earlier that day, there were quite a few more of them who made up this band of mercenaries.

As she picked her way closer to the brook on silent feet, she couldn't see them simply as mercenaries. Especially not after what she'd learned of them. Yes, they were killers. And possibly for hire by the highest bidder. But they were also men of the upper crust. Every one of them she'd met. She could tell in their mannerisms and speech. She also noticed they'd refused to drop her title, keeping formalities in place. Probably on orders by their captain. And that brought her to the train of thought that their alliance with the Black Lily had little to do with money and more to do with the cause.

Of course, the cause of the Black Lily was to bring the humans out of oppression, to do away with the tyrannous rule of Queen Morgrid, to offer humanity a chance at equality. That didn't explain why a band of aristocratic vampire renegades were allying with them.

She stepped from behind a tree where Mikhail's long, roughened leather coat hung on a branch. As she stepped clear of the overhanging flap, she froze.

Heaven above, Mikhail's maker smiled the day he made him.

He crouched over the stream, naked from the waist up. Mina drank in the breathless sight. Lateral muscles bunched and flexed as he wrung his shirt with a tight twist of his hands over the brook. The lines of his muscled back were exquisite. She couldn't imagine what the front of him would look like. She wouldn't have to wait long.

"You'd make a terrible assassin, Your Highness."

He stood and whipped out the excess water with a sharp smack of the shirt tail in the air as he turned toward her. It was his turn to freeze in place.

"Don't do that," he warned.

"Do what?" she asked, unable to keep from letting her gaze wander down the hard planes of his broad chest, along the sinuous line down the center of his chiseled abs, and to the top of a muscular V disappearing into his low-slung pants.

"You know damn well what. Don't look at me that way."

She shrugged, helplessly. "You're...beautiful."

He made no reply, firming his lips together, as if the compliment distressed him. Slinging his wet shirt over one shoulder, he marched toward her. "It's best we get back to the others."

Best for whom?

"No. I need to clean up. Some blood got on my hands as well." She raised a palm to show him the faint blood spatter staining her palm and wrist where she'd held up a hand right before Dmitri had cut the vampire's jugular. Funny how all that violence hadn't unsettled her at all. If anything, her senses had heightened, relishing the fall of those brutal rogues. Nothing seemed to get her blood pumping hard like the man standing before her.

"Fine," he growled. "Go wash."

She untied her cloak and hung it over the branch next to his coat. Stepping toward the edge of the brook, she kneeled on the earthy bank. She caught her unbound hair as it slid over one shoulder toward the water. Irena's maid had woven tiny braids along her temples but had left the rest in its natural waves. She couldn't keep her hair from trailing into the stream while washing.

"Captain? Will you help me?" She gestured toward her hair.

He didn't move at first, staring as he contemplated the request. Finally, he blew out a heavy breath and strode to her side. Kneeling on one knee next to her left hip, his other leg cocked up at her back, he pulled her hair back with one hand, his fist resting between her shoulder blades.

She said not a word but pushed up her sleeves near to her elbows and set to cleaning her hands thoroughly. She then leaned farther over. He anchored her, pressing the fist still holding her hair farther down her back. She splashed the cold water on her face, sucking in a breath at the refreshing chill. Cupping her hands, she drank from the clear-running stream.

Their long run had caused her to sweat, despite the cold. And while she knew what she did next would rouse the man at her back, that was precisely what she wanted.

Slowly, she pulled one sleeve off her shoulder, then the other. Scooping the cold water with her cupped hands, she splashed her neck and chest. A deep growl reverberated from the vampire behind her. The sound hummed up her spine and tingled along her skin till her nipples peaked under her gown. Instantly, electric warmth coiled low in her belly. Her breath quickening, she leaned forward and did it again, splashing even more water up and over her bare shoulders, over the top of her small breasts.

"You don't know what you're doing," his words grated like gravel over stone.

She brought another scoop of water to drink and to moisten her lips before twisting her head over her shoulder, meeting his dark, hungry gaze. She said not a word, her thoughts surely evident in her eyes as she flicked her tongue over her lips. Then she let her gown slip farther down one shoulder.

"I take that back." His expression hardened, his voice husky and smooth. "You know exactly what you're doing. Don't you?"

"I told you last night. There's something between us. I'm not going to pretend it's not there. That would be a lie."

"So you tempt me on purpose?"

"Yes," she answered, unashamedly. "If I must."

He pulled back on her hair gently, arching her neck and clenching his jaw as he leaned his head closer. "This is dangerous."

Rather than cower or succumb to his stormy countenance and menacing voice, she read his true emotions beating a steady drum in the air—fear and potent, hard lust. Empowered by her own instinct, she turned and lifted up onto her knees, facing him, his hand still clutching her hair. She brought her wet forefinger to his parted lips. Tracing gently till he opened wider, she slipped her finger inside and glided the pad along his teeth till she found his protruding canines. Purposefully, she held his darkening gaze and pricked her finger on a sharpened fang. A drop of her blood pearled, but he'd not moved. She stroked the blood onto his tongue, the soft warmth pulling a moan from her throat. He sealed his lips at once around her finger and sucked deep.

The sensation of one drop of his elixir flowed through her body like welcome wildfire, licking flames in all the right places. Slowly, she slid her finger from between his lips. His breath was ragged, like hers, as she trailed her bloody fingertip along his lower lip, watching with heart-pounding fascination, till finally her eyes lifted to his.

Oh, God.

Fierce desire and hot need had never pounded against her this hard. He stared at her with such dark hunger, heat seared through her blood. Inching closer, their breaths mingled and eyes locked.

"Just a kiss, Captain." The heat of him radiated onto her face, cheeks, lips, breasts, belly, like a raging inferno. Yes, his pulse pumped hard as his panting attested. And his desire whipped against her with lashes of aching intensity. "I want to feel it again. Now that I'm awake."

She meant more than having her eyes opened from the

bloodless sleep. She was awake like she'd never been before. Awake to her own heart's desires. And to her body's as well.

He gripped her hair harder, the only signal she had before he closed the inch between them. Their mouths met in a clash of teeth, fangs, and tongue, a desperate, clawing need. A kiss that could block out the world. Or begin whole new ones. Ones where a princess took what she desired, what she deserved, what she was destined to have. And to keep for all time.

She trailed her palms up his hard chest and along his flexing shoulders, settling one hand at his nape. The other she clenched in his hair as their mouths nipped and sucked. Her feminine moans mixed with his masculine ones, weaving them tighter together until he banded a strong arm around her waist and pulled her flush against his body, cradling her close, both of them on their knees, his apart.

He skimmed his mouth up her jaw and down her throat, licking a wet path, laving the drops of water beading on her skin. "You're so sweet," he murmured.

She laced both her hands in his short hair, pressing him closer, before letting them slide down his neck to his hard chest. His groaning growl told her he approved of her exploring touches, feather-light down his abdomen.

"Yes." She whispered her approval when his lips and tongue suckled their way over the swell of her bosom.

She had no experience with men. None. Her first kiss was the blood kiss that had awakened her. She'd heard him in the dark of her prison tower. She'd felt his lips, his mouth, his tongue, his own blood reviving her to full wakefulness, bringing her back to the world with a passion she'd not forgotten since that moment.

And here she was taking more. So unlike her. So far from the staid, poised princess who'd spent her days reading, embroidering, playing piano, and singing music, dreaming of a time when she'd feel alive. Dreaming of this. Of a man like him.

"Mikhail," she moaned as he scraped a canine along the mound of one breast, not breaking the skin but marking her pale flesh with his sharp fang.

He licked the line along her skin. "Mina," he whispered.

She dropped her head back on a gasp of pleasure. Her name on his lips was pure heaven. He skated up her throat, his roughened voice driving her near mad.

"Mina."

He'd let go of her hair and eased his hand to cup the back of her head. He lifted till she met his gaze, his lips hovering close to hers, not touching.

"Mina." His voice had dropped so low, so deep, so dark, with such power, such force, as if he owned her. And in that moment, she knew no man would ever have the right to kiss her lips, to caress her skin, to touch her body. He'd claimed her with a word, with her own name.

His ethereal gaze burned into hers as he swept his lips over hers one last time, gentling his grip in her hair and around her waist, licking into her mouth with controlled tenderness. She could've floated in this place of pleasure forever, but the captain finally pulled away. Panting, he composed himself and lifted her to her feet.

With slow, precise movements, he righted her sleeves up over her shoulders and pressed his palms to the sides of her neck, his fingers tightening at her nape, his thumbs brushing her collarbone, and simply stared at her. It was a look of longing and loss at once, of pain and pleasure, of hope and despair. Something was wrong, more than she could decipher by sensing his emotions. She understood his sense of duty, but she couldn't comprehend why it hurt so much to experience a moment's pleasure.

"Mikhail?"

He shook his head. Taking another controlled breath, he dropped his arms and marched to the tree holding her cloak and his coat. On a heavy sigh, she followed, knowing the moment was gone. He'd already shielded himself behind his mantle of control when he wrapped her in her cloak, tying it at the neck.

He shouldered into his dark-brown leather coat, the tail brushing above his knees. All of the Bloodguard had similar coats in different shades of brown and black with hoods she'd only seen them wear the night they'd rescued her.

"Come. We're almost to Silvane Forest. Once there, you'll be safe."

She nodded and followed him back to the others, wondering exactly who she'd be safe from. She knew he included himself among the dangers that threatened her. What he hadn't quite come to understand was that for once in her life, she yearned for a taste of danger.

Chapter Eight

Mikhail had been rebuking himself ever since that moment by the brook where he'd lost his bloody mind. He'd only barely reeled himself in before tumbling her to the ground and hiking up her skirts.

His goal for this mission had been to save the princess and then to show her the path to claim her throne. With the support of the southern kingdom, she'd have strong, powerful allies and the best equestrian army in all the land to go up against Queen Morgrid and King Dominik's vampire army. His goal had *not* been to attach himself to her in any way, shape, or form that was this intimate. Protect her, yes. Maul her by a stream, suckle her perfect breast, make her come on his fingers—an emphatic NO.

It was the blood kiss. Since he'd tasted her, he'd yearned for more. He wasn't prepared for her reaction to him at the stream. The desire shining in those eyes. He should've had someone else awaken her. Dmitri, perhaps.

Fuck. He knew he wouldn't have. The thought of his brother or any man's mouth or hands on her lit an inferno of fury inside him. It made him even more eager to put quick distance between them and King Dominik's guards. He'd not let that monster get ahold of her. He'd die before he let any harm come to her.

They walked down the last incline leading into the southern edge of the Silvane Forest. It wasn't wise to move at vampire speed into hart-wolf territory. Even if they had allies, not all the hart wolves liked the fact that the Bloodguard had set up camp on the northeastern border by Hiddleston, near Sienna's home. Before they'd left on their mission, he'd learned that the Fire Witch, as some were calling her now, had befriended the princess once before. Arabelle counted Mina as a friend as well, even though she had been betrothed to Marius at the time. Mikhail was glad to know she'd have friends among the Black Lily. It would put his mind at ease so that he could distance himself. The thought struck physical pain in his chest, and yet he knew he must do it.

He had to remain focused. The very reason the Bloodguard took a blood oath to forfeit marriage and family and any attachments to lovers was to maintain their lethal edge. A lack of focus could mean death—for his men, for the Black Lily, for civilians. For Mina.

"Will you tell me about your family?" she asked beside him, jarring him back to the present.

The other men walked ahead and behind, still guarding her from every side. No rogues would wander into Silvane Forest without meeting a quick death by the hart wolves, but they weren't taking any chances.

Mikhail glanced her way. He didn't want to let her in any more than she already was.

That was a lie.

He wanted to bare his soul to the woman. Therein lay danger.

"I am the son of a vampire gentleman and a human

commoner. However, my father was especially loved by King Stephanus. So he honored my father's request to make her vampire when they discovered she was with child—" he glanced at her for emphasis—"with me, of course. And while my father was a favorite of the King of Korinth, he made enemies of the monarchs at Glass Tower."

He reined in the anger flaming up his chest.

"How did he make enemies?" she asked softly.

"My father had radical ideas. Though our estate is extremely small, we support a few faithful tenants to work the land. But my father disagreed with the overwhelming percentage of the tenants' wages going to himself and the crown. So one day, he stopped paying the tithe to the Glass Tower, leaving his tenants with a much larger portion of earnings. Since his appeals to the Tower were consistently ignored, he began to ignore them."

"I don't imagine that went over well."

He could feel her eyes on him, but he kept his own forward. "Not well at all, I'm afraid."

"What happened?"

Flashes of memory. *His mother's cries. His father's mutilated body.*

"While we were all away, except my father tending to the estate, a band of rogue vampires with the blood madness showed up and murdered him."

The princess gasped, remaining silent for a moment. Then finally, "I'm so sorry."

"It's done."

"How can you be sure the rogues were sent by the Glass Tower?"

He looked down at her, remembering his father's decapitated head alongside his crumpled body.

"Because after they assassinated him on the doorstep of our home, they wrote the word traitor in his own blood. It could only be the queen who saw him as such."

She didn't ask anything more. He wouldn't elaborate that his father's radical beliefs stemmed from an age-old wrong done to their bloodline. That this war between his family and the one sitting on the empirical throne was one that began long, long ago. Before he was ever born.

He needed to change the subject before his anger overwhelmed him.

"Arabelle told me you'd met the hart wolves that Sienna kept close to her the last time you were here."

"I don't know about meeting them, but yes, I saw them. There was one very gentle wolf, the white female Sienna called Duchess. Do you know the hart wolf even let her ride her? I remember when Kathleen—" She broke off suddenly, the joy in her voice leeching out as if she'd been struck.

Mikhail had been told of her lady-in-waiting's fate. "I am sorry for your friend."

She kept her head held high as they drew closer to the woods. "Thank you. It was cruel. She'd done nothing wrong. The queen had her killed to hurt me."

"Yes. The queen thrives on bringing pain to others." He cast away that thought, focusing on what was ahead. "The reason I bring up the hart wolves is because there's something you don't know. Didn't know upon your last visit here. And we'll likely be meeting some of them as we enter the forest."

"Meeting?" she gave a curious laugh. "What do you mean?"

"The hart wolves aren't simply wolves."

"No. I never thought so. They're big as bears and have a high intelligence. They also feel emotions on a very pure level."

He slowed and glanced at her quizzically, then remembered. She'd told him she was an empath, right before she said she wasn't ignoring her own emotions. He'd been stupefied by her declaration at the moment, having forgotten that she could sense the emotions of every person, every being. "That makes sense." He said his thoughts aloud as he walked on more swiftly, and she stepped in line beside him.

"What makes sense?"

"You are so forthright and honest. Your own emotions are so obvious. That would make sense for an empath."

She nodded, and they fell silent as they edged into the woods. A thin layer of snow covered the ground, some roots of the thick black oak trees jutting up here and there. No leaves clung to the branches now, where normally they'd be full of silvery leaves.

"I love these woods," she whispered reverently.

"Interesting. Most vampires fear these woods. The magic here."

"Not me. That is why I love them. I can feel the magic singing in the boughs. Can't you?"

He followed her gaze upward, hearing and feeling nothing but a strange chill on the wind. "No. I'm afraid I don't."

"Really?" She smiled like a child beholding a wondrous gift. "It feels like…coming home."

"Perhaps it's because you're an empath. You sense what others cannot."

"Perhaps."

Dmitri flashed from up ahead and stopped in front of Mikhail, the wind whooshing the air around them. "Dane, Allora, and some other clansmen await up ahead. They want to meet the princess."

"Tell them we're coming."

Dmitri flashed away around the bend.

"Who are Dane and Allora?"

"That's what I've been trying to tell you. The hart wolves aren't just wolves. They're a clan—actually, there are four clans from what I've been told—of a people touched by the magic of the hartstone. They are guardians in wolf form."

Mina simply shook her head as they rounded the curve into a small clearing along the path where a row of people stood. The other four of the Bloodguard assumed positions behind Mikhail and Mina, flanking in a defensive mode. Mikhail saw and sensed hart wolves pacing within the woods, watching.

Mikhail recognized Allora first, wearing buckskin pants, a white tunic blouse, and a leather drawstring tie at her waist. Her white-blond hair fell in wispy waves to her thighs. The tips of her tribal tattoo flared with a wispy curl by her collarbone.

Mina slowed her gait but didn't stop. He sensed no fear from her, only curiosity.

"Oh," she finally said just as they stopped before Allora. Dane was on her right.

She seemed to realize what he'd been trying to tell her. A line of four clansmen Mikhail didn't recognize stood on Allora's left. However, their powerful presence was not to be overlooked nor were the golden torques around their necks, crowns denoting their status as kings of their clans.

With a dip of his head, Mikhail gestured to Mina and said, "May I present Vilhelmina Dragomir, Princess of Arkadia."

Allora bowed, rather than curtsied, as both men and women bowed in greeting in their culture, Sienna had explained to him. "I am Allora Godric. Sienna once called me Duchess."

Mina could barely leash the glee shining on her face. "I see." She curtsied. "It is a pleasure to meet you." She cast a wondrous glance up at Mikhail. She truly was a remarkable woman, finding such joy in the discovery that the hart wolves were shapeshifters, touched by magic. Most people would frown in confusion or cower in fear. Not Mina. She welcomed this strange news as she would a glorious gift.

"This is my brother, Dane Godric."

Mikhail bowed his head and smiled as well at the mountainous man who equaled Gregoravich in size. But whereas Gregory looked dangerous, Dane had a fierce, wild edge that never left his hazel-gold gaze. His dark-brown hair hung long past his shoulders. He wore rough-hewn leather pants like the others. His tattoos wrapped down his arms beyond his sleeves to his wrists and cut up in harsher lines around his neck. Mikhail had seen his fighting in action back in King Dominik's palace in Izeling when he and a war party of the Black Lily had come to save the day. Before their arrival that terrifying night, Mikhail wasn't sure they'd all make it out alive. Unfortunately, the king had made his escape alive as well.

Mina addressed Dane. "You were the one Sienna called Hugo, weren't you?"

"Yes, Your Highness," the hard man said with a respectful bow of the head.

Thankfully, she did not question where his younger brother was. The one who'd died in battle against an army of Queen Morgrid's vampires. It was the deciding factor for Dane to join the Black Lily against the evil queen.

"Your Highness," said Allora. "I would like to introduce you to our four chieftains. This is Bain of the Fingal clan, Kiel of the Lochlan, Niall of the Rodan clan, and finally, my father, Hagan of the Godric clan."

"It is a pleasure to meet you," she said, as if it were every day she met the elusive chieftains of the hart wolves.

They all bore varying shades of golden eyes, distinct to the hart wolf. While the chieftains observed Mina shrewdly, Allora's father stepped forward and lifted his hand.

"May I, Your Highness?"

Mikhail tightened every muscle in his body. His protectiveness of her was an instinctual reaction. He tightened his fists, reigning in an emotion he shouldn't be feeling. As her personal guard, of course he'd feel protective. But not to this degree.

"Be not afraid, Captain," said Allora. "He means her no harm."

Mikhail eased his stance but kept close to Mina, who lifted her hand to the chieftain.

When he took her hand in his, he closed his eyes. His hard face broke into a smile. When he opened his eyes, they burned bright gold. Mina inhaled a small gasp but didn't pull her hand away until he released it.

He turned back to the other chieftains and simply nodded. The tension stiffening the three remaining suddenly evaporated like mist in the wind.

"You've tasted magic once before, Your Highness," whispered the chieftain. "You are welcome within the safety of Silvane Forest. As long as you should need it."

"I told you, Father," said Allora behind him.

"Yes, you did, Daughter." He and the other three chieftains marched off into the woods.

Mikhail noted the heavy presence of hart wolves melting away as they wandered off. He smelled their scent growing fainter. Dane and Allora remained, then they marched on together deeper into the Silvane Forest.

"You could've warned me." Mina's arm brushed against his as she whispered close.

"I was trying to."

"Allora," she called to the woman walking just ahead. "What did your father mean? That I've tasted magic before?"

"He means exactly that. You've been touched by magic before."

"But how? What kind of magic?"

Allora laughed, a sort of tinkling sound that echoed up into the empty boughs. She glanced over her shoulder. "The magic of the hartstone."

"But I'd never been to the Silvane Forest before Arabelle brought me here. I've never even seen the hartstone."

"Few people ever have," she said with another enigmatic smile. "Nevertheless. It has seen you. Somewhere." She leaped toward the path when a flash of black wolf slipped between the trees. "Dane, you'll watch them to the encampment, I need to—" She nodded toward her mate.

"Go, Allora. I'll watch them."

Allora ran, pulling her tunic over her head, laughing when Bron caught up to her. Mikhail watched Mina, who had stopped, unable to keep her eyes from the scene, her pretty mouth ajar. Mikhail glanced back just in time to see a naked Allora blur in place, much like when a vampire speeds, then a cracking sound and flare of light. A white hart wolf sprang up, bounding after the black one.

"Come on, Mina," he pressed a light hand to her back to keep her moving.

"Did you just see that?"

"Yes." He chuckled.

"Oh, don't let him fool you," said Dmitri. "He was just as enthralled the first time he saw them do it."

Dane had said nothing, a stalwart tower beside them.

"Dane, why must you watch us?" Mikhail asked.

He exhaled a sigh, glancing to the left and right of the wooded path. "There's a faction of the hart wolves who are angry that vampires are here in the sacred forest. The natural enemy of the hart wolves. We naturally sense when vampires cross into the shades of Silvane. But now that the chieftains have offered sanctuary to the Bloodguard, it chafes those who would rather not have you here. And there are some who definitely don't approve of the princess being here."

The princess was a powerful figure in the vampire world. And would be more powerful if Mikhail had anything to do with it. He drew closer to her, keeping a hand at the small of her back, as if contact would keep her safer. In reality, it simply calmed his nerves.

"There's nothing to fear," assured Dane.

"Then why did your sister seem to think so?"

"The rebellious ones won't go against the chieftains. But there are one or two who might be stupid enough to try something on their own, in an effort to show their worth. If I'm here, they'll cower away." He grinned, making him look more feral than civilized. "Do not worry."

Mikhail had never worried. He had complete confidence in his men, and he never entered a fight he knew he couldn't win. And yet, tendrils of fear had been creeping into his gut ever since he'd pressed his bloody lips to Mina's. A restlessness he couldn't seem to tamp down kept growing. Part of it dealt with the woman walking at his side, but there was more he couldn't quite put his finger on. An ominous tendril circled and hovered. Like a storm rumbling in the distance, he knew danger was coming. He just didn't know when. But he'd be ready.

Chapter Nine

The familiar whisper of magic wrapped around her, growing stronger the deeper they marched into the forest. Like an old friend. She couldn't help but look around and smile. The chieftain's cryptic words swirled in her head. As a vampire, of course, she was touched by magic. All vampires were. But he didn't seem to be referring to her royal lineage. This wasn't the first time she'd been told she was touched by magic.

A conversation she once had with her nurse as a young girl sprang to mind.

"Sweet Mina, your hair and eyes shine so bright. Must've been that fairy dust the good witch gave you."

"What good witch, Nurse?"

"The one who blessed you as a babe, dear girl. That's why you look like the queen of fairies."

Mina remembered how she'd laughed at being called the queen of fairies. Her nurse was taken away not long after that, replaced by strict tutors to prepare her for her role as a proper queen when she was married off to Prince Marius. Steward Thorwald had told her from a young age that she was promised to the youngest Varis prince. Only then would she become queen.

Glancing at Mikhail at her side, who'd remained aloof since their encounter at the stream, she thought of what he'd told her at Wentworth Hall. He'd declared she was heir to the throne of Arkadia. Why had she never thought to claim the throne for her own? She knew why. She'd been the meek, dutiful princess, awaiting the day she'd be passed from one man's care to another. Never had she even once considered the fact that it was her right to demand her claim.

"Are you all right?" Mikhail asked, those all-seeing eyes catching her change in mood.

"No. I'm not, actually." Her blood pumped hard and hot in her veins. The wind gusted through the naked branches above them, knocking limbs together fiercely, as if the forest sensed her ire.

"What is it?" She felt his intense scrutiny, heightened by the deep timbre of his voice. "Tell me."

Tears stung her eyes. It was so sudden and overwhelming that it caught her unaware. She sucked in a deep breath to keep from sobbing, then stopped beneath one of the towering black oak trees. She knelt and fumbled with her laces.

"My boot laces are loose," she murmured, needing an excuse to pull her emotions in check. They never whirled out of control this way. She pulled on her laces forcefully, anger making her actions jerky and fumbling.

"Go on," she heard Mikhail tell the others, sensing they'd all stopped when she did. "We'll be along soon."

He knelt before her and placed his hands atop hers, where she was yanking so hard she nearly broke the laces.

"Let me," he coaxed gently.

She settled back onto her other foot curled beneath her. She swiped the back of her hand across one cheek, then the other, hiccoughing on a shaky sigh. Mikhail didn't say a word.

Slowly, he unwound the now-knotted laces with long, agile fingers. He tightened, then looped, then double-knotted with slow precision, focusing his attention on her foot. Not on her.

She realized he was giving her a moment to gather herself together. This rough and broody and lethal captain was being as gentle with her as with a kitten. When finished, he placed both hands around her ankle, cradling her foot with firm hands, the heat of him seeping through the leather boot.

"There, now." Finally, he met her gaze, his expression serene. "Tell me what has caused you pain."

He was pleading with her, not asking. His brows lifted in quiet patience.

"I am such a fool," she admitted, the shame of it making her squeeze her eyes shut a moment, trying to stop a fresh well of tears. No good.

He lifted one of those perfect hands and brushed the roughened pad of his thumb across her cheek.

"You are no such thing." His usually commanding, even domineering, timbre rumbled soft, as if coaxing a timid mare to his hand.

"I am. You mentioned last night that I would one day be queen. The truth is, I should have been a true leader to my people long ago. Why have I never demanded that position? The steward was to safeguard the throne till I was of age. I've been of age for quite some time. Yet, I never even thought of stepping up and leading my people." She gritted her teeth for a moment, then let out a disgusted exhale. "Actually, that's not true. I had thought of it once. About a year ago, I mentioned it to Steward Thorwald, but he told me it was best to wait till I was married to Prince Marius, then we would ascend together. And I just accepted it. As if I wasn't good enough, strong enough to lead on my own." She let her chin drop, staring at her fingers in her lap, twisting the fabric of her skirt. "I suppose I'm not."

He trailed those long fingers around her neck and lifted her chin with his thumb.

"Listen to me, Mina." The dominance was back in his velvet-dark voice. "You are far stronger than you know. Did you realize that less than half the vampires put into a bloodless sleep actually survive imprisonment for even a week? It's not the starvation that kills them. It's the dark isolation. Those who do survive awaken unhinged, their minds broken."

He squeezed his fingers at her nape, brushing his thumb over her cheek once more. A fervent look hardened his features as he swept his gaze over her face.

"You not only survived for months, you came out whole." He shook his head, a sharp sound of disbelief escaped him. "Not just whole." He cupped the other side of her face, keeping her gaze locked on him as if what he said now was of the utmost importance. "You came out stronger, fiercer, more alive and more brilliant than the Northern Star."

A wave of adoration enveloped her entire body, humming with heat directly from Mikhail. She'd not felt this emotion directed at her in all her life. Not with such intensity and certainty. Her chin quivered, but she bit her lip to keep from making a sound.

"Lesser men have died having endured what you did. But not you. No, not you." His voice dropped to a rough whisper, as if he were almost speaking to himself, not to her. "You bring me to my knees with the strength that is inside you. A woman whose external beauty is nothing compared to the powerful goddess who resides within. Ascend your throne?" He brushed the pad of his thumb across her quivering lip. "Oh, Mina." He shook his head, like a man lost. "You already are a queen."

She wanted to weep again for such lovely words that no one, not a single soul, had ever spoken to her. It was a gift. A greater gift than luxurious silk or jewels or lands or castles.

One that couldn't be bought with gold. It was acknowledgment that she was worth more than what others had seen in her. The steward, the lords, the Legionnaires who'd orbited around her for her entire life, keeping her sheltered, keeping her helpless. They'd seen the little princess whose only worth was tied to the husband she could buy for the kingdom. Mikhail cut them all down in a single conversation, wiping them away with one stroke.

This man. This beautiful, fierce warrior wasn't simply tugging on her primal impulses anymore. He was tugging on her heart. As if he heard her thoughts, those otherworldly eyes widened a fraction before he let her go quickly and stood. He held out a hand to help her up while glancing up the trail.

"We'd better go."

"Of course." She swallowed the lump of emotion still weighing her down.

As she stood, she braced one hand on the trunk of the black oak. The second she placed her palm on the rough bark, a pulse of magic from wherever the hartstone resided in these woods pumped a beat through her palm into her body. She sucked in a sudden breath, relishing the tingle of enchantment coursing through her veins, washing her anew with an electric serenity. A message that all would be well. The forest, the hartstone, was speaking to her.

"What is it?" he asked, having let her go, but still standing close, his features schooled into his grave expression. "Did you hurt your ankle?"

She couldn't explain this sensation to him. It was a knowing she couldn't put into words. She dropped her hand from the tree and smiled. "No. I'm fine now."

With a nod, he gestured up the path. "We're almost to Sienna's cottage."

A cacophony of voices overlapped in the near distance. Then high-pitched laughter.

Mina touched Mikhail's arm, puzzled. "Children?"

He smiled. "Yes. Remember I spoke to you of Friedrich Volya, the Duke of Winter Hill, and his new wife, Brennalyn?"

"Yes."

"They have a cottage not far from Sienna's."

"A duke in a woodland cottage?"

"Aye," added Aleksei, on her right as they rounded the bend where Dmitri waited for them. "And wait till you see how full with children their home is. I daresay the duke has never had to live in such a tight space with so many bustling bodies before."

"Nor has he been happier," added Dmitri, walking on just ahead of them.

Mikhail nodded with a wider smile but said nothing.

"You are close to this duke?" asked Mina.

"Yes. I served him at Winter Hill, knowing he wasn't in league with his grandmother the queen or with his uncle, King Dominik. I'd hoped to discover he might be willing to fight against them. What I didn't know then was that he was already allied with the Black Lily."

The energy of vampires grew, sparking the air with a familiar aura. The stone cottage came into view, its yard full of soldiers—vampire and human. Not quite the same scene she met last time she was here, when the Black Lily had held her captive in hopes of bargaining with the queen. Instinctively, she drew closer to Mikhail as the entire company stopped and turned. Two men who were sparring with short swords paused and looked their way.

"It's all right," he murmured with a comforting hand at her back.

Mina didn't recognize anyone. The cottage door flew open and out hurried Sienna, her beautiful smile bright as she opened her arms.

"Oh, Mina!" she cried as she swept Mina into her arms

and embraced her close.

When Arabelle had kidnapped Mina as a means to negotiate with King Grindal and Queen Morgrid for the Black Lily, Sienna had kept her here at her cottage. Sienna had treated Mina like a dear friend, rather than a captive. She still felt that kinship they'd formed those months ago.

"We were so worried about you." Sienna pulled her at arm's length, gripping her by the shoulders. "You look lovely as ever."

"Thank you, Sienna. It's so good to see you." Her heart melted at such a welcome into the arms of a true friend.

"You look a little tired as well."

"I am." Mina glanced nervously at the entourage of fierce-looking men still staring. "Where is Arabelle?"

Sienna wrapped an arm around her shoulders and guided her toward the cottage, where she saw the former lieutenant Nikolai leaning in the open door. "Let's get you inside and away from prying eyes so we can talk." She flashed a chastising look over her shoulder. "And prying ears. I know they look rough, but they're harmless. Well, to us anyway."

Dmitri, Gavril, Aleksei, and Gregoravich joined the black-clad vampires with brotherly handshakes and pats on the backs, muttering greetings as to old friends. So, these men were other members of the Bloodguard.

Mikhail stood and watched her go, an unreadable expression fixed in place. Part of her wanted to beckon him to follow, to insist upon it, but many eyes watched them. And one thing she was certain of: Mikhail was uncertain of their relationship, if they even had one.

"We expect another snow tonight," said Sienna sweeping her into her pretty little home. "We've had none for over a week, but Nikolai tells me it will certainly snow tonight. We've got a small cottage set up near Brennalyn's home. Actually, it's one of the children's art studios that Friedrich built. The poor duke dotes on those children."

"Or he wants his youngest, Izzy, more occupied," added Nikolai, closing the door behind them and strolling to a cupboard.

"Oh, Nikolai. As if. Izzy has that man wrapped around her little finger. You'll adore Brennalyn's children. They are all so lovely. Seven orphans she took in on her own. Can you imagine?" Sienna urged her to sit on her sofa next to the crackling fire.

"Seven?" Mina was genuinely shocked. "No. I cannot imagine. Brennalyn must be a very energetic woman."

"She'd have to be in order to keep up with Friedrich's demands," muttered Nikolai as he poured three glasses of red wine.

"*Nikolai.* Stop saying such things. Her Highness will think ill of you."

Mina laughed. "No, I won't."

Nikolai arched a brow at Sienna while he handed them each a glass of wine.

"Thank you," said Mina gratefully, taking a large sip. "I must say, I was surprised to see your yard so full."

"Ah, yes. Well, the training encampment is closer to Hiddleston. We've commandeered a wide meadow and valley along the edge of Silvane Forest, but the Bloodguard knew their captain was returning today."

"They did? How's that?"

"Captain Mikhail had told them the precise day and near the hour you all would return, which was this afternoon."

"And no one thought he might've been held up or prevented from his timely return?"

Nikolai scoffed but said nothing, as he gulped his wine while standing at the mantel.

Sienna smiled and shook her head. "Not the captain. If he says he'll do something, it will be done."

Mina understood the man was efficient and resourceful, but she hadn't quite grasped the depth of his own fortitude in achieving a goal. Her heart warmed at his utter devotion to her rescue and her care for the duration of their mission in getting her here. She wondered whether his mission with her was now over. A sudden panic gripped her. What if he moved on and left the encampment for another mission? She hadn't had time to consider that. The stab of loss pricked that soft organ beneath her ribs.

"Is everything all right, Mina?" Sienna asked, placing a hand on hers.

"Oh, yes. Where are Arabelle and Marius?" She sipped her wine, changing the subject, though Nikolai observed her more keenly. He hadn't missed her anxiety at the thought of Mikhail.

"They should be returning soon. They left with a party to speak to King Agnar of Pyros."

"King Agnar?" Mina understood that Marius was closest to this brother who ruled the western kingdom. "Why have they gone there?"

Sienna glanced at Nikolai, her mood turning somber suddenly.

"We sent one of the Bloodguard with a sealed request to King Stephanus a fortnight ago. The east is infiltrated with King Dominik's Legionnaires. We'd hoped that Stephanus would band with us and in return we'd rid his kingdom of Dominik's encroaching dominion as it appears he has designs to take over the east."

"Oh, no." This was more perilous than Mina had realized. "And I suppose Stephanus denied the request."

Nikolai nodded. "He's always been a bit of a coward. I hadn't expected any better."

"And so Marius is hoping his brother in the west will join us," added Sienna.

"What are the numbers of the Black Lily?" Mina glanced from Sienna to Nikolai. "Are there not enough to match them?"

Nikolai drained his glass and set it on the mantel, then squared his shoulders, hands in his pockets. "Your Highness, while you were...incapacitated, Queen Morgrid and King Dominik have been raiding the lands to the north, taking entire villages, turning the men vampire for their army, keeping the women and children as bleeders and as hostages to force the men to fight with them."

"Dear heavens." Mina nearly dropped her glass, but Sienna caught it as it tilted on her lap, then lifted it away.

She set both their glasses on a side table. "It is dire indeed. We have a strong, well-trained army. But not enough. Not against the kind of vampire army they're amassing, many of whom have been infected with the blood madness and will do anything for the queen."

"What of King Grindal? No one has said a word of him."

"No one knows," said Nikolai. "My cousin Riker was the last man we had inside the Glass Tower. Riker said King Grindal seemed to go missing right about the time they started torturing Riker for information. They rightly guessed that Riker was still loyal to me."

"And your cousin? He got out?"

Sienna and Nikolai shared a sad look.

"He did. Barely. They mutilated him, but he is alive. Still recovering on our offshore training center, where the last of our recruits remain. But he is stronger by the day and will be ready for war when it is time."

Mina's stomach churned, acid swirling at the thought of so much evil. The queen and her son had been wreaking havoc across the country while she lay in a bloodless sleep. A flash of her last moments before she'd been imprisoned in her own home. The sneering Radomir coming for her after he'd sliced

Kathleen's throat. She'd been able to do nothing to save her friend or even save herself. They'd grabbed her by the arm and dragged her to the upper tower—cold and damp from lack of use. When she curled up in the corner, Radomir had laughed and murmured, "Sweet dreams," before slamming the bolt home. The memory of loss and pain and her own failure to stop it steeped her in a well of helplessness.

"Your Highness, are you—?"

A soft knock came at the door a second before Mikhail entered. His gaze landed on Mina first as he stepped closer to her side. Strange how swiftly his nearness put her at ease, nearly wiping away the anxiety that had threatened to overwhelm her seconds before.

"Good to have you back, Captain," said Nikolai with a nod. "Your men were growing anxious."

"Thank you for keeping them in line."

"No need. They followed your orders as if you were here. Three trainings a day, alternating the teams every two hours, venturing to town only for feeding, not for drinking ale or making trouble. It was like you never left. I must compliment you on their discipline. I've had Legionnaire troops who didn't follow orders so well."

Mikhail dipped his chin, his stern expression focused on Mina. "Thank you, Nikolai. But they know what is at stake here. They won't let our chances fail because of idleness or lack of discipline."

"Still. It says a lot about you. Your team is an asset to us."

"Thank you." He stepped closer to Mina's side. "I thought I'd get Her Highness settled and let her rest after the journey."

"Oh, of course," said Sienna, popping off the sofa. "I can help and show you where I've stocked everything."

Mina rose wearily, the last memories of her home weighing her down. Nikolai stepped close to Sienna, placing a hand around her waist with a firm grip. "I believe the captain can manage to get her settled on his own."

Sienna opened her mouth to say something. Nikolai's grip tightened at her waist.

"Sure. I'm sure he can get her settled. Then we can all meet for breakfast after you've rested. How would that be?"

"That would be lovely." Mina opened her arms to hug her friend again.

She returned the embrace. "I am so happy you're here. And safe." Sienna pulled her at arm's length, her green eyes sparking with specks of gold.

Mina felt a sudden surge of heart-heavy emotion, like she was touching not just a long-lost friend. But a sister. Funny. They'd only met that one time. And yet, she felt drawn to Sienna.

Sienna's brow rose, her eyes widening. "I believe you belong with us, Your Highness."

"I believe so, too," said Mina, allowing Mikhail to finally usher her back out the door.

Night had fallen quickly. There was not a man in the yard. The only movement was that of a goat in a fenced pen, baaing at them as they passed. As soon as they crossed onto a wooded path, Mikhail pulled her to a stop and wrapped her in his arms, rocking her gently.

Startled, she froze, then sank into his welcome embrace. "Why are you holding me, Captain?"

"Because you need holding. And I need to be the one to do it."

Chapter Ten

He was a fool. A bloody, besotted fool who couldn't seem to mind his own commands. He'd told himself to keep a distance, especially after that incident by the brook earlier in the day. And here he was, running to her aid and comforting her the only way he knew how.

He'd sensed her anxiety from where he stood in Sienna's yard while talking with his men. Immediately, he dismissed them back to camp and rushed into the cottage to be near her, to rescue her. He couldn't seem to keep himself from trying to be her hero.

He wasn't meant for comfort and soft caresses, especially when the relationship couldn't go beyond the physical. He was meant for blood and ruin and war. He couldn't have a lover who would distract from his ultimate goal. Yet here he was, holding Princess Mina in his arms like a lover would, pressing his lips to her hair, feeling her warmth like a balm to the soul.

Her delicate hands slid up his chest to cradle his face as she pushed back to look into his eyes. Starlight sparkled there, luring him to the damnable depths. When she looked at him like that, he was a lost man. Falling so fast he could hardly breathe.

"Kiss me, Mikhail," she pleaded. Yes, the goddess begged for his mouth on hers.

For fuck's sake.

He gave it to her. Gripping her nape, he descended, plundering her sweet mouth, nipping her overfull lips, tasting like a starving man. For her, he was starving. Ravenous to taste every inch of her. He crushed her against him, angling her just right so he could stroke his tongue deeper. A mistake.

She squirmed against him. Not to get away—to rub her body against his, making him painfully aware of his rigid erection pressing against her abdomen. Moaning with pleasure, her soft body responded too eagerly to his hard one.

With an agonizing groan, he gripped her shoulders and pulled away from her.

"What's wrong?"

"Bloody hell. That was a mistake."

Before she could protest, he swept her up in his arms and sped toward the small one-room cottage that would be her home for the time being. He had to get her settled into safety, then get away from her as quickly as possible. Where had all his famed self-control gone? One look from her and he became a besotted, stiff-cocked boy, ready to ravage her without a thought. He'd focus on getting her settled, then getting out the door.

He'd spoken to Friedrich before he and his men had left on their mission. The art studio Friedrich had built for his youngest daughter, Izzy, would serve as the most private abode for the princess's temporary residence.

Setting her on her feet on the front step, he pushed open the door. A crackling fire had already been lit. A bed had been installed, stacked with pillows and heavy quilts. Other amenities had been furnished since he'd left—a wash basin, a bowl and ewer, a small vanity. He held the door open as she entered, glancing toward the main house, where one of the children broke into laughter.

Dmitri had told them of their arrival but had relayed the message that the princess needed a night's rest before more introductions. Mikhail wanted to be sure she wasn't overwhelmed.

"Come in," he urged her more gruffly than he'd intended while he held open the door.

She stepped inside and perused the room, taking in her new home. She walked toward the bed and trailed her fingers on the green-and-white quilt.

"I know it isn't what you're accustomed to."

"It's lovely." She faced him, one hand still on the bed, giving him all sorts of wayward thoughts. "Thank you."

He scanned the room, hands on hips, and gave a tight nod. "I think it will serve for the time being. You're only a short walk to Friedrich and Brennalyn's back door."

"I wasn't referring to the room."

Confused, he stared at her from the open doorway, forcing himself to keep his distance.

She clasped her hands in her lap, her back straight, looking ever like the genteel lady she was. Her lashes were lowered, the black wisps brushing her pale cheeks. "I am grateful for this hospitality, of course." Her gaze lifted. "But I wanted to thank you for today…for what you said in the forest."

Mikhail clenched his jaw, not sure how to respond, other than to say, "You're welcome."

"Captain, I'm not the sort of person who plays games or who ignores my emotions. As an empath, it is impossible."

Her soft voice drifted across the small chamber, seeping into his chest like a hypnotic remedy for an ache he didn't know he had. He'd never known anyone so forthright, so unabashedly honest in every respect of the word—in how she spoke, treated others, treated herself. When he spoke of her inner strength in the forest, she hadn't denied the claim behind false modesty. That would be a lie.

The fact that he'd had to live behind a lie about his own family had twisted inside him for so long. A lie he was forced to live because the queen would kill everyone he cared about if she discovered the truth.

But this princess wasn't who he thought she'd be. He'd thought to find a sweet woman who knew nothing about the world, or a jaded one who thought only of herself. Instead, she was this paragon of beauty—from the perfection of her face, skin, and body straight through to her flawless heart, unmarred by the bitterness of betrayal he'd lived with all his life. Even with her own personal loss, she never let it weigh down her pure spirit. She spoke the truth in every moment, in every way. And it hit him hard at moments like this. Where she sat demurely, sweetly, thanking him for something so little as words.

"It was nothing," he finally said.

She tilted her chin, her glossy fine hair slipping over one shoulder. With a sad sort of smile, she whispered, "It was everything. To me." She laced her fingers together in her lap, squeezing tightly. "I only wish…"

He should've said good night. He shouldn't ask, but goddammit, he couldn't. "What do you wish?"

Wetting her lips, she sat straighter, her eyes glittering by the firelight. "I wish there could be more…between us."

Swallowing the jagged stone lodged in his throat, he spoke his own truth. "I am sorry. More than you know. Do you think it gives me pleasure to turn you away?" he asked, raising his brow as if he expected her to answer. She didn't move, didn't even blink. Shaking his head, he went on.

"Nay. It gives me physical *pain*." His voice was ragged as

he curled a fist to his chest over his heart. "Agony, if you must know." He shook his head on a short laugh that was filled with bitterness not mirth. "You're not what I expected."

She remained silent, watching with those wide, sea-blue, honest eyes, compassion shining bright there. Or some other soft, heartrending emotion.

"I expected a princess. An uppity, perfect model of royalty. A distant, aloof sovereign who would gladly take my assistance at climbing even further toward her crown and farther away from me." He took a step closer, hands at his sides, fisting them in agitation.

She swallowed hard, her voice broken. "I'm sorry to disappoint you."

"Disappoint me?" She didn't understand. "What I didn't expect was *you*." He gestured with a hand. "This beautiful, sensual creature who begs me to kiss her and who looks at me like I'm the only man on Earth. The only man who matters. It's like I'm being pulled straight to hell…and for you?" He shook his head, unable to shut his mouth. "I would gladly burn for all eternity."

Her mouth parted on a sharp inhale. He'd said enough. He'd said too much. Perhaps her honest spirit was infectious, for he seemed unable to even hold his own damn tongue when it came to her. He'd have to try. He turned for the door.

"Good night, Your Highness." And it might as well have been good-bye. He'd keep his distance, emotionally. Physically, he'd guard her with his life. He'd yearn for her, yes. But he was a man of control, after all. Wasn't he?

He pulled the door shut before she could say another word. He didn't trust himself to resist her if she asked him to stay. He'd reorder his thinking tonight and remember how close he was to what he'd been planning since his father was murdered. A goal that would not only bring justice to him but to his entire legacy. To the Romanov family and who they were before they were forced to recreate themselves and hide their lineage in order to stay alive.

His whole plan hinged on Mina taking her rightful place as Queen of Arkadia, of helping the Black Lily alongside the Bloodguard, of winning this goddamned war. Even if King Agnar from the west joined forces with the Black Lily, it wouldn't be enough. He'd already calculated Queen Morgrid's numbers, using his resources to report the number of Legionnaires coming and going from the Glass Tower. His men in hiding in Izeling sent regular reports of the northern villages being raided—the men turned vampire and rabid with sanguine furorem, their women and children taken as slaves to King Dominik's fortress, Dragon's Eye.

He ground his teeth thinking of his mother's home, Kellswater, one of the first to be ravaged by the butcher king and his men. It had broken Mikhail's mother's heart to hear that the village where she grew up had been razed to the ground, the people stolen away like cattle. Mikhail had been grateful her parents were no longer living to have witnessed such an atrocity, but it was little consolation for the poor bastards who'd been set upon by the king's vampire army. Just one more debt the king and his witch of a mother would have to pay.

His thoughts drifted from their army back to the one the Black Lily and the Bloodguard had been building. The westerners were not a warring people. But the southerners were. Aristocratic lines who'd fought in the long-ago Thorn Wars and beat back revolutionaries time and time again, who trained and honed the best equestrian soldiers in all the land. With the force of the Arkadian army, they'd surely win. At least, they'd have a fighting chance.

That was why he must keep his distance from the princess, he told himself as he stormed toward the Bloodguard encampment. Every kiss he stole from her was another distraction from their cause, which was far more important than a lovers' tryst. No one else had figured it out, but Mikhail had. Their success depended upon Princess Vilhelmina. His infatuation with the woman only muddied the waters, clouding what was first and foremost—the future of Varis.

So he'd keep his cock in his pants and his thoughts as pristine and clean as frigid, glacial waters in her presence. Even if the woman drove him insane with desire, he'd stay calm.

"Stay calm," he repeated to himself, combing a hand through his hair, ruffling it in a very not-calm manner.

Downy snow flurried from the sky. Mikhail paused on the trail and turned his face upward, letting the flakes hit and sting his face. He needed it to cool his heated blood, his heated thoughts.

"Is that working?"

Mikhail snapped to a defensive stance, blade in hand, before he realized it was Dmitri. "Don't sneak up on me, Brother." He sheathed his dagger.

"I wasn't." He was leaning against a trunk, arms crossed. "I was waiting for you."

"Why? Do we have news from Marius? From Cutters Cove?"

"Neither. I was wondering if you have news for me."

"Regarding?" Mikhail rolled his shoulders and marched on down the path.

Dmitri stepped in line beside him. "Regarding the princess."

"You'll have to get straight to the point, if you have one."

"All right. I wanted to speak to you regarding your intentions toward her."

"I think that's perfectly clear. Protect her till she takes her place as ruler of Arkadia."

"Protect her? That's all, Mikhail?"

He jerked to a stop. "What the hell are you getting at, Dmitri?"

Unperturbed as always, his younger brother replied simply, "I'm wondering if you're falling in love with her. And if so, does that mean you plan to be king at her side?"

Stupefied into silence for a moment, Mikhail finally found his voice. "Are you utterly mad?"

"Not at all. I've never seen you this way around a woman. You would be a good match. Perfect actually, with our family ancestry. It only seems—"

"She's destined for a royal throne."

"As are you, Brother. And you know you deserve it."

"Stop it." Mikhail marched back down the trail. "We won't go down that road. Not now."

He didn't want to listen to Dmitri's logic, because he was absolutely fucking right. It was as if they were destined for each other. As if that simple blood kiss in the tower wasn't simple at all, but an ordained tap from Lady Fortune's wand, saying "finally." Mikhail stared up, unable to see the stars above the snowy clouds. The heavens seemed to mock him. Or they were forcing him down a path he'd never planned to travel. Of course he wanted to claim his birthright. But this wasn't part of the plan. *She* wasn't part of the plan.

"Why not?" Dmitri kept in step. "Right all wrongs. That's what you told me this was about. The Bloodguard. Our training. Our living away from our home and fighting these bloody rogues. Our alliance with the duke and with the Black Lily."

"And it still is. That has nothing to do with...with bloody marriage, becoming king, or for God's sake, falling in love."

"Falling? I believe you're already there."

"I've known the woman a week."

"You can't take your eyes off her. Won't tolerate any of us

getting too close. This is more than lust, Mikhail, and there's no reason you shouldn't consider—"

"I'm the goddamned *captain* of the Bloodguard," he grit out. "I made a blood vow."

Dmitri sobered, his smirk slipping, showing his tenderhearted brother beneath. "You're right. You couldn't be both." He clasped Mikhail's shoulder in a rare show of affection. "But one of us will eventually have to leave the Guard." Snow fell in soft flakes, catching in Dmitri's black hair. "One of us must have a family. We can't let our line die, my brother." Dmitri rarely ever spoke with such heavy emotion weighing his words. "It's too important. You know that."

Mikhail exhaled a heavy sigh, refusing to acknowledge the truth.

The truth. Something Mina wouldn't let him walk away from. This was too much for him to face right now.

"What I know is I need a good feeding and a good fuck. And that is all." He gestured in the direction of the encampment. "You're in charge of the men tonight."

Then he tore off toward Hiddleston in search of anything, anyone who'd wipe his memory of the fair-haired vixen who did indeed already have her hooks in deep. Entirely too deep.

Chapter Eleven

Mina finished lacing her boot, then settled in front of the vanity to tend to her hair. After brushing it thoroughly, she plaited a small braid to fall alongside her temple. And then on the other side, the same as she'd seen Allora wear her hair. A wildness stirred in her bosom, blossoming more each day. It had started the moment Mikhail had awakened her, the moment he challenged her to drink from him like a natural vampire.

Was that what was happening? She was finally giving into her primal urges and the beast was strengthening her will? She wasn't sure.

Having never had the urge to bite anyone in all her life, now she just wanted to sink her fangs into his muscular form. Anywhere. Everywhere.

Blowing out a breath, she lifted her cloak and tied it on before opening the door to find the prettiest little girl she'd ever seen sitting on a stump. She popped off, her blond ringlets bouncing, and smiled up at Mina.

"Good morning. Have you been waiting for me?"

"Yes. Are you weally a pwinthess?" asked the little girl. Her speech impediment only made her more adorable.

"Yes. And who may I have the pleasure of meeting this fine morning?"

"I'm Isabelle. But evewyone calls me Izzy. Come on!" She grabbed Mina's hand and pulled her along the stone-stepped path to the two-story cottage nearby. "My Mimi wants to meet you. She made me pwomise I wouldn't wake you." Izzy suddenly stopped, her sky-blue eyes rounding in fear. "I didn't wake you, did I?"

"Oh, no. Not at all. I feel quite refreshed. If I must tell you, I've never slept in a more comfortable bed."

And that was the truth. Mina wasn't sure who was fashioning the beds around here, but the warm quilts and comfy down pillows were divine.

Izzy smiled again and tugged Mina along the trail toward the back door. "Well, we've got bweakfast all weady for you."

"That sounds wonderful."

"Oh, wait." Izzy paused again, a despondent look sinking her pretty eyes into despair. "Do you eat bweakfast? You're a vampire pwinthess."

"I do," she assured her. "I love human food. Especially scones." Mina could smell the delicious aroma of cinnamon scones coming from the house. Perhaps with winterberries? "Does your Mimi make those?"

"Oh, my Mimi doesn't cook. It's my sister, Beatwice. And Olog helps sometimes when he's not cooking for the soldiers down near Mr. Hawwison's farm."

"Olog? Is that one of your brothers?"

Izzy giggled, shaking her head, her curls brushing her shoulders. "No. Olog was my Papa's cook back at Winter Hill. But he came with us when we wan away." She turned at the door and glanced to her left and then her right before she whispered, "Can I tell you a secwet?"

Mina leaned down, entranced by the little girl. "Of course. What is it?"

"We wan away in the middle of the night. Took a secwet passage out of the castle and the vampire guards cawwied us on their backs." She grinned as she finished the last.

"Wow. That must've been a great adventure."

"Mm-hmm." She opened the door and yelled, "I've got Pwinthess Mina, Mimi!"

"Heavens, Izzy, stop shouting." A petite and lovely dark-haired woman rushed over to greet Mina. When she drew closer, Mina realized she was more beautiful close up. The young woman's rich, brown eyes sparked with gold. This was certainly the beauty who'd captured the Duke of Winter Hill, Friedrich Volya, the grandson of the evil Queen Morgrid. His mother had been the queen's only daughter.

"Welcome, Your Highness. I am Brennalyn Snow." She squeezed her eyes shut and bit her lip a second, then said, "Actually, I am Brennalyn Volya now. I'm still getting used to it."

"Oh," said Mina, realizing something she hadn't expected when her eyes flared supernaturally. "You're a vampire."

Izzy, who was still holding Mina's hand, said, "My Papa had to save her from the evil King Dominik. So now my Mimi is a vampire. She even drinks *blood*." Izzy shivered. "Gwoss."

"And hot chocolate and warm tea on occasion." She smirked. "Would you like some mint tea? Beatrice has just finished cooking breakfast." Brennalyn waved her hand toward the table.

"I hope you like scones, Your Highness," said a young girl with honey-blond hair. She set a second platter of golden-baked pastries on the table next to a plate of jellies and another of hard cheese slices next to ripe purple winterberries.

"She does," belted out Izzy, popping a berry into her mouth.

"Forgive Izzy," said another pretty-faced girl on the verge of womanhood, with black hair like Brennalyn. "She was apparently raised by wild wolves."

"Hart wolves!" screamed Izzy with a pudgy fist in the air.

"If you'd been raised by hart wolves," said the younger girl with the apron on, "you might be more civilized."

Izzy's response was to stuff her mouth with half a scone.

"Girls, enough. Your Highness, you've met my youngest daughter, Izzy, of course. These are my other two, Beatrice and Helena." They each gave polite curtsies, then took their seats.

A flurry of five boys ran down the staircase, making a hellacious racket like thundering hooves.

"*Stop.*" Brennalyn's one sharp word stopped the line of them at the door, the eldest with his hand on the knob.

They turned at once, guilt shadowing their adorable faces.

"Your Highness, may I introduce my four boys, and a fifth who has joined the wild pack? The eldest, Caden."

He dipped a bow, still holding onto the door, his long, gangly frame that of a teenager lacking the muscles of a man, though his keen eyes said he was wiser than his years.

"And this is Emmett and Jack." The next two in line bowed like Caden. Mina could see a blood resemblance in these three with familiar facial structure and brown mops of hair. "And my youngest son is Denny."

Denny was closer in age to Izzy, perhaps a few years older, his black hair and fair skin setting him apart from the other three boys.

"And that rascal is Nate. His father is one of the founding members of the Black Lily."

Nate, a russet-haired boy with dirt on his nose and mischief in his eyes, made an exaggerated bow, nearly sweeping his head to the floor. "Pleased to meet ya, Yer 'ighness."

"Very pleased to meet you, Nate. To meet you all."

Brenna leaned close to Mina. "Nate is actually one of the undercover couriers for the Black Lily. Arabelle holds him in very high regard."

Nate preened, puffing his skinny little chest out.

"Well, we are so grateful for your service," added Mina with a bow of her head.

He waved a hand. "Aw, it's nothin'. I like being sneaky. Best fun there is."

Denny and the other boys laughed.

"I'm sure you do," added Brenna, raising a brow. "Now, have you boys eaten breakfast? I don't want you at the training camp without any food in your bellies."

The four youngest looked to Caden, who sighed. "No, Mimi. But we can't be late. Grant and Dmitri are showing us how to use a bow and arrow today."

Brennalyn pointed to the table. "Food."

Their shoulders slumped at once as they dragged their feet toward the table.

"Heaven forbid." Brennalyn tsked. "Just grab some and go."

Like a pack of wild animals, they leaped at the table, each grabbing a handful of scones and berries and running out the partially opened door.

"The door, for heaven's sake!" shouted Brennalyn, picking up a scone they'd dropped on the floor.

A moment's pause, then the kind-faced one, Denny, popped his head back in and smiled at Brennalyn.

"Thank you, darling," she said. He nodded and closed the door. Their boyish whoops and shouts faded as they fled into the woods.

"They are quite active, your boys," said Mina.

"Quite," agreed Brennalyn.

"Animals," muttered Beatrice, sweeping the crumbs they

left behind onto a napkin. "Whenever we return to Winter Hill and away from the training camp, I hope Papa gets a tutor to teach them to be gentlemen."

Helena took the steaming pot of tea from Brennalyn after she'd poured a cup for both Mina and herself. "Leaving the training camp won't change their behavior. They'll just spend all day in the sparring yard with Captain Mikhail and his men."

Mina's pulse rocketed at the sound of his name.

Brennalyn's dark eyes glanced in Mina's direction over the rim of her teacup before aiming her response at Helena. "Once we are back at Winter Hill, they'll be taking up their studies again. And yes, Beatrice, I suspect you'll all be receiving tutors in the proper etiquette of both gentlemen and ladies."

Mina's heart swelled at the thought of Friedrich Volya, the Duke of Winter Hill, taking in these seven orphans as his own children. "And may I ask how you girls feel about that? Becoming ladies of the gentry?" She finished off her buttery scone.

Helena dipped her poised chin. "I am very happy at the prospect. Though I'm not so sure Beatrice is."

Beatrice twisted her hands in her apron in her lap and bit her lip before eyeing Brennalyn. "My only fear is I'll not be able to cook if I become a proper lady."

"Beatrice, you know the duke wouldn't allow you to be unhappy. He only wants what's best for you."

Izzy set her empty glass of water on the table. "You'll have to learn to be a pwoper duchess, too, Mimi."

Brennalyn's teacup rattled as she set it in the saucer. "Don't remind me. Let's just get past this war first, then we'll worry about all the rest. For now, this is our home. And we'll try to make the boys behave as best we can." She wiped her hands on her napkin in her lap. "Though it is hard when they are living out their dreams to become warriors."

Helena tossed her head with a little laugh. "Or soldiers or pirates or any manly occupation that allows them to wield a sword and stick something with it."

They all laughed at that. Even Mina.

"Here we are, prattling on about ourselves. Forgive me, Your Highness. How are you feeling after your journey? And after—" Brennalyn stopped herself.

"It's all right. I'm doing quite well, if you must know. But apparently, I was in the most capable of hands under the protection of Captain Mikhail."

"He's the bestest evew," said Izzy with a gleam in her eyes. "Except Papa, of course."

"Of course," agreed Mina, smiling at Brennalyn.

"Mimi, can we go watch the boys shoot bows and awows?" she asked.

"I don't think Princess Mina wants to go and watch a bunch of boys and men learning archery."

"Actually," said Mina, folding her napkin on her plate. "I'd like nothing better. Archery was one of my favorite pastimes at Briar Rose."

"A princess—I mean, a lady can learn archery?" asked Beatrice, incredulous, wide-eyed with excitement at the prospect.

"Oh, yes. I was quite good." She smiled. "I'm afraid I spent many hours learning such skills and few in the company of others. My steward was very protective." She frowned with a flicker of memory.

"Are you all right, Your Highness?" asked Brennalyn.

"Yes." She wiped away her frown, but the bitter memory of her lonely life at Briar Rose stuck. She rose from her chair with new vigor, "I say we go and see what all the boys are up to."

"Yay!" shouted Izzy, rushing for the door.

They laughed and filed out in a more ladylike fashion. Mina smiled, but that memory pricked like thorns. Steward Thorwald had pretended to show her the greatest respect, presenting her to the House, but making them all bow and never allowing her to have a voice. Then he'd send her off to a ball or the theater, fully chaperoned by Legionnaires and Kathleen, before shuffling her back to Briar Rose. For the first time, she saw the reality of what he'd done. Cut her off, shut her up, cast her out of her rightful domain. The monarch of Arkadia was the leader of the House. But she'd only ever been so in name. Steward Thorwald had ousted her and taken that right when she was a young orphan and had never allowed her the opportunity to reclaim that role.

Mikhail was right. She must garner her strength. Prepare for the inevitable. For the time was near when she'd need her voice to be heard, whether Steward Thorwald wanted to hear her or not. Whether the lords of Arkadia wanted to hear her or not.

"Yes, ladies." Mina took Izzy's outstretched hand. "Let us go show the boys how a proper bow and arrow is to be shot."

They smiled in feminine conspiracy, their laughter rolling up into the boughs of Silvane Forest. Once more, Mina inhaled deep of the magic here, as if it were calling her toward her destiny. Guiding her to a fate she never knew would be hers but had been intended for her all along.

Chapter Twelve

"When will the last troops come over?" asked Aleksei.

Mikhail observed the archers from his stance behind them, arms crossed and mood foul. "In a fortnight, I imagine. Nikolai's cousin Riker will lead them across the Cimmaron Sea and leave the families in the safety of Cutters Cove."

Aleksei nodded, his own countenance grave as he glanced up at the mass of clouds growing heavy. "Is Riker healed enough to fight?"

"Nikolai says so."

Mikhail heard Friedrich's boys tromping through the woods before he saw them launch onto the training field. Nate, the wild one whose father forged weapons for the Black Lily, was with them, as usual. Caden thrust an arm out to stop them from running out like fools in front of the line of archers. He'd be a good leader one day.

"Those fucking Legionnaires at the Glass Tower did a number on him," he continued. "They should've killed him when they had the chance. According to Nikolai, he's full of fire and fury, ready for combat."

Aleksei chuckled. Mikhail watched the boys as they stepped up to Dmitri, who was leading the morning training. One of the Black Lily's human soldiers patted Caden on the back as he handed over a bow. The soldier then ambled toward the sparring pin where Gregoravich, Gavril, and Yuri were training on a variety of weapons. Gregoravich demonstrated one of his deadliest moves with an ax in one hand and a dagger in the other, thrusting animatedly in the air. He had a rapt audience. Mikhail had seen him perform that particular move so many times he'd lost count. Subdue the vampire enemy with an ax to the head, then slit his carotid before he could blink.

"Good job, Emmett, but your aim is a little low," said Dmitri, drawing Mikhail's gaze back to the line of archers.

Dmitri was coaching both Caden and Emmett on proper stance and aim when the breeze carried the mouth-watering scent of sunshine and jasmine down the line. His canines extended at once.

"Good morning, Dmitri," said Brennalyn, Mina close at her side.

Beatrice and Helena walked nearby, watching Caden and Emmett. Izzy ran down the hill, following Nate, Jack, and Denny to the sparring pit, her blond ringlets bouncing.

The sight of Mina—tall and fair and blindingly beautiful—knocked the air from his lungs. It also overcast him in a shadow of regret. He'd fled to Hiddleston last night, seeking a willing blood whore to fuck and feed his lust away, then *maybe* he could get Mina out of his mind. He'd found a lovely barmaid at the Bull's Eye who was more than eager to oblige him, right there in a back room of the tavern. As soon as he sank his fangs deep, she'd hiked up her skirt, moaning and grappling with the lacing of his trousers.

When he'd stopped her, Mikhail actually felt remorse for misleading the woman. She'd not asked for payment, but he dropped three sovereigns on the ale barrel anyway and left her in the dark. He'd heard her call him *bastard* the second before he tore away again into the night. He didn't stop at the encampment but continued on into the forest, winding up in the shadows outside the little cottage where Mina slept.

She was a magnet, ever drawing him closer. He'd watched over her till dawn, at peace just knowing he was keeping her safe. But also in turmoil for wanting what he couldn't have. Shouldn't have. She was right. Dmitri was right. He could have her. If he revealed his family's tragedy and rewrote the past. All he wanted now was to right the wrongs of the present. Losing himself in the beauty that was Mina was a mistake. A distracted captain was a perilous one.

Yet, here he was, completely enraptured at the first sight of the fair-haired goddess. She approached Dmitri.

"May I have a try?" she asked.

Emmett handed over the bow while Dmitri smiled in his charming way. "Of course. So, stand with your feet square facing in that direction."

Mikhail refrained from growling when Dmitri placed a hand on her back to guide her.

"Like this?" she asked.

He couldn't help himself, sidling closer as Dmitri gave her instructions.

"Yes. Now grip the bow and—"

"She needs an armguard first," Mikhail interrupted, lifting one off the post where they kept the quivers, arrows, and guards. Dmitri smirked at Mikhail as he stepped aside to stand next to Brennalyn.

Ignoring his brother's implicit accusation with a look, he stood in front of her and lifted her left arm. Without meeting her gaze, he wrapped the guard around her slender forearm and buckled the straps.

"Have you shot a bow before, Your Highness?"

He felt the weight of her gaze, but he remained focused on tightening the straps so it wouldn't slip. He didn't want her silken skin to be marred by the snap of a bow string.

"A little," she whispered intimately.

Unable to deny himself any longer, he lifted his gaze to hers as he dropped her arm. Why he felt the need to torture himself, he wasn't sure. She held him there with the most serene, gentle expression he'd ever beheld. Her calm exterior only agitated him more, especially when his own emotions were in turmoil with one glance.

He stepped behind her and squared her hips. "Keep your body facing this direction, like Dmitri said."

"I see."

"Since you've shot a bow before, you know to keep your elbow out and your inner arm flat, correct?" He raised her arm now gripping the bow, aiming it toward the target, a bale of hay with a canvas bull's-eye.

"Like this?" Her elbow still angled toward the ground, jutting out her inner arm. And though she now wore the guard for protection, his blood rose at the thought of her injuring herself while playing at archery.

"No," he practically growled and stepped close behind her.

She focused on the target. With his body aligned behind her, he mirrored her stance, gripping his hand over hers on the bow's handle.

"Look at my arm. See how I've turned my arm where my inner arm is flat? That will keep you from getting hit with the string when you let loose. It also gives you more control of the aim."

"Oh. I see."

Her heart rate picked up speed. That was when he realized he had a death grip on her waist, keeping her body perfectly molded to his. What he wanted to do was to nuzzle his face into her hair and breathe deep of her essence. Instead, he stepped away and crossed his arms, facing toward the target.

"I think you've got it. Just notch an arrow, aim, and let loose."

"Here you go," said Dmitri, handing her an arrow from the quiver on the stand.

"Thank you." She notched the arrow and pulled the string back, her bow tilted slightly upward.

"No," Mikhail corrected gently. "You're aiming too high."

She didn't reply but aimed a second longer before letting the arrow fly. It hissed through the air, arching upward toward the overhanging tree beside her lane, struck through a single leaf dangling from its branch, then sailed onward in the perfect curve, hitting the target dead center of the bull's-eye.

Brennalyn laughed behind them. But his eyes were on Mina as she glanced over her shoulder. "Like that?"

So, the princess could be deceptive after all. That was a new discovery.

"You weren't exaggerating," said Brennalyn, a bemused expression lighting her face.

He arched an accusing brow at her. "You've practiced more than *a little* archery."

She placed the bow back in its wooden stand and unbuckled the armguard with quick, deft fingers, like someone who'd done it a thousand times. "A lady should never be too vain about her abilities." She quirked a smile at him. "Perhaps I was born to be a warrior, not a princess."

You were born to be a queen, he thought with conviction. He took the guard from her and tossed it to Dmitri, who grinned like the fiend he was. "Would you care to take a walk with me, Your Highness? I'll show you our training camp."

"I would love nothing more."

She placed her hand at the crook of his arm. Her touch both rattled and grounded him. The woman had the strangest effect on him. He led her along the ridge toward the sparring pit. Brennalyn and Dmitri walked down the hill toward the ring where Helena and Beatrice stood off to the side. Dmitri positioned himself a yard behind Helena, hands at his back, eyes watchful. He'd been protective of her ever since they'd saved her from King Dominik's prison fortress. Mikhail wondered at that, then Mina broke in.

"So, the Bloodguard is training the human army for the Black Lily."

He brought her to a stop as they watched Gavril wielding a thin-bladed short sword, demonstrating in slow motion on Yuri where to stab a vampire through at the back of the neck and into the skull in order to kill with one strike. Gavril and Yuri were two of his best men.

"Not entirely," he answered. "Nikolai has already taught most these men both on Cutters Cove and those we've recruited here the essentials of hand-to-hand combat as well as battle strategy. My men are also training them in deadly force and use of weapons." He pointed off to the right of the sparring pit, where a group surrounded it. The burly human, Ivan, had his brother in a choke hold as they demonstrated evasive moves in slow motion for newer recruits. "Do you see those two men down there?"

"Yes."

"That's Ivan and Evan Barrow."

"Yes, I know them. They were kind to me when Arabelle had me kidnapped."

Mikhail slid his gaze down to her. The chilly wind lifted strands of her white-gold hair, a tendril gliding over her lips. She swiped it away, then looked up at him, a sweet, innocent expression softening her face.

"You didn't know Arabelle had abducted me when I was

sent here to the Glass Tower for my wedding?"

He flinched at the thought of her marrying Marius. Of her marrying any other man.

"Yes. I heard." He watched the sparring session, Friedrich's boys leaning on the wooden fence surrounding the small arena. "I suppose it's difficult to imagine, seeing where we are now."

"Yes, you've all been hard at work since I've been... gone."

His heart clenched at where she'd been the past months. "So, you learned archery growing up at Briar Rose."

"I did." She smiled with confidence.

"And what else did you learn with such proficiency in the south?"

Her smile faded. "Nothing else very exciting, I'm afraid." She heaved out a sigh. "The typical makings of a lady. Embroidery. Dancing. Painting. Music. Though I did enjoy riding. Did you know the Arkadian horses are considered the finest breed across all four kingdoms?"

"I did." He liked hearing the pride in her voice. "Friedrich has two Arkadians."

"Really?" She glanced down at the fields, stopping their leisurely pace. Soft flakes of snow began to fall. "Where does he keep them?"

"One of the men is a farmer who has a sizeable barn on his homestead nearby, just outside Hiddleston. Harrison keeps a few horses for the Black Lily. And there are others who are doing the same within the vicinity of the forest."

She nodded. "It seems you've all been planning well for quite some time."

"We have."

"And everyone's playing their part. Even Sienna and the hart wolves."

"Yes. Nikolai and Sienna risked their lives recruiting

toward the north. That's when they heard from Friedrich about you and where you were. And Sienna, she..."

She gazed curiously up at him. "What did Sienna do?"

"She had a sort of vision, actually. She's, well, I'm not sure how to say this. She's been gifted with prophetic sight... among other things."

"I see. And apparently she had a vision that involved me, didn't she?"

He gave a stiff nod.

"Well?"

Clenching his jaw at the vision Friedrich told him of, one he'd be damned to hell before he let come to fruition, he stared down the hill. "The full vision is disturbing, to say the least. She remembered a dark fairy tale her grandmother once told her. But this time, she saw the faces of those within the tale clearly. She saw you."

"Me?"

"Yes. You were married to King Dominik. You bore him a child. And the queen—" he forced himself to face her—"she took your newborn babe and killed him. Drank him dry."

Mina's eyes widened in horror, but Mikhail would withhold nothing from her. She must understand all that was at stake. Not simply the breaking of the caste system and equality among human and vampirekind.

"She used black magic and sacrificed the pure-blood vampire child to plunge our world into eternal darkness, where she would reign supreme, unfettered by laws or rules. Where she could spread her wickedness and the blood madness far and wide until all who lived were slaves unto her."

Mina wobbled. He gripped her shoulders.

"But that was Sienna's vision, you said." Her face paled. "That doesn't mean it will come true."

"No. It won't come true. I promise you that."

He smelled a friendly scent and heard someone approaching in a run.

"Your Highness!" Allora shouted.

They both turned to see her step from the woods. She ran to them, her buckskin coat with fur hood protecting her from the falling snow. She panted puffs of white when she finally reached them.

"Marius and Arabelle have returned. They called for you as soon as they arrived. And you, too, Captain. They're with Friedrich at Brennalyn's cottage."

"We'll join them immediately," said Mikhail.

Allora nodded and swept down the hill toward the sparring pen.

Soft flakes were sticking to Mina's hair. He reached up with both hands and lifted the dark green hood of her cloak. Though a vampire could withstand the cold, he couldn't bear the thought of her being uncomfortable in any way.

"I hope they bring good news," she murmured.

Tucking his hands back in his pocket, he crooked an arm for her to take to escort her back. She did so, leaning softly toward him as if they'd walked side by side a thousand times. He wondered what that would be like. For this to be commonplace, to walk beside her.

"I do as well." He heaved out a heavy sigh. "But I doubt it will be."

"You don't think King Agnar will support his brother?"

Mikhail gave a tight shake of the head. "I have sources who tell me the king is unlikely to side against his mother."

Mina's grip tightened on his arm. Her eyes narrowed. "That witch has put the fear into everyone, hasn't she? Not just the commoners she tramples on. But even her own kin."

"Yes. She has."

Her steps quickened, meeting his long strides, quickening their trek back through Silvane Forest.

"You don't appear to be afraid." He pushed a low-hanging branch aside as she passed under it.

"I'm not. I'm furious."

Mikhail smiled. She caught him.

"You think that's funny?"

"No," he answered soberly, though he still smiled. "I think that's wonderful. We need anger, Your Highness, to fuel us till the end. To wipe out her armies and to raze her kind from this land. To destroy her and King Dominik and start anew."

He glanced to see if his words frightened her. For they were honest words. He chose to be as forthright as she was with him. Her fierce expression of determination never wavered. If anything, she appeared downright warrior-like, ready to march into battle.

"I believe we must do whatever necessary and pay whatever cost in order to end her reign."

They rounded the bend, Brennalyn's cottage coming into view. A plume of wood smoke unfurled from the chimney.

"Indeed, Captain. I'm ready to play my part, whatever that might be." Grim determination burned bright in her steely expression as she released him and stepped up to the cottage door. "Whatever the cost."

Mikhail's heart skipped a beat at the look on her face. For it was the exact same expression he'd seen in the mirror these many years since his father had died. Both he and Mina had lost much at the hands of Queen Morgrid. They were united in their need not just for vengeance, but for justice. It appeared fate continued to find ways to bind them together. At least in this regard, Mikhail had no objections.

Chapter Thirteen

"I'm just so happy Captain Mikhail and his men got you out of there safely." Arabelle had just hugged the breath out of Mina then led her to a quaint parlor where Friedrich, Sienna, and Marius were already gathered. Mikhail followed behind them. Mina and Arabelle took a seat on the sofa. Another man Mina didn't know stood next to Friedrich. He wore the clothes and strapped weaponry of a Bloodguard and had a rebellious tilt to his mouth. But he was human, not vampire.

"Your Highness." Friedrich stepped toward her and bowed regally. "It is a pleasure to see you safe and sound." He flicked a glance over her shoulder. "Though I had no doubt Mikhail could do it." He waved to the human. "This is my brother, Grant."

"Brother?"

Grant stepped forward and bowed with less finesse, though it somehow came across as alluring. "The better-looking one, Your Highness." He winked.

Mina laughed.

"Behave yourself, Grant," said Brennalyn, coming in

behind them with Helena and Dmitri.

The parlor was filled with too many bodies and not enough seats. Brennalyn closed the door and moved to Friedrich's side.

Grant aimed a devilish smile at her. "Are you hungry, darling? I'd be happy to oblige you now."

"Don't you think that joke is getting old?" asked Friedrich, scowling.

"What joke is that?"

"That my wife wants to feed every time you're near. As if you're just *that* tempting."

"No, it will never get old, because it always gets a rise out of you. And she does want to feed from me every time I'm near. Don't you, darling?" He tapped her under her chin.

"Stop it, Grant," she said playfully, biting back a smile.

Friedrich stood behind her and wrapped his arms around her waist. "I'll be making you a vampire within the fortnight, Brother. That'll solve that problem."

"Promises, promises."

Marius anchored himself against the wall next to the sofa on Arabelle's side. "Then we'll have two new vampires in our party soon."

Arabelle shot a scathing look over her shoulder at him. "Must you announce it to everyone?"

"It's not a shameful secret, sweetheart."

Mina couldn't help but ask, "Are you going to become a vampire, Arabelle?"

She rolled her eyes to the ceiling with an exasperated sigh. "Yes."

While her demeanor showed frustration, she sensed both excitement and fear rolling off of the vibrant leader of the Black Lily.

Mina arched a brow at Marius, the prince she was once betrothed to marry. "You are not forcing her, are you?"

"Forcing her? Of course not. As if I could." He laughed as if it were a foolish idea, crossing his arms over his chest. "Strongly coercing? Yes. That I'm doing."

Mina observed Arabelle a moment. "Well, you will be even stronger and more formidable with vampire strength."

Marius scoffed. "See? What did I tell you?"

She ignored him and answered Mina directly. "That is the reason I've agreed to the idea. Among others."

Marius whispered low, though every vampire in the room could obviously hear. "It has nothing to do with my threat to withhold particular—"

Arabelle whipped up a hand for him to stop and shot him a daggered look. "Hold your tongue, husband," she threatened, though there was a smile in her voice.

The door opened. Allora and Dane stepped in.

"Oh, my," said Sienna. "Aren't we a large party?"

"Not large enough," said Marius.

They joined the circle, Nikolai moving to Marius's side. "Tell everyone how your mission went."

The lighthearted mood darkened at once. Marius shoved off the wall and stepped slightly forward so all could see and hear him.

"I bring good and bad tidings from my brother, Agnar, in the west. He has sent resources in the form of coin for food as well as blades forged by the most revered craftsman of the four kingdoms."

"But?" asked Nikolai.

"But he will not fight with us."

A heavy sigh and murmuring of dissent circled the room. Mina felt the sting keenly, glancing up at Mikhail. His steady and composed expression never wavered as he addressed Marius.

"How long will the coin last for food provisions?"

"That depends," said Marius, glancing at Nikolai. "How

many soldiers do we have returning from Cutters Cove? And when do they arrive?"

Nikolai stared at the floor, mentally calculating before raising his head. "They'll be here within two weeks' time. Then we will have approximately two thousand. Those who have families who joined the cause will add another seven hundred mouths to feed."

Marius gave a sharp dip of his chin. "Then we have coin to last two months even with the additional families. We will need to set our course for Izeling not long after the last ship arrives from Cutters Cove."

"It's not enough." The soft but steady voice of Helena quieted everyone in the room. No one said a word, but everyone swiveled in her direction.

"What do you mean?" asked Dmitri gently, standing next to her.

"The number of soldiers," she clarified. She glanced up at Dmitri then back to Marius. "You don't know what just one of the vampires in King Dominik's army can do." She gulped hard. "Much less the hundreds, perhaps thousands he has by now."

Dmitri moved protectively closer to her.

Arabelle sat forward on the sofa, her expression grim but determined. "We don't simply have the human soldiers, Helena. We also have the Bloodguard." She waved a hand toward Mikhail and his men. "We have the Fire Witch." She nodded to Sienna. Mina wondered what that meant but thought to save it for another time. "Do we have the hart wolves?" she asked Allora.

Allora eyed her brother Dane. "You will have some. But the clans are not united on whether to involve themselves in this war."

Helena gave a frustrated huff, fear lining every groove of her pinched forehead and mouth. "You *don't* understand."

She wrung her hands together. "When I was held captive in the king's stronghold—in Dragon's Eye—it wasn't the ones with the blood madness I feared. Those infected by Queen Morgrid were out of control, wild with their need to feed. But it was the king's men, the vampire soldiers he created, that I feared the most. They would do anything...*anything* the king ordered them to do. The king—" she gulped hard before continuing—"he would come to Dragon's Eye. He would make people do unspeakable things...to demonstrate his power. And always within the center arena where so many of us captives could see from our cages." She inhaled a deep breath, a tear slipping off her cheek onto her blue gown. "I watched a man impale his own son on a spike because the king ordered him to do so." She turned her gaze to Arabelle. "I saw a woman give her body to two men while her husband watched." She swallowed hard and moved her gaze to Brennalyn. "I saw a mother hand over her young child to three new vampires infected with the blood madness. All simply because King Dominik had bitten them, injected his persuasive elixir in their blood. And commanded it be done. They could not resist."

Heavy silence pervaded the room. The unthinkable visions Helena had seen while she was in captivity lingered in the room like a dark premonition of what the world would be like should King Dominik and Queen Morgrid win this war.

No. It could not, would not happen. Mina seethed with anger at what sweet Helena had witnessed, that royals who should use their position to protect instead used it to brutally subjugate with violence and terror. She couldn't allow that to happen any longer. Mikhail was right. They must be destroyed, whatever they had to do to make that happen.

"She's right," said Mina, all eyes swiveling to her. "It's not enough. The Black Lily army, the Bloodguard, the hart wolves, all of us here, we are not enough to defeat the kind of evil Dominik is amassing in the north. We need an even more formidable army with the strength of the vampire."

Arabelle shook her head and said softly. "Mina, though I've agreed to be remade vampire, this is a personal choice. It is not what my people would choose for themselves. They want only to be freed of the yoke of the vampire monarchy, to live their *human* lives in peace."

Mina smiled. "Yes, and they shall when we win this war. But it isn't them I speak of when I refer to gaining a vampire army of our own."

"Please enlighten us," said Nikolai gently.

Standing, she moved forward where all could see and hear her. "The Arkadian army has always been known for its strength and skill."

Nikolai folded his arms over his chest. "Yes. This is true. But they would not ally with the Black Lily, a mostly human army, against their own brethren. The Arkadian army serves the southern kingdom, and only the southern kingdom. Steward Thorwald ensures it."

"True," added Friedrich. "My grandfather used to complain how they never joined the north in past wars unless it suited them and their interests alone."

"I hear what you're saying, gentlemen. But they will ally if their queen commands it."

She felt Mikhail's passionate response ripple at her side, but she didn't meet his gaze. She continued while the room stared in stunned silence.

"I have been asleep longer than the few months I was in that tower. I've been asleep my whole life, truth be told." She faced Marius. "I never thought beyond what Steward Thorwald told me. That I was destined to be queen but only next to the Varis king who would rule at my side. I never gave a thought that I could rule on my own." She smiled, finally looking at Mikhail. "I never realized that I should've been queen all along."

No one said a word. Mina held her breath, waiting for someone to laugh or gently protest her lofty idea. Still, her heart pricked at her conscience. This was what should be done. What must be done.

"Indeed," said Friedrich, the vampire duke she'd met on occasion when he visited the southern kingdom. "No one here would question your right to the Arkadian crown. But I imagine there are a few lords in the House of Arkadia who would."

Brenna nodded. "I believe Friedrich is right. It may not be as easy as you think."

"It won't be easy at all." Mina thought a moment. "I imagine one of the lords you're referring to is Lord Rathbone, Earl of Devonshire."

A look of surprise lit both their expressions.

Brenna stepped from Friedrich's arms, closer to Mina. "You know Lord Rathbone?"

Mina tilted her head, sensing a spike in Brenna's heart rate. "Of course. He's one of the three high counselors of the House of Arkadia. My question is, how do you know him?"

She glanced with a nervous smile at Friedrich who was not smiling at all. But he answered before her.

"Brennalyn met him at King Dominik's ball a few weeks ago."

"Oh. I imagine you met Lord Maksim and Steward Thorwald."

"Yes," answered Brennalyn. "They were all there together."

Mina dipped her chin. "Though I was never allowed to participate in the political affairs of the House, I attended parties and balls hosting politicians and diplomats. The three high counselors—Rathbone, Maksim, and Thorwald—hold the power of the House. Thorwald thinks he holds the most, but he's merely Rathbone and Maksim's puppet."

"You seem to have a plan already in mind," cut in Marius.

Her stomach twisted in knots at the idea of confronting the three most powerful men of her kingdom. *Her* kingdom. She notched her head a little higher.

"I believe the best course of action would be to pay a visit to Lord Rathbone's estate in Devonshire. Then—" she inhaled and blew out a deep breath—"if I'm lucky, I'll inform him of my plan to call the House to order and demand my coronation. I'll also inform him of the threat Dominik and Morgrid pose to Arkadia."

"That may not take much convincing," said Friedrich. "Maksim and Rathbone are well-aware of my uncle's threat to them. They left the ball quickly after the queen announced his intentions to marry you."

Mina swallowed the lump in her throat. Mikhail stiffened at her side.

Nikolai finally spoke up. "That's because they know if Dominik married Mina, he'd rule the southern kingdom as well as his own."

"Right," agreed Friedrich. "Which means they may very well be amenable to a strong ruler who holds Arkadia's interests at heart. But the southerners are a stubborn lot."

"Not to counter that lovely sentiment," interjected Grant, "but how will Arkadia allying with the Black Lily be in Arkadia's best interest? Especially if as you've said before—" he looked to his brother, Friedrich "—they've always bowed out of conflicts where there was no advantage for them."

For the first time since they'd entered the room, Mikhail spoke up. "Because without Arkadia, we will lose this war. And if we lose this war, then Queen Morgrid and King Dominik will dominate the people and the land with brutal violence, spreading the blood madness and building their vampire army until Arkadia has no chance of defending themselves against such a force. Arkadia will fall if they wait and stand alone."

Tension sparked the air as the truth of Mikhail's words settled in the room. Marius was the one to finally break the silence.

"You're right, Mikhail. But I know these men. Even worse, I know the pompous politicians of the House of Arkadia. They will not be persuaded easily."

"To hell with them then." Arabelle scoffed and slapped a hand at her side. "We'll go straight to the people of Arkadia."

"Arkadia is a prosperous, healthy land," said Mina. "The people trust the noble lords of the House."

"And so how do we persuade them?" asked Arabelle. "Obviously my normal strategy of brute force won't work. What do we have so that we can show this is the only course of action? That they must ally with us?"

Dmitri stepped from the outer circle and bowed before Mina, punching a fist against his heart. "You have me, Your Highness."

Nikolai took a step forward as well with a slight bow. "You have a former lieutenant to the Legionnaires of the Glass Tower."

"And a Fire Witch." Sienna smiled beside him, gold sparking in her eyes.

Mina still wondered what that meant exactly but felt the magic swirling in the air around her red-haired friend.

Friedrich followed suit. "You have the Duke of Winter Hill, royal nephew to the Varis crown."

Brennalyn made a bow of assent beside him, then Helena as well as Grant.

"And you have a prince of Varis," said Marius, falling in line.

"The leader of the Black Lily." Arabelle winked.

"You have our clan of the hart wolves," Allora promised.

Mikhail turned to her with fierce adoration in his gaze.

"You have the Captain of the Bloodguard," he whispered. "But you already knew that."

With tears welling in her eyes, she scanned the room, unable to process her own emotions brimming to the surface. But it was the emotion rippling from the black-haired man closest to her that swallowed her heart whole. He had enough hope and belief and determination to build a new world. With him at her side, she could easily build that world. One where humans weren't trampled on as inferiors, but given the rights and respect and opportunity they deserved. One where the monarchs ruled not simply with a just hand but with generous hearts. One where she would be happy and loved and whole.

Inhaling a ragged breath, she said with regal confidence, "Then we set out for Arkadia at once."

Chapter Fourteen

Mina had little to pack other than the extra gown, chemise, corset, stockings, and slippers given to her by Aleksei's sister at Wentworth. She'd stuffed all into a small bag and set them by the door for the morning. For the journey, she'd wear the practical gown for riding that Sienna had designed for her and the sturdy boots Arabelle had acquired from Hiddleston. She stood in front of the small looking glass hanging on the wall, admiring her new attire.

The skirt of the emerald-green gown hit her mid-calf, but her leather boots laced high to her knees so no skin was bare. The black outer bodice laced at the front, giving her support and also comfort, unlike the suffocating corsets she normally wore.

Helena had asked to style her hair. Mina couldn't deny the sweet girl anything. Though she'd survived a harrowing experience in the hands of King Dominik's men, she still bore a sweet innocence about her. She'd woven several tiny braids together, tapering from her crown to fall loosely with the rest of her long, unbound hair. She looked more like one of Allora's clan than the Princess of Arkadia. Not to mention the conventional dress and coiffure. Somehow, it suited her better. She looked like the warrior she'd teased Mikhail about at the archery field.

A soft knock came at the door.

Smelling his mulled-spice-and-leather scent, her heart raced ahead despite her efforts to remain calm. She opened the door to the devastatingly handsome sight of Mikhail in a loose-fitting black shirt with a lace tie at the V-neck and his black leather pants, the moonlight giving his hair a blue-black hue.

He roved her body from top to toe, then finally said, "I brought you a gift of my own."

He held up a black belt with a dagger in its sheath.

"Thank you."

"May I?" He gestured toward her waist.

"Of course."

Standing in her doorway, he looped it around her hips and cinched the buckle tight. Mina refrained from leaning into him and pressing her lips to his neck. The temptation was palpable. Once buckled, he leaned away.

"Now, remove your dagger. I want to show you a few things."

She did, then stared at the finely crafted eight-inch blade. It was narrow, thin, and fang-tip sharp. The metal itself was black with a sliver of gold embedded on the sharpened tip. The hilt bore a single emerald stone at the base near the handguard. "Remarkable. This is almost too beautiful to wield."

He wrapped his hand around hers on the hilt. "Beautiful things can often be the most deadly." He arched a brow to which she smiled. "Now. If you're in close combat with a vampire, there are several quick ways to bring him down with a dagger like this."

"All right."

He moved her hand with the tip of the blade under the edge of his jaw. "Plunge straight up at an angle into the skull here." He moved her hand and dagger tip toward his ear. "Right here. Less resistance on the entry. And if you're unable to get a clean entry into the brain, then just slash through the jugular here." He moved the flat of the blade to the exact spot for her to slice.

She nodded with grim determination, her primal instincts kicking in, her vampire liking this lesson very much.

"Got it?"

"Yes."

He guided her hand to slide the dagger back into its sheath then let go. "Of course, I won't leave your side if I can help it."

"Do you think I'll be required to use such deadly force on our journey?"

"There's no telling who we may encounter already allied with King Dominik. There are already whisperings in Hiddleston that King Dominik will give ten thousand sovereigns to whomever turns you over to him unharmed."

She noted his sudden shift from serene temper to volatile. Though his expression hadn't changed at all, his fury rode him hard, sharpening his features into frightening angles.

"Thank you, Captain."

With her new zeal to return to Arkadia and unite her people behind the Black Lily, she now understood something she didn't before. Mikhail's sense of duty wasn't just an important part of him, it was an *essential* part. A tree was merely branches and fluttering leaves without the sturdy trunk holding it up. His honor was the trunk that held him up.

She knew that she was in the wrong now, that by tempting him to betray his vow to the Bloodguard—no matter that she yearned for him body and soul—she was asking him to break himself in half. To set aside what was the essence of who he was as a man. Noble and fine and steadfast till the end. A pang of remorse stung her, knowing what kind of lover, what kind of husband he would make. She was going to say good night, then he took a step closer and gestured behind him.

"I have another gift for you." He frowned, his demeanor becoming rigid. "Not a gift actually. But a pledge."

"A pledge?"

"Come with me."

He offered his hand. She took it and let him guide her away from the cottage and the natural trails, into the thick of the woods. Darkness wrapped around them, as did the pervading pulse of magic that Mina always sensed here. The electric tingle vibrated along her skin, then through her flesh, to her bones. It wrapped inside her chest as if holding a secret for her, waiting to be discovered. She gasped at the rightness of being here at this moment, holding Mikhail's hand as he led her deeper into the dark.

They stepped through the brush toward an open grove of black oaks. Before they stepped into the clearing, she saw the circle of men, the familiar faces of the Bloodguard, each of them shirtless beneath the light of the full moon. The sight took her breath away.

"What is this?" she asked in a whisper, feeling as if she interrupted a sacred rite.

He didn't answer but led her between Dmitri and Gavril to the center of the circle where a silver goblet stood on the ground. He lifted it and wrapped both her hands to cradle it.

"Hold this. You'll know what to do when the time comes."

Stepping back, he reached his arms over his shoulders to his back and removed his shirt in a swift move. Dropping it at his feet, he marched to the one open space next to his brother.

"Bloodguard, *ready*," he commanded in a clear, loud

voice.

In unison, they knelt, left knee then right. Including Mikhail.

Mina tried not to react, but it was impossible. The sight of a circle of forty muscular, shirtless warrior vampires on their knees around her under the moonlight was enough to make a weaker woman swoon. She did her best to remain poised, her breath puffs of white air in the cold.

Mikhail continued in his commanding tenor. "This pledge of devotion and fealty is given by free hands and free hearts." He held her gaze with fiery intensity. "This rite is our seal and vow to you, Vilhelmina Dragomir."

Then they spoke as one.

"We are the Bloodguard. Noble by birth, brothers by choice. We smite the evil ones. We avenge the innocents. We right all wrongs. We are the cold blade in the dark night. We give our swords, our bodies, our strength, and our blood. We bleed as one. We die as one."

The chorus of voices echoed in the silent grove as Dmitri unsheathed his dagger and sliced open the fleshy part of his palm.

"For Vilhelmina." He stretched out his arm, blood dripping onto the snow-dusted ground.

Mina understood and moved swiftly to him, catching droplets of his blood in the cup. He then swiped his palm across his chest, over his heart, smearing a line of crimson.

"Vilhelmina," said Gregoravich at Dmitri's left, slicing open his palm in the same way.

Again, she collected the blood sacrifice. A few drops fell into the goblet, then he marked his bloody palm over his heart.

"Vilhelmina." Aleksei was next. Then Gavril.

Mina went from one warrior to the next, meeting each one's gaze, hoping they recognized how much their pledge meant to her. She circled around till she was finally left standing in front of Mikhail.

With a swift slice of his dagger, he raised his hand, blood dripping in a steady line. "Vilhelmina," he annunciated clearly with his dark, melodic voice. The one she recognized that awoke her from the bloodless sleep. The voice that called to her helpless heart, beating frantically.

She collected his offering, watching in fascination as he crossed his heart, marking himself with his own blood. Then all was silent as they remained on their knees. Watching her. Waiting.

She knew what was expected of her but not what words were usually said after such a sacrificial rite. She could only say what she felt down to her bones once she'd taken her place at the center of the circle once more.

"I accept your pledge."

She raised the goblet in salute, moonlight glinting off the silver, her voice trembling with emotion. With one hand, she eased her left sleeve off her shoulder, exposing the skin over her heart.

"I will honor and cherish it."

Dipping two fingers into the goblet, she smeared their mixed blood across her own heart, turning in a circle as she did so that they all could see the visible sign of her own vow to them.

"I give you my loyalty as you give me yours."

Holding the goblet up to the sky, she scanned the perimeter, her eyes landing on Mikhail, then tipped it back and drank the blood of the men who'd just devoted their lives to her safety.

For a human, this might be hard to stomach, but for her, it was like drinking the nectar of the gods, the essence and strength of every man energizing her body. She accepted them not just as her personal guard, but as her devoted knights for the duration of her life and their own.

When the chalice was empty, a drop trailing from the corner of her mouth, she held the goblet between both hands and watched as they quietly lifted to their feet one by one and disappeared into Silvane Forest. Until finally only Mikhail was left, standing where he'd knelt, looking at her with his otherworldly eyes, thinking deeply of she knew not what.

Mina trembled from the ritual, the power of it, the devotion of it. "Why?" she asked, swiping away the blood at her mouth with the back of her hand.

He remained statue still, carved in perfect lines by moonlight and shadow. His bare chest hardly rose with his shallow intake of breath while Mina felt as if she'd run a lap around the world.

"What do you mean?" he asked, still not moving.

She walked toward him. "Why did they do that?" Her voice quivered. "Because you asked them to?"

"No," he answered calmly, though the flare of his eyes said he was anything but. "The Bloodguard is an order of brothers. Not a military dictatorship."

She finally reached him, her body thrumming with the energy of their blood and the utter beauty of their pledge. Fire pumped hard through her veins while the chill of the winter night cooled her skin. Once more, she felt so magnificently alive. She wanted to thank Mikhail, but words felt insufficient for such an act of devotion.

His mouth ticked up on one side as if he knew her thoughts. "It's time to get you indoors." He took her hand and roughly led her back through the dark woods.

Laboring to keep up with his swift stride, for her limbs still shook from the magical ceremony in the clearing, she said, "You must think me in grave danger to need the allegiance of the entire Bloodguard."

"That's not the entire Bloodguard, if you must know.

There are more of us."

"There are?"

"Yes."

"Where are they?"

"Not here."

"Why?"

"They are needed elsewhere."

She sighed, shaking her head at his vague response, then tripped on a fallen branch. He spun and scooped her in his arms, without a word, then sped vampire-swift to her cabin.

He nudged the door open and set her on her feet, but she kept her hands locked at his neck.

He glided his fingers up her arms, gripped her wrists and tugged gently, but she held fast, gazing up at the strong lines of his grim countenance. The devotion of the Bloodguard brought the cutting realization that she didn't have *his* devotion. Still, she couldn't ask him for more. She wasn't a selfish creature, but her vampire instincts still pushed her to kiss him, to take him, to keep him for her own. The contradiction of need and doing the honorable thing twisted her heart.

Jerking her hands from his neck, she spun and walked away, wrapping her arms around herself. Standing before the fire, she stared at the dying embers, the orange-gold coals bringing her no warmth at all.

"What is wrong?" he finally asked.

She didn't want to tell him. But she also did. How did this man twist her into such a maelstrom of stormy emotions? She'd always been quiet and composed, even sage-like with others. Her empathic gifts had helped her steady the keel, keep the balance of the world around her. But not since Captain Mikhail had stepped into her life.

Glancing sideways, she once more noted his flushed complexion at the jawline, his eyes glittering more brightly, his pallor less stark. All signs of a good feeding. She'd ignored it before, but the thought of him feeding, being with another woman ripped her insides out.

"You've fed well recently."

"A vampire must feed."

"Earlier today, you told me you heard rumors of Dominik setting a ransom on my return. Did you overhear that in Hiddleston?" Her heart pounded violently in her chest, not wanting the answer but needing it all the same. "Where you fed on a bleeder?"

His expression darkened, not in anger, but in something close to guilt. "Yes."

She turned her gaze back to the fire, not wanting him to see the hurt in her eyes. Swallowing the lump swelling in her throat, she unbuckled the belt and dagger he'd given her and tossed it to the floor. The door closed.

"You know I must feed," he said gingerly, stepping farther into the room.

"Yes. Of course." She lifted the poker and stabbed at the embers, doing little more than causing sparks to spit up in the air. "You're a man with other needs as well, so…" She shrugged and let that thought die before it could cross her lips, putting the poker back in its place against the stone mantel.

He stalked closer with heavy steps. Facing him, she forced her gaze to meet his, taking two steps back.

"Yes," he grated. "I *do* have needs. But I didn't…it's not what you're thinking."

Angry heat flared up her neck and into her cheeks. The beast within her breast demanded voice, and she couldn't stop herself. "Did she taste good?"

"Stop it." With long, steady strides, he closed the small space between them.

Crossing her arms in defense, she matched his steps in

reverse till the backs of her thighs hit the bed. "Did you feed before or after you...bedded her?"

He gripped her around the upper arms, pressing his chest to hers, though her crossed arms formed a barrier. "I didn't fuck her," he grated with dark intensity.

"But you wanted to."

"No." He tilted his head lower till his lips hovered in aching closeness to her own. "I wanted to fuck you." His voice shook with passion. "I still do."

Her body trembled once more with the desperate need of this man, her eyes sliding closed on the blissful thought of him being inside her.

He was honorable and loyal and true, eager to follow the noble path. But he was also strong and passionate and sensual. Though he may not know it, his aggressive demeanor and tantalizing strength were a beacon to the woman newly awakened within her bosom. He held it all so in control. The she-beast inside wanted it unleashed...on her.

"You're killing me slowly, Mikhail," she whispered on a trembling breath, leaning closer, her bottom lip brushing his. "I won't ask you to betray your brotherhood. I couldn't dare. Not after tonight. After what you all did for me." Her voice cracked, but she held it together, sucking in a deep inhale as she pressed her palms over her abdomen. "But it hurts, Mikhail." A tear slipped down her cheek. "It hurts so much."

He manacled his large hands around her arms. "Don't," he commanded.

She knew he meant the tears, the angles of his face growing sharper by the dying firelight.

"I can't help it." As if her admission opened the dam, tears fell freely.

"Goddammit. I can't, either," he breathed on a harsh breath before he tossed her on her back diagonally on the bed. He was on his knees, straddling her waist, whipping off his belt with a snap of leather and a clink of buckle.

Startled by the explosion of action, she sensed the sex-laced tension whipping from the man on top of her. "What are—"

He grabbed her wrists and wrapped them with the belt twice, slid her body up, and buckled the belt around the wooden bedpost.

"Mikhail—"

His lips were on hers. Not a sweet, questing kiss. But one of control and dominance. Before she even felt her bodice loosen, it was unlaced and opened, then Mikhail's large hand mounded her breast and squeezed. She arched into his touch and moaned, long and loud. He broke the kiss, staring down with the wildness of a frantic beast, caged too long with the need to dominate his prey.

"The pain in your eyes tears me to the heart." His voice was gravel-rough. "I'm going to take care of you." He murmured the dark promise against her lips, trailing his tongue along her lower lip.

"Like before?" she asked on a relieved sigh.

"Better than before."

He pinched her nipple through the thin fabric of her gown and chemise. She whimpered and nodded. "Yes."

He unlaced the drawstring between her breasts and scooped the blouse down to expose her breasts, the bottom of the bodice jutting them up. The cool air heightened her sensitivity, her nipples budding under his hungry gaze. Dipping his head low but holding her gaze, he licked a path around one nipple before sliding down the slope of her breast and across her sternum to the other.

"Is this what you want?" he ground out.

She nodded and bit her lip to keep from moaning too loudly.

"Answer me. I want to hear you say it."

His hand was under her skirts, hiking them higher, his calloused fingers skimming up the inside of her thigh.

"You want my lips on your skin?" he asked in an authoritative tone, sounding more like a command than a question.

She nodded with a breathy, "Yes."

His long fingers found the apex between her legs and teased her swollen bud. "*Fuck*. You're soaked for me." He lowered his mouth to her nipple again, covering it and sucking hard before commanding, "Open your legs wider."

She did, then rocked her hips as he slicked his fingers into her folds. As she pulled her arms, his leather belt strained and creaked.

"No," he said, gazing up with a dark smile. "You'll keep your hands to yourself."

She closed her eyes and thrust her hips up, aching for more.

"You want my fingers inside you?" He teased around her entrance, dragging a choking sound from her throat.

Her canines were long and sharp, pushing her mouth open, so every little sensual sound crept from her throat and filled the room with her desperate need.

"Tell me, Mina, and I'll give it to you."

"Yes," she said more violently than she meant to.

He lowered his head and nicked the mound of her breast with a fang, releasing a drop of his elixir into her body. It felt just like the man who owned it, burning through her like an avalanche of potent aggression and power. Just one drop sent her body shuddering on a wave of ecstasy. She couldn't imagine what it would feel like to have his long fangs embedded in her throat, releasing the full power of the man in his elixir.

"Oh, God," she cried as he teased and circled her sex, slicking around and around the engorged bud.

"You'll have to speak clearly, Mina."

"Yes, Mikhail. Put your fingers inside me."

Closing his mouth over a taut nipple, he pushed one long finger inside, her tight flesh yielding to his intrusion. Sweet bliss. She thrust up and clamped her muscles around his finger. He lifted over her and stared down.

"Bloody fucking hell." He pulled out.

"No," she protested. "Please, Mikhail. *Please* don't stop."

"Easy."

He glided two fingers in, pumping slowly, letting her body welcome the foreign intrusion. Without removing his fingers, he leveraged down her body, flipping up her skirts. She was bare to him, her knees bent, her hips making tiny thrusts as he pumped inside her. She squeezed her eyes shut, unable to watch him stare at her so intimately.

"No, Mina. Look at me."

She had to obey. When she did, she found he'd laid between her legs, holding his body up on one forearm, his face just above her mound.

"I want you to watch me give you pleasure."

It wasn't a request. She nodded. Then he lowered his head and opened his hot, wet mouth on the bud of her sex, pumping his fingers in a long, slow glide. She fisted her hands, pulling the belt taut, pressing her pelvis toward his wicked, wicked mouth.

"Please," she begged.

He flicked down her center with his tongue and thrust his fingers deeper, harder, faster. She ground her sex against his hot mouth and lapping tongue, her own violent need stoking her higher. His other hand slid under her ass, gripping one cheek, his thumb spreading her wider for his feast.

He lifted his head, still stroking his long fingers, staring at her with palpable heat and longing.

"Beautiful," he murmured.

Her own sensuality drove her now, as she thrust her hips up against the downward stroke of his fingers. Her she-beast wanted free. Jerking one hand with a surge of strength, she pulled it loose, the other cinched tight in the belt loop. His gaze flicked up to her as she mounded her breast and pinched the taut nipple with thumb and forefinger. The answering growl from Mikhail pebbled her skin on the erotic sound.

He bent his head again to his wicked work, licking with new vigor.

"Mikhail," she whispered, bucking harder against his mouth.

He clenched his fingers around her ass and pumped his fingers deeper, harder. Her vampire guiding her now, she reached down with her free hand and clenched a fist into his hair, holding him in place as she stroked herself up against his hot mouth.

"Yes," she breathed, her voice unusually low and dark, her keening cries quickening, louder and closer together.

"Come for me, Mina," he whispered before clamping his lips over her clit and growling, the vibration shooting her over the edge.

"Mikhail!" she screamed.

Waves of pleasure rippled around his thrusting fingers. She let out little moans of ecstasy with each throbbing pulse, even as he licked her sensitive bud while she came down from her fevered release.

White spots appeared in her periphery. She'd nearly fallen unconscious at the violent pleasure tearing through her. He slipped his fingers out slowly, and she whimpered in protest. He placed a sweeping kiss on her inner thigh, brushing his stubbled jaw in a tender caress.

"Fucking beautiful," he murmured almost to himself. Then he was over her, pressing her body into the mattress with his own. His large, stiff bulge pushed against her hip.

She'd never taken her fist from his hair. Holding his weight on a forearm, he placed his other hand on top of hers in his hair, lacing his fingers between hers.

"Better?" he asked, arching a brow.

A giddy joy rose up inside. "Much." She let it bubble up into laughter before she squirmed, her hip bone pressing on his erection.

His eyes widened, his gaze falling to her lips once again. He lowered his mouth to hers. Like the brush of wispy clouds, he skated in light, torturous touches. So light, he might've been brushing her lips with a feather.

"You've been honest with me, Mina." Another tantalizing touch of lips, a small slip of tongue. "So I'll be honest with you."

She kept her eyes open, as did he, his vampire burning bright in every taut line of his face.

"I want you." He let loose his hand lacing her fingers, then gripped her nape, squeezing gently. "I want you so much, I feel like if I don't make you mine soon, then some part of me will break away and disappear into the unknown. Then another will break away and another, until there's nothing left of me at all but a hollow void. A shell of a man." A trail of his tongue along the slightly parted seam of her lips. "I didn't know I'd ever have to choose between a woman and the Bloodguard." He brushed his thumb across her cheekbone. "But I didn't know I'd ever meet you."

Her heart in her throat, she whispered, "I don't want you to have to choose between me and the Bloodguard."

"I don't, either, Mina." He pressed a harder kiss to her lips, stroking sweetly with his tongue before pulling away, a pulse of fervent adoration seeping into her empathic senses from this virile man. "But I also want to be whole. Sometimes, I think the heavens put me in that tower in Briar Rose and sealed my fate with that blood kiss. Like fate is against me."

"No," she whispered fervently, brushing a lock of his dark hair away from his brow. "I've felt the same since that very moment. Fate is *with* us. You were meant to be the one to awaken me."

He pressed his forehead to hers. "We'll find a way, Mina, we'll—"

Without warning, he lurched off of her and leaped to the window.

"What is it?" Mina listened but heard nothing. Not at first.

Then a blood-curdling scream pierced the darkness from Brennalyn's house. It sounded like Beatrice or Helena. Mikhail slammed the inside shutters closed over the window and latched them tight. That was the first time Mina realized they were made of iron not wood. Only painted to look like wood.

He pulled his dagger free and charged for the door, but turned before he opened it.

"*Quickly.* Bolt the door when I leave and hide behind the bed. Keep your dagger close, just in case. I'll be back shortly."

Then he was gone.

Chapter Fifteen

Mikhail flashed to the back door, but it was locked. A crash to the floor inside and someone grunted.

"Get Izzy and Denny!" screamed Brennalyn, panic and fear so ripe he could taste it through the wall.

Without hesitation, he smashed through the window, glass shattering around him. Brenna stood blocking the hall to where Izzy and Denny slept, wielding a gold-tipped dagger at the ready. Gold, the one element poisonous to vampires. She bared her fangs, even though her two attackers were twice her size. Her sleeve was sliced with bloody claw marks at the shoulder.

The two bulky vampires had turned at the sound of breaking glass. Their eyes were flat black, a sure sign of sanguine furorem. The madness would make them strong and lethal, but not as deadly as him.

"Well, look who it is. Cap'n of the Bloodguard," said the bigger one, puffing up his chest and creeping forward.

"Take 'im, Jeb." He turned to Brenna. "I'll take the pretty little vamp."

Mikhail didn't have time to wonder how they knew who he was, but he took about two seconds to process that these were commoners turned vampire, one of the thousands taken by force from villages across Varis for Queen Morgrid's army. These two were apparently rogues, lost and looking for easy prey. They threatened Brenna and her children. They were dead men.

Mikhail launched at the big one who gripped his wrist before Mikhail could slice his throat. Grappling, Mikhail twisted in a blur, breaking the vampire's grip and coming up at his back. Before the vampire could even turn his head, Mikhail gripped his throat from behind and shoved his dagger into the base of his skull at an upward angle with a satisfying crunch.

As Mikhail spun back to the second one, Brenna leaped out and slashed, scoring the intruder's face, a spurt of red spraying the air, flesh sizzling from the cut with gold.

"Bitch!"

Mikhail was on him before he could leap onto her. They tumbled sideways against a sideboard, a vase of flowers shattering as they rolled. Mikhail straddled his chest, fisted his scraggly hair, and slammed his head to the floor. The vamp was skinny but strength pumped hard in his newborn veins, the blood madness doing its work. He gripped Mikhail's blade before it slid into his jugular. Squeezing the blade, his fingers dripped blood. The creature scented the air, baring his fangs at the smell of his own blood.

The door crashed open. Mikhail faltered. There, silhouetted in the doorway was the frightening figure of Radomir, the queen's consort and personal guard, his bald head shining by moonlight. The vampire who'd killed Mina's lady-in-waiting, then imprisoned her in a bloodless sleep. Fury lit within Mikhail's chest. Several of the queen's guard in royal colors, blue and silver, strode in with Radomir.

The sudden distraction was enough for the skinny vamp to leverage his weight and push Mikhail off.

Mikhail leaped in to a defensive stance. Brenna ran away down the hall toward the children's room.

Radomir's gaze followed her before he uttered a silky, menacing command. "Get her." Four vampires launched down the hall. Radomir pulled a curving scimitar from his belt and instead of coming forward for Mikhail, he flashed down the hall behind the Legionnaires.

At the exact moment, Friedrich, Grant, and Gregoravich blurred into the house.

A thump sounded against the wall in the bedroom.

"Noooo!" screamed Brennalyn.

Friedrich, with death in his eyes, sped toward them. Grant and Gregoravich engaged with the two Legionnaires still standing in the room. Mikhail followed Friedrich.

Friedrich had already snapped the neck of one in the three seconds it took Mikhail to get there. The duke swung his sword and cleaved in two the head of another Legionnaire who was entirely too close to Brenna, who hovered over and whispered to the crumpled, unconscious form of Beatrice.

Radomir stalked toward Izzy and Denny, the children clinging to each other in a bed in the corner, their wide eyes frozen in terror. Mikhail launched at Radomir only to feel a sharp stab in the middle of his back.

Mikhail roared and spun on his attacker. Not a new-born but a seemingly skilled officer of the queen's guard, his fine blond hair shining by the moonlight streaming through the bedroom window.

"Come on, traitor," he beckoned, grinning, his canines sharp, but the sword in his hand sharper. "Let's see what you can do with your little dagger."

In a flash, Mikhail pulled two finger-size blades from his belt and sent them home. They embedded in the officer's eyes. He fell back, bellowing and bleeding. Before he could hit the floor, Mikhail was on him.

"More than you can do with your pretty sword," he answered, shoving his serrated blade into his carotid artery and slicing deep.

"Hold!" screamed Radomir.

Mikhail was on his feet, shoulder to shoulder with Grant, whose face was splattered with crimson—not his own. Friedrich stood in front of Brenna and the fallen form of Beatrice, his fist white-knuckled on the hilt of his bloodstained sword.

But not a soul moved. Radomir held Izzy off the floor, an arm banded at her waist and his scimitar at her tiny, pale throat. The one who'd gotten away from Mikhail had Denny with his claws already pricking the tender skin of his neck, a dirty knife poised over his heart. In one second, they could kill them both.

"Radomir." Friedrich beckoned his attention to him, Brennalyn standing only a foot behind him. She stared at her two hostage children, fear radiating through the room in her quickened pulse. "Whatever you think to gain by harming my children, think again. You'll die the second you do."

The narrow-eyed consort of the queen smiled, his canines thicker and longer than most vampires', making him look far more monster than man. "You don't understand, Your Grace." His gaze flicked to each of them, seeming to gauge his chances. "I didn't come here to kill the children."

Friedrich took a step forward, but Radomir tightened his hold and pressed his blade closer. Izzy squeaked, a single drop of blood sliding down her slender throat.

"Mimi," she cried, tears falling from her pale-blue eyes.

Brennalyn clenched her hands together, her voice shaking. "It's okay, Izzy darling."

"What did you come for then?" Friedrich demanded, his

beast riding his vocal cords.

Radomir grinned, his eerie gaze sweeping the room, landing on Mikhail, then locking back with Friedrich.

"Not even your Bloodguard can help you now, Your Grace."

He glanced at his man holding Denny, and with an almost imperceptible nod, he crashed through the glass window, taking Izzy with him. In the same second, the scraggly vampire stabbed his dagger straight into Denny's chest, the sweet-faced boy's brown eyes going wide then glassy before he'd even hit the ground.

Brenna's blood-chilling scream filled the room as she leaped for her fallen boy. The killer had already blurred after his master.

"Stay with them!" Friedrich yelled at Grant, falling to the floor to pull Denny's limp body into his arms.

Mikhail followed, speeding into the night, rent with screams and clanging metal and the overpowering smell of black smoke. Not just wood smoke but the distinct foul scent of burning flesh. That's when Mikhail realized this wasn't an attack on Brennalyn's home. This was a full-scale attack on the Black Lily. Grant was fast on the heels of Radomir, and Mikhail on the child killer.

Catching his prey as Mikhail leaped a snow-covered log, they tumbled to a stop, once more with Mikhail straddling his chest. He didn't waste time but slit his carotid artery, finding some overwhelming satisfaction in the sight of his blood spilling onto the white snow.

"Rot in hell, you fucking bastard."

He laughed on a gurgle. "You shouldn't've taken the princess, Cap'n." He grinned, mouth bubbling his own blood. "She wasn't yours to take."

Icy fear sliced down his spine like the reaper's blade. He raised his dagger and with a powerful force hacked once, then twice, the killer's head rolling away.

Mina.

He fled back toward the cottage with horror on his heart, sending up a brief prayer to the stars if anyone was listening on this cold, black night.

Chapter Sixteen

Screams and cries filled the night. Mina huddled behind the bed gripping her dagger, sensing the fear and turmoil taking place in Brennalyn's cottage, and even farther off. In the distance, she sensed rage filling the air. The furious bellows of men at arms, engaged in a battle for blood. The howl of a hart wolf broke through the din of death, a haunting call to their pack. The weight of dark, sinister emotions threatened to cripple her.

Then someone rattled the doorknob. She didn't call out. Mikhail would've let himself be known.

"Yasha! Bring your ax," barked a commanding voice. "She's in there. I can smell her."

Then the fear was her own, spiking adrenaline through her body, igniting her she-beast to the forefront.

Crack. Crack.

The wood around the door splintered. The frame disintegrated under the vicious blows of the vampire named Yasha on the other side.

Crack.

Mina refused to be dragged out like some defenseless lamb. They knew she was here.

Crack.

Someone's boot kicked the fractured door in. But before anyone stepped in, the thumping sounds of combat echoed into the chamber. Grunts and metal on metal and bones crunching and blood spilling. There were more than two or three men fighting outside the cottage. Mina could make out the thrumming of ten heartbeats. Then nine…then six…five…and finally two.

The panting of the victors drew closer. Mina held her ground, her vampire claws sliding out of her fingertips for the very first time. She recalled Mikhail's teachings, where to thrust the dagger in easiest, as they sidled through the doorway.

The officer wearing Queen Morgrid's Legionnaire colors strode confidently into the room, a scarlet-stained short sword in one hand. Then a burly beast of a man in commoner's clothes entered, eyes as black as the devil's heart, his ax in hand.

"There now, Your Highness," crooned the officer, holding up his hands in a calming manner. "Best come easy, sweetling."

As they crossed the fireplace, now only a few feet separating them, the officer stopped and inhaled deep.

"Oh, my." His blue eyes dilated, his fangs elongated more, thickening his speech. "Seems our little princess has been naughty." He shook a finger at her like she was a child. "Tsk, tsk. I don't believe King Dominik will like that at all."

The beast called Yasha grunted, his nostrils flaring. Mina knew sanguine furorem made men feral. Not just like animals, but like crazed monsters. Craving blood above all, but their primal instincts to dominate rode parallel to the bloodlust. At this moment, Mina's empathic senses felt the air changing around the ax-wielding creature.

His black gaze shifted down her body in a caress of menace. His emotions were a blistering concoction of malice, hunger, hatred, and sinister lust.

"Yasha!" The officer put his hand to the creature's chest. "Wait outside. I'll handle her."

Yasha didn't move as the officer advanced. Mina readied herself. No way would she be taken without a fight. She hissed a warning at them both.

The officer smiled one second before he was on her.

. . .

Mikhail smelled the pungent blood before her small cabin came into view. Bodies lay in the snow outside her shattered door. The two closest to the entry caused Mikhail's heart to stutter, his stomach clenching in grief. Not now.

Someone struggled inside. He flashed over the bodies and into the dark room. A Legionnaire lay dead on the floor, Mina's emerald-studded hilt jutting out beneath his chin.

Then Mikhail's entire body lit into scorching rage. A giant vampire pinned Mina down, one hand on her throat, the other ripping at her skirt, trying to subdue her struggling body. In swift succession, Mikhail lifted the ax on the floor, gripped the bastard by the hair, lofted him off Mina and onto his back, then started chopping.

The head rolled off in four hacks, tongue lolling, but it wasn't enough. Mikhail aimed where the beast's heart lay. It might still be beating. He wanted it stopped. He wanted this foul fucking beast to be nothing but an unrecognizable mass of mutilated flesh and bone.

On what must have been the twentieth upward swing, he heard her call his name.

Heaving, he turned. She stood straight and tall, her dress

bloody and torn, starlike eyes filled with pain but bright and burning. He dropped the ax and swept her into his arms, fearing she might still be swept away from him.

"Are you hurt?" he rasped. "Did he hurt you?"

"No." She shook her head and wrapped her arms tight around his neck, squeezing him as hard as he was.

A mournful wail echoed on a sob from Brenna's cottage. Mina gasped and pushed back.

"What happened?" she asked.

"Come on." Taking her hand, he guided her out the door.

At the doorway, Mikhail stopped, the fury cooling, replaced with hollow-souled grief. Kneeling beside his blood brother, he looked into the lifeless eyes of Aleksei one last time before closing them for good. His body was already cold. The bitterness of it, of a man who'd made him laugh so many nights around the fire, who'd fought beside him and shed blood with him time and again, his last act to give his life for the princess. Then he stepped over him to the Black Lily soldier, Ivan.

Aleksei and Ivan had always gotten along so well, with their mutual love of good ale, fine women, and warm laughter. The sight of his vampire guard and the human soldier side by side in death reminded him what this war was all about, what they were fighting for. And how much they had to lose.

"Oh, God." Mina knelt beside Aleksei. "They'd come to protect me."

"Aye," he agreed, glancing at the six bodies they'd felled before they breathed their last. "They did their duty," he said gently, not meaning for it to sting, though it did. "Not out of obligation, but because it is who they are." He glanced down, a lump swelling in his throat. "Who they were."

Mina's eyes pooled with tears but didn't drop until she leaned over Aleksei and placed a kiss on his forehead. Then she moved to Ivan and did the same.

"Come," he murmured, anxiety riding him to find his brother. But first, he must see to it that Mina was in safe hands.

They ran through the brush, off the trail, the shortest route to the front door. They quickly passed the dead bodies and followed the mournful sound of Brennalyn coming from the children's room.

Brenna sat on the floor next to Beatrice, the limp body of little Denny in her lap, his dark head against her chest as she combed her fingers though his hair. Gregoravich stood over her, guarding. The two dead Legionnaires were piled against the far wall near the door.

Mikhail knelt onto one knee next to Beatrice, checking her pulse, when two pairs of light footsteps and a set of heavy boots sounded up the hall. Helena, Sienna, and Nikolai rushed into the room, all three battle-worn. Helena's pale face bore a purpling bruise on her cheek, her black hair falling in wild disarray. Sienna's eyes glinted gold with her fire magic, the residual scent of it like charred honey lingering in the air. Nikolai carried his sword, bloodied from his kills, his face a mask of tamped rage.

"Oh, Mimi!" Helena fell down onto her knees, cradling Denny's face.

Brenna swallowed the grief she'd been pouring out through tears and sobs as Helena wept instead.

"Not Denny, Mimi," she cried, shaking her head. "Not sweet Denny."

"Oh, my darling." Brenna brushed her hand over her head and pulled her close. They clung to each other with the boy's lifeless body between them. "He's with the angels now, my love."

Brenna's voice cracked as she tried to comfort her daughter with words that could never alleviate the pain of this innocent's untimely death.

"Where's Friedrich?" Mikhail asked Gregory.

The somber giant nodded toward the crashed-open window. "Went after you and Grant after he gave Denny his elixir."

Mikhail knelt beside Brenna, noting Friedrich's elixir wasn't strong enough. Without even thinking, he gently pried Helena back and eased his arms around Denny.

"Let me have him, Brennalyn."

She shook her head. "Not yet. I need another moment with him."

"I may still be able to save him. Let me have him."

Brenna's night-dark eyes, glassy with tears, fixed on him. Shaking her head softly, she whispered, "You can't. Friedrich tried. His heart has already stopped."

Mikhail slipped his hand beneath the boy's slim nape, then firmed his voice. "His blood is still warm. Give him to me, Brennalyn."

She let go at once. With the frail child across his lap, the lifeblood staining his chest, Mikhail ignored the tense silence as everyone watched him. Tearing open Denny's shirt, he bent and sank sharpened fangs into his jugular, releasing the potent elixir that poured through his veins. A powerful potion he carried from his family's secreted lineage—more powerful than Friedrich's, a grandson of the original Varis vampire.

After a breathless moment, he heard and felt against his lips the soft murmur of a birdlike pulse, then another. He pulled out his fangs, sealing the wound with a swift lick, then pressed his fingers to his throat. There again, the soft flutter of a heartbeat. Raising his head, heaving from the intensity of the moment, his gaze swept the room, everyone watching in awe.

Mikhail avoided Mina's questioning gaze and landed on Brenna. "He is alive."

She gasped and cried, pulling Denny into her arms gently. "Oh, Captain. How? How did you—?"

"Best get him to another room, keep him warm. I'll see to Beatrice."

Brenna was on her feet, carrying the boy to her own bedroom with Helena on her heels.

"Let me help," said Mina, hurrying with them.

Mikhail scooped Beatrice into his arms to take her into her bedchamber next door.

"Oh, Helena. What about the boys?" Brenna asked from the next bedchamber, panic gripping her again.

"They're fine. They're all okay. They were with me and Dmitri. And Marius and Arabelle, too."

"Marius, Arabelle, and some of the Black Lily are with the boys at our cabin," added Nikolai, now standing in their doorway.

"Where's Dmitri now?" asked Mikhail, stopping beside Nikolai and peering into the room.

"He went looking for you," Helena answered, sitting on the edge of the bed where Brenna brushed Denny's hair away from his face and Mina pulled the quilt up tight.

Gregoravich cleared his throat behind him. "Captain, he came here with Yuri and Gavril. I told him you and Grant, then Friedrich went after Radomir. And…the girl."

Mikhail noted that his bear-size friend couldn't even say her name. He was fond of Izzy. Everyone was. The girl had wrapped every member of the Bloodguard around her sweet, pudgy finger. *Why in heaven's name did the queen kidnap her?*

Helena gasped. "Girl? Where's Izzy?"

Brenna just shook her head, unable to speak it aloud for a moment. "They took her."

"No. No. *No.*" Helena shook her head, as if she could change reality if she denied it enough. Brenna pulled her back into her arms.

Everyone knew what Helena had suffered at the hands of King Dominik's men when she was imprisoned at Dragon's Eye. The constant abuse as their bleeder, the neglect, the terror. But a little girl couldn't be used as a bleeder for long before she died. They would've taken Beatrice if that were their goal. She'd last longer as their blood slave. No, it was some other reason.

Mina had remained silent all this time, until now when she sucked in a sharp breath. The pain emanating in this room was palpable, a raw scraping against the skin. Mina stood beside Helena and Brenna, placing her hands on their shoulders. He couldn't see or smell anything different, but the air changed all the same. A wave of numbing peace radiated from her, spreading like morning mist. He'd heard of some empaths with the gift to impart a healing kind of serenity. Brenna and Helena continued to weep, but the grief seemed to subside to a bearable pain as Mina wrapped them both in her arms. She murmured low, soft words of compassion to ease this ungodly weight.

Mikhail had to get out of there and find Dmitri. He glanced at Gregory. "You'll stay here."

"Aye, Captain."

"I will, too," added Nikolai.

"I'll help you," said Sienna, following Mikhail to the next room.

Sienna pulled back the rose quilt so Mikhail could lay Beatrice down.

"Are Marius and Arabelle all right?"

"Yes." Sienna's brow furrowed as she felt the lump on the side of Beatrice's head. "Arabelle was badly injured. They'd broken her arm, the bones sticking out and cracked her rib cage. She couldn't breathe, one of the bones must've punctured her lung. Marius gave her his elixir, but it wasn't enough. Blood was coming out of her mouth, and we knew"—she choked up, glancing at him—"we knew she'd die if he didn't take action quickly."

Mikhail didn't need to hear the rest to know what happened next. "He made her a vampire."

Sienna nodded, brushing Beatrice's hair away from her face.

"Then she will be fine."

"Will Beatrice truly recover?"

"Yes." He sat on the edge of the bed beside Sienna and lifted the girl's arm, rolling up the sleeve of her blue dress. "After I give her my elixir."

"How, Captain? How is your elixir more powerful than Friedrich's? He is a Varis."

The most potent elixir of healing pumped through the veins of a pure-blood Varis. The closer one was to the original source, Queen Morgrid, the more potent the power of healing.

He caught Sienna's curious expression. "I saw what you did for Denny. You brought him back from the dead."

"His blood was warm and his spirit still close. It would've been too late had we waited another second."

"But it wasn't too late. How, Captain?"

"A tale for another time."

He leaned his head and bit into the girl's thin forearm. He didn't suction her blood but allowed his potent serum to be released from the needle-thin glands in his fangs. He counted to ten, then pulled away, hearing her faint pulse thrum faster into a healthy, strong beat. She turned her head to the other side of the pillow, the first sign of consciousness.

Sienna stared at Mikhail questioningly. But he wouldn't tell her what she longed to know. How and why his elixir was as powerful as that of a Varis prince.

"I must find my brother and Friedrich."

He blurred from the room and away into the woods in the direction he'd gone after Radomir. The night was lit with the orange glow of an inferno beyond Silvane Forest to the west. Anxiety rode him when he smelled the familiar scent of his brother, Friedrich, and hart wolves. He sped past the body of Denny's would-be killer toward the sights and sounds of those he knew.

Dane—naked in human form from a recent shift—had Friedrich's arm wrapped around his shoulder as he helped him walk. Allora and her mate, Bron, in wolf form, flanked them, as well as Dmitri, Yuri, and Gavril. Allora's white coat glistened by moonlight. Bron's sleek black fur helped him meld with the trees. Their gold wolf eyes glinting in the dark.

Dmitri's eyes widened in relief when they landed on Mikhail. The two jogged to each other. Dmitri gripped his shoulder, squeezing hard.

"I didn't know where you were." Which was the closest he could come to saying, *I thought you might've died.*

Mikhail grabbed his brother's nape and tightened his hold, thankful to the heavens for sparing him. For he was sure there would be a high count of the dead from this night.

"I'm hard to kill, Brother. You know that."

"You mean you're too damn stubborn to die."

"Aye. There's that."

They shared a knowing but brief smile. No need to say what was surely on both their hearts—sheer relief. The others caught up to them.

Mikhail broke away to walk on Friedrich's opposite side. "Are you badly injured?"

"Hell no. The bloody bastards nearly cut my leg off, but it's healing." He gripped his thigh, the blood-soaked trousers sliced open from a blade where a deep gash slowly mended. "But I couldn't follow them," he added bitterly. "I'm worried for Grant. He went after them alone."

"Gavril, Yuri," snapped Mikhail. "Follow Grant's trail. If I'm right, they were prepared to be followed. He will need help."

Gavril and Yuri chorused together, "Aye, Captain."

They blurred away. Bron and Allora sped after them, a streak of black and white disappearing in the gloom of the wintry forest.

"Get home, Your Grace," said Mikhail. There was time to plan strategy to get Izzy back later. But for now, they must end this unhallowed night and mourn their dead and pray for the dying. "Denny is alive."

"What!" Friedrich's eyes snapped wide. "Alive?"

Mikhail nodded, not ready to explain that it was he who'd brought him back. "Brenna needs you now."

Friedrich's gaze peered in the direction of his cottage as if he could see his wife and children in pain, in need of him. "Faster, Dane." He quickened his pace with Dane's help.

"Dmitri," said Mikhail. "The encampment."

"Aye. Let's go."

They spirited away, the icy wind turning colder by the second, as if winter deepened with the loss of so many souls to keep the forest warm. The forest full of magic that had sheltered humans and vampires alike, brothers in arms, against a dark evil. Their loss slowed her pulse, as if she wept with them.

The stench of burning flesh grew stronger when they wound out of the forest's edge to Harrison's farm—the center for the soldier's tents and weapons armory. They stood on the hillside near the archery training site.

The farmhouse was ablaze as well as the barn and every tent along the forest's border. The field was littered with bodies, both their own and Legionnaires', their uniforms setting them apart. The soldiers still standing had a chain of buckets from the well to the barn. Some of the Bloodguard flashed in vampire speed to and from, dousing the flames as fast as they could.

The brawny form of Harrison was at the helm. His wife and children stood to one side near the boy Nate, holding the reins of Friedrich's Arkadian horses. Nate stared at the burning barn, where his father worked and they both slept each night. Mikhail didn't see the silhouette of Nate's father, the blacksmith who'd forged many weapons for their army. As horrific as the sight was, it wasn't their dead men burning that wafted that unholy smell up into the night.

"Dear God," muttered Dmitri at his side.

In the distance, a hellish haze glowed up into the wintry sky as if the netherworld had opened up right where the town of Hiddleston stood. Amid the roar of flames came the quieter sounds of stifled cries and screams of women and children.

"They burned the whole fucking village."

Hiddleston had been a friend to the Black Lily. And so was an enemy to Queen Morgrid.

Dmitri sped off toward the cries for help. Mikhail was right behind him. He stared up, watching his hope that they'd ever escape the queen's evil rising with the smoke and ashes of Hiddleston.

Chapter Seventeen

The black oak grove stood quiet but for the faint whisper of wind. Sable-silver leaves tumbled over the snow-dusted ground. A pile had delicately fallen on the six-by-two-foot dirt mound where Nate's father lay since they'd buried him yesterday. The silvery leaves blanketed his grave, as if the forest longed to keep the man warm. But he was no longer here.

Mina stepped silently, not wanting to disturb Brenna and Nate. Brenna stood beside the boy, a slender arm draped around his shoulders. The cut of death dug deep for everyone, including the villagers of Hiddleston. But nothing hurt more to a young boy than the loss of his father.

Brenna spoke gentle words to the boy at her side.

"They're walking together, Ivan and your father," she was saying, just like she was telling a bedtime story. "Remember how Ivan would admire your father's forge work. No one could craft a sword or dagger as strong or as beautiful as your father."

"Papa loved these woods." Nate's voice was rusty but

proud.

"I know." She squeezed him closer. "That's why the hart wolves thought it best he be laid to rest here. I think he'd be proud of that. Don't you?"

"Aye. 'e would." He wiped his sleeve across his nose and heaved out a big breath. "Best get back to camp. Still cleaning what weapons we still got."

"Yes. You'd better get busy."

Nate tore away, running toward the Harrison farm—what was left of it. Brenna didn't look surprised to find Mina behind her. She would've heard her regardless, or smelled her, being a vampire herself.

"Is Friedrich asking for me?" Her eyes were rimmed red, though no tears stood out on her cheeks. She must've wept all that she possibly could by now. For the dead, for her injured children, for Izzy now gone.

Brenna met her on the trail, and they fell in line together.

"Actually, we've been invited to the burial rite of the Bloodguard men. Everyone is there already."

Brenna paused mid-step and met her gaze. A sad smile quirked her lips. "That is an honor, as I know they are such a private lot. I still don't even know where any of them came from. Where they were born, if they have parents, siblings, anyone we should write."

Mina linked her arm with Brenna and led her deeper into the forest where she knew the ceremony was taking place. The exact place where the forty guardsmen pledged their fealty to her, now only thirty-four.

"Aleksei has a mother and a sister," Mina mused, a pang striking her at the core for how painful this loss would be for them. "Irena is a lovely mirror of her brother. I fear they will take this very hard."

Brenna lifted her chin. "I must pay them a visit and thank them personally for his service."

"I feel that I should be the one. After all, Aleksei was killed while—"

The rest stuck in her throat. Mina couldn't admit the guilt she felt because men had died to protect her.

Brenna squeezed closer as they walked along, hooked arm in arm. "And do you think if Aleksei had lived that he would regret having risked himself to protect you?"

Mina shook her head, knowing he wouldn't.

"Of course not."

Brenna's gaze fell forward as Mina guided her around a thick bramble of brush she recognized. They were edging closer.

"Aleksei was the one who carried Izzy to safety from Winter Hill." Brenna's voice sounded distant as she stumbled back to that memory. Then she laughed. "I remember her remarking they had the same color hair."

It was Mina's turn to squeeze her friend closer. "We'll get her back."

Brenna's lips drew tight, but she tried to smile anyway, then they were rounding the bend up to the meadow Mina remembered.

The black-clad and hooded Bloodguard stood in a perfect circle around the six bodies on pyres. Their dead brethren dressed exactly like them, as if they were headed into battle, each holding their weapon of choice across their chest, ready for combat.

Vampires typically had family tombs where they would be buried, but the Bloodguard followed an ancient ritual. One where the warrior went up in flames.

Arabelle and Marius stood side by side at the head, Marius with his arm around her waist, holding her up. Arabelle's injuries had been extensive. The dark circles under her eyes, which now shone bright with her new vampirism, revealed the wounds and the new change were taking their toll. New-borns needed rest for the body to make the change. But of course she would never lie in bed for this.

Mina walked ahead of Brenna toward where Friedrich, Helena, and the boys stood on the other side of Nikolai and Sienna. All in one line at the head of the pyres where Aleksei lay. Grant stood next to Caden, an arm around the gangly teen's shoulder. Grant had been subdued in his pursuit of Radomir and Izzy by a dozen Legionnaires. And though not drastically injured, he lost his chance at catching them before they crossed into the border of the Glass Tower where hundreds of new-borns with the blood madness guarded the grounds. His forehead bore a deep cut and his jaw and eye nasty bruises, yet he seemed unaffected, his focus intent on the men on the pyres.

Mina's breath caught at Mikhail standing apart with torch in hand. He didn't look at her as he approached, staring down at his men from a grim mask of calm.

The only sound was the crackling of the torch and their quiet footfalls across the meadow. Friedrich pulled Brenna close to his side when they reached them, brushing a kiss atop her head. He'd left Olog, his chef from Winter Hill, behind with Beatrice and Denny. Mina should've been surprised by the oafish man's soft heart for young Beatrice and the duke's children, but nothing surprised her about these people anymore. They cared for one another the way people ought to, especially in a cold world where evil washed the land in blood and ash.

"Brethren!" Mikhail's booming voice snapped everyone's attention to him. "The creed."

In unison, they fisted right hands over their hearts and recited with vigor.

"*We are the Bloodguard. Noble by birth, brothers by choice. We smite the evil ones. We avenge the innocents. We right all wrongs. We are the cold blade in the dark night. We give our swords, our bodies, our strength, and our blood. We bleed as one. We die as one."*

Tears pricked Mina's eyes, having heard these words from all of them, from the six men lying atop their pyres who would speak no more. She knew the other five men's names now, wanting to know who had given all they had for the cause, promising to never forget them. The Black Lily had begun as a human cause for equality. Vampires could simply sit back impassively and let Queen Morgrid and King Dominik rule the land if they so chose, especially children of noble birth like these men. But they didn't. They took up arms in their own way among their brethren. They went into this quest against evil, against the crown, knowing death might be their likely end. And yet, they did it anyway. Bravery took on new meaning as she stared at the still warriors.

Mikhail stepped to the head of the line next to the dead guardsmen Mina recognized as the one who sparred with Yuri on her first day here.

In a clear voice, Mikhail said, "Farewell, Anton." He lit the pyre at his feet.

The Bloodguard chorused in a low rumble. *"Anton."*

Mikhail stepped to the next man, quiet and unassuming, but who tended to the horses in Harrison's barn.

"Farewell, Ilya."

The Bloodguard again chorused his name as Mikhail set his pyre aflame. Then the next man, Petyr. Then Stanislav and Sasha.

Finally, Mikhail stood before Aleksei. His grave, sharp-angled countenance softened for the briefest of seconds. No one could sense what Mina could—this proud, unshakeable warrior's heart breaking in two—and for once in her life, she wished she didn't have this gift. For to feel the man she loved—yes, *loved*—falling apart inside, and without the ability to run to him, to take it all away, cut her too deep.

Mikhail raised the torch. "Farewell, Aleksei."

The final chorus echoed in the crystalline morning air. "*Aleksei.*"

Mikhail tossed the torch on his pyre, the flames licking up with a sharp crackle, rising into a conflagration, the heat pressing on Mina like the weight of emotion of every person here, pushing on her with need for release.

"Go in peace, brothers." Mikhail's deep voice resonated the final parting words of the Bloodguard. "Rest in the stars where you belong. Until we meet again."

The remaining members of the Bloodguard thumped their fists once against their chests then slowly took their leave, one by one, not unlike they did the night of their pledge to Mina. Helena and Dmitri walked solemnly away with Caden, Emmett, and Jack toward their cottage, until those left were Arabelle, Marius, Sienna, Nikolai, Brenna, Friedrich, Mikhail, Grant, and Mina.

Silence stretched. Nothing but the pop of the dry oak logs burning and the whir of wind dancing through the flames. All of this devastation fell solely upon Queen Morgrid. How many lives had she destroyed in her quest for tyranny? How many more would fall and suffer at her hands?

Her army hadn't marched into battle against the Black Lily but had crept up behind them by way of Hiddleston, like thieves in the night. No one had heard or sensed them coming. They'd all assumed the queen had used her black magic arts in some way to skirt the sentries without detection. However she'd gotten them through, it had worked. The Black Lily army was devastated, Hiddleston had been razed to the ground, innocent women and children were dead, and Izzy was gone.

The fury that had stirred Mina's she-beast when she awoke in that tower rose within her once more.

Friedrich's gaze shifted from the burning guardsmen to

Mikhail. "Grant and I are leaving today to find Izzy."

"I'm not sure if they kept her at the Glass Tower," added Nikolai. "I went into Sylus covertly to see what one of my sources at the local tavern, the Silver Crown, could tell me. He's seen movement of many troops, heading north, including the queen's royal carriage."

"That's not surprising," sighed Friedrich. "Probably bringing her to Izeling Tower." Brenna made a small, choking sound. Friedrich pulled her close. "He won't hurt her, kitten. He'll be using her to bargain something from us."

"But what?" asked Brenna. "Surrender? They've already defeated our army."

Friedrich's expression tightened. Brenna was the first to say aloud what no one else could admit.

Arabelle turned her face into Marius's shoulder. This was her revolution that appeared to die last night with the fallen. Not if Mina could help it.

Marius lifted her into his arms. "I need to get Arabelle to bed. She's still too weak." Then he sped away with her in his arms.

Mikhail stepped toward Friedrich, his expression pensive. "I'll bring Gregoravich. He can detect where they might have taken Izzy if we can find their tracks."

"No." All eyes swiveled to Mina. "That's what they want."

"Your Highness," said Mikhail, keeping her at a distance by using her title. "Regardless of—"

"No," she quipped in a sharp tone. "We won't do what the queen wants. Or what King Dominik wants."

"What would you have us do, Your Highness?" asked Friedrich. "Give up? We've already lost—"

"Too *much*." Her voice broke with fury as she settled on Brenna. "We've lost too much. Hiddleston. Half our army. The precious lives of those we loved." She gestured back to the burning pyre.

No one said a word, the air crackling with Mina's ire. Mikhail didn't take his eyes from her.

Her tenor vibrated as she enunciated clearly, "I am the rightful Queen of Arkadia. I am going home to get my army." She felt his piercing gaze but didn't look at him. "Then we'll go to Izeling Tower and *take* Izzy back. And be rid of the damned queen and her son once and for all."

"Now that's what I like to hear." Grant finally spoke, his jaw tight.

"Aye," agreed Brenna.

"Indeed," added Friedrich.

Mina turned to Sienna and Nikolai, who nodded. Sienna smiled like a woman who understood the depth of Mina's need for justice. Finally, Mina turned her gaze up at Mikhail, who'd inched closer to her side. She raised her brow in question.

His grief-weary expression—deep grooves seemingly fixed in his forehead—transformed to one she hadn't expected to see. One of hesitant hope. His wide mouth ticked up on one side before his soft rumble reached inside and quickened her pulse.

"Aye."

Chapter Eighteen

The horses slowed as they evened out onto flatter, smoother roads. They were in the valley, closer to Lord Rathbone's home in Devonshire. Mina remembered his palatial estate from one visit many years ago with Steward Thorwald. Mikhail led the line of riders off the main road and through the silver-plated gateway and under the name of Rathbone's home, *Sommersby*, in perfect script.

Mina rode atop Friedrich's Arkadian mare, Asphodel, a white beauty, reminding her how many resources her kingdom could offer the Black Lily. Once she'd truly claimed it, that is.

"Don't tell Brennalyn this," said Friedrich as he rode beside her on his massive black, "but you look more natural on that horse than anyone who's ever rode her."

Mina smiled, leaning forward to brush her neck. "She's uncommonly beautiful. And has such easy manners."

"Indeed."

Yuri's chatter continued a few paces behind while Gavril remained silent and listening at his side. Gregoravich's baritone chimed in every now and then, but it was mostly the talkative, easygoing Yuri keeping their conversation lively.

"Perfect mount for you, Princess," added Grant with a wink, riding on the other side of Mina. "Though I daresay your beauty exceeds sweet Asphodel here. Watching you ride the past three days has been a pleasure all its own."

Mikhail cast a brief but dark look over his shoulder at Grant, then galloped ahead as they closed in toward the estate manor. Mina arched a brow at Grant, trying not to grin at his impropriety. He couldn't help himself. He seemed to glory in breaking etiquette in the most devilish ways.

"I'm not sure if I should say thank you to such a compliment."

"No, you should not." Grant placed the hand not holding the reins over his heart. "I should be thanking you. For I'm the one who has enjoyed the view."

Friedrich chuckled for the first time since that night Denny almost died and Izzy was taken.

"Best watch yourself, Brother. You'll rile the captain. I don't believe he likes you flirting with his lady."

Mina's pulse jolted at that. He knew? Not that she felt much like *his lady* anymore. Since the attack, he'd not been alone with her once. Nor had he given her any assurance that the fragile bond they'd forged just before the attack was still intact. She wondered whether Mikhail regretted saying such words now, whether he felt guilt for being with her that night when he could've been on guard. No one could've been prepared for what happened, but she felt his deliberate distance keenly.

"Hmph. The captain needs riling if you ask me." Grant tilted his handsome face toward Mina. Even bruised from the battle, the man could make a nun swoon with those eyes. "Besides, the princess is going to be a queen soon. She may want to hire a personal bodyguard. Or better yet, her personal bleeder." He waggled his eyebrows at the last.

Friedrich laughed louder. Mina sensed Grant's bad behavior was partly to entertain and revive his brother from his deep melancholy. She loved the scoundrel for it, then her gaze flicked to Mikhail. He'd slowed his horse's gait farther ahead, but still she caught the stiffening of his back.

Grant leaned his torso toward her with a hand braced on his thigh and whispered conspiratorially. "Come on, Your Highness. Brenna says I taste awfully good."

"I swear, one of these days I'm going to beat you senseless," the duke added casually.

"You can try. But everyone knows I'm the better warrior."

Mina found her voice finally. "Is that so? Better than the Bloodguard?"

Grant straightened with confidence, not that he ever looked less than confident. "I'm as good as any of them. Ask Friedrich."

The duke heaved out a sigh and rolled his eyes.

"Even as a human?" asked Mina.

"Well, I don't have preternatural speed. Hell, when I am a vampire, I'll be better than your captain."

Mina glanced toward the man himself. "He's not *my* captain," she said low.

Grant chuckled with a shake of the head. "Oh, yes, he is. Whether the bastard likes it or not."

Mina made no reply as the lane opened to a circular drive, the gravel finer than on the entry road, leading to a pristine white-stone manor stretching wide and tall. A thick-trunked, gold-leafed elm stood oddly alone to one side, as if the owner couldn't bear to chop it down when he built the home. Mikhail tethered his horse on a low branch and drew close to the portico as their party made their way to the entrance. His stern expression revealed his temper hadn't softened at all on their journey. She wondered whether he'd hardened his heart to her as well. She longed to speak with him alone. It would have to wait.

Now, she must meet with Lord Rathbone and hope he'd support her claim.

...

Mikhail watched as Friedrich held his stallion Ramiel's reins, saying something to Mina while she nodded and stroked her hand down his muzzle. Her slender, pale fingers against the coal-black coat was a pretty sight.

She was always a pretty sight.

"We'll take the horses to the stables, then encircle the estate," said Gregoravich at his side.

"Good. Be sure to scout Rathbone's estate for rogues. Or spies."

Grant walked up. "Do you believe Rathbone may already be allied to King Dominik?"

"Possibly. But from what we gathered in Izeling, Rathbone wasn't eager to get into bed with a power-hungry tyrant set on expanding into his territory."

Gregory grunted. "But he signed a contract with the king, you said."

Mikhail gave him a wry look. "Contracts can be broken."

"Aye then. We'll keep watch out here." Gregory followed the rest of the Bloodguard toward the stables.

"Where's Dmitri?" asked Grant, ever watchful.

He wished the bastard would stop watching Mina quite so closely. But he also knew the damn man just enjoyed getting under people's skin. It had become apparent to him, as well as others, that Mikhail's protectiveness of Mina extended beyond mere duty.

He actually had a notion to invite Grant to join the Bloodguard when Friedrich transformed him to vampire, which was to happen soon. Friedrich had confided that he'd held out keeping his brother human long enough. Too long. The duke wanted to take care of it before they traveled to Arkadia, leaving Grant behind. But he would have none of it.

"Dmitri's gone ahead of us."

"Fine," Grant heaved a sigh. "Don't tell me. I'll set up a perimeter with Gregory. And leave the bowing and scraping to your lot."

"My lot?"

"You're a gentleman, Captain."

"And you're the son of a duke." Though Friedrich's father had never claimed his bastard son, he still bore noble blood.

Grant grinned like the cat who stole the cream. "That doesn't make me a gentleman."

"Tell me, what do you know of Izzy's parents?"

Seeming stumped by the change in conversation, Grant remained pensive a moment. "Actually, we know nothing about them. Brenna said that someone she knew in Korinth found an abandoned child outside the city, so she made arrangements for the child to be brought to her home in the north, where she's had her ever since." Grant flicked his gaze from Mina and Friedrich to him. "Why? Do you suspect something?"

"Not exactly. Just rationalizing Queen Morgrid's motives."

"You don't think she was taken to force Friedrich to heel?"

"Not likely. They don't need him anymore. They've built a strong army without his Varis blood to help create it." Clenching his jaw, he shifted his attention to Grant, knowing the man's intellect reasoned the way his did. "Why would an all-powerful queen who practiced black magic need an unspoiled innocent child?"

Grant's thoughtful expression darkened to a murderous

scowl. "Blood sacrifice," he hissed with disgust.

"Aye," agreed Mikhail, shifting back to Mina and Friedrich as they approached. "Don't mention this to Friedrich."

"Not on your life." Countenance stormy now that he saw what hell might await them if they ever caught up to Izzy, he nodded toward Mina and the duke. "You enjoy yourself. Friedrich says Rathbone is a nice piece of work." He strode off after Gregoravich.

Mikhail followed behind Mina as Friedrich led their party to the door. He couldn't help but admire the svelte line of her neck. He preferred when she wore her hair down, but he also enjoyed getting a full view of her moon-white skin, reminding him too well how it felt beneath his fingers, his lips.

He was well and truly caught. With the Black Lily having fallen—on a night when he should've been more on guard, not absorbed in Mina—he tried to maintain focus on their goal. And yet, he knew that was impossible. He could no longer look at her and see anything but a woman he longed for even more than he cared to avenge his family's betrayal that stretched back long before he was born. None of it seemed to have meaning when she stood within his sight. All that mattered was...Mina.

The door swung open, snapping Mikhail from his trance. A waif of a man with thinning hair and a large nose, the butler, bowed at the site of gentry at the door, though Mikhail chose to remain in his mercenary garb. He wanted the earl to understand his purpose at this meeting right away.

"Good afternoon, my lord. May I tell Lord Rathbone who is calling upon him?"

"Yes." Friedrich took the dominant position at the front, carrying himself with the arrogant confidence of his station. "You can tell Rathbone that Friedrich Volya, Duke of Winter

Hill, is on his doorstep."

The butler's squinty eyes popped open as he gulped down two swallows of air. "Forgive me, Your Grace," he bowed deeply, then swung wide the door. "Please, please come in. You can wait in the blue parlor." He stepped lively on his long legs, giving him the look of a loping praying mantis.

Friedrich quirked a brow at us with a lopsided smile and whispered, "I believe we were unexpected."

They followed the butler through the foyer with a dangling crystal chandelier, where he gestured toward the first parlor on the left.

"Please, make yourself comfortable."

"Thank you, um—" Friedrich paused with his hand aloft, waiting for the man to fill in his name.

"Graves, Your Grace. At your service. I'll let Lord Rathbone know you're here right away, Your Grace. And your lovely companion?"

He didn't recognize Mina for who she was.

"Introductions will be given in person," said Mikhail, not wanting the earl to know who was standing in his parlor just in case he had thoughts of sending out an alarm in secret.

Though Mikhail's men would have the entire estate surrounded and would intercept anyone trying to leave or enter the earl's manor, he would take no chances. When the butler loped off to find his master, the three of them took in their surroundings.

"You have never been here before, Your Highness?" asked Friedrich. "I thought you said you'd visited once."

"Yes. Once," she confirmed. "But I was quite young." She stood demurely, like the perfect princess, nodding to the door. "Though Graves may appear to be one step away from achieving his namesake, he is human and wasn't even alive on my girlhood visit to Sommersby."

"The blue room isn't very blue," observed Friedrich,

tapping a finger on the sun-yellow drapery.

"It was once blue from floor to silk-papered ceiling," came the smooth baritone of the Earl of Devonshire standing in the entrance.

His comely and well-fashioned appearance presented a vampire entirely unruffled by the surprise visit. Though his steady gaze on Mina ruffled Mikhail at once. The earl smiled in a way that put one on edge, rather than eased the tension.

"My, my. So the rumors were true." He strode into the room before Mina and gave a regal bow. "I am happy to see you safe, Your Highness."

"Are you?" she asked.

His smooth expression faltered. "Why wouldn't I be?"

"Seeing as I was held in a torturous, bloodless sleep, imprisoned in my own home at Briar Rose, and not you nor any other southern lord came to my aid, I'm just curious if you are truly pleased. Or if you're playing diplomat in your non-blue room." Mina had never spoken with such bite, but she couldn't keep the thread of betrayal from her voice.

"Your Highness—" He stepped closer with an arm raised to touch her.

Mikhail took a protective stance at her back, his hand on the hilt of his dagger. The earl noticed. Rathbone raised his hands in a disarming gesture.

"No need for violence." He stepped back. Smart move. "I would never harm Princess Vilhelmina."

Her hands clasped before her, she said in her regal, authoritative tone, "That's quite reassuring, my lord." Her voice still sharp. "But the fact remains, you allowed your sovereign to be detained by force without even calling the House to arrange a rescue."

For the first time, the earl's composure slipped. Rather than fear, his expression pinched with pain. "I did not know."

"Liar," said Friedrich. "How could I know all the way at

Winter Hill but you had no knowledge right here in Arkadia?"

"And how did *you* know of this atrocity?" asked Rathbone.

Friedrich opened his mouth to snap off an angry retort and paused before saying, "My uncle."

"Right." Rathbone gave a stiff nod. "Well, he did not inform us he had our princess imprisoned and starved into unconsciousness. He said she was under his protection and guard because of this Black Lily that had kidnapped her once already. Steward Thorwald then told us the king's men were slaughtered at Briar Rose, the princess awoken from her bloodless sleep, and abducted by a band of brigands. The king and his mother, the queen, are scouring the land in search of her."

"I take it, this is the leader of that heroic band of brigands," Rathbone nodded to Mikhail.

Mina gestured to her right. "Lord Rathbone, may I introduce Captain Mikhail Romanov of the Bloodguard." Mikhail stepped to her side.

"Captain Mikhail?" His examining gaze shifted to admiration. "We have heard much of you."

"Oh?" He remained soldier-still, unreadable but for the lethal edge in his voice. "All good, I'm sure."

Rathbone chuckled lightly, measuring the three of them a moment. "Tonight, dinner will be interesting for once." He ambled toward the door, "Graves."

"Lord Rathbone, we have urgent news to discuss with you."

When he pivoted at the door, he bore the first expression of gravity since they'd walked in the room. "I've already heard about Hiddleston and the rumors of the decimation of the Black Lily. Therefore, I also know you've traveled nonstop to get here. And with the Duke of Winter Hill and the Princess of Arkadia standing in my parlor, I can only surmise you've come with a request of some import. I understand this. But first, you'll rest, and we'll dine. Then we'll discuss the matters at hand." He repeated out the door, "*Graves.*"

"Yes, my lord." The spindly butler practically leaped into the room, apparently listening to every word. "Will you show our guests to their chambers for the night? I'm sure they all need a rest after such a long journey from...well, from wherever they came."

"Yes, my lord." The butler bowed in obedience as if he were always given odd directives such as this. "Right away."

Friedrich frowned but followed the butler. Mikhail allowed Mina to walk on. He stepped up beside the earl and stopped him with a hand to the chest at the doorway.

"Lord Rathbone, since you apparently know of the Bloodguard's reputation, I should think there is no reason for me to warn you that if you try to send word out of this house regarding who is currently residing under your roof, my men will gut them before they reach your borders." Mikhail faced him and enunciated each word as evenly as a sharp knife slicing a peach. "And then I'll gut you."

Mikhail wouldn't step foot from his presence until the earl understood quite clearly that he was looking at his own death should he step out of line. Earl or no.

The earl didn't blink or flinch at such a promise of bloodshed in his home. He pasted on an amiable smile, which he probably wore for the most arrogant men of his station. "There is no reason at all, Captain. I quite understand your meaning."

"Mikhail?" Mina had returned, fear written in the knitting of her brow and tightening of her mouth. "Is everything all right?"

"Oh, yes, Your Highness. The captain and I were just coming to an understanding." Rathbone stepped away.

"I'm sure," she replied, suspiciously.

"I'll be in my study should Graves or my housekeeper, Ms. Ward, not be able to find what you need." He turned as if he remembered something. "My father will be pleased to see you again, Your Highness."

"Your father?"

Mikhail noted her high-pitched surprise.

"Yes." Rathbone laughed. "He's still alive, believe it or not. We'll see you all at dinner." He turned toward what appeared to be his study from Mikhail's vantage point. "Interesting night, indeed." The earl chuckled to himself.

Mikhail walked at her side as they ascended the carpeted stairs. "Why were you shocked his father is alive?"

Mina smiled. "Do you mean to say that I know something the great and fearful Captain Romanov does not?"

He huffed out a breath. "Tell me, Princess."

"His father beget him when he was over a thousand years old. The earl is his one and only child."

"Wait. Then why is Rathbone the earl while his father still lives?"

Mina tripped on her skirts. Mikhail caught her by the arm. Her breath hitched, but she kept moving up the stairs. He didn't let her go, holding her till they reached the landing.

"The former earl displeased Queen Morgrid over I know not what, but it was enough that King Grindal and Queen Morgrid stripped him of his title. They allowed him to live only if he remained here at Sommersby all the rest of his days. You see, the former earl was around as far back as when the king and queen first claimed Glass Tower as their own."

"You mean when the queen murdered her twin brother in cold blood, usurping his throne so that she could rule."

Mina continued walking slowly up the corridor where Graves had led Friedrich. "Yes. I keep forgetting that."

"I don't," he bit out harder than he'd intended.

She paused and turned to him. "Are you all right?"

He combed a hand through his hair, anxiety riding him at the turn of conversation. "I don't know."

Her light touch on his arm both calmed and stirred him. "Mikhail. Are you all right?"

When she looked at him like that, like she was his woman and she intended to make the world right again, he wanted to fall to his knees and surrender once and for all.

Instead, he repeated, "I don't know." Then turned up the corridor and away from the woman he wanted more than life itself. Even his justice…and his revenge.

Chapter Nineteen

Lord Rathbone didn't lie. Dinner *had* been interesting. The conversation light. The meal heavy, finishing with a goblet of warm blood instead of dessert. Typical of a formal meal in the house of a vampire aristocrat. What Mina found the most interesting was the way Rathbone's father, the former earl, who went by Lord Petrov, kept most of his comments to himself and his eyes on Mikhail. He watched him as if trying to remember something. Or perhaps trying to remember some*one*.

In appearance, Lord Rathbone's father was a mirror image of his son, just less formidable in stature and breadth of chest. While his eyes held all the fire of a young man, his face and demeanor were brittle. He was one of the few vampires left who was there at the beginning, when Queen Morgrid had become ruler of the realm.

The lilting laughter of one of Rathbone's three concubines who had joined them for dinner interrupted her thoughts. The stunning redhead placed a dainty hand on Mikhail's sleeve.

"Oh, come now, Captain. I'll bet in your line of work you

have a thousand fascinating stories."

"They may be a little rough for your liking, my lady," he responded leisurely, though Mina noted the tightness around his eyes.

"I don't mind 'a little rough,' Captain."

Mina's empathic gift showed her the redhead, Lady Sasha, wasn't simply pretending. Her lust for Mikhail practically hummed in the air around her. Not that Mina could blame her, but the thought of her in his arms made her clench her fists in her lap. There was no reason, since Mikhail gave the lady no encouragement whatsoever.

"Shall we adjourn to the parlor?" Lord Rathbone stood, the candlelight gilding his auburn hair gold. "I believe some musical entertainment is in order." He smiled down at his concubines. All three standing, with demure bows of the head, they led the party into the large parlor with the grand black-lacquer piano in the corner.

Mina had no parents, so she had never experienced a household where the master and mistress had blood harems. Though Lord Rathbone's three ladies of nobility couldn't quite be called a harem, they were still ladies of questionable morals. They reminded her of the women she encountered when Steward Thorwald had sent Mina off to the opera or balls or musicals. They said one thing but meant another, manipulating men with a flicker of lashes, and cutting women who got in the way.

Thankfully, they weren't at a ball or an opera. And she wasn't just any lady of the gentry.

She glanced at Mikhail, wondering whether he'd ever had a harem. No. He might be born a gentleman, but he wasn't of royal blood. Even so, she didn't imagine he'd ever keep a collection of women for his pleasure.

Mina joined Friedrich on the settee. Mikhail remained standing to the side. Lord Rathbone took a position next to

Mina. His father ambled in and seated himself in a well-worn leather chair, the nailheads on the arms having long lost their sparkle.

"Do you have a particular request, my lord?" asked Lady Sasha, her glossy red hair hanging over one pearlescent shoulder.

The brunette seated herself at the piano, flipping through music sheets. And the blonde, beautiful though not as captivating as Lady Sasha, seated herself on a high chair behind a harp.

"You ladies always know better than I."

Lady Sasha smiled, her beauty shining so bright that Mina felt even more nauseous than before. Lady Sasha whispered something to the brunette, who nodded and began playing a plaintive tune. The blonde joined in with a melodious strumming of the harp. Then Lady Sasha sang, and Mina understood why Lord Rathbone would want to keep such a woman in his possession.

However, as she began to sing about lovers parted at sea and their ardent reunion upon the soft sands by night, and as Mina's gaze lingered overtly upon Mikhail, her thoughts drifted to the last time they were alone. To his hands on her skin, his lips on her breast, his mouth between her legs.

"Your Highness, you look a bit flushed," Lord Rathbone whispered close to her ear. "Might I escort you to the balcony for some fresh air?"

She shot up without a word, allowing him to take her through the open doors out onto the darkened and chilly night. What she needed was to speak to Mikhail alone, but even more urgent was her need for Lord Rathbone's help. Now was as good a time as any to acquire that aid.

He immediately removed his coat and wrapped it around her shoulders. She crossed her arms and gripped the lapels to keep it tight around her, though the frosty night was welcome on her heated cheeks.

"I'm glad to have you alone, my lord."

"That makes two of us."

She ignored his flirtation. "You know you haven't once asked why we are here or what we've come for."

"I can guess."

She leaned against the stone banister, the half moon peeking through wispy clouds. "Then please do."

"As I've mentioned, the Black Lily army was destroyed. They've lost their numbers. The Bloodguard has rescued you from a horrific fate, so you feel obligation toward them. As the Princess of Arkadia, you seek help in recompense."

His demeanor changed not one iota, his flirtatious tone ever present, as was his knee-buckling smile. He leaned against the banister, facing her. He tilted his head, his perfect features appearing all the more dazzling by the pale moonlight, but he didn't interrupt her. Simply waited.

"You are still the lead counselor of the House of Arkadia, are you not?"

"I still share that role with Lord Maksim and Steward Thorwald."

"I may have looked only like an ornament all of those times I visited the House, but I observed well. We both know that no matter what is decreed on parchment, you are the lead counselor."

His mouth ticked up into a smile. "I won't deny it."

She lifted her hand from his sleeve and gripped the cold banister, needing the tangible feeling of the stone beneath her fingers, of holding onto something sturdy and true. That unfurling bloom within her chest pressed wider, seeking the light that would finally open her to the world.

Lord Rathbone lay his large hand atop hers.

She flinched but didn't remove her hand from beneath his.

"Your Highness," he started gently, "tell me."

Deep breath in, then out. "My lord, I intend to present myself to the House and demand my rights as Queen of Arkadia. Steward Thorwald has kept my throne warm for long enough. I intend to exert my power as the rightful heir of the Arkadian throne, and I am requesting your support. Not just for me, but for all of Varis."

His winter-blue eyes sparked with supernatural fire. "You will have it."

She blinked, not expecting it to be quite that easy. "You understand what I'm asking of you? Of the people and the army of Arkadia?"

"Let me see if I have it." His devilish eyebrow shot up. "You've come with full armed guard, intending to stake your claim as queen—as you should—then you plan to rally the resources of the south against King Dominik, since he is trying to force an unwilling alliance of marriage between the two of you. Furthermore, you will ally with the army of the Black Lily, as you are now in the company of the exiled Duke of Winter Hill, to overthrow Queen Morgrid and start some kind of new world order."

Mina could only stare for a moment, completely at a loss for words.

"Is that your intention, Your Highness?" he probed softly, brushing his thumb over her knuckles.

"Yes," was the only answer she could think to say. "The punishment for treason is death. Supporting my claim would go against Queen Morgrid's wishes. You have much to lose."

"Precisely," he agreed, his tone grave. "I have too much to lose for that power-hungry King Dominik to come in and take it all. Do you know what would happen to Arkadia if you should marry him?" His perfect features hardened, and she saw the charming facade vanish and the vampire thrust forward. "He would rule with an iron fist, and the freedoms and prosperity we've enjoyed in the southern provinces would vanish overnight."

"Then why did you sign contracts with him in Izeling?"

His composure slipped for a second. He glanced through the balcony door opening where Friedrich sat, clapping at the closing of another song.

"Damn, that vixen of the duke's overheard everything, didn't she?"

"Yes." Mina refrained from smiling. "She did."

He launched forward as if it mattered not at all. "The contracts were to appease the king and keep him out of our territory. We'd counseled with the lords of the House and all were in agreement to sign over some of our resources—equestrian soldiers and Arkadian stock horses. Then the queen made that damned announcement, and we abruptly changed our minds. We left at once without engaging the king on the matter till we could figure out what must be done." He smiled, and this time Mina did feel her heart race at being the recipient of such a godlike smile. "And here you are, our angel straight from heaven to save us all."

"I'm not so sure about an angel."

He edged forward. "You certainly look like one. You are quite breathtaking, Your Highness."

Laughter lilted from the open doorway. "Wouldn't your concubines disapprove of you flirting with another woman?"

He let out a full-throated laugh, his breath white curls in the air. "My blood concubines are not mine. They are free to come and go as they please. If they decide to leave Sommersby, they can go without a moment's notice. And I am not flirting with another woman, I am attempting to get the attention of my future queen."

Her gaze drifted back to the open doorway.

"Princess Mina, an alliance of our houses would strengthen your claim of the throne."

Pulled back to Lord Rathbone, she refocused on what he'd said. "Our houses? As in you and me?"

"Is it so far-fetched? You already know I hold the most influence in the House. My support is one thing, but my word as a man at the side of his future bride would be quite another. There would be no dawdling from the cantankerous lords in the House who like to take three months to make a decision. And there is the other dilemma of Steward Thorwald. True, he is only a steward, but he is supported by the queen and has made many allies over the years."

"So you're offering me marriage, a political alliance to ensure I am given my birthright?"

"I am offering you marriage because you are a beautiful, intelligent, and beguiling woman whom I would be honored to marry. And whose right as the monarch of our land I would protect with my own life."

He curled his large hand around hers and pulled it to his chest. She tugged, but he held her, opening his mouth to speak when someone's footsteps sounded behind them.

"Your Highness." The rough timbre of Mikhail's voice rolled in the air.

Mina pulled her hand from Lord Rathbone's, tucking her arms back under the coat. *His* coat. "Yes, Captain?"

"His Grace is retiring. Lord Rathbone, we request a private audience with you early in the morning."

"Private?" asked Mina, frowning.

"Private among our party," Mikhail clarified, meaning without the concubines and Lord Petrov.

"Granted," said Lord Rathbone.

Mikhail's steely gaze dipped to the ground as he gave a tight bow and retreated back inside.

Mina must go to him. He mistook what was taking place out on the balcony. Or did he? The earl had just proposed marriage.

"Captain Mikhail is certainly in earnest about your protection, Your Highness." His tone was accusing. Knowing.

"The Bloodguard are devoted to me."

"The captain most of all."

His expression sealed his knowledge with a smile. "I believe I know the answer to my proposal."

She smiled with sympathy. "I'm sorry, my lord. I cannot accept."

"Too late, I see." He smiled and swept her hand up in a parting kiss. "He's a bit gruff for one as gentle as you, but I see that in your eyes, I'm already outmatched." With a deep bow, he filed back through the balcony doorway, but she stopped him before he crossed the threshold.

"My lord?"

"Yes?"

"Steward Thorwald is not a dilemma. Neither are the lords." She lifted her chin, the strength of her she-beast steeling her backbone. "Arkadia is already mine. I will claim it as their rightful queen."

Then she would save Izzy and the rest of the world by showing Queen Morgrid what decimation truly looked like.

Lord Rathbone studied her a moment, his wide mouth sliding up into a scintillating smile. "Perhaps you're a good match for the captain after all." Then he was gone through the empty parlor.

With a deep inhale of the crystalline air, she enjoyed the righteous passion stirring her blood, willing her to take what was her own.

She walked back into the parlor and draped Lord Rathbone's coat over the settee for she'd forgotten she still wore it.

"I know who he is, you know."

Mina spun and gasped, her heart leaping into her throat, only to find Lord Petrov still sitting in his chair in the corner, staring into the fire.

"Pardon, my lord? You know who *who* is?" Perhaps this was the onset of dementia, sitting in a room all alone, divining strange things from the flames.

Then he turned his gaze on her, his eyes as sharp and intelligent as any vampire she knew. "Mikhail Romanov. I know him." He smiled like the devil with a secret, chuckling to himself. "And he's not a lowly lord's son of Korinth."

Heart hammering, she asked, "Who is he?"

"Sit down, my dear. I have a story to tell."

Chapter Twenty

Mina seated herself in the chair opposite the former earl. The firelight danced across his face, illuminating his sharp nose and broad brow. He looked much older, though once more his keen gaze fixed on her with a vibrant intelligence.

"Once, long ago, there was a good king who ruled the land of Varis."

His voice was husky with age. Mina didn't realize he intended to tell her a fairy tale. Perhaps he wasn't so lucid after all. Still, she remained seated, hands in her lap.

"His name was King Rodin. The people were at peace, and they loved him. Then one day, his twin sister returned after a long absence. She had left the kingdom the year before in spiteful anger and dabbled in the black arts. Still, King Rodin welcomed her home. In return, his sister, now a creature of the night, bit into his throat so viciously he fell prostrate before his throne."

Mina gasped. He was telling her the story of their origins, the beginning of vampirekind. Not a fairy tale at all. He turned his piercing gaze on her, seeming to step out of the past for a moment.

"I know this to be true, my dear, because I was there when it happened."

Mina wanted to ask him a hundred questions. So few vampires still lived from the early days. As a matter of fact, other than Queen Morgrid and King Grindal, Mina had never spoken to any of them.

"Please, my lord. Go on."

With a dip of his head, leaning back into his chair, his arms draped languidly, he stared back into the fire.

"The stories passed down have all spoken of the Massacre at the Glass Tower. And indeed, it was a massacre." His gravelly voice rolled dark and bitter with memory. "Queen Morgrid demanded loyalty on the spot. Anyone who fought against her was killed at once. I lost many friends that day." His eyes misted. Sorrow pooled around him, like a cloak of mourning billowing down to his feet. "But there is one person the tales have all forgotten, mainly because Morgrid thought her dead."

"Who is that?" asked Mina, breathless with anticipation.

"Queen Tamora, the good king's young wife."

"King Rodin had a wife?"

"He had a queen," he corrected. "She was so beautiful and so kind. Ebony hair, lovely smile." His brittle features softened by the firelight as he remembered. "Morgrid wandered the castle and infected one man after another with the blood madness, the ones who swore allegiance to her. Killing all the rest. She didn't know that Queen Tamora had used the secret passages to get to the throne room to her husband. The poor queen held her husband's head in her lap, thinking him dead." Sharp eyes met Mina's. "He was not. Morgrid had infected him with the blood madness and though savaged, King Rodin was a Varis. He'd absorbed his twin sister's power into the blood they shared, giving him the same power of creation that she held. Had he lived and survived the blood madness, I believe he would have ruled the new land with justice."

"But what happened?" Mina sat on the edge of her chair, her fists tight in the folds of her gown.

"The blood frenzy was too great. King Rodin didn't know who leaned over him, her throat so sweet, her pulse pounding, beckoning him to taste. He bit her. She screamed as the king threatened to savage her. Then her knight stepped forward and chopped off the king's head to save her. For the king would surely have killed her in the throes of the blood madness. Her knight was devoted to her and carried the queen away into hiding. And this is where the story gets interesting, my dear."

"It isn't interesting already?"

He chuckled, and with a heavy blink of both eyes, he said, "Listen." He laced his fingers together across his lap. "The queen's knight tucked her far away in the woods, where no one would find her and where she could give birth to her unborn child in privacy."

"She was with child by the king?"

"Indeed." His glassy eyes sparkled. "The child, her son and the rightful prince of Varis, was the first vampire born."

"Oh, my stars."

"Her son, whom she named Rodin after his father, the king, grew tall and strong. By the time he was a man, Queen Morgrid had established all of her vampire loyalists as aristocrats across the land. She'd also created her Legionnaires, her own vampire army. And she had taken her king, Grindal, as her husband. He was the one who'd encouraged her to establish laws so that her vampires didn't savage the humans mindlessly. Grindal saw that if there weren't laws in place to protect the humans, then there'd be no humans left to feed upon. And so the peasant class and commoners became the feeding ground, the human aristocrats helping enforce the laws to ally themselves with the vampire monarchy."

Mina's stomach twisted. The brutal enslavement of a people had over time become an accepted, commonplace practice. Yes, there were laws protecting humans from mindless slaughter, yet it still occurred. And the peasants were kept in the darkness of poverty to ensure their continued obedience to the vampire's will and reliance upon them. When Mina was queen and when they'd won this war, she would ensure no one was forced to serve another being—human or vampire.

"But what happened to the son, to Rodin?"

"I'm getting to that, my dear." Squinting as if to see the memories better, he said, "Tamora raised her child and lived in peaceful quiet until she died of frail health. Though she was vampire, she had never recovered from the loss of her husband."

"So it's true one can die of a broken heart?"

His sad smile said enough. "It is also true one can live too long with a broken heart."

Mina pleaded, "Please continue, my lord."

"The knight took the young man to the east, away from the eyes of the Glass Tower. He pretended to be the boy's father and invented a new name. He'd had enough sovereigns to set them up as local gentry. There, young Rodin met a lovely woman of the vampire aristocracy and married. The knight went away, thinking it safer for Rodin, for if he ran into the king or queen or anyone who was there at the Massacre, they would know him on sight."

"That's so sad."

"Perhaps. But necessary. And so Rodin and his wife had a son they named Christov. Rodin lived long, but he died in a battle during the Thorn Wars. Christov met a lady, a human, at a Harvest Holiday in the north while visiting friends. I'm not sure if you're familiar with Harvest Holiday, but it is a night of revels…and passion." His blue eyes twinkled.

"So Christov and his lady…?" Mina couldn't quite state the obvious to the grandfatherly Lord Petrov.

"Yes." He chuckled lightly. "She became with child and Christov loved her, despite the fact she was not vampire or even an aristocrat. It is rare for such a thing, but Christov was beloved by the King of Korinth, Stephanus Varis, and so he bestowed the gift of vampirism on Christov's bride. Therefore, their child, a son, was born vampire."

Mina's heart thrummed wildly in her breast, dawning realization sinking in. "Where did you say Christov's wife was from?"

"I didn't, Your Highness. But if you must know, she was from Kellswater."

A feverish wave of heat flushed through her body as she tightened her fists in her lap, her panting more pronounced. "And what was the name the queen's knight gave Rodin?"

He grinned, seemingly satisfied she'd come to the correct conclusion. "Romanov."

"Christov's son is…was…Mikhail Romanov."

"Yes, my dear. I never thought to lay eyes on him. But he couldn't deny the genes of his great-grandmother Tamora if he tried. Same ebony hair. Same eyes."

Her mouth had gone dry at all that had just unfolded. "My Lord. You knew Queen Tamora?"

His gaze remained on the fire, now little more than gold-red embers. "Very well."

"You were the knight who saved her, weren't you?"

He smiled at her, and Mina saw the young, noble knight who so many years ago saved a queen and her unborn child. And therefore, Rodin's son, Christov, and Christov's sons, Mikhail and Dmitri.

Leaning forward, he gripped her hands in his older ones. "It is not coincidence that you come to my house seeking aid from my own son in your quest to be queen. That Mikhail Romanov serves as your protector, your knight. The man who would have been king. *Should* have been king."

Mina's mind reeled from the revelation, her heart racing with joy. But then she wondered, "Do you think he knows of his heritage?"

"He knows." He squeezed her hands. "Though he does not know I was the knight who saved Queen Tamora. No one does but Queen Morgrid and King Grindal."

"And that is why you have been put on house arrest all these years, isn't it?"

"Indeed. They recognized me here in Arkadia. They knew I had disappeared that day with the queen. I confessed, saying that she died of her injuries from the king's bite. They believed me."

"I am surprised they only stripped you of your title and didn't kill you."

He arched a brow with a haughty smile. "By then, I had many allies in the House of Arkadia, including the king, your father. He was the one who anointed me earl after my marriage to my late wife. Killing me would've injured diplomacy. When my son was born many years later, they allowed him to reclaim the title they'd taken from me. This was all long before you were born, and they had plans to ally their kingdom with your father's."

"You knew him?"

"I did. He was a good man. When you were born and your mother had died in childbirth, he held a gathering to celebrate your birth. He loved you so. When Queen Morgrid visited and declared that her son Marius would marry you one day, your father refused. Did you know that?"

A queasy sensation twisted her stomach. "No. I didn't.

But I *was* betrothed to Marius."

"Hmph. After your father was killed."

Mina leaped to her feet, pacing away and then back. "She had my father killed, didn't she?"

"There has never been any proof. But it was shortly after your father was ambushed on the road by rogue vampires that she installed Steward Thorwald."

"Steward *Thorwald*," she spat like poison from her mouth. "The man who kept me prisoner in Briar Rose all my life, making sure I was kept in comfort but had no free will of my own."

"That certainly sounds like the man."

"Well, damn him. *Damn* them all. I will be queen. No one will have control of me ever again."

"Only perhaps your heart," he teased, sounding very much like his son.

"Perhaps. What do you know, my lord, that you are not saying? For I can see a glint of merriment in your eyes?"

"That celebration at your birth, Queen Morgrid threatened revenge upon your family. Because she dealt in the dark arts, everyone feared that she had indeed placed a curse upon you and the king. But then a woman appeared, dressed all in white. She was a white witch, to be sure."

"A white witch? I've never heard of such a woman."

"They are rare and live apart, for fear of being burned as witches."

Mina shivered. "But my nurse spoke of such a woman once. Before she was taken away. What did this white witch say or do?"

He hopped up and ambled to the far shelf, his long, bony fingers tracing over the spines of old books. "Ah. Here it is." He snatched the tattered book from its shelf and shuffled back toward the dying firelight.

"What is that? *Grimmstone*?"

"Yes. A first edition. I pen many things in the notation section as my memory fades." He flipped through the back.

"Well, you are a man of many years." Mina wondered what other interesting memories he had penned.

"Here we are." He cleared his throat and read. "*The white witch dusted a piece of hartstone onto the infant princess's face and said, 'A prince will awaken your heart with a blood kiss. Not long after, you will drink fire into your soul and awaken the beast of vengeance and righteousness. And courage and hope. Blessed child, you will awaken the white queen with emerald eyes and smite the evil one with one bite. You will be the savior of them all.*" He snapped the book shut.

Mina peered up at him. "I was awakened with a blood kiss."

He nodded. "And soon you will be the white queen to save us all." His voice cracked, tears brimming.

Mina threw her arms around this old man who was a mere stranger till an hour before. Her heart poured out with love for him, this vampire who'd risked his life to save his queen and who'd lived a life of exile for it. For it was his bravery and devotion that allowed Mikhail to come into the world.

He squeezed her tight and whispered, "You must be our white queen, Your Highness. You must be."

Chapter Twenty-One

Mikhail had been waiting in the dark of her bedchamber for quite a long time. Long enough for Mina to accept Lord Rathbone's proposal and seal their betrothal with long, lingering kisses. Perhaps more than kisses. He fisted his hands on the arms of the chair in the corner.

Finally, he heard the quiet *snick* of her door opening and closing. She entered on silent feet, carrying a single candlestick, which haloed her face, making her appear even more angelic. His heart ached at the sight of her. She set it on the sideboard near the window and looked out. Was she thinking of him? Or Lord Rathbone?

Mikhail swallowed bitter bile, for this was all his own doing. He'd been confused on how to handle his undeniable feelings for her with the slaughter of their army, and his blood brothers, in Silvane Forest. He'd kept her at a distance, trying to work through it all. Well, no more.

He watched her slide off her slippers and stockings with a soft rustle of silk, then unlace the bodice of her gown. She could use some help, but he remained there in the shadows, watching and wanting. Before she could slip it from her shoulders, he spoke.

"Did you accept him?"

She gasped and squeaked at the same time, spinning toward him. "For heaven's *sake*, Mikhail. Don't frighten me like that. What are you doing sitting here in the dark?"

"Did you accept him?" he asked, the words scraping against his throat.

She paused, her arms crossing her chest, still holding up her gown. "You overheard Lord Rathbone's proposal?"

"No. But I know men like him and how they think. He deduced why we were here the moment we stepped into his blue parlor and will have realized that an alliance of his house with the Arkadian throne would be a strong one. And beneficial to him."

"I see." She continued undressing, pushing the gown down over her hips and stepping out of the circle, standing in only her sheer chemise, tied with white silk ribbons at the shoulders. "And what do you think?"

Starting at her bare ankles, he looked his fill—at the slender curve of her thighs, the dark thatch of hair between her legs, the indention at her waist, the subtle curve of her breasts, pink nipples hardened against the transparent fabric, her slender arms at her sides, and svelte neck tall with her chin raised. A paragon of beauty and royalty. And pure woman. A possessive vise gripped his chest and squeezed, his beast murmuring in the dark. *Mine.*

His fangs throbbed in his gums, extending and forcing his mouth open. He wanted to sink inside her in every possible way, slip into the sweet oblivion of Mina.

"I think he's right." The truth of it ripped him in half. "He would be a strong partner and ally to win the favor of the House as well as the people of Arkadia." He should stop talking, the thought of losing her like a knife slitting up his spine. But he had more to say, to make her understand. "But it will never happen. You don't belong to him."

After a moment's pause, she unpinned her hair and shook out the waves around her shoulders.

"Come to me, Mikhail," she beckoned, and he was sure his soul slipped from his body at her command.

"Did you accept him?" he asked yet again, softer but shaking, gripping the arms of the chair.

"Come to me, and I'll tell you."

Slowly, he shoved out of the chair and stood, then strode toward her with long, hard steps, stopping only when he was mere inches away. She didn't reach up to touch him. And he didn't reach out to touch her.

He couldn't understand the expression on her face, both adoring and somber at the same time. "I did not accept him. Because you're right. I belong to another."

He couldn't move, relief washing over him so fast his vision hazed.

"You asked me once what it was like when I was in the bloodless sleep." She licked her lips, emotion shaking her voice.

"Yes."

"There were times I could hear people moving in the room around me, even talking like I wasn't there, like I was invisible. While I lay there in pain."

Mikhail wanted to break the bones and slash the throats of every man in that tower. Again. He kept his fisted hands at his sides while she continued.

"Other times, I drifted in this dreamy place where the sun shined and the birds sang. And then there were the nightmares where monsters chased me, trying to pull me down and devour me. But every time I had one of the nightmares, a faceless man would come and save me. I called him my dark prince." She reached up and skimmed the tips of her fingers along his defined cheekbone and down his chiseled jaw. "Then you did come. You...my dark prince... son of Christov Romanov, grandson of Rodin Romanov, and great-grandson of Rodin Varis, the rightful, good king of the Glass Tower. Of the Varis Empire."

He couldn't breathe as she whispered his secret and traced the lines of his face, the pads of her fingers sliding over his lips. The secret he and Dmitri had kept, lest they be murdered like their great-grandfather, the twin brother and first victim of Queen Morgrid.

"How did you know?" The rolling timbre of his voice sounded like the low rumble of thunder before a storm.

"While you've been thinking I was downstairs courting Lord Rathbone, I've been visiting with his father."

"The old man who wouldn't stop staring at me all night?"

"Yes." She smiled, her hand sliding down his throat, where she began to work on the buttons of his shirt. "He was staring because he recognized you."

"Me? I never forget a face. I've never seen him before." His attention shifted to her fingers. "What are you doing?"

His shirt gaped open. She skimmed her delicate hands over the ridges of his abdomen and the planes of his chest. He flexed beneath her touch, holding himself rigid as stone.

"I need you, Mikhail," she whispered—hesitant—the sound of her desperation cracking his shell of stone. "Please be my dark prince again. Be the man I need...and desire."

Mina skated her hands up over his bare shoulders, sliding off his shirt till it fell in a soft whoosh. But she went no further.

The look of yearning in those ethereal pools of blue brought him to his knees. He could no more turn away than he could tear out his own heart. And yet, that's exactly what this felt like. Ripping through sinew and bone, exposing the vulnerable, raw part of him he'd kept behind a wall of vengeance and rage. He'd only had room for his brother, the Bloodguard, and the fervent will to annihilate Queen Morgrid and her order for so many long years. To the great disappointment of his mother, he rarely returned home. How could he? When his father was not yet avenged?

But now, the world fell away, his body and soul demanding he take what was his, divined by auspicious stars and bewitching fortune, tempting him to break every vow and promise, if only to have this woman as his own.

Lightning swift, he lifted her by the waist and backed her into the wall. Sliding his hands up over her ribs, skating her breasts, lifting up her arms and smoothing his hands up till they were palm to palm, he laced his fingers with hers and pressed them to the wall.

"I'm thinking you've ruined me." He nuzzled her lips but didn't go in, then dragged his mouth across her jaw to her ear and settled his weight against her, letting her feel every hard inch of his body pressed to hers. "Whatever plans of ambition and justice for the Bloodguard, for my family, that I had, they are now gone."

"I wouldn't take that away from you," she said breathily. "You don't have to give up anything for me."

"It doesn't matter. It's too late." He scraped the tips of his fangs along the tender spot beneath her ear down to her pulse point, pressing hard enough to mark her but not enough to draw a drop of blood.

"No, Mikhail. It isn't."

Bending his leg to slide between her own, he pressed his thigh to her hot core. "I tried to keep away. Tried not to touch you. *Impossible.*"

He trailed his tongue from her pulse down the curve to her shoulder. Clamping his teeth on the end of her ribbon, he pulled the bow free. The tie fell, the flap over one breast falling with it. He shifted back to gaze at her rose-pink nipple, puckered and waiting, the rise and fall of her lovely chest, the roundness of her eyes, filled with yearning. For him.

"But I'm done, Mina mine. I'm going to touch and taste every part of you." Dropping his head down, he sucked her taut nipple on a groan, then lifted back up till his lips whispered gruffly against hers. "I'm going to drive so deep inside you, you'll forget everything but me"—he stroked his tongue along the seam of her lips, prying them apart with erotic leisure—"and when you've come on my tongue and on my cock for the fourth or fifth time, you might finally understand what it feels like to be me. To be utterly devastated with need."

He crushed his mouth against hers, unlacing his fingers from hers to cup her face and hold her hard. He kissed her roughly. Thoroughly, wholly, deeply. Her fangs sharp, she pulled back and nicked his lips with a lust-filled gleam in her eyes. Her aroused scent filled his nostrils, hardening his cock to pain.

He twisted her around and flattened her palms to the wall. "Keep them there."

He wasted no time jerking up the hem of her chemise, sliding his hand over her hip, dipping his fingers lower between her folds, over her tight bud. He wrapped his other arm across her chest and slid his hand under the chemise to squeeze her breast and tease her nipple.

"Please," she whispered, grinding her hips against his hand, the globes of her ass brushing against his cock still constrained in rough leather.

"Who do you belong to, Mina?" he grated in her ear.

With her hands planted on the wall, she pushed back more forcefully, drawing a hiss from him when she ground against his crotch. "You, Mikhail."

"Yes." He rolled her nipple between index and thumb more roughly. His need for possession amped his blood to liquid fire, his body hardening in response, ready to plunder and mark her deep. "Mine."

She moaned in response.

He pushed a finger inside her—so tight—planting rough kisses along her neck. "Soaking wet, Princess." She tilted hear head to one side for him, her hair sliding away so he could see, hear, feel her rapid pulse humming in the air. He was drowning in the musky scent of her arousal and the call of her blood.

"Fuck."

The need to be inside her blacked out his brain and any other thought. Making short work of his laces, he gripped his thick cock and stroked the head into her folds just once without breaching her. A virgin, for certain, he kept hold of the reins, coating himself in her warm heat. A slow glide through her cleft tore a sweet whimper from her throat.

"Yes." She arched her spine, lifting her bottom higher.

He slid in just enough for his tip to be fisted tight. The agonizing torture it took to restrain himself nearly broke him. His beast urging him to thrust and take. Not like this.

Withdrawing, she released a plaintive cry, arching back to offer more of herself. He stripped to nothing in a blink, then swept her up into his arms. She made a giggle-gasp in surprise, wrapping her arms around his neck, her warm breath on his cheek.

Stretching her out on the bed, he ripped the chemise up over her head and tossed it away. She lay back, her golden hair spilling over the sapphire counterpane, half-lidded eyes glinting bright, fingers clawing into the fabric beneath her, moon-pale skin a delectable feast for his eyes.

He knelt above her, gazing his fill, in utter rapture at her erotic beauty. She stared up at him as if he were a conquering king, finally taking what was rightfully his. Perhaps he was. Her perusal swept down his face, his chest, and torso, stopping at his stiff cock. It hardened even more under her widened gaze. Taking himself in hand, he stroked as she watched, her slickness still there, the musky scent an aphrodisiac he inhaled deep.

"See what you do to me."

Sweeping his thumb over the tip, he slicked himself more, coating his cock. There would be no foreplay tonight. He'd taste her after he came hard inside her body. That was paramount.

"I've been like this since the moment I touched your lips in that tower."

He recognized his voice had dropped to a dangerous, grating decibel, but she showed no fear as his vampire reared forward in triumph that this moment had finally come.

"Aching for you." He stroked, his cock growing impossibly thicker. "Like fucking torture."

Her gaze lifted, her pink tongue darting across her lips as she raised her arms, "Then come to me and let me ease the pain."

"Open for me, Mina."

She spread her legs, and he was lost. Falling forward onto one hand beside her head, he lifted her right leg over his hip. Notching his cock at her entrance, the heat of her pulling him in just an inch, he groaned like a dying man, bracing his forearms on the bed, caging her in.

"This may hurt at first."

"Good." Her eyes glittered with sensual mischief, her fingers gripping his broad shoulders. "I want it to hurt." She added, breathlessly, "I want to remember this first time, the first man entering my body."

A guttural growl rumbled from deep in his chest as he spoke so close, their lips brushed. "I am and will be the *only* man, Mina." Then he thrust up inside her body, tearing past her barrier with brutal force.

She cried out, her neck arching, vampire claws biting into his shoulders. Her perfect small breasts pressed up, peaked nipples grazing his chest.

Primal desire pulled his mouth down to her alabaster skin. He licked a line along the curve of her neck and shoulder, finding her rapid pulse with his tongue. Holding his cock deep, not moving, her tight sheath stretched around him.

"Mina." He ground her name out like a curse to the heavens or a prayer to hell, hoping his sanity didn't slip as he bit into her soft flesh, his fangs sinking hard.

"Ah!" She dug her claws in deeper till Mikhail scented his own blood. A primal possessiveness exalted in the beauty of her beast rising up to meet his. This would be no gentle coupling but one where a vampire queen and vampire king bound themselves to each other with sweat and blood and a primitive conquering of each other.

Mikhail groaned in ecstatic pleasure, sucking her blood into his mouth. The sweet tang flooded into his limbs, sending a pulse of power through his entire body.

As he drank and his elixir poured into her veins, she rocked her hips up, willing him to move. He obliged, pulling out to the tip and gliding back in on a groan. Finally unlatching his fangs from her flesh, his lips found hers.

"You undo me, woman," he breathed, cupping the back of her head in his palm, stroking in slow inside her.

"You make me whole," she whispered, then he opened his mouth over hers and started to move.

Pumping inside in a slow but steady grind, he swallowed her moans, stroking his tongue along hers. She encouraged him with soft sighs as their mouths came apart, as they drifted into each other in a way he'd never experienced with another woman.

He lifted away, hovering close to see the look of ecstasy in her eyes shining back at him, her mouth ajar, full lips swollen, canines long, curved, and sharp. Keeping her body immobile with his chest, he stroked deeper, harder, furiously pounding his thick cock, the erotic sound driving him to the brink.

A fierce look of determination crossed her face as she planted her hands on his shoulders and pushed. He let her have her way, rolling with the momentum till he was on his back and she was mounted on top of him like a golden goddess upon her erotic throne. A bark of laughter slipped free from his throat, melting into a rough groan when she ground her hips down hard.

"Come on, then," he murmured, spreading his hands on her slim hips, "take what you want." He thrust upward, her eyes slid closed. "Fuck me good," he commanded, even while her beast reveled in taking the reins.

Her hands on his chest, pushing her pert breasts together, pink nipples jutting up, she rode him, accepting the rhythm he set beneath her. He leaned up to lick and suck one nipple, which spurred her on to rock faster. Feeling her orgasm quicken, he fell back to watch—the look of carnal pleasure sweeping her face, the beauty of her lithe body moving on top of his, the slick eroticism of his cock entering her heat.

Then she cried out, mouth open in pure ecstasy. Holding her hips down, he groaned as her tight cunny pulsed around his cock until the ripple finally ebbed and her sated gaze found his. She lay her sweet torso atop his, her silken hair trailing on his chest, and tilted her head forward, her mouth at his ear.

"I want to feel you come inside me." Without warning, she bit into his neck near the shoulder, her slender fangs a mere pinprick. But then her elixir. Pure, raw, sweet ecstasy.

"By the stars, you're going to kill me."

Sliding his hands to cup the globes of her ass, fingers digging into her flesh, he drove up harder, his entire body sleek with sweat. "Yes," he groaned, still pumping hard. "Drink from me, Mina mine. Take it all if you want to. My heart…my fucking soul, too."

He was lost. Gone. Undone. Riding on pure erotic bliss and a headier, stronger emotion he knew could only be one thing. For it filled him with a terrifying kind of joy.

She wrenched her mouth away, though careful not to mar his flesh, her head falling back with a swing of her golden hair, the tresses sliding over the backs of his hands squeezing her ass. The ripples of her second orgasm milked his cock to the point he could hold back no longer. With one long, slick stroke, he speared her deep, burying his face into her neck as his cock pumped his seed, hot and hard.

For a long moment, he simply held her there as she draped herself on top of his chest.

When he could finally draw breath slow enough to speak, he admitted, "I'm a bloody fool."

She propped her cheek in her hand, elbow on his chest. "Why?"

"No man living and breathing could deny you anything. I promise, Mina mine. I won't deny you ever again."

She smiled, a pretty pink flushing up her neck to her cheeks. "If I'd known that's all it took, I'd have seduced you back in that cave in the Novak Mountains."

He laughed, one that echoed the absolute joy blooming inside him. Yes. This woman could certainly command a kingdom. Just as she now commanded his heart.

Chapter Twenty-Two

Mina didn't know she could feel like this. She lay with her head on Mikhail's bare chest, his fingers languorously tracing lines from her hip to the small of her back then repeating the trail. His lovemaking was intoxicating, but the man himself? Riveting. Mesmerizing. Like she'd fallen under the sweetest of spells. And this time, she didn't want to wake up.

But more than that, this man, this emotion burning through her with meteoric fury, felt like being shot into fate's precarious hands. She was focused only on what the stars deemed important. And at this moment, that was her dark prince. Not the war. Not her coming confrontation with the lords in the House of Arkadia. Nothing at all but this precious gift weaving her into a sensual web.

The rough pads of his fingertips as they swirled over her skin, the soft rise and fall of his chest as he breathed, the strong thud of his heartbeat beneath her ear—this was where her destiny lay. She was sure of it.

"What are you thinking about?" he asked, voice rumbling deep.

"You."

His fingers stilled, then began roving again. "Good things, I hope."

She lifted up onto one arm, her loose hair falling down to his chest. "The best." She smiled.

He reached up and cupped her cheek, fingers combing into her hair. "Then what worries you?"

He seemed to always know. She couldn't tell him she feared now that she'd found her purpose, found him, that he would disappear. And she'd fall back into that slumber where everything was cold and quiet. No life at all. She didn't want to rule without him at her side.

"You can tell me," he urged. But she wasn't quite ready to voice those fears.

She turned to thoughts of Lord Petrov again, gliding her fingers along his pectoral and sternum, her fingers lazily dipping and rising in the hard grooves.

"You know, Lord Petrov told me of a white witch visiting my birth celebration. I remember when I was a little girl, my nurse used to say that a white witch visited me as a babe and made me the fairy girl that I was. Then she was taken away from me, and I forgot. Or I thought it was only a tale to make me laugh. It didn't seem important then, and I've heard no one speak of it since." She paused her exploration with her fingers, meeting his gaze. "Have you heard of that before?"

"Yes. I know those who dare to speak of that witch. But not many do. It's as if Queen Morgrid cast a spell to make everyone forget."

"How do you know about it then?"

He smirked. "I made a point to discover all I could about you when the queen set her sights on using you as a pawn in her plans."

"You did?" She was surprised he'd investigated into her past before they'd met. "Why did you do that?"

"If the queen had made a point for her son to marry you when war was raging across the land, I knew there was another reason other than a merry wedding. Nefarious reasons."

"I see. And what did you discover?"

"I found that a white witch visited you on your birth and proclaimed you would be Queen of Arkadia and would rule them all. That's how I know you were meant to be queen."

Mina frowned and shook her head. "That's not exactly what she said. Not according to Lord Petrov, who actually wrote the words down."

Smiling, something he was doing more than usual as of late, he asked, "Would you care to enlighten me?"

Smiling at his teasing request, she thought a moment, remembering the words exactly as they were scrawled into his book. "You will drink fire into your soul and awaken the beast of vengeance, righteousness, courage, and hope. You will awaken the white queen with emerald eyes and smite the evil one with one bite." She paused, hesitant about the last. "You will be the savior of them all."

"What frightens you?" he asked.

She shrugged one shoulder, her hair slipping over her breast with the movement. "All of it, really."

In a blink, she was beneath him. He held himself up on his forearms and wedged a heavy thigh between her legs.

"Being queen frightens you?"

"No. Not exactly. What does all of that *mean*?" She let her hands wander to his shoulders. "Drinking fire? Beast of vengeance? Smiting with one bite?"

He laughed, brushing a kiss on her pinched brow. "It's a metaphor. The southern army will help us win against the Glass Tower."

"But I won't be that kind of queen. I'm not that kind of person."

"What's that? The kind who fights for what is good and

right in this world?" When she opened her mouth to speak, he slanted his mouth over hers, silencing her protests with his probing tongue. His invasion caught her off-guard, melting her worries away. She clenched her nails into his muscular shoulders on a soft moan. When he broke the kiss, his eyes blazed starbright. "You will be the queen we need."

"I'm not a beast," she whispered.

"I'm not so sure." He spread open her legs with his thigh and settled lower, pushing inside her with a slow roll of his pelvis. He held her gaze, his own mere inches above her. "I can see a queenly beast in there staring back at me."

She planted her feet on the bed and rocked up to meet each sinuous slide of him inside her.

He grinned, fangs sharp and ready. "A she-vampire of the highest realm," he grated. His gaze drifted down their bodies. He glided his hand down her outer thigh, crooking his fingers under her knee. "With a throne I long to mount every moment of every day." Another languid roll of his pelvis. "I could worship at this throne forever."

"Stop torturing me, Mikhail—" she clutched a hand in his hair—"give me what you promised."

His brow pursed together in a frown as he paused in his too-slow tempo. "What promise was that?"

"I believe you said four or five times. I've had but two." She pulled his mouth down to hers, feeling as if there was indeed a beast inside her, yearning to claw her way out. "More, Mikhail." She nipped his lips. "Love me hard."

He bent her long leg high, pressed a kiss to the inner side of her knee and hooked it over his shoulder. "Whatever you command, my queen."

Then she experienced the power of the man, the vampire, covering her body with his own, consuming her from the inside out, pressing home his masculine strength with such intensity she heard a whispering from the inmost part of herself.

This. This was what was missing all her life. This feeling of being vibrantly alive. Of finding she loved the strength within herself that she'd kept hidden so long, too afraid to let her vampiric qualities rise to the surface. Mikhail awakened her most primal instincts in such beautiful, delicious ways. While the idea of being a less-than-genteel creature had once frightened her, Mikhail adored every part of her, including the animal within that had awoken on the night he gave her a blood kiss in the tower. The night the fates first joined them, divining this fierce, electric kind of love.

And now, as he drove deep and hard inside her body, just as she'd asked him to, she could only repeat a mantra of "yes" against his lips, their gazes locked. Like their bodies, they were held fast and hard to each other, reaching for that moment of ecstasy together, and something else. Something more.

When she opened her mouth in a soundless scream, her orgasm crashing through her like a violent tidal wave, he melded his mouth to hers, groaning as he spilled inside of her. She dug her nails into his back, relishing the heaviness of him buried deep as he found his release, growling his satisfaction.

Even as he kissed her down from the pinnacle of orgasm, the burning need remained. An unquenchable fire.

She broke the kiss, panting. "Will it ever go away?"

His mouth quirked up on one side. Not exactly a smile. More an expression of acceptance. "No. I don't think it will." He brushed away a strand of her hair sticking to the dampness of her neck. "Not for me."

She cupped his sharp, angular jaw gently, sweeping her thumb to the corner of his mouth. "What will happen to us? After the war, will we—I mean, you are the great-grandson of Rodin Varis. You are a prince yourself, the highest rank I could marry."

She couldn't keep the hope from her eyes, wishing he'd make that sacrifice for her. She couldn't bear the thought of ruling alone, for she'd never take another man but him at her side.

Angling his head just enough, he pressed a kiss to the pad of her thumb. "Hush now, Mina mine. Let's not worry about tomorrow." He hovered close, sweeping his lips across hers, gliding his tongue across the seam as he rolled his spine, stroking inside her. "You just relax and let me keep my promise."

She laughed, her breath catching on a gasp when he pounded once, deep and hard. "Yes, Captain."

He pressed a desperate kiss to her lips, sweeping his tongue in swiftly before lifting away. His expression transformed to one of storm and midnight, a dark gravity hovering over him as he expressed himself with his unearthly eyes and magnificent body. She couldn't hear the words, but she felt the emotion with her empathic senses and with her own heart. The most deep and reverent emotion of all pouring from the man thrusting deep inside her.

She closed her eyes and whispered her mantra of "yes," accepting his wordless vow that there would be a future beyond the veil of blood and death that loomed ahead.

Chapter Twenty-Three

Standing at the top of the stone steps leading into the Grand Forum—a circular building made of white stone, the floors of white marble—Mina exhaled a deep breath.

"As we said, I'll go in first and call the House to order," Lord Rathbone said, leaning close to her ear. "Then I'll relate there has been a new proposition put to the House, one not in their current registers. That's when you will enter."

"Right." She nodded.

"Smile, Your Highness." He stood tall, smoothing his waistcoat. "All will be well." Then he winked and walked with long, commanding strides into the hall where the overlapping voices of the many lords fell to a hush at his entry.

"Don't be nervous," said Friedrich on her right.

"I'm not nervous."

And that was the truth, strangely enough. She'd always been nervous upon her annual visits to the Grand Forum. But now she understood why. Steward Thorwald paraded her in as an ornament, for her to show her face and never open her mouth. She'd always felt out of place because she'd had no place there. But not today. Today, she would be seen *and* heard.

"We'll be right behind you. To be sure they understand you're not alone."

Mina turned to Friedrich and gave him a warm smile. "I've been alone all my life, Your Grace. It was what I was taught at an early age by Thorwald. A princess is a solitary entity who must live a solitary life. Not until I awoke from the bloodless sleep did I finally come to understand the truth."

"What truth, Your Highness?"

"That a princess alone is a dying flower on the vine." She shifted her gaze forward, hearing the staccato wrap of a gavel, bringing the House to order. "And a strong queen is never alone."

"Quite right, Your Majesty."

She smiled at his slip of a queenly title. "Not yet, Friedrich. Let's get through this first."

She marched forward, feeling the presence of her entourage at her back, sensing Mikhail closest on her left behind her.

"What new proposition?" She heard the blustering voice of Steward Thorwald as she crossed from the shadows of the arch into the light of the amphitheater. The oculus at the center of the dome let in sunlight, the rim of the dome ringed with large windows as well, bathing the white marble room in a vibrant air.

Rathbone arched a superior brow from the helm of the hall on the raised bench, gesturing toward her. "One that I believe Princess Vilhelmina Dragomir will present to us."

A wave of gasps and murmurs echoed in the large chamber as she made her way across the hall with Friedrich and the Bloodguard at her back. Grant filed in as one of the Bloodguard. Mina took in the gaping, awestruck steward who had abused his position as her keeper all her life, then stepped up to the podium facing the amphitheater.

The tiers of lords all turned their eyes on her. They were separated by province. Their unique banners and scepters marked the first row of each province. She scanned them all, recognizing the leaders of the provinces, their eyes fixed on her. She nodded to Lord Grable of the Pierson Province, known as the greatest breeders of the fine Arkadian horses. She looked to the right, catching the eye of Lord Steele of the Creed Province, known for their superior craftsmanship in armor and weaponry.

Reaching out with her empathic gift, she sensed no menace—excepting the steward at her back on the bench with Rathbone and Lord Maksim—but felt pinpricks of surprise and curiosity. And perhaps a little fear as a few heads turned nervously to the entrance, many glancing at the black-clad Bloodguard standing in two lines facing opposite sides of the hall. Rumors had surely spread far and wide that she'd been a captive of King Dominik and that he was now on the warpath to recapture her.

"Greetings, my lords." Her voice lifted to the domed ceiling easily in such an acoustic chamber. "I come today with a royal petition, but first I must digress to dispel any erroneous reports circulating throughout my kingdom."

Thorwald huffed out a blustering protest at her mention of ownership of Arkadia. For she never had before. "This is preposterous. What can she possibly—"

"Close your mouth, Thorwald," said Rathbone with such malevolence that Mina turned to find him staring daggers at the man. "Or I'll shut it for you."

Thorwald glanced away, his face mottled red.

Mina faced forward, inhaled a deep breath, chin up, back straight. "I must also confirm the truth of some of these reports."

She waited while a few lords muttered to one another, but

most of them remained riveted upon her.

"It is known that my father King Holland was a good and just king. He was the one who unified the provinces under the House of Arkadia and built this Grand Forum so that every lord might have a voice for his people." Nods of approval. She waited till all was silent again. "If you were at the celebration of my birth, then you are aware he rejected Queen Morgrid's demand that I, his only child, be betrothed to her son, Marius."

No one made a sound. Not even Thorwald at her back, whose seething anger she felt like a burning fireball.

"Interestingly, this truth was kept from me till quite recently. All that I ever knew of my dear father was that he'd loved me. And he was killed by the hands of brigands when I was far too young. I never knew that love after he died. I was put under the care of Steward Thorwald."

She flicked a hand over her shoulder without turning.

"He made sure I had the best of nursing care and I was kept far...*far* away from the rest of *my* kingdom. For my protection, he assured me."

She heard the cynical twist of her words, but she cared not. They would hear it all. Right here. Right now.

"And so I was raised to be the perfect princess. Obedient. And silent. Awaiting the time when I would marry Prince Marius, since Steward Thorwald upheld the queen's wishes that I should marry her son. Reminding you that this was against the wishes of your king before he was murdered."

She couldn't help but let her gaze flick to Mikhail. He remained steadfast, his gaze straight out toward the right of the hall, but his mere presence strengthened her still.

"I understand why none of you defied the placement of Thorwald at the helm of Arkadia. Queen Morgrid is a powerful force, the empress of our land. But I want to remind everyone here that your proper and true king did not want an alliance with the Glass Tower. Why? Because my father knew her evil would infect our land as soon as she held power over it."

She paused, sweeping her gaze across the quiet auditorium.

"And so, understandably, you all accepted him as your ruler."

She gestured a regal hand over her shoulder again.

"Even though he was in alliance with Queen Morgrid. When Prince Marius fled the Glass Tower to marry his human wife, Arabelle, of the Black Lily, defying his mother because he discovered she was the one infecting the land with sanguine furorem, the blood madness in the vampires killing rampantly at will, she blamed me for his betrayal. My punishment?"

She swept her gaze from one side to the next. No one moved.

"I was dragged back to Briar Rose, where my lady-in-waiting, my lifelong friend and blood host was murdered before my eyes. My only friend up till that point in my life. Her throat cut by Queen Morgrid's right-hand man, Radomir. Then she was fed to his men like cattle."

Her voice cracked with grief for Kathleen, but she held back all tears, wielding righteous anger in its stead.

"I was locked in my own tower in my own home and starved into a bloodless sleep."

A few lords glanced and whispered low, nodding. Many had heard this rumor. It was nothing new. But they didn't know what it was truly like.

"Being in a bloodless sleep is beyond any of your imagining. Beyond any nightmare you could possibly conjure. The constant gut-ripping pain in my abdomen from starvation wasn't the worst of it. The paralysis wasn't, either. The times where I could hear officers moving and talking in the chamber struck a new kind of fear in me. Can you imagine hearing men talk about the vulgar ways they could and would like to use your body while you lay prostrate and helpless? Never mind me. Can you imagine your own wives being in this helpless situation? Your daughters?"

Nervous shuffling and movement rippled along the rows of men. Mikhail's shoulders stiffened, but he didn't swivel or move his head an inch. Mina softened her voice but not the strength of her words.

"Thankfully, their fear of the queen's command kept them at bay from using me unlawfully, but only because I was apparently to be saved as a prize for her son, King Dominik. Otherwise, I'm sure there would have been little left of me to save when the Bloodguard came to my rescue."

Mina swept a hand toward the line of twenty men who'd accompanied her on this mission. The lords examined them more closely, realizing these were the mercenaries spoken of in many dark corners, but few had ever seen with their own eyes. They were indeed a formidable force, even when only half were standing here. Their expressions and demeanors fiercer than any troop of Legionnaires.

"Yes. Five of the Bloodguard saved me and killed all but a few of King Dominik's Legionnaires."

Gregoravich turned to her and held up three fingers, winked, then faced front again. She smiled.

"Correction. All but three men. From there, I was taken to safety in the home of Sienna of Silvane Forest."

"She's a witch! Burns men alive!" yelled Steward Thorwald.

A sharp crack. By the time Mina turned her head, Rathbone stood over Thorwald, slumped forward on the bench, Rathbone palming his fist.

His glare swept up the rows of lords. "I declare Steward Thorwald, who is in service to Queen Morgrid and not in service to this realm of Arkadia, to be unfit for his position as lead counselor. Do you agree, Lord Maksim?"

The gruff reply was swift from the steely-eyed man at Rathbone's right. "Agreed."

With a stiff bow, Rathbone said, "Please continue, Your Highness." He straightened his waistcoat and resumed his place.

Mina swallowed hard, realizing what Rathbone had just done for her. He'd publicly denounced the steward of their land, not to mention punched him unconscious. He, the man whose voice and opinions everyone respected above all others, had just declared the steward no longer trustworthy. And the second high counselor, Lord Maksim, had concurred, removing the steward from their trust and their counsel. This meant any allies Thorwald held in the room would be committing political suicide to stand with him now.

Clearing her throat, she continued. "Sienna has been bestowed with a gift from the hartstone, it is true. And she's not burned one innocent man alive, only the vampires set upon her forest to do her harm along with those she loves. That includes Nikolai, former lieutenant to the Glass Tower's Royal Guard. I was also under the protection of the Black Lily. They've all allied together against the army the queen and her son are amassing."

"Your Highness," said the deep, gravelly voiced Lord Maksim at her back. "We are thankful for this information, but what petition do you have?"

His countenance was as dark and stormy as his voice. He and Lord Rathbone were dear friends besides being high counselors together of the House. He was a no-nonsense kind of man, which also made his loyalty invaluable. He wasn't a man to be persuaded to anything other than what was right and best for the land of Arkadia. She couldn't be sure, but she hoped Rathbone had apprised him of today's proceedings and that he was fully on board.

"Thank you, Lord Maksim. Here it is." Lifting her eyes to the tiers of lords who held her fate in their hands—everyone's fate for that matter—she said, "I petition this most reverent House to bestow upon me my birthright. To crown me as the sovereign Queen of Arkadia."

Loud murmurs and grumbling swept the chamber. Lord Rathbone hammered the gavel several times as one of the lords in the lowest tier stood.

"Lord Hanson, you have the floor," said Rathbone.

"Your Highness," he began respectfully. "By what right do you ask for this petition now?"

"By what right do you keep it from me?"

She kept her voice level and steady even as her knees trembled. She needed these men behind her. To claim the crown wasn't enough. She must have a kingdom behind her or it was pointless. She must not cower but show strength.

"Begging your pardon," Lord Hanson continued, "but you have laid out before us that you have as much allied with the Black Lily, the exiled prince, and this Bloodguard."

Friedrich raised his hand. "And don't forget the exiled Duke of Winter Hill."

Now the murmurings escalated to new heights. They obviously saw Friedrich and understood his reason for being here, and yet not until he made it quite clear where he stood did they react.

"As you can see, Lord Hanson," she continued, stepping from behind the podium but remaining on the dais, her hands folded demurely before her, "factions of the Varis family are breaking away from the queen. But let me answer your first question." Her voice rose, and she sensed an internal fire sparking to life, tingling along her skin like a magical mantel to protect her, to guide her. "I have the right to petition for my immediate coronation because I am Vilhelmina Dragomir, daughter of the just and rightful King Holland Dragomir. The blood that flows in my veins flowed in that of our founding father, my great-great-grandfather King Thormand Dragomir, who conquered this territory and claimed it for his people, the *only* kingdom still not under the tyrannical rule of the Glass Tower." She spoke treason against the queen, and yet it felt more like victory. "As the last living descendant of Thormand Dragomir, I am your rightful sovereign of this great land, and I pledge my life to rule as my father did before me."

Her voice had reached a fever pitch, roaring to the height of the dome. Lords lifted up their scepters and banged them on the stone, cheers swelling high.

"Hold!" Lord Grable of the Pierson Province stood and raised his hand.

Lord Rathbone hammered the gavel again.

"Your Highness!" The knocking of the scepters on the floor dimmed, giving this particular vampire lord due respect. "You are correct. You are our rightful sovereign. But is it your intention to force us into war against the Glass Tower? I admire the heart of the human army of the Black Lily and these few men of the Bloodguard, but this force of her vampire army along with King Dominik's is too formidable."

"My lord, I cannot and will not force anyone to do anything. I am *not* the tyrant Queen Morgrid." She emphasized the last with vehemence. "But mark me well. War is coming. If you ignore this call, you will fall, just as the Black Lily will without the help of the Arkadians. You will lose more than your queen into the hands of King Dominik, for I can promise you I will die before I become his wife."

She caught the slightest movement of Mikhail below her, his hands fisted at his sides. She continued.

"The queen will not be satisfied until she owns us all under the dark veil she plans to spread over our lands. Until our soil is soaked in the blood of your wives and sons and daughters. The blood of *my* people." She pressed a fist to her heart. "Do you really want to wait until that shadow falls on your doorsteps—for it will should the Black Lily fail—and then you will wonder why you didn't fight when you had the chance? When your queen asked you to."

A hush fell upon them all. She waited, holding Lord Grable's gaze. Finally, he lifted his scepter and raised it in the air, "Hail, Queen Vilhelmina!"

A cacophony of cheers and resounding echoes of Lord Grable reverberated in the forum, scepters pounding on the floor. Mina's heart swelled with such love and pride she could hardly bear it. Then Lord Rathbone was at the foot of the dais, offering his hand near the steps. He had a square of cloth tucked under his arm. She let him lead her down to the hall floor while cheers continued.

He leaned in close. "Well done. You nearly had me swooning at your feet."

"I find that highly unlikely."

He chuckled before sobering his face for the crowd with a hand in the air. When they'd all taken their seats, he continued, "Due to the dire state of the land abroad and because a formal coronation would put our sovereign's life at risk, we can afford no formal ceremony as Her Highness deserves. Therefore, we will proceed immediately."

He unfolded a scrap of green silk embroidered with her sigil, the white dragon, the edges frayed from time.

"Here is the banner carried by King Thormand's army into battle in these southern lands. The original banner that waved over the fields of victory for our people."

He whipped it out and laid it upon the marble floor.

"Please kneel, Your Highness."

She swallowed the lump of emotion lodged in her throat as he helped her to her knees. Lord Maksim was suddenly behind him, holding the silver scepter of the high counsel of the House. Apparently, he had been apprised of this plan somehow. Lord Maksim held the sacred scepter to the people of Arkadia. Automatically, she bowed her head as he recited a litany of words from the Arkadian Book of Order. It held the laws and rights of the people as well as the role of their sovereign ruler.

She heard hardly any of it at all, trembling where she knelt, realizing she'd done it after all. Mikhail was right. She was strong. Her voice was heard. And they believed in her. The responsibility of her new role was overwhelming and wonderful all at the same time. Destiny smiled upon her. She snapped back to what was happening when she felt the scepter touch her right shoulder.

"Do you promise to uphold the Arkadian Book of Order, to rule by law, justice, and mercy in all your judgments?"

"I solemnly promise."

He touched her left shoulder with the scepter. "And will you uphold your oath of loyalty to the people of Arkadia, vowing upon your heart and soul?"

"I will."

He touched her right shoulder again.

"By the heavens above, under this sacred roof, and before the eyes of the House of Arkadia, I pronounce you Vilhelmina Dragomir, only child of King Holland, the sovereign Queen of Arkadia." He pounded the scepter with one heavy *thwack* upon the floor. "Hail, Queen Vilhelmina!"

Once more, joyous voices arose. Lord Rathbone lifted her to her feet. Friedrich was at her side, bowing deeply.

A rumble of marching feet could be heard coming up the outer steps. The sudden joy in the air was squelched by the rhythmic pounding of boots entering the double doors of the hall.

"Oh, hell," Rathbone whispered, grabbing hold of Mina's arm.

"Bloodguard!" Mikhail bellowed. "Front!"

But rather than ready themselves into attack mode, the two rows simply pivoted and faced one another, leaving the space between open as if they welcomed the army, which could only be the queen or king's army stomping closer.

Through the archway and out of the shadowy vestibule marched three lines of black-clad men. Wait, and there was one woman on the front row. They weren't Legionnaires. They were Bloodguard soldiers. Dmitri at the front of the line. And they just kept coming. Mina swiveled to Mikhail, who still had not once looked at her through this entire interlude.

They marched in their single file columns till the first row halted where Mikhail and Gregoravich made up the front of the line. Mina stared in awe. There had to be at least two hundred of them within the chamber, and she couldn't see the end of them disappearing out of the forum archway.

That was when Mikhail stepped forward to stand directly in front of her. He knelt onto one knee.

"Queen Vilhelmina. As Captain of the Bloodguard, I hereby formally offer the services of our *full* force."

As one, the Bloodguard knelt in perfect unison. Forty of the men had pledged their fealty in Silvane Forest, but that wasn't nearly the full force.

She smiled down at Mikhail, "Captain, we need to talk."

"Indeed." He smiled back and stood, gazing down at her. "Your Majesty." He gestured toward them. "Will you walk with me and examine your troops?"

She nodded. Hands clasped at his back, he led her toward the front row. They parted with a smooth movement, stepping aside, then pivoting to face inward. Dmitri winked as she passed. The female guardsman seemed familiar somehow. With a salute of their fists to their hearts, they bowed their heads in respect as she and Mikhail walked side by side, Rathbone, Friedrich, and Maksim behind them. As they exited through the archway and the vestibule then out through the open double-doors, Mina's jaw fell open. The black-clad Bloodguard extended in a perfect quadruple line down the stone steps of the Grand Forum. Beyond the steps was a row of guardsmen on horseback, circling the forum and lengthening down the main cobblestone street of Arkadia.

Shopkeepers poked their heads out of their shops. Women of the aristocracy on their way somewhere had stopped in their tracks, pointing and whispering. One fanned herself furiously, sending her blond ringlets swinging.

"How many?" Mina asked, still in disbelief. Though why, she wasn't sure. Mikhail continued to surprise her.

"Five hundred strong, Your Majesty."

"Five hundred Bloodguard?" asked Friedrich at Mikhail's side, incredulous. "Damn it, Mikhail. One guard is worth five regular soldiers. At the very *least*. This isn't a secret you needed to keep from us."

"On the contrary, Your Grace. Information is key to winning any battle. But it was time to assemble." He turned away from the magnificent view of his Bloodguard force, gazing down at her with a look she'd seen before. A heady mix of need, adoration, and something stronger. "We are ready to face Queen Morgrid, Your Majesty."

The tolling of bells from a distant tower drew all eyes toward the hills. It echoed into the square in a distinct repetition of *gongs*. Two short, one long. Mina turned to Lord Rathbone.

"How could the town know of the coronation?" she asked.

He stepped forward. "That's not the toll for coronation." His brow pinched into a frown.

They all followed his gaze. Beyond the hills to the north, the clouds coalesced into a dark, heavy mass, swirling violently.

"A snowstorm is coming."

Chapter Twenty-Four

Mikhail stood inside his tent, the map of the north spread across the table. Friedrich and Grant leaned over it with him. The duke wore a grim expression of both determination and of fear in equal measure. No one needed to say that everyone's thoughts weighed heavily on finding Izzy safely. But none more than Friedrich.

Mikhail had successfully avoided private conversation with Mina since the coronation. He was in charge of organizing the full force of the Bloodguard for the journey to Izeling, all five hundred of them, so he kept busy. Lord Rathbone stayed behind to assemble the Arkadian army, including its elite force of equestrians. Now that word would spread of Mina's coronation, Queen Morgrid and King Dominik would be acting swiftly. Mikhail had to push his forces to move at once in order to assemble what was left of the Black Lily army for the march north. The great battle was near.

It wasn't that he didn't want to speak to her alone. It was that he wasn't sure what to say. He didn't know he'd feel this way after his goal had been achieved, after she'd faced off the

House of Arkadia and demanded they'd crown her. And then they did. He didn't know he could love her more.

Damn it to hell.

Yes. He loved her. *God, save him.* He loved her with every fiber of his being. She'd won, after all. He could no more allow her to take another man to her bed or to her side than he could cut out his own heart. They'd be one and the same, really. And so he was trying to find a way to tell her this without sounding like an utter fool. How did a man confess his love? It was done every day all over the world, and he couldn't find the words. What if she didn't return his love? Yes. Captain of the Bloodguard, slayer of rogues, leader of mercenaries, hardened, battle-ready warrior was afraid…of love.

"Something funny, Captain?" asked Grant.

"No." He cleared his throat and pointed down at the map. "There's only one way in or out of Dragon's Eye. That's where their forces will be. Though we don't know whether he'll be holding Izzy there or in Izeling Tower."

"This plain here will be ideal for battle," said Friedrich. "The mountains of Belaya Noch won't allow for any covert movement."

"Hmph," grunted Grant. "The king's intention was to hide his fort from the rest of the world. While doing so, he effectively cut himself off from escape."

Friedrich stared down, arms crossed. "That's because he never intended to be caught there."

"Which is exactly why it's the best place of attack," added Mikhail. "A separate force can sweep the castle at the same time and discover if Izzy is being held there."

"I'll be with that troop," said Friedrich, his expression grim.

"Of course."

They'd all suspected that Izzy was taken for some special

purpose none of them could quite predict, but it was more certain that she'd be kept close and not away at the fortress.

The tent flap popped open and Katya stepped in. He'd not seen her in nearly a year as she'd been working in the west of Pyros and reporting what she could about the queen's movements within King Agnar's regime. Much to Mikhail's dislike, as the only female of the Bloodguard—especially wearing the close-fitting black leather garb and gear of a soldier, her dagger harness crossing her chest—she drew the eye. Especially Grant's, it appeared.

"Captain." She stopped in front of Mikhail with a tight nod. Pulling back her hood and shaking some of the snow piled on her cloak, her dark rope of a plait fell forward over her shoulder.

Grant crossed his arms and grinned. "Captain, if I'd known you were letting girls in the Bloodguard, I'd be asking to join."

She tensed and swiveled her head in his direction. "And what makes you think we'd *ask* you to join—human?"

He put his palm over his heart. "Ouch."

"Gentlemen," Mikhail interrupted, trying to hide his grin. "This is Katya Romanov. My sister."

Grant started, shrugging apologetically to Mikhail. Friedrich chuckled with his gaze to the ground.

"Katya, this is His Grace, Friedrich Volya and his brother, Grant."

She gave them both a stiff nod of greeting.

"Lady Katya," said Friedrich, giving her the title she deserved as a nobleman's daughter.

"Just Katya, please."

Grant winked. "Charmed."

Katya narrowed her gaze then pivoted to Mikhail. "Barracks tents are complete. As well as for the horses. This blizzard was unexpected."

"Indeed." Mikhail was pleased Katya had returned from Pyros with over a hundred horses as promised. They'd need a strong cavalry to lead the advance. With the troops Lord Rathbone was assembling, they'd have a mighty force. "We'll give the horses a night's rest, then push on."

"Yes, Captain. Any other orders?"

"I want to be sure we have a secure perimeter. Check with Dmitri about patrol duty."

She rolled her eyes. "Mikhail," she complained, then remembered herself. "I mean, Captain. He'll give me the worst shift in the most difficult position."

"He wants to challenge you."

"You mean kill me."

"Mother would kill him if he did."

She huffed out a sigh. "If only I were so lucky." Then she turned for the door and exited with a snap of the tent opening, a gust of frigid air sweeping in.

Friedrich turned to Grant. "You may have been charmed by her, but I don't believe the feeling is mutual, brother."

"Oh, give her time. Wait till she sees me in action with a blade."

Mikhail chuckled. "Wait till you see *her* in action with a blade."

"She's good?" he asked.

"Let me put it this way. Gavril is by far the finest assassin with a blade in my entire Guard. Except for her." Gavril's skill with the blade had become legendary around the Black Lily camp. "She always bests him. She'd best you as well."

"Heaven help me." He clutched at his heart. "I think I'm in love."

Friedrich and Mikhail laughed, when the tent flap opened again and Dmitri stepped in, shaking the snow off and stepping up to the low-burning fire on stones in the corner. Each of these wartime tents was made with a small, round ventilation flap that opened outward in the corner. The fires set in a dugout hearth and kept burning low to keep the temperature comfortable and even.

"Colder than a witch's tit out there." He rubbed his hands together over the fire. "I'll freeze my stones off if I don't take a break."

Vampires could regulate their own body heat but extreme cold and drastic changes in temperature shocked their systems just as they would a human's.

"Did you see Katya?"

Dmitri looked over his shoulder, grinning. "Aye."

"Don't start a row with her. I need everyone level-headed."

"Who's starting anything? I just gave her a patrol assignment. Like she asked."

"Where?"

He waved a hand. "Over on the north peak."

"Where the wind is blowing hardest."

He turned, warming his back with a boyish shrug. "She wants to be treated like one of the men. Well, that's what I'm doing."

Mikhail sighed, pulling on his leather gloves. Sibling rivalry wasn't what he needed on his mind right now. "I'll make the rounds for a while. Did someone take your place on duty?"

"Yeah." He blew into his cupped hands, heating them. "Gavril took my place at the eastern point of camp."

Mikhail nodded to Friedrich and Grant. "Get some sleep if you can. We'll ride hard tomorrow, no matter if this blizzard is still blowing or not."

He flipped up his hood and headed out. Strangely, there was little snow falling now but a glacial gusting wind whipped the fresh layer into curling torrents. He pulled the kerchief tied around his neck up to his eyes to shield from the sting.

There'd been no snow on the ground when they'd left the Grand Forum; the storm sweeping in supernaturally fast.

He froze and looked around, fear sliding down his spine like a trickle of ice. The tents were set in orderly rows. He listened above the screaming wind. Rumblings of men. Laughter. Shuffling of the horses in close quarters. Blades sharpening on whetstones. Nothing out of tune.

He marched directly toward Mina's tent, stationed at the center of the encampment and surrounded by guards. He shot past the two out front and entered her tent, only to be stunned still by the sight within.

Mina sat on a carpet tossed on the ground by the stone hearth. She had uncoiled her crowning braids and brushed them out. Her hair fell in golden waves, shining by firelight like the rays of the sun.

She turned at the sound of him entering, a frown etched on her brow. "Mikhail."

Warmth spread through his stiff limbs as she stood and came to him. For their journey, she'd changed from her formal gown and garments back into the dress Sienna had given her. She'd forgone the bodice, apparently readying for bed now in her bare feet. Sienna's styling suited her well. He found her even more alluring than in her queenly garb.

"What's wrong?" he asked, pulling her into his arms.

She pressed her head into the crook of his shoulder, her body quivering.

"You're cold."

"I can't seem to get warm enough." Her voice was half muffled in his cloak. "I feel it even on the inside."

"Come." He took her hand in his gloved one and pulled her toward the cot, covered in a bear pelt, the inner lining smoothed and cured to the softness of silk. He knew because it was his pelt. He needed to know she'd be kept warm at night when he couldn't be there to do the job himself, so he'd made sure the pelt found its way here.

Sitting, he hauled her onto his lap, holding her as close as he could. "You've had an unbelievably taxing day."

Wanting to feel her, he removed his leather gloves without jostling her and tossed them aside. Then he stroked his hand over her silken hair down her back. She snuggled close, slipping one hand beneath his cloak to rest it on his shirt over his heart.

"Yes. I suppose you're right. But I can't shake the feeling that something might happen to you. Or to us."

"Shh. All is well." He continued rubbing her softly, her body becoming pliant in his arms. "Why are you so worried? Is it Izzy?"

"Yes. And no. I'm also worried for you." Her tiny hand fisted in his shirt. "If anything should happen to you, I don't know how I could bear it."

"Shhh. Nothing will part us."

A wave of fierce need for possession swept over him. He tilted her head up, a finger beneath her chin, and pressed his lips to hers. Firm at first, she softened beneath him, opening her mouth and letting him in. He tasted her leisurely, as if a savage storm didn't blow outside the door and an impending battle didn't await them. A battle that could indeed take his life. He was a great warrior, but there was a good chance he marched to his own personal doom. He wouldn't be content until he'd severed King Dominik's head himself. He was smart enough to know one-on-one combat with the butcher king might end his life.

She moaned into his mouth. He cupped the nape of her neck, then sucked her full bottom lip, letting it slide out slowly. He licked along the seam to one side then back. Wanting to taste more of her skin, he swept up her jaw to the sensitive spot beneath her ear.

"Is that better?" he asked.

She clutched a hand in his hair. "That depends what you mean by better."

Smiling against the creamy silk of her neck, he trailed his tongue down to the hollow between her collarbones. Her nails dug into his scalp.

"Are you warmer?

"Oh, yes," she breathed huskily. "But now I'm also aroused."

He returned to her lips, his hand sliding to her unbound breast, loving the softness of it beneath the wool fabric. He mounded gently, sweeping his thumb over the tip, knowing she could feel the slight abrasion beneath the layer.

"Mikhail." She slid her nose up the side of his. "Please tell me you're going to do something about that."

"What do you want me to do, my queen?"

"I want you to spread me out onto this bed, climb on top, and bury yourself inside me."

He stilled, watching her closely. Her sea-glass eyes were engulfed by her dilated pupils. Her boldness choked off his voice with lust. He thought his cock was hard before. Now it was a steel rod. No way was he leaving this room without doing just what she wanted. What he wanted.

"Very well then."

He slipped her sleeve down over her shoulder till the breast he'd been teasing was exposed, the dusky-pink nipple puckered for him.

"As my queen commands."

He cupped her chin with one hand, pressing his index finger to her lips. "Open your mouth."

She did, so he slid his finger inside, stroking slowly in and out. Once. Twice. Then he pulled away and used the same finger to circle and wet her nipple. The pink of her areola tightened further. She watched him circling, then pinching softly with forefinger and thumb. The sight of her watching made him painfully hard.

Lifting his hand to her mouth, he stroked two fingers back inside, her gaze fixed on his. He slid his hand up under her skirt, where she opened her legs for him. Rubbing his fingers along her hot, slippery cleft.

"God, woman. So wet for me already."

"Always," she replied breathily, eyes falling to half mast as he stroked those two fingers inside her tight heat, his thumb circling on her swollen bud.

He leaned down and took her nipple in his mouth, teasing with his tongue. And teeth. She gasped. Her arousal scented the air. In a swift movement, he had her on her back and was pulling the dress over her head. She helped him, shimmying to release her body from the garment.

He unclipped his cloak and tossed it aside. She was already at the laces of his trousers. And hell, it was all he could do to pull the lacing free without ripping them. His cock sprang straight up against his abdomen, thick and ready.

She gasped again and lay back, clutching his shoulders to bring him with her. He wasted no time spreading her wider with his body, slicking the head of his cock along her cleft as he held his weight on one forearm. Her eyes slipped closed.

"Tell me what you want, Mina mine."

She smiled. "Your beautiful, big cock inside me."

He gave it to her with one hard thrust. Her tight heat squeezed around him. "So good," he whispered. "You feel so good."

"Ah!" She arched her neck and rocked her pelvis up.

"Do you want it hard or gentle?"

Her eyes opened, her vampire staring back at him. "Hard."

"That's what I thought." He shifted, both forearms on either side of her head. "Wrap your ankles around my back."

She did, tilting her pelvis up at the perfect angle. He

pulled out to the tip, then thrust back in, burying himself so deep in this position. Her mouth fell open in ecstasy. He lowered and whispered against her lips. "Did I hit your sweet spot?"

"Yes."

He did it again, and again, building a steady rhythm, making sure to hit home hard. Her whimpers of pleasure and the tightening of her thighs around him as she tilted up farther drove him near mad. His need for her had become a desperate, frightening thing, demanding relief.

But there was no end. Even when he came inside her body, it wouldn't be enough. It was never enough. The fear of wanting her beyond reason made him drive harder, thrust faster, his cock swelling as she lifted her head to his ear and said, "Yes, Mikhail. Make me your woman. I am yours and yours alone."

Without even thinking, he pulled out and flipped her body onto her stomach, her sun-yellow hair spilling across the bearskin. So beautiful. His beast wanted that beauty. Wanted her for his own, to cling her tight like a dragon with his treasure.

He gripped her hips, spreading her thighs with his and gazed down at her swollen, glistening pinkness. With a guttural groan, he pushed inside her. She curled her fingers into the dark fur, her pearl-white body spread and opened. For *him*.

He stared down, watching his thick cock tunnel into her soft, wet sex. "Mine," he groaned. Clenching his fingers into the fleshy part of her hips, he pistoned faster, slapping his flesh to hers with a satisfying sound. His primitive beast liked it. Loved it. Wanted it. Wanted her.

"Mina." He pounded. "Mine." Again. "Forever." He ground inside her in a circle at the end.

"*Yes*." She wailed on a long moan, her orgasm rippling

around his still-stiff rod. He continued grinding hard against her ass while the vibrating waves milked him. "Yes," she whispered, her panting breath blowing strands of blond that had fallen in front of her face.

Before she'd come fully down, he fell forward, still clothed except for his trousers halfway down his thighs, pressing close to her body, his mouth at her ear. In a slower tempo, he pulled all the way out and pumped in, over and over. He nibbled her ear then her neck as she panted and whispered "yes" with each thrust of his pelvis.

He may have awoken her in the tower, but she'd awoken his heart. And he was strong enough of a man to own what this truly was. He brushed his mouth close to her ear again, still pumping inside her.

"I love you," he whispered, the truth of his words swelling his heart and raking his insides with the need for her to feel the same.

She reached out and clutched her hands atop his, which were pressed into the bearskin fur. She tilted her bottom up higher and turned her head to him. "Kiss me. For I love you, too."

He melded his mouth to hers. Her tongue flicked inside so sweetly and tenderly. He came on a feral groan, but she didn't let him break the kiss. She sucked his tongue inside her mouth as he emptied his seed inside her body.

And it was heaven. As if the stars had aligned and blessed them both for recognizing love when they saw it. And giving it voice the moment of its birth.

He pulled out of her body and rolled her over to press a smiling kiss to her lips. "I love you, Vilhelmina Dragomir."

She laced her slender arms around his neck, a tear slipping from one eye even as she smiled. "I love you, Mikhail Romanov."

"Is it that bad that you must cry?" he teased.

"It's that good."

He shook his head, feeling almost dizzy. "I thought love was supposed to be painful and heartbreaking."

She laughed, the sound reaching straight inside him, winding him ever closer.

"Now wherever did you hear a thing like that?" she asked.

He shrugged a shoulder. "I don't know. Isn't that what they say in all the books?"

"What books have you been reading? Tragedies?"

"I only read books on military strategy and weaponry."

"Of course, you do."

She combed her fingers through his hair. He wanted her to do that forever. Well, perhaps not forever. He'd like to tup her as often as possible in between her soft caresses.

"Well, let me explain something to you, Captain. There are many books that portray love as the pinnacle of happiness. As the zenith of the heart's delight."

He swept his mouth softly against her kiss-swollen lips. "And is your heart at its zenith, my love?"

Her expression sobered as she cupped his face. "Yes. It absolutely is." She pressed a soft kiss to his lips. "But I'll be happier when this war is over."

"Bloody hell." He pushed up off of the bed and tucked himself back into his pants, retying his laces as quickly as possible.

"What is it?"

He laughed. "What is it?" He picked up his heavy cloak and hooked the clasp, lifting the hood. Then picked up his gloves and slid one on. "One look from you and I forgot the whole world outside this tent."

She smiled, so beautiful with her fair skin flushed pink from his kisses and caresses. He leaned over the bed, fisting his hand gently in her unbound hair with the ungloved hand, then kissed her. A light peck. Those half-lidded eyes, slits of the purest blue stared back with satisfaction. And he'd put that look there. He puffed with pride, wanting to tumble her back down to the bed.

"Heaven above, woman. I believe you've ensnared my very soul."

She turned her head and placed a kiss inside his palm. Her sweetness would ruin him, soften his tough exterior as the formidable leader of the Bloodguard. He smiled at the fact that he didn't give a fucking damn.

"Don't worry, Captain." She helped him put on the second glove, making sure it was snug and tight. "I'll take good care of your soul." She peered up, a vulnerable expression making her appear childlike. "Will you take good care of my heart that you've stolen?"

He curled his gloved hand around her delicate fingers, pressing her palm to his lips. "The greatest care." His throat was thick with emotion. "I'll treasure it forever. And I'll never break it."

"Is that a promise?"

"Upon my life."

Then she smiled. And all was right with the world.

"Now you need to get some sleep. We'll leave at the break of dawn. I want you well-rested because we've got a long ride ahead."

"We're going straight to Izeling, aren't we?"

He lifted her toward the head of the cot so she could tuck under the bearskin fur. He needed to know she was safe and warm before he went out on patrol.

"Yes. How'd you know?"

"I listen to you men more than you think. I've heard you talk of the king's fortress where he keeps his rabid vampire army in Izeling."

He tucked her in and brushed his hand over her golden hair. "You'll be a mighty queen, Mina."

"With you at my side," she whispered. Hesitantly. Questioningly.

"Yes, love." He smiled and pressed a kiss to the crown of her head. "With me at your side."

She sighed heavily as if a weight had fallen. He hadn't even realized he'd put it there. How much he'd meant to her. But now he did. And she meant more to him than life itself.

He marched for the entrance and turned back one last time to find the most beautiful creature on Earth smiling at him.

"I'll wake you in the morning."

She arched a brow. Her smile turned wicked. "I look forward to it."

With a laugh, he left her.

He nodded to the two vampire guards on duty at the entrance, sensing six sets of heartbeats nearby, surrounding the back of the tent.

"No one leaves their post till I send your replacements."

"Yes, Captain." They snapped in unison.

Feeling assured, he marched toward the southern perimeter to start his rounds. It would be a long night in the storm.

Chapter Twenty-Five

After Mikhail left, Mina couldn't fall asleep. Not after what had just transpired between them. She threw off the pelt, which was indeed quite warm, then used some water from her canteen and a cloth to clean herself. She set to redressing completely, all the way down to her knee-high boots and belt with her dagger.

Something stirred in the stormy winds outside. She curled up near the low-burning fire, wondering at her life now. She was queen of her kingdom. Her home. And she loved the man who loved her. She wanted to dream of a life at Briar Rose with Mikhail, but the war still loomed.

The burning embers glowed deep orange and burnished gold. She blew out a breath and watched them spark, shimmering in a wave of mystical light. Almost as if there were answers to be found there. She peered closer, the heat radiating not on her skin but through it, reaching straight through flesh and bone into her chest, pulsing, awakening some secret she should know.

What did this mean?

She'd felt it before at certain times in her life. Especially when she walked the path of Silvane Forest. Like an otherworld whisper. She was close to the answer, to discovering the secret. One that held mighty power. Reaching out her palm to the heat, she tried to divine whatever mystery was glittering supernaturally in the fiery embers, somehow sending a line directly to her rapidly pounding heart.

"I don't understand," she whispered.

Remembering Lord Petrov's tale of her birth celebration, of the white witch, of the hartstone, she knew it was connected to this supernatural stupor. Then the embers sparked wildly, crackling, sending up an eerie green flame that licked into the air in a straight line, snaking sinuously back and forth. A warning.

The tent flap crinkled, snapping her out of her trance. Just within the entry stood Gavril, his eyes cast to the ground. She stood slowly, sensing his unease.

"Gavril?"

His gaze shot to hers. She gasped. There was always a halo of emotional pain surrounding the quiet assassin Gavril. Mikhail had told her of some haunted past he still hurt from. But now, in his storm-blue eyes swirled a tempest of crippling physical pain. The knuckles in his fists were bone white.

"*Gavril.*" She rushed toward him. "Tell me. What has happened?"

Blood splotched his neck and soaked his dark shirt beneath his cloak, the pungent tang filling her nostrils.

"You're hurt."

She reached out to help him but stopped with her arms aloft. His head tilted to one side then the other in an unnerving movement, like a snake raising his head from the long grass, his eyes never leaving her.

She took a step back, realizing too late her danger. He was on her, twisting her body so her back was pressed to him, his hand clamped hard over her mouth, pinning her head to his chest. When he spoke in her ear, it was the voice of a man drowning in pain. It filled her so completely, tears pricked at her eyes as if it were bleeding into her own body. Her empathic senses quivering under such torturous pain.

"I'm s-sorry...my queen."

Then he moved in a blur out into the cold, where the snowy gale howled in violence. She saw nothing as they flashed through the darkness, away from the camp. She couldn't make out anything at this speed and in this storm, which seemed to breathe menace and violence, a pestilent air on the wind. Her hair, tangled by the gale, covered her eyes as Gavril held her in an iron-clad grip, speeding toward some unknown evil.

And yet, she knew what it was, who it was, before they even finally stopped on an outcropping of a cliff. Gavril halted so quickly she fell to her knees in the snow. He did the same but apparently of his own volition, as if in utter defeat, his chest heaving in great painful gulps of air.

They were in the foothills of the Novak Mountains, the northernmost point of Arkadia. Not far from the Glass Tower.

"Why have you brought me here?" she asked Gavril, whose shoulders slumped and head bowed.

Shadows materialized into men moving toward her on the snow-swept cliff. The largest of the figures sent her pulse racing in a maddening frenzy. He wore the pewter armor for battle, the red crest and black dragon emblazoned on the chest plate.

"No," she gasped, looking up as he stopped before her.

"Yes." King Dominik grinned in that feral way that had always given her shivers when he stalked her with those hungry eyes at royal assemblies. It wasn't unknown to her that he'd watched her, tracked her like prey, even when she was betrothed to his brother. This man, this monster, obeyed no boundaries.

She was paralyzed, frozen from cold and fear, as he reached out and cupped her cheek roughly.

"Finally." Even as the storm whipped around them, his black cloak billowing, he spoke in a low, commanding voice. "I like you on your knees, Vilhelmina. I'll put you there often when we're married."

She jerked out of his grasp and glared at him as she rose to her feet, unsheathing her dagger beneath her cloak. She didn't reach his shoulders, but she could aim well enough under his chin the way Mikhail had taught her, the way she'd killed that Legionnaire in the cottage in Silvane Forest.

"I will never marry you." Disgust seeped from her every pore as she thrust up lightning-fast, his large hand clamping her wrist just as she nicked the underside of his chin.

He squeezed her wrist till she was forced to drop the dagger. His slash of a mouth broke into a cruel smile, canines thick and sharp. She flinched. His giant hand fisted in her hair at the back of her head as he pressed himself close. One of her hands flattened on his armor, cold and unyielding. The other grasped at his wrist, his ruthless hold stinging her scalp. She couldn't look away from his eyes—those that had seen untold horrors done by his own hands. And would see more, she was sure of it.

He lowered his mouth almost to hers, his thunder-deep voice rumbling against her lips. "You'll do whatever I want you to do, Princess." He raised his brow in mocking surprise. "I mean, Queen Vilhelmina."

Despite the sliver of dread and prickles of icy menace pouring through her veins, she glared back at him. "You have no idea what's coming for you."

Her dark prince.

He chuckled and pulled her head sharply to the right, finally dropping her wrist to clap his other beefy hand on her bottom.

"You have no idea what's coming for *you*."

"Ah!" She cried out at the stab of pain when he pulled hard at her scalp.

"You think I'm afraid of your little toy soldiers?" His mouth was at her ear. His tongue licked a slow line down her throat and back up. "You're going to be my willing slave, Vilhelmina. Begging me on your knees nightly." He scraped his sharp fangs down to her pulse.

"No!"

She struggled, powerless against a vampire as strong as him.

"Yes. Fight me, little dove. That feels so good."

His rumbling laugh sent a spike of anger through her. She hauled back her hand and slapped him across his right cheek. Hard.

His expression darkened, hardened, shifted to more beast than man, his vampire eyes glowing like a burning comet.

"I think my bride needs to learn a lesson on who her master is."

He opened his mouth wide and sank his fangs deep into her flesh, between shoulder and neck. She let out a choking scream, the pain so intense, sudden, violent. His elixir pumped hot and hard into her veins, flooding her, crippling her with his malevolent dominance and sinister control. Both her hands on his armored chest curled inward till she gouged her nails into her own palms.

He moaned as he suckled deep, his hand on her bottom squeezing and crushing their bodies together in some parody of a lover's embrace. A tear finally slipped off her cheek, flaking to ice before it was swept away by the glacial wind.

"Please," she whispered, the pain of his bite and elixir sending her to the brink of consciousness.

Groaning, he pulled his fangs from her flesh and licked the spot thoroughly. His touch making her stomach churn with acid.

"It seems my little dove has been at play," he murmured in her ear, biting her earlobe till it must be bleeding. She gasped. He didn't lick her wound this time to allow it to heal.

Rearing back to his full height, he glared at her accusingly.

"You smell of another man." Crushing his lips to hers in a mockery of a kiss, he stroked his tongue in so deep, she gagged. Then he yanked back, nicking her bottom lip with a fang. Again, leaving the wound open. A drop of blood pearled on her lip. "But not for long."

He let go of her so fast, she stumbled but didn't fall.

"You are mine now, Vilhelmina. You will do as I command you to do."

"No, I—"

Like a serrated knife gouging down her spine, the pain bowed her back in agony. She screamed.

"Just say, 'Yes, master,' and it will go away."

"Y-yes, master," she whispered barely above the wind.

A roll of pleasure washed over the pain as if it hadn't happened. His elixir was frighteningly powerful.

"Louder, little dove."

He lifted her chin, forcing her to look at him. The fear of pain ripped a quiet answer from her mouth.

"Yes...master." She may have said the words, but defiance burned brightly in her chest.

He grinned, for he knew it. "I'm going to enjoy making you say that over and over again."

"Your Majesty! We should be leaving. Trackers will not be too far behind."

"Yes, Kostya," he said over his shoulder.

Without warning, he leaned down, gripped her hips, lifted her, and tossed her over his shoulder, keeping a firm hold across the back of her thighs.

"Your Majesty, what do we do with him?"

Upside down, she glanced toward the Legionnaires on either side of Gavril, who still kneeled in silence in the snow. His head cast down. Unmoving.

"Toss him over the cliff. If the fall doesn't kill him. His blood brothers will."

"No!" Mina screamed as they dragged a nonresistant Gavril to the edge and threw him into the cold darkness.

"Don't worry your pretty head," said King Dominik, gripping her thigh tightly. "I'm sure it was a painless death. Aye, men?"

"Aye," replied the chorus of a dozen soldiers.

"Let's get home." He laughed, and his Legionnaires with him, as they flashed into the night, speeding away from Arkadia. Away from Mikhail.

Closing her eyes, she sent a prayer to the stars above, smudged out by the gray tempest, pleading for the answer she'd sought a short while ago in those flames to burn back to life inside her. There was a way out of this, a way of escape, a way to victory. But she couldn't see it. Only feel it. She begged the fates to show her how, to guide her hand. And her heart.

"Please," she whispered. The wind snatched the word and swallowed it like a ravenous monster.

Still, she held onto hope. No matter that the devil himself held her captive in his hands. No matter that she knew his intentions were foul and twisted. No matter that the queen had even more diabolical plans for her. It was hope that flew on the wind next to her, like a gale-swept lark, tattered but fighting to stay alive. Never giving up and staying with her till the end, even when its wings were frayed and torn.

Mina closed her eyes and cradled that hope within her chest, not allowing fear to destroy her now. Her prayer took on new form as she whispered so softly that only she could hear the mantra that gave her strength.

"Mikhail…Mikhail."

Chapter Twenty-Six

Mikhail shouldered into the wind. It had picked up speed as he'd made his way along the southern perimeter of camp to the western edge, where he'd spent some time chatting with each guardsmen and even longer speaking to Gregory about provisions some of the men had picked up before leaving Arkadia. All was quiet, except for the howling wind. Nothing out of the ordinary at all.

He headed up the incline, where a hill protected their encampment from the harshest winds. Katya stood like a solid tree planted in the ground on the ridge. She spun at his approach, dagger drawn.

"Hold, sister. I'm not the enemy."

Her eyes were all that were visible, her head hooded and face shielded by a kerchief like his. She rolled her eyes at him. "Dammit, Mikhail." She dropped the captain title when they were alone. "This wind is playing tricks on me. Messing with my senses."

"Aye." He frowned, crossing his arms over his chest and standing in the wind to block her as best he could. "Mine, too."

She crossed her arms in a similar fashion. "I know what you're doing. I don't need you to shield me from a little snowstorm, Brother."

He scoffed. "Katya. You're the toughest, meanest, hardest woman I know. You've proven it, aye?" He nudged her with his elbow. "But you're still my baby sister."

Her indigo eyes crinkled with her unseen smile. "All right then. I'll allow it." She sighed. "To keep my big brother from feeling insignificant." Her eyes narrowed mischievously. "Though I believe someone else has convinced him of his significance."

He stiffened. "What do you mean by that?"

Another roll of those eyes. "Please, Mikhail. The whole camp knows you and the queen are smitten with each other."

"Smitten? I'm the Captain of the Bloodguard. I do not get smitten."

She laughed. "Liar."

He smiled beneath his kerchief and shrugged. "So I am."

Katya sobered. "You'd be right to marry a queen, Brother. It would be fitting. Don't you think?"

He glanced down, unwilling to travel down that path again. He made a promise to Mina, and he would keep it. He'd never leave her. Never. But he wasn't sure how he'd fit in her world exactly. Time would tell. Rather than answer his sister's question, he noticed her gloved hands trembling as she gripped her crossed arms. "You've been out here long enough. Why don't you get some sleep? I'll take your place."

"Are you sure? I can remain on duty longer."

He chuckled. She'd always been stubborn beyond reason. Even as a small girl, she'd face off with the biggest bully in the schoolyard. He didn't stand a chance in convincing her to stay home with their mother after their father died and he set off to form the Bloodguard. She swore she'd just follow if he and Dmitri left her behind. So she'd become the one and only female of their band.

"Go. But before you do, go 'round to the eastern perimeter and tell Gavril to break now and tell his replacement to relieve him. I didn't make it to him."

She nodded and flashed away.

Mikhail faced into the wind, away from the encampment. He conjured images to keep him warm. Alabaster skin. Ardent sighs. Soul-stealing promises. Sea-blue eyes.

He smiled, a curl of contentment warming him from the inside out. This wasn't the plan. She wasn't the plan. So far from it that he chuckled at his own lack of foresight. The man who strategized every maneuver, rethinking every possible outcome before he took steps. She'd stepped directly in front of him. In his mind, she'd been the means toward their victory. An instrument to destroy the old monarchy and bring in a new one. A just one. He'd never calculated the possibility that the princess he awoke with a blood kiss would ensnare him so completely.

A distant thrumming sounded on the wind. Coming from the northeast. He stared into the darkness, knowing there was an open plain in that direction, though the snowstorm blocked him from seeing far, even with his vampire sight. The repetitive thrumming morphed into the recognizable thud of hooves. He drew his sword, double-fisted the hilt, and stared into the gloom, awaiting whatever threat drew nearer.

He inhaled deeply, unable to smell anything but ice and snow. The riders materialized, four of them, just off to the left. He lowered his sword as the distinctive red cloak of the female rider, and their familiar scents washed over him. He raised a hand in the air to get their attention.

Nikolai saw him first, jerking his mount toward Mikhail. The other three following, galloping right up to him. Nikolai leaped from his mount and shot to Sienna, lifting her from the saddle before she'd had a chance to dismount. Sienna pulled down the white scarf she'd wrapped around her face, her breaths puffing out white clouds.

"Nikolai. Sienna. What's wrong?"

Sienna's expression appeared desperate.

"Captain, we must see Mina right away."

"Tell me what this is about."

His gaze shifted to the other two riders. One was Dane Godric, the hart wolf, who rode in his human form, his amber-gold eyes shining like burning suns in the dark. The other man, hooded but without any shield over his face, which revealed the hard countenance of a dangerous vampire, a patch over one eye, a vicious scar trailing from beneath.

Nikolai noticed Mikhail's discerning observation of the men. "This is my cousin Riker, back from Cutters Cove." The vampire with the patch nodded.

Mikhail remembered the tale Nikolai told of his cousin who'd been tortured at the Glass Tower for information on himself, Sienna, and the Black Lily. The man had been battered and gouged with blades of gold to be sure the scars would remain. Apparently, they had.

Nikolai nodded to their other companion. "And Dane came along as well. We rode hard to get Sienna here as quickly as we could."

"Please." Sienna stepped forward, a wisp of her red-auburn hair caught on the wind, an urgent plea in her eyes. "I must see her."

"What's happened?" Foreboding dripped in the air like a black pestilence.

"Can we get inside, Captain?" Nikolai glanced around. Even as he spoke, the wind died down from the constant roar it had been for hours.

Before Mikhail could turn and lead them away, Sienna gripped his forearm with a gloved hand. "Two nights ago,

I had a dream. A premonition." She glanced sideways at Nikolai.

Nikolai stepped closer. "The hartstone is speaking to her again."

"Go on," Mikhail urged.

"I dreamed of a great hall in a beautiful castle. The white dragon sigil of Arkadia hung behind the throne dais, where a king sat near the cradle of his babe. Queen Morgrid was there, demanding the babe be given to her youngest son in marriage when she was of age."

Mikhail frowned. "This isn't a dream. This is the true story of Mina's birth." Why would they come all this way to tell him a tale they already knew?

"Yes," said Sienna, still clutching his arm. "But listen. Queen Morgrid cursed the babe and left. Then the white witch came and gave her blessing."

He nodded. He knew all this. What was going on?

"Do you know what the white witch decreed?"

"Yes. She will become queen and save them all. I don't understand why this is so urgent." Mikhail's agitation prickled along his skin.

"*No*," said Sienna, shaking her head. "She said, 'You will drink fire into your soul and awaken the beast of vengeance and righteousness.' This is what will bring about the victory."

Mikhail glanced at Nikolai then back to Sienna, at a complete loss why this was important.

"Hear me, Mikhail." Sienna pressed close, gripping him with both hands, a desperate urgency vibrating in her voice. Her green eyes glittered with sparks of gold. "*I* am the fire Mina must drink. The fire magic that races in my blood. I saw it. In the vision, I lifted the babe in my arms from the bassinet, then she transformed to herself as Mina is now. We were holding hands then she drank from my throat."

Mikhail couldn't help but wonder if this was all some

effect of living within the Silvane Forest too long. So strange. And surreal.

Sienna seemed to see his doubt. She edged closer, intimately so, and cupped his face in her hands.

"This is no figment of my imagination, Captain." Her palms heated against his skin, sending a tremble of energy into his mind. He saw the vision unfold.

Mina drinks from Sienna's throat. A blast of white light. A field of dead soldiers dressed in black-and-red livery. Dominik's army. And finally the tall green banner bearing the Arkadian sigil, the white dragon, whipping in the breeze in victory.

When he snapped from the vision, stepping out of her grasp, his heart pounded like a battle drum.

"This is urgent, Captain. I can't sleep. Can't eat. The magic has been pushing me hard since I awoke with the vision."

"Come," said Mikhail.

The other two dismounted, leading the horses by their bridles down the hill into the encampment.

Katya appeared at the bottom of the hill, wide-eyed and breathless. Not from fatigue. From fear.

"Mikhail!" She rushed to him.

"What is it?" He gripped her shoulders.

"Gavril is gone. He's not at his post and there's—there's blood in the snow."

A sudden blast of dread ripped through his body. The timing of this storm with the coronation and the intense darkness that swept over the land with it. The erratic wind hindering his vampiric senses. The constant nudges to his psyche that something wasn't quite right.

Black magic.

He snapped his head in the direction of Mina's tent. "*No.*"

Without a word, he left them, flashing through the

encampment lightning-fast. The two guards at the door were crumpled on the ground, legs contorted unnaturally. Sweeping past, knowing what he'd find, he sped into the tent, finding exactly what he'd feared he would. Nothing. No one.

Combing his fingers against his scalp, he circled the room like a caged beast, looking for something. There on the rough-shod rug covering the ground, a single spot of crimson. Kneeling, he dabbed his finger to it and sniffed deep.

It was Gavril. He'd shed enough blood with the man over the years to know his scent. So he hadn't been killed on watch, then dragged off and shoved in a ravine so that the king's men could bypass him into camp. Of course not. *The king.*

"Fucking hell!" he roared.

He spun back outside and crossed paths with Sienna and her party with Katya. He didn't stop when Katya called out, flashing back to his tent. By the time he'd tossed off his cloak and thrown open the chest of weapons, arming himself with razor-sharp, double-edged blades in every sheath and scabbard he could carry, filling the dozens of slits along his crisscrossing harness with finger blades, Dmitri was at his side in a rush of violent wind.

"How did it happen?"

Shouts echoed across the encampment as word spread.

He didn't recognize his own voice, the malevolent timbre growling out of his throat like a cornered animal. "Dominik, the fucking butcher king, bit Gavril and injected his elixir into his body, then commanded he abduct Mina."

It was the perfect plan. They'd scent a stranger among the encampment, but no one would stop Gavril, one of his Elite, from going into the queen's tent.

He'd seen what the king's power of persuasion could do even after the elixir had worn off. He and Friedrich had interrogated one of his bitten minions back at Winter Hill. The rogue vampire fell unconscious and died after disobeying a command of the king's by giving them information. Gavril had been freshly bitten. He hadn't stood a chance.

"What are you going to do?"

Mikhail cut a glare at him. "What do you think I'm going to fucking do? Get her back."

He unbuckled his belt and slipped on two more scabbards in addition to the one already there. He'd have serrated daggers to rip sinew and bone on both hips and one at his back.

"You're not going alone." Dmitri stood in his path before he could make it back to the weapons chest. "You'll be killed."

Nikolai entered with Sienna, Dane, and Riker behind. Then Katya.

"Do you think my life matters more than hers, Brother?"

Ice poured from every word. He'd lost his ability to reason like the captain he was. Only one driving force moved his feet and pumped blood to his heart at this moment. *Mina.*

"I'm just saying we need a plan. If you'd stop long enough to think, we could form one."

"We're going with you," said Nikolai.

Friedrich entered with Grant.

"Is it true?" asked Friedrich.

Seeing Friedrich was the only thing that made him pause. His wife had been under the power of that cruel bastard. Brenna had felt the cold icy fingers of his dominance in her veins, pulling her strings like a puppet. She'd felt his violent will when he slit her throat with his own claw right before Friedrich's eyes, powerless to stop him.

"Yes." He glanced away, unable to see the horror in his eyes any longer. What Brenna had experienced might very well be Mina's fate, under the thrall of that evil bastard.

A gaping hole opened up inside of him. A chasm filling with the darkest kind of dread. The king wouldn't kill her. He knew that. They needed her alive to fulfill Queen Morgrid's plan to perform the black magic rite to blight the world in darkness. However, fulfilling that plan would also require the king to impregnate Mina so Morgrid could sacrifice the newborn pure-blood Varis at the hour of its birth. The thought made his vision blur, spots in his peripheral vision.

King Dominik may not kill her, but he was the one man in this world who could do so much worse. Mikhail had heard the horrors of his brutality.

Black thoughts flooded his frame, thinking of Mina in the control of such a monster. He shook it off, unwilling to allow his mind to spin out of control. Guilt of his own negligence threatened to make him insane. While he should've sensed that this storm was wrong in a supernatural way, he'd been too distracted by his emotions and need for Mina. The very reason he'd called for the Bloodguard vow to forsake love or marriage had been why he'd failed her. Why she was now in the ruthless hands of the butcher king.

Focus. Stay sharp. Cool thoughts. Deft hands.

He lifted the double-bladed sword, custom-crafted and forged by a friend in Korinth. The hilt at the center, made of black oak from Silvane Forest, was smoothed and honed to perfectly fit his fist. The black-iron blades—razor-sharp on one side, serrated on the other, curving in opposite directions—extended three feet from point to point. The edges of both blades sparkled with gold. Gripping hard, he bent his wrist, cutting the wind on one side then the other. Perfectly balanced. The supreme weapon for decapitating one's victims. And he had only one victim in mind at the moment.

"Mikhail!"

His eyes snapped up, everyone staring at him. He'd been in his own trance.

"Did you hear me?" Dmitri stood close, fear and frustration on his face.

"Aye, Dmitri." Though he hadn't heard a word. "Fetch Gregoravich quickly. And alert my Elite."

Dmitri disappeared out the tent flap, a gust of glacial wind blowing in. Mikhail's Elite were his most highly skilled assassins. He slid a sheath onto one blade of the sword and a second on the other blade, then buckled it to the harness crossing his chest. Lifting his cloak, he hooked it at the neck and swept the room with an assessing gaze.

"Nikolai, your party is welcome to follow, but I'm not slowing down for anything." He glanced at Sienna. "Or anyone."

Nikolai nodded. "We'll keep up."

Dane stepped forward, the mountainous hart wolf in human form sparking the dimly lit tent with his amber-gold eyes. "I'll carry Sienna." He shivered as if the need to shift was on him now. "We'll be close behind."

Nikolai nodded agreement. Mikhail had heard Sienna complain often enough of the nausea she experienced traveling at vampire speed in Nikolai's arms. Riding on Dane's back while he's a hart wolf would be infinitely faster than on horseback, but not at the dizzying pace of vampire speed.

Dmitri reentered with Gregoravich behind him, standing next to Dane, almost as tall with the same beefy build.

"Gregory, I'll need you in lead for tracking."

He was a memory reader, born with the vampire gift where he could recapture memories of people by touching places they'd been.

"Yes, Captain," answered Gregory, scowling.

There was no time to discuss Gavril and his forced betrayal or where he was now, but the tension rolling off Gregoravich, who was a close friend, told him enough. The man wanted answers as much as he did.

"Dmitri, I need you to report to Prince Marius and

Arabelle what has happened. Assemble the army and get them moving toward Izeling. You're the fastest, so don't argue with me."

Dmitri closed his mouth, since he apparently was about to do just that.

"Are you sure that's where he'll have taken her?" asked Nikolai. "The Glass Tower is not far. He may have gone there."

"Doubtful," interjected Friedrich. "They've been amassing their army at his Dragon's Eye. He'll have returned to Izeling, where his forces are largest. My uncle is arrogant, but he's also smart enough to know that the army set up in Silvane Forest could overrun the forces at the Glass Tower, even at our diminished state."

"Katya, you'll follow us with the Bloodguard. Send word to Lord Rathbone."

"Yes, Captain." She spoke like the perfect soldier, but her eyes shone with distress.

Anxiety riding him, Mikhail swept toward the door, stopping in front of Friedrich. "Your Grace, I'll be parting ways with you here."

Mikhail had worked as the duke's personal bodyguard for months since Friedrich had released his Legionnaires of their duties, knowing there were spies for King Dominik within their ranks. Mikhail had continued to serve when they left Winter Hill, escorting and protecting Friedrich, Brennalyn, and their children in Silvane Forest. Now was the time he needed to sever that formal arrangement. He was moving of his own accord from here on out with one and only one objective.

Save Mina.

"Of course, Captain. We'll follow Dmitri to Silvane Forest." He clapped a hand to Mikhail's upper arm in farewell, a look of fierce determination written in the duke's eyes. "I'll see you in Izeling."

He swept from the tent out into the cold, where the winds had died away, a shimmer of moonlight peeking from behind wisps of cloud. His Elite stood in a single, silent line outside the tent, armed and ready, black hoods up shadowing their eyes, though he felt their keen watchfulness. Their sharp alertness. No movement but their cloaks billowing around their legs. All of these men were at the blood rite ceremony in Silvane where they dedicated their allegiance to Mina. Electric energy sizzled in the air, rippling between them. A vibration only an otherworld creature could feel, beckoning like a call from the hartstone herself. Or from hell.

A growl rumbled from the depths of his gut, the need for blood and crushing bones singing through his limbs, the beast within yearning for wrath and death.

"The butcher king used our guardsman, our blood brother Gavril, to betray us." The timbre rumbled more growl than words. "And he took…our *queen*." The eyes of his Elite glowed with blue fire and fury beneath their hoods. "Now let's go fucking kill him and bring her back."

Chapter Twenty-Seven

Dominik slung Mina on the bed, *his* bed, a behemoth piece of furniture with tree-trunk-thick posts and laden with red silk curtains. His bedchamber was dark and opulent, dripping with black satin, red brocade, and crystal chandeliers. Even so, gray morning light peeked through the heavy folds of draperies. They'd traveled at vampire speed without resting at all. The trip to Izeling Tower should've taken longer, but Dominik was far stronger and faster than she'd realized.

He towered above her, hands on both hips, the firelight casting his silhouette in shadow. She could see nothing but his flaring eyes and gleaming smile, canines still sharp. She shivered. They'd hurt puncturing into her neck. Not like Mikhail, who eased into her slowly. Dominik bit with brutal force, seeming to enjoy her pain.

"Where's the little girl, Izzy, you kidnapped?"

"Get cleaned up, little dove. Mother requests your presence."

"Tell me what you've done with her."

"Get cleaned up, and I'll show you," he said with a grin,

watching and waiting.

Three maids hurried into the room, carrying buckets of steaming water into the connecting chamber, keeping their heads bowed. She heard the rush of water as it poured into the tub.

Her eyes darted back to him. She lifted her chin. "I'm not bathing in front of you."

He laughed, the hard sound twisting her insides into a nest of snakes. "No?" He bent over, bracketing his hands on either side of her hips, his massive frame threatening. "You'll do whatever I want you to do."

Her breathing accelerated, fearing whatever command he was about to give her. Because she knew she would obey, even as she screamed on the inside. She'd heard of people dying from defying Dominik's commands while under the thrall of his elixir. She had to survive.

His gaze roamed down her neck to her heaving chest then back up, locking his malevolent eyes to hers. "If I tell you to lean back and spread your legs, you'll do it."

She shook her head, tears pricking.

He only smiled wider. "If I tell you to get on your knees and suck my cock, you'll do that, too."

She squeezed her eyes shut, trying to even out her breathing, trying to keep the welling panic at bay.

"Open your eyes, little dove."

They popped open without her even thinking it, her body already obeying his will.

"No, Your Majesty," she said with a plea in her eyes, using his title as some way to appeal to his ego. "I am the Queen of Arkadia. You can't—"

His hand clamped under her jaw, arresting her speech.

"Yes. I heard about your ascension to the throne. Did you think it would help you and your traitorous friends who are allied to the Black Lily?"

She could say nothing with his giant paw holding her jaw in place. His fingers loosened, and he slid his hand down her throat, his fingers nearly encapsulating it.

"Who did you spread your legs for, Vilhelmina?" Malice laced his voice now, sending a tremble of dread through her frame.

"Mikhail Romanov, Captain of the Bloodguard."

His countenance darkened to a murderous glare. "The one who took you from Briar Rose?"

"Yes."

"And killed my fucking men," he growled, fingers tightening.

"Yes," she rasped, feeling some kind of triumph in telling him who he was and what he'd done.

"You'd best forget him. You'll be my queen soon enough." He grinned, voice dropping even deeper. "You'll be *my* woman after tonight." He roughly let her go and stood, bellowing to the three maids standing at the entrance. "Scrub her good." He started for the door, boots clomping on the slate floor. "And get the stink of that bloody vampire off her."

・・・

Though the snowstorm had cleared, it had muddled the trail. Mikhail paused as the craggy silhouette of the Novak foothills rose up in the night. He halted their party with a hand in the air, having caught a whiff on the wind. Not of Mina, but of another familiar scent.

"Captain!" yelled Yuri, off to the right, kneeling in the shadow of a cliff face.

Speeding to his side, his gut clenched at the sight. Gavril on his back, one leg folded backward, a pool of blood seeped into the snow beneath his head. The near-full moon shining through vaporous clouds illuminated his deathly pallor. Yuri had a finger to his pulse, listening.

"It's faint, Captain. But he's alive." Desperation rang in his voice, for he and Gavril had also been close friends. "Gavril, can you hear me?"

Mikhail reined in the thoughts of Gavril stealing Mina away from him and handing her over to Dominik. Not to mention wounding his blood brothers. Dmitri had assured him none of the guardsmen at her tent were killed. Their necks and legs had been broken so that they couldn't heal quickly enough to set off a warning in the camp.

Gavril's eyes opened to narrow slits, pain etched in his brow when he looked beyond Yuri to Mikhail standing at his side. "God, no." His voice was little more than a weak rasp. He closed his eyes. "Leave me."

Mikhail knelt and gripped his shoulder. "Listen to me, Gavril. You did not betray your brothers. Or the queen." He squeezed his shoulder harder. Gavril opened his eyes, despair swimming there. "Or me, my brother. You had no choice. You could've killed your blood brothers, for I imagine Dominik ordered you to silence anyone in the way. Correct?"

Gavril didn't move or speak, his hopeless gaze unmoving from Mikhail.

"You're going to survive. Then make amends and fight alongside your brothers again."

A faint nod, then he pointed up. "Bring Gregory...up there." His voice cracked, barely a whisper.

Mikhail glanced over his shoulder. "Soren!"

The broad-shouldered vampire snapped to his side. "Yes, Captain."

"I need you to carry Gavril back to Katya. She'll be sure he's tended to."

"Yes, Captain."

He helped Yuri gingerly lift the battered man to Soren's shoulder, then they flashed away.

"Gregory!"

"Over here," he bellowed from off to the left.

Mikhail and Yuri joined him where he was already climbing, having found a particularly jagged facing.

Gregoravich glanced down. "I can smell traces of the queen."

Mikhail leaped up, climbing fast. "Gavril said to go up." He gripped each notch in the mountain and launched himself up, clamoring to the top first.

He gasped, inhaling deeply of that sweet jasmine and sunshine scent. Something half covered in the whirling snow caught his eye. Kneeling, he lifted the dagger he'd given her and smelled the drop of blood at its tip. Not her blood. But certainly not a death wound by the mere drop left here.

Gregoravich was at his side, puffing out a great lungful of air.

"Damn, Captain. You were up that cliff like a cat."

Yuri followed.

"Here, Gregory. Touch here." He pointed to the snow where the dagger had lain, sliding the dagger into his belt.

Gregory did so without hesitation, bowing his head as he read the memory upon this ground. His shoulders tightened and heartbeat accelerated. Mikhail's own pulse kept pace, fearing the worst. When Gregory lifted his head, his eyes were sparking with blue flame, wild with otherworld energy vibrating through him.

"Tell me," commanded Mikhail. "Everything."

"It is definitely King Dominik." Gregoravich stood, and Mikhail with him. "He...he bit the queen and injected her with his elixir. She is under his thrall."

A fierce growl erupted from Mikhail's gut and up his throat.

"They definitely took her to Izeling." His expression grew sharper under the moonlight. "And they tossed Gavril over the cliff. Assuming we would kill him if he survived the fall."

Mikhail suffered a pang of remorse for thinking ill of Gavril even for a second. "The king doesn't know us."

They stepped away toward the edge. Mikhail gripped Gregoravich by the forearm, asking low, "Did he hurt her?"

The pitiable look on his face told him enough, tightening every muscle in Mikhail's body.

"He was not gentle with her, Captain," he finally said quietly.

Mikhail vibrated with restrained violence, his voice low and lethal. "Yuri."

"Yes, Captain."

"Lead the way. We need to find a way into that tower."

A surge of fresh fire burned through his body, igniting his need for vengeance. To bludgeon. Claw. Maim. Until nothing was left of the infamous butcher king. It was time to wipe his kind from this world. Not just for the people of Varis, but for Mina. He would regret ever touching her.

Before Mikhail cleaved his skull in two, he'd make sure the bastard understood just that.

Chapter Twenty-Eight

Moving robotically down the long crimson-carpeted hall and escorted by four militant Legionnaires, she focused on breathing, on calming herself. She'd been dressed in a red-velvet gown that dipped too low for her liking. Though she was unsure where it had come from, King Dominik possessed a large blood harem. One of his concubines was apparently her size.

She pretended the revealing garment didn't unsettle her, even as fresh lust emanated from the Legionnaires marching her toward her destination. Especially the blond to her right whose eyes kept straying to her breasts.

She ignored him, glancing instead at the floor-to-ceiling paintings as they marched on. She'd never been to Izeling. And though she'd heard of King Dominik's grotesque taste, she didn't understand until now. Each painting depicted one more horrific scene than the next. An angelic woman in white clutching a tree in a storm. Her gown had slipped past her breasts and was drenched from the pouring rain while a godlike vampire laughed from the clifftop. His canines were sharp and ready.

Another painting depicted a nude woman racing bareback on a black horse across a snowy plain, a look of stricken fear upon her pretty face as she looked over her shoulder at whatever was chasing her. A third showed a feast of men laughing and clinking ale goblets, hovering around some unseen spectacle at their center. All that could be seen through a break of men was the painfully flexed arch of a pale, slender foot in the air. Terror and menace. That's what this entire castle reeked of.

She swallowed the bile rising and kept her eyes forward. Soon enough, she heard low voices ahead. Dominik's rumbling timbre she recognized as he said, "—how you did it, but it worked."

Then the definite, melodious, and yet chilling voice of Queen Morgrid. "Easy feat, my son. For one adept at the dark arts as I am."

The soldiers marched Mina up to the open double doors of a large parlor, ornamented in the same reds and blacks that covered the entire castle like a morbid, repetitive nightmare.

"Here she is, Mother. My blushing bride."

Mina cringed and stepped inside, stopping before the gray wolf fur rug, her eyes on the queen not Dominik. She glanced for a second time at the wolf fur, for it was quite large. She sickened at the thought that it must be a hart wolf.

"Hello, Vilhelmina," said the queen, draped across a red-velvet chaise, a glass of blood held aloft. The queen was the embodiment of beauty and evil in the flesh. Very similar to her son, the larger, masculine version of herself stretched out in a massive brown-leather armchair. The queen shifted her legs on the chaise, her silvery gown glittering like scales under the candlelight, her black hair coiled in tiny braids atop her head and gleaming like snakes.

Her man, Radomir, the hard-looking, square-shouldered

one who never left her side, stood at ease next to the mantel, his gray eyes watching Mina, his hands clutching the shoulders of little Izzy in front of him.

"Izzy!" She started to run, but the two soldiers grabbed her arms on either side and kept her still.

Izzy's wide blue eyes blinked furiously, her chin quivering, but she said not a word. The nightgown she'd been kidnapped in was smudged with dirt, her white slippers soiled as well. They hadn't even given her a change of clothes.

Mina reined in her rage for Radomir, who'd imprisoned her in the tower at Briar Rose right after he'd murdered her dearest friend. Now, it burned brighter than ever at the wickedly gleeful expression he wore, holding a child prisoner as if he enjoyed it.

"Why have you taken her?"

Mina was easily controlled by Dominik's elixir. They didn't need the child to force her obedience. There was another sinister reason, she was sure. A strange tingling, almost a tickling of her empathic senses. It was the secret that kept itself hidden from her, wanting to spill out.

Dominik stood and strode toward her with ominous steps. His ice-blue gaze lingered on her before flicking to the blond holding her right arm. "She looks good in that dress, doesn't she, soldier?"

The Legionnaire stiffened, realizing his mistake too late.

With a lethal swipe of his claws, Dominik opened the soldier's throat, his tight grip on Mina's arm knocking her sideways. The other soldier caught her before she fell; the warm spray of blood splattered her face and chest. She watched in shock as Dominik put a boot on his chest, reaching down to grip his head, "No one looks at what is mine."

The soldier only gurgled in response before Dominik twisted with his powerful hands, the snapping of bone and sinew as he wrenched and tore the soldier's head free with a final grunt. Bile rose up Mina's throat as she turned to Izzy.

"Close your eyes, Izzy," she commanded. The girl obeyed at once, squeezing them tight.

Dominik stood, wiping his hands on his pants legs, "Dispose of this mess," he commanded the other Legionnaires, who quickly obeyed him. He then took his place, sinking back into his leather chair.

The queen didn't bat an eye or seem surprised at this display of murderous violence for something so small as a lustful glance. Mina was truly in the hands of monsters.

Morgrid sipped her glass of blood, ignoring the men dragging the bloody corpse from the room, her gaze on Mina. "Oh. I almost forgot." She stood, setting her glass on a scalloped, black-lacquered table, and glided forward. "I believe I owe you a curtsy," she said, mockingly. She dipped her knees but not her head or her eyes, her lips tipped in a slash of mockery. "Your Majesty."

Rather than cower or wither under the queen's ire, she remembered who she was. And who she'd become since she'd come awake at Briar Rose. "I am the rightful heir of the Arkadian throne, Your Majesty. I hardly see how it is a surprise that I should claim it."

Morgrid studied her, fingering a string of black pearls at her throat. "I will admit it was quite a shock. Not that you claimed what was rightfully yours but that it was *you* who did so, my dear." She examined Mina, presumably expecting a break in her composure at the insult. When Mina didn't even flinch, she went on. "It matters not anyway. You'll take my son as your husband."

"No. I will not—"

"Yes, you will," Dominik said.

A lightning rod of pain bowed her spine. She crumbled to her knees with a sharp gasp.

"Pwinthess," Izzy cried on a tiny sob.

Mina shook her head at her.

"Say yes," he commanded.

"Yes," she grated through clenched teeth, the pain subsiding at once. Catching her breath, she finally looked up at the queen with burning anger thrumming through her body. The queen quirked a brow.

"Well, well. It seems someone has grown more defiant since her bloodless sleep, rather than more obedient, my son."

"Yes. She has," he noted from his lounging posture, a predator at rest but still watching its prey with interest, picking all the places he wanted to gouge his teeth and claws.

"You'll have to tame her, darling," the wicked queen crooned. "If you're going to get a child in her."

Acid churned in Mina's belly at the thought.

"Unless she has one in her belly already," he said with menace.

The queen hissed. "What?"

"She's lain with another man."

"Who?"

"The Captain of the Bloodguard that Friedrich hired to replace his Legionnaires."

"Stand up," commanded the queen.

Mina didn't try to refuse, especially when Dominik stood and circled behind her. The queen moved close and pressed her palm hard against her abdomen, closing her eyes in concentration. She smiled, a triumphant smile creasing her eerily beautiful face. Dominik was at her back. The heat of him too near, but she didn't dare try to inch away.

"Good." Morgrid glanced to her son over Mina's shoulder. "Nothing to worry about. She's not with child." The queen exhaled a ragged breath as if she'd actually been scared for a moment. "All is well, though she nearly ruined it. We would've kidnapped the whelp there for nothing."

"What are you talking about? Tell me why you've taken

her!"

The queen's icy eyes glowed white hot, then she cocked back a hand a slapped Mina so hard she stumbled. Dominik grabbed her by her upper arms from behind, straightening her.

"That's for giving yourself to someone other than your husband. A royal should know better."

Izzy whimpered and cried behind them. The queen glanced over her shoulder. "That little girl is going to ensure my success."

"How?"

"Didn't that schoolteacher ever want to know who she belonged to back in Korinth?" The queen shrugged. "I guess not. The wench took in whatever peasant fell on her doorstep. It took me entirely too long to find Stephanus's bastard he beget with his favorite mistress."

"What?" Confused, Mina's heartbeat pounded faster with new dread. "Why do you need your son's child to ensure your success?"

The queen leaned forward, narrowing her eyes to serpentine slits. "Varis blood is potent, my dear. The perfect sacrifice to get a child in that belly of yours."

"No!" The horror of what she spoke turned her blood to ice.

Mina could take the stranglehold of their horror and disdain no longer, rage making her voice tremble. "No matter *what* you do, whatever black magic you use, I will *never* be yours to rule."

Dominik laughed at her back, still clutching her arms. The queen smiled.

"Don't worry your pretty little head, my dear. We need you alive." She turned and lifted her glass of blood. "For now. Your husband can decide what to do you with you after your first child is born."

Mina's stomach churned with acid. "The one you plan to murder in a blood rite the hour he's born."

She froze, her cutting gaze knifing through Mina like the sharpest blade. "How did you know?" Morgrid's scowl darkened. "Do you have the sight?"

Dominik shook her from behind. "Answer the queen."

"I do not," Mina replied just as the edge of an icy sting pricked at the base of her spine. "But a friend of mine does."

Morgrid sipped from her goblet, casting a look past Mina to Dominik behind her. "It's that Red Witch in Silvane Forest, no doubt." The queen laughed. "Yet again, it matters not. You'll do your part and give me what I want, even if we have to chain you to the bed for the rest of your life."

"Not a bad idea." Dominik pulled her back against him, the hard press of his body against her bottom and back a frightening presence. "But there will be no need. She'll know her master soon enough."

"See that she does."

"And what about King Grindal?" asked Mina. "What does he think about your plans to spread sanguine furorem and cast the world in an eternal black magic veil?"

Mina had known King Grindal to be a cold, calculating vampire, but he was the one who'd always enforced the laws so that humans wouldn't want to revolt. Though it had happened anyway once the queen started spreading her blood-maddening disease, which flowed in her own blood.

"He doesn't think of anything…anymore."

"You killed your own king?" Mina didn't understand why she was so shocked. Morgrid was maniacal beyond imagining.

Morgrid turned away. "Put her in her room till tonight, my son." She sashayed toward Radomir, whose worshipful yet cold gaze was fixed on his queen. "And, Dominik?"

He tugged Mina by one arm toward the door.

"Yes, Mother?"

"No bedding her till after the midnight ceremony. The child we need must be legitimate from conception."

He said nothing. Mina didn't dare look at him.

With a hand resting upon Radomir's chest, the queen looked over her shoulder, still holding her glass of blood. "Son, I only need the firstborn. Then you can beget as many as you like on her."

"Of course, Mother."

Mina locked on Izzy's gaze and mouthed, *Be brave. It will be all right.* Izzy nodded, her springy curls limp on her shoulders, but she swallowed hard and lifted her chin as Radomir pushed her toward another exit from the parlor.

Dominik marched Mina back out, not bothering to slow his strides for her. Though she was tall, she wasn't nearly as tall as him. He didn't speak to her the entire walk back to the bedchamber, a place of dread. Turning into his bedchamber, he strode through the door, opening and slamming it closed.

Without warning, he pushed her back to the door, opened his mouth with fangs sharp and thick. Her fight instinct took over in a flash, her vampire claws extending as she swiped at his face. When she reached for his eyes, he jerked up just in time. She raked his cheek and gouged hard.

A fierce growl rumbled from his chest.

"Fucking bitch," he snarled. Hauling back, he backhanded her to the floor, the sharp pain radiating across her face so hard her vision blurred.

Rolling to her back, she saw him coming, reaching for her. She kicked hard, barely missing his groin, hearing the satisfying whoosh of air leave his lungs as her foot landed in his gut. Then his body crushed her to the floor. Clawing out again, she drew blood at his throat, wincing at the bitter tang of his scent in the air.

He manacled her wrists and pressed them above her

head, his other hand at her throat.

"Settle down," he growled, bearing his teeth like a wolf to its prey. "I could kill you so easily."

His fingers squeezed till she couldn't breathe, and she saw her own death in his eyes. He wanted to kill her. And would have.

Then his clutch loosened. She sucked in air in gasping breaths. His gaze shifted from raging fury to dark lust. His great paw roamed to her breast, where it squeezed hard. Even corseted, it was more sensation than she cared to feel from him.

"I hate waiting."

Self-preservation took root, keeping her wits about her. "Queen Morgrid said you must. You can't go against her."

He chuckled, squeezing her breast to a painful point. "Like you care what the queen wants."

He lifted up, hauling her by the wrists from the floor, then swiftly flung her facedown onto a midnight-black counterpane. Before she could push up, he was on her again, pressing her into the mattress, his erect shaft at the cleft of her bottom. Pinning her wrists again to the mattress with one hand, he gripped a fistful of hair and yanked her head, arching her neck back.

She screamed, unable to keep from crying out in pain though she refused to beg him to stop this time. That didn't work with Dominik.

He ground his pelvis into her bottom with a rumbling growl at her ear. "I can wait till tonight." He licked along the crook where her neck met shoulder. "But I'll give you something to remember me by."

His fangs sank deep, spearing pain into her shoulder. She wept silently, furious at her helplessness, at this malicious, sad, horrific twist of fate. He groaned and sucked her blood, injecting more elixir into her bloodstream. The wave of violent power flooding her veins and rippling through her frame wasn't a shock this time. It hurt, nevertheless.

When he extricated his canines, he was breathing heavily. He didn't lick the wound to help it heal. Her body could self-heal if she'd fed recently, which she hadn't. He remained with his heavy body pressing her into the mattress, almost suffocating her.

When she started gasping for air, he eased up a fraction. Suddenly, he jerked her off the bed and planted her in a silver-brocade chair facing the bed.

"You will not leave this chair, do you understand?"

She nodded.

"You will sit here in this chair all day and night. You won't sleep. You'll think about me and watch me and listen to me fucking and drinking from my concubines until it's time for our wedding rites." He bit her again, higher on the neck.

She cried out as he punctured but didn't suckle, giving her the pain of his bite for no other reason to show her he could. For his own sadistic pleasure.

"Then I'm going to teach you about pain. And who your master is."

He wrenched her hair till she felt some of it pull loose, her scalp stinging till her eyes pricked with tears. Her head arched back, though she could see his dark gaze looking down over her.

"Say *yes, master.*"

"Yes, master." She didn't hesitate.

He didn't loosen his hold as he bent low and suckled her bottom lip gently into his mouth, as if he were a true lover.

"Mmm." He licked her lips, but she didn't move. "Don't look so scared, little dove. You'll be begging me for more by the time I'm done with you."

He released her and was out the door in a flash. Mina lifted her legs and curled into a ball, the tears flowing hot and steady now. Ignoring the pain of her body, she coiled around that hope still cradled to her chest. A hope that felt small and crushed and barely breathing. But it was there all the same. Just like the tiniest of whispers telling her to hold on, for Izzy, for herself, for Mikhail.

So she did.

Chapter Twenty-Nine

The afternoon crowd at Boar's Head was a raucous one. The place looked as if it had seen its fair share of brawls that had ended in bloodshed. The bartender was built like a bull, his nose broken one too many times. The tabletops were nicked and stained from years of use, the chairs and stools mismatched and well-worn. Yuri had said this was the place where no one would care who they were or why they were there. He seemed to be right. Their serving wench had asked for their order without casting them a second glance. Except for Riker, whose fierce disposition radiated danger even more than the gruesome scar running beyond his patched eye.

It had been a while since Mikhail had been in a pub in a city the size of Izeling. Korinth was equally as large. A good place for strangers to get lost. Perfect for his group, tucked in the back-corner booth.

Mikhail guzzled the rest of his ale, still watching the door for signs of Yuri. He'd clenched his jaw so tight for so long, his teeth ached. His need to get to Mina made him want to crawl right out of his skin and barrel toward Izeling Tower, despite his head telling him to be smart and calculated. The king would have his tower well-guarded, so Mikhail was forced to sit here and glower at every man who laughed at a joke with comrades when he was dying a slow, torturous death inside.

Gregoravich sat next to him with Nikolai and Sienna across from him and Riker in the chair at the end of the booth. Dane had decided to remain in the woods behind Izeling Tower. Even in human form, his wolf scent would set off any Legionnaires they came across in the city. The rest of the Elite scattered and milled in pairs either in the pub or on the street. Though Izeling was the kind of place where people didn't bother foreigners, they certainly might take note of a large group of lethal-looking vampires and inform the king at the tower sitting above the city.

"So how in the world did you get a guardsman who was born and raised in Izeling?" asked Nikolai, his blond hair falling forward and concealing his wary look around the room. Sienna leaned her head on his shoulder.

A serving wench bumped the next table over, where four rough-looking working men enjoyed their pints. The hardest of the bunch clapped a hand to her hip and pulled her in his lap with a bawdy remark.

"Git off, Dirk!" she slapped him but laughed when she jostled off him.

"Yuri had...family troubles with the crown. So he headed east, where he heard of a guard independent of the throne. He's a resourceful man, so he found us."

Gregoravich huffed. "Every one of the Bloodguard has had *troubles* with the crown."

"Not just the Bloodguard. Every one of us at this table," said Riker. A rare moment, since he hardly spoke at all. His troubles had done more than scar his body and give him a noticeable limp. They'd done serious damage to his psyche. But that's exactly what had happened to them all.

"Aye," agreed Mikhail. "It's about time to even the scales."

Sienna sat up. "As long as we have a well-conceived plan. The wild emotions humming off you men at this table are unsettling me more than I already am. And they're bound to make you all do stupid things if you're not careful."

Nikolai quirked a smile at her.

"Don't even give me that look. You're the worst. No one is to go off half cocked."

"I'll be fully cocked when I do," Nikolai whispered under his breath.

"*Hush.*" She jabbed him with her elbow, then swept her green gaze from one to the next. "We all know the depths to which the queen and her son will go to win. We must tread carefully." She compressed her lips together in thought for a moment. "That being said…I need to get into that castle as soon as possible."

"Bloody hell, woman." Nikolai shed his cavalier demeanor. "The plan was to get Mina out and bring her to you. Not the other way around. You want me just to toss my woman into the devil's den?"

She turned to him, intimately close. "Nikolai. You don't understand. I must get to her as soon as possible. I can't explain it." She glanced at them all. "I can't tell any of you how I know. Only that it's *dire*. I can't wait." Her voice shook with brittle tension. "It must be soon."

Her eyes flashed gold, then simmered to their cool shade of green again. Mikhail exchanged a glance with Gregory. Mikhail had expected another protest from Nikolai, who held her hand in her lap.

"If you go, then I go."

"We'll all go," said Mikhail. "Whoever is willing. The rest can wait for the army."

Gregory slung back his tankard of ale and pounded it on

the table. "Captain, you're a dumb son of a bitch sometimes."

"What?" Mikhail was taken aback.

The big man smiled wide. "Who the fuck here is not going to be willing to go into hell with you if you ask?" Then he remembered Sienna. "Pardon, my lady."

"No need." She smiled.

Riker, ever somber, nodded to the door. "I believe it's time to go to hell, gentlemen."

Yuri stepped inside long enough to capture Mikhail's eye and gesture toward the street.

"So it is." Mikhail's pulse pounded faster.

Soon, Mina.

The streets teemed with people shuffling here and there on a late afternoon. What little sun was left was covered by wintry clouds. No snow in the air, but the biting wind of the north was ever constant. Mikhail followed Yuri up ahead, who turned down an alley off to the left behind a street vendor with a cart, his scraggly son yelling, "Meat pies! Hot 'n' fresh!"

Not for the first time, Mikhail wondered why no one batted an eye at so many vampires who weren't the king's Legionnaires wandering these streets of a human tenement neighborhood. Then again, he'd forgotten about the many rogue vampires who roamed Korinth, dealing with all manner of men in the underground black markets.

Yuri strode not far in front of them, finally ducking into…a brothel? A run-down one at that. As Mikhail crossed the threshold, he caught the small, square placard hammered into the wall beside the doorframe—black with a red crown. The universal sign that they serviced vampires looking for blood as well as flesh. A slip of a young woman in her corset and an underskirt led a man up a narrow staircase. Yuri had stepped into a dark parlor on the right.

"Oh," came the soft voice of Sienna as she entered behind

him. Likely, she'd never been in a place like this before.

The parlor was finer than the appearance of the exterior of the building and the entry. Though the frayed furniture was draped in vibrantly colored satin and gossamer fabrics to disguise its age, the decor was more tasteful than one might expect. Leaning against a sideboard was a curvy prostitute with jet-black hair and an ample bosom on display.

"Vietka," called Yuri to the woman.

She turned, her hand still on her hip, measuring the party filing into her small parlor. Though her mouth was soft, her eyes were flinty hard.

Yuri gestured to him. "Vietka, this is the man I spoke of. My captain." Yuri had kept their specific identity hidden as he'd requested. Though he trusted Yuri to find the right kind of allies for this mission, Mikhail knew everyone could be bought by the crown.

"Pleasure," said Mikhail with a polite bow.

Riker clicked the door closed as the last one into the room.

There was no need to go through introductions. It was understood that the least amount of information that was traded the better. Anonymity was sacred among those who dwelled in the underworld of these cities. But it didn't keep the woman from casting a measuring glance to each and every one of them, stalling longer on Riker. Of their party, he appeared to be the most dangerous. Little did she know that behind Mikhail's cool exterior, he was meticulously rehearsing the many ways he'd carve King Dominik into pieces once he was within distance. His beast crouched low, watching and waiting, savoring the moment when he could flay the man alive for daring to take his woman. That was the only thing that kept him calm and composed.

"Interesting crew you bring in here, Yuri. Seems you've been up to all manner of mysteries since you left Izeling."

Her voice was a sensual caress, practiced for her trade. Or perhaps it was the trade that matched her voice.

"Yes, Vietka," said Yuri, grinning with pride. "I have."

Vietka's velvety gaze landed on Mikhail. "Yuri tells me you need a way into the castle. Unannounced."

"That is correct."

"There's no way to get you all in." She swept the room again with dark eyes, tilting her head as she glanced at Sienna. "She wants in?"

"Yes," said Sienna. "It's most important that I go."

Nikolai tensed at her side. "And me with her."

Vietka's brow rose. "What in the hell is goin' on, Yuri?" Then she snapped a hand in the air. "Never you mind. Don't want to know."

"What's your plan?" Yuri asked.

She poured herself a tumbler of amber liquor and took a lazy swallow. "The change o' the guard is at midnight. That's when I regularly send me girls to relieve the men as they come off duty. They'll open the south gate to let them in." She glanced at Gregoravich and Riker, then swiveled back to Mikhail. "Seems you men are equipped to handle the few guards at the south gate. They'll be tired, with nothin' but blood and sex on the brain." She knocked back the rest of the liquor. "I do expect to be paid handsomely for such a risk."

"What's your price?" asked Mikhail.

Her brow pinched pensively, her lips tightening into a line, seeming to consider as she took in their quality of clothes and weapons. "One hundred sovereigns. And you do exactly as I say. Otherwise the deal is off. I won't risk me girls or me own life for any amount of money." She glanced at Yuri. "Or whatever 'noble cause' you be chasin' these days, Yuri."

Mikhail withdrew a satchel of sovereigns and tossed them on the sideboard next to her decanter of liquor. The jingling of coin caught her attention.

"There's five hundred sovereigns. You get a handful of us in the door with no questions asked. We'll do the rest."

Her dark eyes widened as she lifted the satchel, opened the drawstring, and peeked inside. She looked up from beneath dark lashes. Her tilted smile showed Mikhail how she'd seduced many a man.

"Well, then. I'd say we have a bargain."

Chapter Thirty

Once more, Mina was being escorted by guards down the long corridor. Dominik had awoken from his blood and sex-coated bed two hours earlier and released her from being confined in the chair where she'd watched the horror of her future husband's conquests.

The memory of what she'd been forced to watch all night flickered anew. Three of his concubines writhing in his bed, all of them roped and bound in different postures. He favored the blonde, who was fair, her hair braided in a long rope. He bound her hands and ankles with her bottom straight up in the air so he could beat her with a black riding crop. Mina had heard of such sex games, of course, but these weren't mere tantalizing games. Dominik took each of them beyond pain to the edge of death before he was done with them.

He placed the one he bound with her bottom in the air facing Mina. "Look at my future queen, Melinda. Isn't she beautiful?" He'd whack her with the crop as she cried out, "Yes!" Then he took her from behind, and when Mina tried to look away, he wouldn't have it. "Look in my eyes, little dove." And Mina did. "Watch what I'm going to do to you tonight." Then he wrapped Melinda's braid around his wrist, gripping it near the scalp, and yanked her head back till she screamed as he pounded into her body and lashed her back with the riding crop, leaving red welts crisscrossing her porcelain skin. The woman whimpered, tears streaming down her face as she stared at Mina, humiliation and pain written on her face. The whole time, Dominik forced Mina to gaze into his eyes, grinning with unnatural delight.

"Tonight, little dove," he kept saying, reminding her over and over that this fate would soon be hers. Then he'd beat the girl with the crop again, just to hear her pain-filled cries.

The nightmare ran on for hours, till he finally tired and released her from her chair, dragging her by the wrist to an adjacent chamber, where two lady's maids awaited next to a steaming bath.

He commanded her to drink the blood they brought in a carafe, then to bathe and prepare for the midnight ceremony. She shuddered at being forced to marry him, her heart sinking at what tonight would behold. "Be sure you put her hair in one long braid," he'd said as he clenched his fist.

Mina shivered with dread, remembering the concubine he'd abused all night, pretending she was Mina. Then he'd left with little more than a gloating smirk at her as she stood there, frozen in fear at the thought of bedding him. Of becoming his slave to brutalize and humiliate.

He'd given her a dress of red lace overlaying black silk, scalloped at her neckline and dropping to a sharp vee down to her sternum in the front and to the small of her back. He'd also instructed she not wear a chemise, a corset, or underskirts. In a mockery of modesty, the lace sleeves extended to her wrists. She wanted to refuse to wear such a monstrosity, but what use was it? He'd only command her, and through pain or a beating, he'd make her submit to his will.

As the guards led her down a long corridor, unadorned with a rug to soften their steps, rather than down the grand staircase as she'd expected, her mind wandered again to Mikhail. Where was he at that very moment? Would he have been able to follow their trail in the blizzard? Her spirit darkened, remembering how they'd tossed Gavril off the cliff as if he were an animal carcass to be discarded. The cruelty of these men, of Dominik, of the queen, set her emotions aflame once more.

She glanced down every corridor and through every open door, hoping to get a glance at Izzy, praying she was still unharmed. Though fear lit in her eyes, Izzy was still unhurt. Mina had to find a way to save her after this blasphemy of a wedding ceremony.

One of the guards stopped before a door with a rounded wall. When he unlocked and open the door, revealing a winding staircase within, she realized it was one of the turrets leading to the battlements. Holding the door open, he gestured for her to go ahead. She walked up the narrow, spiral staircase, catching a whiff of the cold night air above.

So she'd be married on the battlements of Izeling Tower? So be it. A strength she'd never experienced welled up inside of her, a tingling along her skin. She could do this. If she could survive a lifetime of loneliness and neglect at Briar Rose and the pain and agony of the bloodless sleep, then she could survive King Dominik.

She stepped out onto the battlement and saw the hulking figure of the man himself. He stood on a square of red fabric—the matrimonial cloth in his royal colors—at the far end of the battlement, overlooking the northern road winding down into the city. The lights of Izeling glittered like the stars above them, the night unusually clear. Queen Morgrid stood beside Dominik in a shimmering black gown. Two dozen Legionnaires made up the square of the battlement, which happened to be the tallest.

As she walked toward them, the only sound was the sigil banner rippling in the wind. And her heart beat in her throat. She approached like the queen she was, shedding whatever fears had made her cower within a shell her whole life.

The gaunt priest in black stood on the other side of the matrimonial cloth, his back to the parapet wall, his head bowed in prayer and cowl billowing in a gentle breeze.

Yes, the night was gentle. Even the moon—full and bright—cast an air of serenity on those below. An ironic twist of fate as a war waged within her.

"Welcome, my bride." Dominik appeared tense and eager, not quite the relaxed beast that was his usual demeanor.

Morgrid appeared equally tense. "Let's get on with it." If not more so.

Something shining behind the queen caught Mina's eye. It was a swath of black silk draped over a waist-high table, oddly shaped—narrow and not especially long. Then Mina noted the cross-like extensions with iron restraint cuffs at the end, her gaze dropping to the cuffs on short chains and the pillow at the head above the cross restraints.

"*No.*" Mina shook her head in horror. "*A consummation altar?*" Savagery.

She'd read about them, used by kings long ago. Public consummation so there was no argument whether the marriage was legal. It was a barbaric ritual for the king to display his husbandly rights the moment the vows were said. To force his bride's submission in front of witnesses only exhibited his strength and power. And brutality.

Dominik laughed. The queen didn't, her piercing gaze twinkling under the moonlight.

"You will beget the infant I need *tonight.*"

Radomir appeared, dragging Izzy by the wrist. Three of the Legionnaires stepped out of line, revealing another horrific surprise, a stone altar with dark stains upon its flat surface. Radomir lay Izzy roughly on her back. She whimpered. With assistance, the Legionnaires cuffed her tiny wrists and ankles, the wind billowing her frayed nightgown at her knees.

"You can't!" she screamed. She turned to Dominik. "I'll do anything. *Anything.* Just don't hurt the girl. Please, I beg you." She looked up at him, thinking herself insane if she would find any sympathy or mercy there.

"I can." Dominik gripped her arm and jerked her next to him. "And I will."

Facing the priest, whose eyes swam with compassion, Mina couldn't find the answer to escape this nightmare, even while that whispering voice inside told her to be calm. That help was coming.

"Get on with it, priest." Dominik squeezed her arm in a viselike grip. "And make it quick."

...

Mikhail was on edge, crouching from the line of trees near the south-gate entrance while Vietka and her girls sauntered up the winding drive, cackling and carrying on like it was any other night. They had to be especially cautious with the sudden clearing of the night sky, making every movement visible from Izeling Tower. The tall brick wall that surrounded his estate was manned by guards. But their first target was the battlements. If they attacked the guards at the walls first, those on the battlements would send out the alarm. The best strategy was to get in covertly, then silence the men on the battlements.

Dane growled right behind him, his fire-gold eyes narrowed on the gate as a dozen Legionnaires loitered, obviously those who'd just come off duty, awaiting the women.

He'd shifted back into human form, but his beast simmered on the surface.

Vietka laughed raucously as if inebriated, though the woman was as sober as could be. The gate opened. Mikhail's muscles tensed, the need to invade a primal urge. Vietka's girls and Sienna meandered in, crooning and giggling to the Legionnaires.

"New girl, eh?" said one of the guards, offering his arm to Sienna.

"Bloody hell," growled Nikolai. "She'd better hurry the fuck up."

As if she'd heard Nikolai's impatience, Vietka lifted her skirt, pretending to adjust her stocking and garter. "Brontus, luv!" she called out.

Brontus was the lead guard on this shift, the one who was most experienced and the most dangerous, according to her. Vietka never serviced the men, and she typically had one of the girls bring back the weekly wages. She'd said her girls wouldn't be able to lure Brontus out the gate easily. But she could. He'd always had an eye for her.

The tall vampire sauntered out the still-open gate. Even from here, Mikhail could smell the man's lust for her driving him forward.

"You got something for me, Vietka?"

She straightened. With one hand on her hip, her breasts thrust up, she crooked a finger at Brontus. "Was thinkin' you might come keep me company tonight."

He strolled closer, body still in an alert posture. "You've never come looking for me before."

"I've never been without a good man in me bed this long."

He scoffed, stopping right in front of her. "A good man?"

"By good," she lilted sweetly, "I mean one who can keep it up long enough for a girl to get some relief. You think you're good enough for the job?"

"Aye." His hands found her hips, lust making him sloppy. "Let me get just a taste of you, then I'll take you on inside."

"Come on, then," she took his hand and dragged him toward the shadow of the trees.

His eyes were locked on her. He smelled and heard the danger too late. Before he could even draw his blade, Riker was behind him, one hand on his forehead, snapping his head back, and slicing through his jugular with the other. Vietka leaped back as Riker cut the rest of the way with a serrated blade, completely taking the sergeant's head off before he dropped it next to his crumpled headless body without a whisper of exertion.

"Now," said Mikhail, noting the gate slightly ajar as Brontus had left it.

As one, they shot in a blur through the gate and set upon the lingering guards. Vietka's women didn't make a sound, as she'd ordered them not to. No cries or screams to alert more guards as, one by one, Mikhail and his men put them down and dragged their bodies into the shadows near the castle wall. All within seconds.

Wiping his bloody blade on his pants, Mikhail turned to the group of silent, wide-eyed women. "Best get back to town, ladies."

They didn't wait, slinking out the gate and down the road where Vietka waited for them. All except Sienna, who stood silent as the grave with her red cloak and hood shrouded around her. Nikolai stood protectively behind her, scanning the area for signs of other guards.

Yuri was at Mikhail's shoulder, pointing to the right. "South battlement entrance."

They strategically planned to take down the guards on each battlement overlooking the four corners of the Izeling grounds. If all seemed well from the battlements, then no reinforcements would be alerted. They could get in, get Mina and Izzy, and get out much swifter. The longer this took, the slimmer their chances were of getting back out alive. Speed was crucial.

With Mikhail at the helm, they entered the south turret door and wound in vampire speed up to the first landing. Yuri, Gregoravich, and Dane nodded with ten other guardsmen behind them, taking the first-tier battlement. Izeling Tower had a lower and upper tier of battlements. Mikhail swept up to the highest landing and pushed out into the night. Three guards swiveled from the parapet overlook, but they were no match for the fury riding Mikhail.

Before Nikolai, Riker, or the other guardsmen could even fall out fully onto the square, Mikhail had gutted one and slit the throat of a second. He turned on the third, but Nikolai swept in behind him and cracked his neck, dropping his body soundlessly to the ground. Riker finished off the gutted guard before his moans could be heard.

An upper passage led to the next battlement. Mikhail strode on swift feet, hearing the scuffling below and someone gasping for breath as the others were making quick work of the Legionnaires. Soundlessly, they sped through the shadows, finding five Legionnaires guarding the next tower. Dane kept back near Sienna while Nikolai fought alongside Riker, sweeping wide and dispatching the Legionnaires with little to no effort at all. They met back on the next passage leading to the north battlement.

"Either these men have seen few battles or they've never been trained properly," said Nikolai, ten-inch blades in both hands.

"I'd say a little of both." Mikhail glanced behind them at the crumpled bodies they left in their wake. "Dominik has spent his time raiding human villages and taking them prisoner. It will be the vampires infected with sanguine furorem and his compulsion elixir who will be the true challenge."

"Seems he's keeping them all at Dragon's Eye," said Riker.

"He didn't expect an invasion this quickly," added Mikhail. "We just need to—"

A harrowing scream pierced the clear night, raising goose flesh on his neck.

"*Mina.*"

Without thought, he fled like a madman toward the sound, the north battlement. Spilling out onto the large square, his heart plummeted. Two Legionnaires were cuffing Mina onto her back onto some sort of table. Mina's expression—half horror, half fear—ripped him open. Dominik stood behind her, unbuckling his sword belt. In a flash, Mikhail took in the priest, the matrimonial cloth on the ground, and the queen's determined expression as she stepped toward a stone table, where little Izzy was chained. *Good God.* He'd been right. She was going to kill Izzy and use her blood with black magic. And Dominik was about to consummate his forced marriage to Mina on the battlement.

"Over my fucking dead body."

A new kind of hatred expanded in his chest. The kind that razed villages to nothing but blood and ash. The kind that overwhelmed all else within its vicinity, sucking the enemy into a gaping maw of black, black death. The kind that made him uncage his beast and push aside the man. His claws pricked, his fangs sharpened, and he knew his eyes rolled black with the beast.

Mikhail bounded across the space, unsheathing his double sword, throwing the scabbard into the air, but was tumbled to the ground mid-leap by Radomir.

Chapter Thirty-One

Mina was trapped, her hands still cuffed to the barbaric consummation altar as Dominik unlaced his trousers and edged closer. Her heart was full of fear and relief at the sight of Mikhail, storming toward Dominik like a demon come to collect his soul, but he'd been catapulted aside by Radomir. And this crazed animal was still intent on raping her right here and now.

She recognized Nikolai and some of the guardsmen who'd pledged their loyalty to her now engaged in fierce combat with the Legionnaires. And another grave warrior with an eye patch, whom she didn't recognize. More of the king's men flooded onto the battlement, having heard the fighting upon the towers. There were more men on the second tier of battlements for she could hear the cries of the wounded and the clang of steel.

A distant thudding sound vibrated from the ground through the stone castle. Queen Morgrid hissed as she swept away toward the parapet. While the Bloodguard were entangled in battle, the sound grew louder. Then a horn bellowed up into the crisp, clear night.

"Hurry, my son," commanded the queen, rushing back to the altar where Izzy was bound, her black mantle whipping behind her. "It must happen at the same time." The queen assessed the scene below. "Get to Dragon's Eye. Summon them *all*," she snapped at an officer standing at her side.

"Yes, my queen." His dark voice was a whisper on the wind as he sped away.

A fireball burst upon the queen's cloak. In a whirl of icy wind she summoned out of the air, it snuffed out. Crossing the battlement between men in fierce combat strode Sienna. She raised her hands, palms up, and flicked her wrists. Tendrils of ropelike fire snaked down and coiled on the ground, the ends of the fire whip gripped in her hands. She raised her arms and snapped the fiery ends with a loud *crack* in the air.

"*Let them go.*" An orange aura of flame enveloped her from head to toe.

She snapped a man in half who dived at her, his body sliding in two charred pieces across the pavement.

The queen backed up a step, whispering some incantation under her breath.

That whisper, that inner secret sprung to life once more, rising out of a maelstrom of emotions. The one ringing clear and true above all was righteous anger. Singing to her a dark lullaby.

The growing awareness of the magic, that whispering that had kept her company for so long, intensified. The aura of flame billowing around Sienna in a mystical shroud and the knowing look in Sienna's golden eyes told her what she couldn't understand all this time.

Drink the blood of fire.

"It's Sienna," she whispered, her heart leaping with joy, even as Dominik snapped to two guards to go after her.

Sienna's fire whips cracked in the air, wrapping around

their necks. With a hard tug, the two decapitated men fell at once. Sienna locked on Mina's gaze and smiled, the second before a burst of power threw Sienna across the battlement, knocking her head into the pillar with a crack. She fell at once, blood pooling from her auburn hair, the fire halo dimming until it evaporated into smoke.

"No!"

A cold electricity sparked in the air where the queen had closed her eyes and lifted her hands to the heavens, calling on some dark spell. Where the sky was clear before, a gathering of black clouds swirled in a maddened tempest, flashing with menacing magic.

Izzy squeezed her eyes closed, looking away from the queen, who stood over her altar, hands raised to the sky.

"Now, Dominik!" bellowed the queen over the winds.

Grief swept over Mina, watching Sienna's prostrate form bleed out while the world went to hell around her. Then Dominik was on her again, yanking up her skirts. As he gripped a handhold near her head and leaned his large body over her, his expression set with grim determination and a hint of sadistic pleasure, her grief melted away, replaced by such dark rage she could only think one thing.

Survive. And kill.

His hand gripped her upper thigh, leaning forward just enough. She lurched up and latched her fangs in deep at his pulse, sucking so hard he screamed, squeezing her thigh harder.

"Let go, bitch."

She clamped even harder, drinking him down, molten fire burning through her body like a volcano spewing lava into her veins. Burned. It burned, but she wouldn't relent, determined to take his life in any way she could.

He jerked up, screaming, but she didn't unlatch. Finally, he gripped her throat, blocking off her swallowing his blood, then finally her breathing. When she saw black in her periphery, she let go. He flew back off of her, blood dripping from his wound. Before he could set upon her the black vengeance in his gaze, Mikhail tumbled him to the stone ground.

The burning persisted as the potent blood of Dominik pumped hard. His blood blazed like liquid fire through her body, igniting a conflagration of its own.

"It wasn't Sienna," she whispered, staring up at Dominik's banner, the black dragon sigil with fire-gold eyes. "Dominik is the blood of fire."

Without a thought, she pulled on her restraints. They broke at once. She stumbled off of the altar and gripped the parapet wall. She heaved in breaths of the night air, taking in the sight below as a strange sensation swept through her body.

Far down the hill filtering through the now-open double gates and spilling into wide lines was the army of the Black Lily. Mina caught her breath. Merging with the human army on their left was Lord Rathbone leading his force of Arkadians, riding astride a great black horse, his silver armor glinting under the moonlight. Lord Maksim was at his side. The equestrians filled the fields beneath Izeling Tower by the hundreds, including the black-clad Bloodguard.

A great blast exploded a hole in the western exterior wall. Katya and Dmitri rode upon their mounts through the opening, leading the Bloodguard cavalry onto the western slope. Behind them came the armored men of the Black Lily and a solid force of hart wolves flanking Friedrich, Marius, and Arabelle. The white coat of Allora beamed under the moonlight. Her black-furred mate at her side.

Even from here, Mina could see the difference in Arabelle. Her proud stance, wearing a man's armor with her blond hair tied in a tight rope of a braid, her skin gleamed pearlescent white like that of a vampire. She'd finally done it. The revolution that this peasant girl started would end this night. Mina laughed.

The king's right hand, that vicious viper called Kostya, was down below on the snowy ground, calling out commands as lines of Legionnaires marched into place to face the onslaught preparing to charge across the open field.

And all this time, Mikhail went at Dominik full force. Mikhail bore a streak of blood across his cheek, though he appeared as strong as ever. He dove at Dominik, taking him around the chest right over the parapet. Mina gasped, leaning toward the parapet wall, finding them both back on their feet on the lower tier, where Gregoravich and Yuri fought side by side. Bloodied, but not fallen.

A roar of overlapping battle cries sounded from the field where raging vampires—no doubt infected with the blood madness—ran in a frenzy from the thick of the woods across the field toward the Black Lily army.

Morgrid cried out in rage, staring across at Mina, who'd escaped her dismal fate. The wicked queen held her hands to the sky, summoning the storm. A blistering wind swept across the battlements, filled with the crackling energy of malice and death, building stronger and stronger. A cacophony of snarls, howls, clanging metal, tearing flesh, and breaking bones echoed up to the ramparts as the mayhem of battle raged on down below. Mina glanced to Mikhail and Dominik, still locked in combat, though Mikhail's side bled profusely, gushing onto the stone floor.

"Mikhail." Then she found Izzy, still bound helplessly, still precariously close to the witch who wanted her as a blood sacrifice. "No," Mina panted, standing tall.

The whispering grew louder, overlapping voices colliding into one voice, a woman's melodious voice as she spoke clear and loud.

Awaken the white queen from her long, long slumber.

Strange words. Dominik's blood scorched like living flame through her body. A burn that didn't hurt but purged all weakness away, leaving a tower of strength and power in its wake. A purge of the girl who was afraid to hold her head too high or to acknowledge the beast that lived within. The beast that Mikhail had taught her to embrace. To love.

A sudden memory whirred through her fevered thoughts, her nurse walking her through the gardens of Briar Rose.

"You know the bones of the white dragon lay right here beneath your feet."

"No. That can't be true. That's just a fairy tale."

"Aye, sweet girl. 'Tis true. And that magic lives in your own blood, did you know?"

Mina's mind snapped back to the present, but she answered her sweet nurse over time. "Yes. It does."

She could feel it, the fire blood of Dominik melding with the magic inside her own, awakening something she knew was there all along but was too afraid to face.

The gathering storm of Morgrid's making swirled with enraged violence, blocking out the stars and the moon. Morgrid finally opened her eyes and bellowed to the night sky. "Winds of night! Heed my call! Take my blood. Make them fall."

She'd taken a blade from one of the fallen soldiers and sliced open her palm, raising it to the freezing gale, which thickened with icy crystals. The crystals crackled and grew as they rocketed down from the dark heavens. Nikolai cried out as he ran to where Sienna lay, blood pouring from her head, when a six-inch spike of ice embedded in his back, knocking him to the stone floor, immobile.

Mina backed up to the parapet, shaking her head in helpless rage as the deadly shards crashed into stone and into her friends and warriors. None of the icy spikes even touched her. They wouldn't. The queen needed her alive. But it could kill everyone she knew and loved. Panicked, she leaned over the parapet wall to see on the battlement just below a dagger-size shard impale Mikhail's wrist, forcing him to drop his sword. Dominik slung his weapon and scored Mikhail across the upper chest, just missing his neck as Mikhail leaned away. Mikhail's blood spattered the air. Two more ice daggers impaled his thighs, dropping him to the ground. Dominik grinned like the feral predator he was, edging toward his wounded prey.

Mina screamed, gripping the stone of the parapet wall, claws pricking, blood burning.

Far down below on the field, ice daggers and ice swords fell from the sky, piercing the soldiers of the Black Lily army. A rain of ice daggers fell upon Lord Rathbone, his horse squealing as it fell and rolled over the vampire who'd helped her to become queen and had joined her cause.

Another hail of ice blades fell upon Arabelle, Marius, Friedrich, and Grant, who fought back to back, the shards hitting their marks and felling Friedrich to the ground, unmoving.

Kostya pushed his army of rabid vampires forward, bellowing the call to kill them all. In a swarm of screams and blood, the vampires descended and leaped upon the Black Lily army, ripping and clawing them all to the ground. The human army fought, but few could stand up against the rage-filled monsters the queen and her son had created.

Another troop of them filed in from the gaping hole in the wall, coming up behind Lord Rathbone's army, behind her own Arkadians, slicing through throats. The vampires were on more equal grounds, but with Queen Morgrid's ice daggers felling Mina's people one by one, soon there would be no one left standing.

They were losing. And if they lost, she would be a slave to

Dominik, for a child to be born of her, ripped from her womb and sacrificed in a black rite to bring an eternity of darkness across the land.

Panic seized her as she watched in helpless horror. "No."

Then, she heard the call of the white woman inside her. *Mina.* It was the white witch of legend who spoke to her from within. *It is time. Awaken the white queen from her long, long slumber.*

Morgrid laughed behind her, a sinister chill filling the air. "What's wrong, Princess? Not what you had planned with your little army?"

Mina swiveled to face her.

Morgrid flinched at something she saw in Mina's eyes. Yet her haughty demeanor remained unchanged. "Oh, I'm sorry. I'm speaking to a queen, aren't I?"

Morgrid narrowed her menacing gaze as the ice daggers she summoned from the black sky continued to rain down upon Mina's friends. Upon her own love. Hart wolves yelped and howled on the field as they were stabbed through.

"Yes," said Mina, crawling up onto the parapet and then standing slowly as the wind threatened to tip her over. "I am a queen."

The burning fire of Dominik's blood coursed through her veins with savage fury, lighting her up with palpable energy that crackled in the air around her. Magic sizzled along her skin.

"I am the white queen of legend."

Mina's voice deepened. Darkened. A beast speaking the words. Her body pumping hot and hard, no longer with blood, but with pure powerful magic. Pouring lavalike through her body as her senses intensified, amplified well beyond a vampire. All she could think and feel and yearn for was fire. She smelled it come from her lungs as she breathed deep, smoldering to life inside her own body, the furnace buried at the core of her being.

When she spoke again to Morgrid—now stupefied in place, staring with blatant shock at Mina—her words were barely audible through the earth-deep growl resonating with peril and doom.

"And I am going to kill you."

• • •

Dominik smiled, his throat dripping blood where Mina had bit him, easing in a circle. Mikhail didn't move, his stance straight, his fist clenched on the hilt of his double sword, the gold-tipped blades winking under the moonlight.

"So you're the one who stole what was mine. Some untitled nobody who couldn't even make the Legionnaires. Had to start your own little guard."

"She was never yours." Mikhail bent his wrist, twirling the blades menacingly. "She never will be." The moonlight cut the butcher king into harsh angles and lines, but all Mikhail saw was the perfect point and angle he'd slice to remove the bastard's head. "There are many reasons I want to kill you." His words were smooth as silk, low and sonorous like a poison that slid into one's veins without one ever knowing. "The innocents you've butchered over the years. The villages you've raided and destroyed, including my own mother's. The countless number of people you've terrorized for your own pleasure. But you'll die tonight for one reason alone." He took a threatening step forward, his gaze sharp on his opponent's movements. "Because you dared to touch one hair on her head."

He scoffed, puffing up his barrel chest. "I touched a lot more than that."

Red dominated his vision. Mikhail dove onto his enemy. They met in a violent clamor of steel on steel.

Bleeding from the icy shards that had pierced his body in at least seven places, Mikhail crawled up the parapet wall to reach for Mina's dagger, sheathed in his boot. Pain lacerated his body. Dominik drew closer with certain intent to make the killing blow. Another needle-thin shard of ice hit Mikhail directly in the chest, piercing deep. The shock of the sharp pain distracted him long enough for Dominik to slice across the wrist of his one good hand. The severing of his tendons forced the dagger from his fingers, clattering to the stone.

An ice dagger had cut his other wrist, leaving him literally helpless to even hold a weapon. He bared his sharpened fangs, nevertheless, as the butcher king drew closer.

"Know this, Captain Whoever You Are, before you die." He inhaled and exhaled a great puff of white air. "I will enjoy Vilhelmina's sweet body and sweet blood day and night till she gives me an heir." He tossed Mikhail a haughty smile, swinging his sword up to lay flat against his shoulder in a too-casual manner. "Then I'll let my Legionnaires have a go at her. None of them have bedded a queen. That will be entertaining. And in all that time, you'll be rotting in a cold, dark grave."

Mikhail charged the animal and brought him to the ground, burying a knee on his throat. Dominik leveraged up and launched him off. Cries erupted on the parapet, not cries of pain and death, but of exclamation and surprise. The clanging of swords ceased. Both Mikhail and Dominik looked up to the upper parapet wall, where all eyes had swiveled.

Mina stood atop the banister, her arms outstretched, her unbound hair whipping in the glacial wind, and a haunting vibrant green aura rippling in flames around her body.

"Magic," whispered Mikhail. "The legend."

Her body rippled with power, then she roared, letting loose a sound that no human could produce. Her arms extended, stretching outward, long black claws like a bear's growing from the ends. Then her legs lengthened and widened, as did her torso and her neck.

"Heaven save us," whispered one of the Legionnaires standing nearby.

Her neck continued to stretch and stretch, her skin changing, shimmering like scales. No, not *like* scales. They were scales. Her face extended, jaws opening wide. Wider. Her long blond hair stiffening into a jagged spiky spine extending along the back of her lengthening neck until she wasn't a woman any longer at all.

"My God," he whispered as she grew taller, until the parapet wall crumbled beneath one of her mighty back claws, her body filling up the entire battlement. And the force of the promise, the vision given to her at her birth when Morgrid had cursed her launched upward in the behemoth form that towered on top of Izeling Tower and roared to the stars. A great white dragon.

She was fixed on something, someone beyond Mikhail's vision from below. Her neck coiled back like a cobra, then snapped at the unseen object. A piercing woman's scream echoed into the night as Mina, the dragon, lifted Queen Morgrid in her jaws, clamped around her torso.

"No! Guards! Help me!" screamed the queen who'd murdered and brutalized hundreds, thousands of her own people, just like her son now staring up in stupefied horror. "Nooooo!"

Mina's eyes glittered bright emerald green with a shocking spark right before she snapped her jaws closed and severed the queen in half. The black storm of ice shards evaporated in a blink, the evil mass of clouds dissolving into the ether. Ice shards falling without force from the sky.

The white dragon queen reared up her head toward the night sky and released a deafening roar. Her head then snaked around and snapped down to the parapet where Mikhail stood, her serpentine green eyes focused on Dominik.

"Oh, no, she doesn't."

The wrist where the ice dagger had cut through him had knitted together and healed enough for him to bend over and pick up his double sword. While Dominik stared up in shocked horror at the dragon queen, Mikhail grabbed a fistful of his hair and jerked back.

"I am not a nobody. Know this, before you die. I am Mikhail Romanov, great-grandson to Rodin Varis, the first king of the land before your bloodthirsty mother slayed him on his throne. And I will restore his world of peace while you lie rotting in a cold, dark grave."

Mikhail then tore through Dominik's throat with his blade in one slice, jerking his head loose of his spine and slinging it up and over the parapet wall.

Mina's dragon snorted a satisfactory huff of smoke. While Legionnaires scrambled to get away, she unfurled her white wings and flapped. The gusting wind was now caused by the storm of Vilhelmina Dragomir as she lifted off the battlement into the air, her body glittering like diamonds under the moonlight. She was horrifyingly beautiful. Mikhail smiled.

"My queen," he whispered to himself as she circled down toward the battlefield.

With a hissing intake of breath, swooping down toward the retreating vampire army, she blew out a stream of electric-green flame, incinerating the screaming vampires in a flash. Dmitri and Katya, still mounted, led the charge against the retreating enemy.

"Yah!" bellowed Dmitri, letting fall from his hand a gold-tipped grappling hook on a chain, one of the many weapons forged in Cutters Cove for this day.

The Bloodguard and Arkadian equestrians still standing launched toward their enemy and let fly their grappling hooks, winding them above their heads as their cavalry pounded down the fleeing Legionnaires. A dozen hart wolves lay in pursuit with them, careening toward the woods.

The rabid vampires with sanguine furorem, and especially those pumped with Dominik's elixir, didn't retreat but fought like the maddened beasts they were. Marius, bleeding and roaring with rage, battled three at a time. Arabelle, not far away, engaged two more with Allora swooping in to take down a vampire coming at her back.

The pounding of boots reverberated on the battlement below as Legionnaires stormed upward to defend their queen and the king of Izeling. They circled Yuri, Gregory, and Dane. Dane tossed down his weapon and with a growling howl, ripped open his shirt the second before electricity snapped in the air and a flash of light blinded them all. In his place stood a towering, fierce hart wolf. A low growl rumbling from his throat, his tail whipping. The soldiers took a step back and raised their swords.

With a satisfied grunt, Mikhail heaved his weight off the wall, gripped his double-edged sword tight and leaped the parapet wall to land directly in the center with his men and Dane. The landing jolted his leg injuries. He winced but shook it off.

"Good of you to drop in, Captain," said Gregory, grinning and wielding a battle ax with a head nearly the size of his own.

Mikhail smiled at the man's humor at a time like this. He scanned the numbers. "Looks like ten to one."

Yuri shrugged, blood dripping down his temple from a gash on his head. "We've had worse."

"Indeed, my brothers. Let's kill the bastards."

With Dane's agreeing growl, they lay into the enemy. The fight was far from over.

But above them, the roaring white dragon, the white

queen of legend, burned away the enemy of the people, of the good and righteous. Creating a new world, ending the old in green flame. The night wasn't won yet, but it assuredly would be.

He smiled, remembering the prophecy at her birth. *"And she will be the savior of them all."*

Mikhail sliced through one attacker on his left then his right, taking a quick panting breath to glance up into the sky where she soared. The strength and power of beauty and beast in one body.

"Mina mine."

Chapter Thirty-Two

Propped against a tree amid the other wounded, Mikhail watched Izeling Tower burning in green flames, the eerie aura rising high into the heavens. Mina's dragon flame had caught the castle on fire when she returned from tracking down those who'd tried to flee back to Dragon's Eye. Mikhail had already been down on the battlefield with the rest of his men when she flew over in a roaring rage, burning the north battlement.

Next to him, Brennalyn wept over the prostrate Duke of Winter Hill, with Izzy wrapped tightly in her arms, now asleep after her ordeal. Friedrich bled from numerous battle wounds, but one had made a definitive mark. Brennalyn had stayed behind in Izeling, waiting for the fighting to end. And now she lay her head to Friedrich's chest, her black hair sprawling over him as she wept and wept.

"Kitten, you'll have to stop crying like that." Friedrich pulled himself up against a tree trunk. "I've still got one good arm to hold you with." To exemplify, he tugged her close and caressed her back, the stump of his left arm now stitched and mending since he'd fed from one of Vietka's girls. Then he placed a hand atop Izzy's golden head with a smile.

Strangely enough, Vietka and her women had traipsed back to the battlefield to help those holding onto life, knowing the vampires would need blood to self-heal and the humans would need tending. The people of Izeling had swarmed out in droves to help, carting many back to the church, which had become a hospital for the wounded victors of the Battle of Dragon Fire, a name one of the locals had already dubbed it.

Brennalyn shot up off his chest, fury pinching her brow. "I want to *kill* the one who did this to you."

"No need, darling," crooned Friedrich, playing with a lock of her black hair. "Riker took care of that for me." He nodded appreciatively at the man, standing with his arms crossed and leaning against a tree.

"You're quite welcome, Your Grace."

"I want to kill him again," muttered Brennalyn, seething.

Friedrich smiled up at her. "Now, kitten. We've had enough death for one night. And look at Riker. He does quite well with only one eye. I'll do well enough with one arm." He glanced to Riker. "No offense."

"None taken."

Arabelle strode up with Marius at her side, a severe cut on her forehead already mending itself. Marius, a gash torn through his armor and shirt below the ribs, knelt beside Friedrich.

"Are you all right, cousin?"

"Good God. I'm fine. Everyone, stop fretting over me." His severe tone shifted when he looked at Brennalyn and cupped her face. "I'm alive. And that's what matters."

Arabelle blew out a heavy breath. "Quite right, Friedrich. Many lost their lives."

Marius glanced back at the burning tower, an otherworldly flame consuming the evil dwelling brick by brick. "But many more would have had it not been for Vilhelmina."

"How is Sienna?" asked Arabelle. "Someone told me—"

"She'll be fine," said Mikhail. He had bitten her right after he killed Dominik to ensure healing began at once. Her injury wasn't as bad as it had appeared at first, though she wouldn't be out of bed for a long while if Nikolai had anything to say about it.

Arabelle crossed her arms. "You know, Marius? I hated Mina for being betrothed to you when I first met her. It seems I should've befriended her from the start. We might've ended this war before it had ever begun."

"Kind of hard to befriend your kidnapping victim." Marius smirked.

Arabelle rounded on him. "She was a bloody royal vampire. My enemy."

"And now you're a bloody vampire. And a royal one as my wife."

"Has anyone seen my damned brother?" asked Friedrich.

Grant marched up at that very moment with Katya and Dmitri. "Miss me already?"

"Thank the stars." Friedrich scowled. "I hadn't seen you since that damned queen plagued us with ice-pick hail."

Grant glanced down at his brother's missing arm, a severe frown pinching his brow with anger and concern.

"Oh, for God's sake," snapped Friedrich. "Don't you start, too. I'm all right."

Grant cleared his throat, seeming to swallow his anger. "I only want to know one thing."

Friedrich rolled his eyes. "What's that? If I killed the bastard who did this?"

"No." He shook his head lightly. "How the devil all you vampires look like you've been beaten to shit and I'm rosy as a day in spring?"

Friedrich grinned. Marius laughed, then grabbed his

injured side with a wince. Grant knew what his brother needed.

Mikhail glanced at his own brother, Dmitri, who knelt beside him. "Do you need a bleeder? They're kind of on short demand at the moment."

Mikhail shook his head. "I'll be fine. Let those worse off get tended to first."

Dmitri glanced at his blood-soaked stain, scenting the extent of his injuries even though Mikhail's black attire didn't show how badly he'd been hurt. The truth was, he was weak. But he'd certainly heal.

"Oh, my dear Katya. Seems you've sustained a few injuries as well." Grant arched a devilish eyebrow at her as he sidled intimately closer. "Brennalyn says I taste awfully good. I'd be more than willing to sacrifice my blood for you."

Mikhail and Dmitri exchanged a knowing glance. She didn't enjoy the flirting kind of man.

She tilted her head and whispered softly, "If you and I were the last two on Earth, I'd fall into a bloodless sleep before I drank your blood."

He grinned wider, pulling at a loose leather strap on the harness crossing her chest. "The lady doth protest too much."

She slapped his hand, vampire swift. "I'm not a lady." She stormed past him and marched off.

"Perhaps not." Grant watched her walk away with ardent admiration shining in his expression. "But you are a very fine woman," he whispered mostly to himself.

"Mikhail!"

He swiveled to the sound of Mina's sweet voice. She'd donned someone's heavy cloak, her bare legs and arms exposed as she ran toward him, her eyes still glittering green with the residue of magic. A line of Bloodguard marched behind her, including Gregoravich and Yuri.

She knelt and crushed herself to him. "I was so scared

you didn't make it."

He buried his head in her hair, inhaling the wondrous scent of sunshine and white jasmine. The scent of joy and passion. And love.

"You're shaking." He slipped a hand beneath the cloak, gripping her waist to determine that she was indeed naked beneath. He hauled her onto his lap, snuggling her closer.

She pulled back enough to look in his eyes, her emotions bright on her face. He smiled and wrapped her nape gently, stroking a thumb along her jaw and whispered, "So the white queen wasn't exactly what we thought, was it?"

She laughed, cupping his face. "No. It was more."

Without a care for propriety, he melded his mouth to hers, slipping his tongue inside to taste his woman, to remind her she was his and he was hers. He quickly learned that not all parts of him were so injured.

"Ahem." Marius.

They broke apart and looked at their staring audience.

"Sorry to interrupt," he continued. "But we couldn't see everything that happened on the battlements. The ice storm was thick. I need to know…is my mother dead?"

Mina's expression softened to compassion. "I'm sorry, Your Highness. She is dead. I—"

He raised a hand and sighed relief, squeezing Arabelle closer with a kiss to her crown, their armor clanking together. "Thank the stars."

Mina relaxed in Mikhail's arms. "I'm afraid your father is gone, too."

He glanced toward the burning castle. "I knew that. I knew she wouldn't let him live."

Gregoravich, covered in bloody scrapes on every piece of exposed skin, leaned against a trunk. "Her damn man Radomir escaped."

"We'll find him," assured Dmitri.

Yuri nodded in agreement as they shared a silent vow to track down all who'd escaped.

"Did everyone get out of the castle? The servants?" Mina's eyes were round with dread. "The king's daughter?"

Mikhail squeezed her close, knowing she feared in her rage she'd killed innocents with her dragon fire. "The Bloodguard swept the entire castle when the flames caught on the rooftops. Everyone was taken clear of the castle."

"But we never found Lucille, the king's daughter," added Yuri.

They were all silent for a moment, wondering what might've happened to the young, frail princess. Hopefully, a servant had helped her escape like the knight who'd helped his great grandmother Tamora so long ago.

Mina turned her attention back to Marius. "You must take the throne at Glass Tower, Your Highness. With your queen, Arabelle, at your side."

Arabelle grinned, her vampire-bright hazel eyes widening. "Queen!"

Marius laughed. "Unless you plan to abandon me."

"Hell no. I'm going to be the best damn queen Varis has ever seen. Oh, except you, of course, Mina." She prattled on, her face lighting with ideas. "We'll start legislation right away, change the caste laws and property laws." Her eyes gleamed brighter. "And open charity houses for those who've lost too much. Oh, and orphanages."

"I second orphanages," said Brennalyn. "I can help you with that."

"First," interjected Friedrich. "We'll return to Winter Hill. With our children." He glanced at Mina. "And you'll return to Briar Rose. We need to put all back in order, assure the people they are protected. Then we can start on Arabelle's plans to change the whole world."

"Yes," said Mina softly, turning her gaze on Mikhail. "I'll

return to Briar Rose." She clutched a fist in his shirt, as if he planned to break his vow and not go with her.

"I heard what you said," said Nikolai, stepping up out of the shadows. "I also know it was your healing bite that helped Sienna. Only a powerful elixir could heal her so quickly."

No one realized Nikolai was there until the silence drew his gaze away from Mina and to the sober, blond-haired vampire. All other eyes rested on him as well.

"What was that?" asked Mikhail.

"I heard what you told the butcher king. Before you ripped his head off and threw it over the wall."

Silence settled among the group, all intent on Nikolai. There was import in his purposeful gaze and slow words. Mikhail waited, knowing his secret would be no more. Now was the time to own it.

Nikolai stood straighter. "You're the great-grandson of Rodin Varis. The brother and king who sat on the throne before Morgrid murdered him."

Brennalyn gasped. All eyes locked on Mikhail, except Dmitri, who stood beside him, arms crossed over his chest.

"Aye," said Mikhail. "I am he. King Rodin's wife was with child when Morgrid bit him. He didn't die right away. When Queen Tamora fled to his side to help him, he bit her in his raging bloodlust, turning her unborn child vampire. My forefathers changed their name and hid among vampirekind." He gripped Mina tighter. "But I'll hide no more. I am a Varis, and I'll take back the name that was stolen from me by that dead witch burning up on that hill."

He nodded toward Izeling, sweeping his gaze back to the shocked faces around him. All except Dmitri who grinned from ear to ear.

"Aye," agreed Nikolai, his mouth quirking on one side. "Then you are the rightful heir. Your Majesty."

Mikhail frowned at the title.

"Oh, hell!" exclaimed Arabelle. "That means the Glass Tower is yours."

Marius opened his mouth to speak, but Mikhail silenced him with a hand in the air. "I don't want the Glass Tower. I just want my name. My true name." He turned to the woman on his lap and cupped her sweet, beautiful face. "And Mina."

She smiled, the emerald green fading from her eyes, returning to the deep sea-blue that had caught him from the moment she opened her eyes in that tower at Briar Rose. Lacing her arms at his neck, she nuzzled close and whispered against his lips, "You have me. My king. You've had me from the very start." She leaned close, pressing her cheek to his, her mouth near his ear. "I dreamed my dark prince would come and save me. And you did."

He murmured against her ear. "I believe we saved each other, my love."

She embraced him tighter and he her, for there was nothing more to say. Mikhail had always followed his strategic plans—a captain's best asset—seeking the goal of triumphant victory. But in the end, he'd only needed to follow his heart. A lesson he was sure Mina would teach him over and over again. And he looked forward to every one of them.

Epilogue

"Hail! Mikhail Romanov Varis, King of Arkadia!" Lord Rathbone shouted to the dome of the Grand Forum.

The lords and ladies of Arkadia leaped to their feet, erupting in cheers and applause. This was never the goal he'd sought, but Mikhail welcomed it. He would be a strategic and cautious king next to his compassionate and wise queen.

She took his hand, led him to the center of the Forum floor, and circled with him to greet his people. As well as some visitors.

A line of the Bloodguard stood at attention on the Forum floor, clapping—his Elite and Katya. Dmitri smiled at the head of the line, now the Captain of the Bloodguard. One concession he was forced to make to his new wife. A king couldn't be running around the country chasing rogue vampires. As difficult as it was to lay that task down at his brother's feet, he did so and took up his new mantle.

Friedrich stood on the bottom tier of the amphitheater. He couldn't applaud, but he beamed with pride, the man who'd trusted him and joined him in his plan toward this better world. Holding to his hook hand was the pretty little blond Izzy and Denny and Nate beside her along with his other five children, those Mikhail had protected as if they were his own at Winter Hill. At Friedrich's side was Brennalyn, happy tears streaking her cheeks, the mound of her unborn child beginning to show. Grant grinned like a man who'd found out a secret. Perhaps he had, staring down at a king who'd always professed to be no more than a hired assassin. Mikhail nodded with a smile.

Next to the Duke and Duchess of Winter Hill and their children stood the general of the newly appointed Legionnaires of the Glass Tower, sworn to keep peace and protect the people—all people, both human and vampire—of the land of Varis. Besides his sharp new uniform and the Black Lily insignia upon his lapel, Nikolai wore his usual crooked smile, his lovely bride Sienna at his side. They'd come straight from their home, Nikolai's family estate not too far from Briar Rose. Beside them stood Dane, Allora, and Bron, emissaries of the clans of the hart wolves of Silvane Forest. Though not all of the clans had fought at the Battle of Dragon Fire, many had. Those who did showed their support for this new world built on equality, not hierarchy.

Next to Nikolai and Sienna stood Lord Petrov, whispering something to Mikhail's mother, who smiled at whatever he'd said and smiled brighter down at her son. He'd long hoped for the day when he'd avenge his father and put a smile back on his mother's face, but he never thought it would happen like this.

King Marius and Queen Arabelle applauded from the dais on the Forum floor. Mikhail noted that if Arabelle, the peasant girl raised in the oppressive shadow of the Glass Tower under Morgrid's rule, could rise to the confident queen in her white regalia, then perhaps he could rise to the occasion as well. It was in his genes, after all.

He realized that his fear never stemmed from being unable to achieve his goal of avenging his family name. It had risen from not being able to live up to it. To be the man he was supposed to be. The king he was supposed to be.

He looked down at Mina. Her golden hair unbound, the emerald-and-diamond crown of Arkadia atop her head, the silken gown of green falling in thick folds to the floor. She caught his gaze, the applause still a deafening roar.

"What are you thinking?" she asked.

Leaning toward her, he said, "I'm thinking about how quickly I can get you out of that dress. And everything else." He glanced up to her head. "Except the crown."

Her eyes widened, a pretty blush crawling up her neck. "Mikhail." She smiled and waved to the crowd.

"Yes?" His eyes remained on her.

"I don't believe a king is supposed to talk like that."

"Oh, darling. You've never known a king like me. My queen's pleasure comes before anything else."

She laughed. "It sounds to me as if you're thinking of *your* pleasure."

"Perhaps a little," he admitted, then sobered. He reached up and cupped her cheek, an unusually public gesture in front of the populace, but he didn't care. "As long as you're happy, then all is right with the world."

She met his gaze and placed her palm over his hand against her cheek. "I didn't know a person could be this happy."

"Then I'll endeavor to keep you so."

She glanced away coyly. "Well, I wouldn't mind being as happy as Brennalyn."

Mikhail glanced at her in the crowd, rounded belly and seven children at her side. Eight if one counted Nate, who was as good as hers.

"Are you telling me you want eight children?"

"Well, I'd be happy to start with just one."

"My queen. I am at your command." He swept her up into his arms and carried her down the corridor toward the exit. More applause and not a little bit of laughter followed them.

She caught her crown. "Really, Mikhail. That was a little dramatic for your first appearance as the new monarch of Arkadia."

"I'm a man of action."

"Yes, I know." She glanced down the marble steps, the people of Arkadia waving and cheering outside the line of Legionnaires, the fragrant smell of roses on the wind as they tossed petals in the air. The warm sun of a spring day beamed down on them. "We're not going to the reception? Where everyone wants to congratulate you?"

He marched down the long steps and carried her into the awaiting carriage, pulling her into his lap and drawing the curtains. "I don't want anyone's attention but yours, Mina mine." He started on her lacings at the back. "Now, let's get started making a baby."

She fell into a fit of laughter, both of them pulling at each other's regal clothes, stripping the pieces off one by one. He set his crown aside, but when she went to take hers off, he shook his head and forced it back in place. Lifting her by the hips to straddle him, he positioned her and thrust up into her body on a satisfying groan. She sighed, molding her sweet mouth to his. And Mikhail lost himself in her kiss, in her body, in her sultry, sweet sounds and jasmine scent.

For once in his life, he didn't have a plan. But he had a compass, her soft warmth surrounding him in love. And she would forever point him home.

Acknowledgments

A huge thank you to my readers. Without you, I'd just be the crazy lady who hears voices in her head. You've not only made the *Vampire Blood* journey possible, but you've warmed my heart with your encouragement and excitement for the characters and the world.

To my dearest friends, who keep me going when the writing road gets rough. Love to all of you—Erin Kelly, Rhenna Morgan, Kyra Jacobs, Naima Simone, and my Early Birds—A.S. Fenichel, C.D. Brennan, Gemma Brocato, and Janna MacGregor.

About the Author

Juliette is a multi-published author of paranormal and fantasy romance. She calls lush, moss-laden Louisiana home where she lives with her husband, four kids, and black lab named Kona. From the moment she read *Jane Eyre* as a teenager, she fell in love with the Gothic romance—brooding characters, mysterious settings, persevering heroines, and dark, sexy heroes. Even then, she not only longed to read more books set in Gothic worlds, she wanted to create her own.

Discover the **Vampire Blood** *series...*

THE BLACK LILY

THE RED LILY

THE WHITE LILY

Also by Juliette Cross

THE DEEPEST WELL

DARKEST HEART

HARDEST FALL

COLDEST FIRE

Discover more Amara titles...

MAGNOLIA MYSTIC
a Sentinels of Savannah novel by Lisa Kessler

Skye Olson is a psychic, but a bad break up with the man she thought was her soulmate has left her confidence in her abilities shaken. Colton Hayes spent his mortal life plundering royal ships with his pirate crew, but one holy relic changed everything. Now he and the rest of the crew protect the port of Savannah from their captain. When Colton discovers the captain wants to build a hotel in the heart of historic Savannah, he sets out to stop him, but nothing could prepare him for the sexy smile and violet eyes of the Magnolia Mystic.

WOLF OF HER OWN
a Salvation Pack novel by N.J. Walters

Mikhail stays in Salvation to be close to his sister, and to be near Elise. He's wanted Elise for years, but being with her could cost him his life. After escaping her abusive mate, Elise made a home in Salvation. She never expected to have her emotions stirred up by the always serious and seriously handsome Mikhail. When danger creeps into the pack, both she and Mikhail have to be willing to sacrifice everything to have a chance at love.

BITTERSWEET CHRISTMAS
a novella of the Order by Nina Croft

Winter, the half-pixie daughter of Father Christmas, has a chance to make her own Christmas dream come true. For years, she's longed for a job at The Order. Now, she has a chance at that job, while fulfilling an orphaned boy's dream of having his uncle back. Little does she guess that finding Liam's Uncle John will fulfill a few dreams of her own...

Made in United States
Troutdale, OR
05/15/2024